"Get out!" Valeria pointed to the door. "You think you're such a goddamn adult, take your goddamn lunatic and get out!"

It wasn't supposed to *be* like this! First Valeria promised they'd never separate, then it was only supposed to be for *two days.* Sarah never imagined anything like this when she agreed to let Dmitri take charge of her, and now two days is stretching into a lifetime. How can she tell him how unhappy she is, when he had to sacrifice everything he had for her? She's trying to be patient, but she'd give just about anything to go home again. Disaster follows disaster, and still Dmitri won't listen to reason. Time is passing, and things are changing at home. They're changing for Sarah, too - she's growing up, and she can't make it stop. Can she hold herself together in the process? Will Dmitri ever realize that *responsibility* and *maturity* are two very different words?

Sarah's desperation is growing, and the depths to which she'll sink to stop Dmitri's plans may just be unforgivable…

Best Efforts. Everyone tries.
Not everyone succeeds.

1

Best Efforts

Susan Staneslow Olesen

This is an original work of fiction. Names, characters, places and politics are the work of the author's imagination. Any similarity to persons living or dead is entirely coincidental.

With love and thanks to
C.R.M. & D.M.M.
who taught me what
brothers are about

And with sincere
apologies for Chapter 28.

The Kirushenko Family
as of February 7, 2264

Alexander Kirushenko - (48) 6'9" and 350 lbs, the widowered father of 13 children. A once-brilliant archaeologist, he is serving 7 to 15 years in prison for the accidental death of his daughter Elizabyeta.

Valeria - (23) - Eldest of the Kirushenko clan, she is the legal guardian of David, Nikky, and Marina. A tall (6') brown-eyed blonde, she's been in charge of the family for the past year, through the most trying times of their lives.

Galina - (23) - Valeria's identical twin. Legally, she has custody of Sergei and Vladimir.

Alexei - (21) - Having left home after the death of his mother, no one knows of his whereabouts.

Viktor - (19) - The responsible one everyone still worships, even though he fled to the military six months previous.

Ekaterina - (Katya) (17) Caught in the middle of every direction of struggle, Katya tries to stay positive.

Dmitri - (16) - Girl-crazy, full of schemes, always looking for a good time, all he ever wanted was to have his opinions respected. Being on his own has pushed him further than he ever thought he was capable, but as usual, what he envisions, and the results, are often two very different things.

David - (14) - A brawny, troubled teen with a temper to rival his father's, betrayed by the brother he considered his best friend. He's suddenly at the top of the ladder - in the presence of an adult who has the gall to respect him – and the world is a very different place.

Sergei - (12) - It used to be easy for introverted Sergei to hide in a large, chaotic family, but the changes will force him out of hiding.

Vladimir - (10) - Anxious, undersized and immature, he's lost the person who led him through life. The wound of separation from his sister is larger than he is, but his salvation will come from the most unlikely of places.

Sarah - (9) - First a nervous breakdown, then a shaky recovery; now her soul is bleeding for the brother she's been torn from. Brilliant, with an IQ over 180, she's still a very fragile nine emotionally. Haunted by obsessive demons in her past, anxiety can still get the better of her. To her greatest horror, Sarah's growing up - and she's absolutely helpless to stop it.

Nikolai - (4) and **Marina** (1) - Nikky can't really remember his mother, and barely remembers his loud, angry father. Marina has never known either. They hear the stories, but they're growing up in a very different lifestyle than that of their older siblings - and free of the same prejudices.

Tomas Ivanov - (45) (b. Nov. 21, 2218) - Having lost a sister he cared deeply about, guilt drives him to make right through her children - the extent of which no one could have foreseen. His own family destroyed by tragedy, he won't let this one get away.

I. Fast Lane

Ten-year-old Vladimir screamed.

The ground-flyer shuddered, lifted, and pulled away from the long castcrete house in the desert. He'd been dragged into the flyer very much against his will, and he no longer cared what happened to him. They were leaving his sister Sarah behind, his best friend in the universe, and he wouldn't have it.

"No! You can't! You can't!"

His older sister Galina held him, but he wrenched free and threw himself at the side hatch, pulling at the handle even though he knew the safety wouldn't release until the flyer stopped.

Galina grabbed for him. "Shhh, Vlad. It's only for two days. You've been away from Sarah longer than that before. Stop."

Vlad slithered over the middle row between his brothers Sergei and Nikky to the pilot's seat, where Galina's identical twin Valeria sat. Vladimir wasn't very big, but no one was taking him off-world without a fight. Not without Sarah.

Every second carrying him farther from the house, Vladimir pounded his small fists on Valeria, then grabbed the control bar and pulled with all the strength his twenty-two kilos could muster. The wallowing hovercraft pitched sharply to the right and dove downward fifteen centimeters, rattling the passengers and the mountain of luggage in the cargo area as it fought to maintain a safe cushion from the swells. The emergency thrusters engaged, but the overloaded craft lurched dangerously close to the sand.

"Turn around! You turn around and get them!"

Valeria locked the controls on auto. "Vladimir! What are you doing? You could have made us crash!"

His third sister Katya wiped away tears in the other forward seat. "Vlad, you're not helping things…"

"I don't care! Let me out! Right now! Let me out!" He grabbed for anything in reach as Galina squeezed forward and dragged him back to their row. "Let me ooout!"

He bucked and thrashed, but statuesque Galina towered more than half a meter taller, and so much stronger. Vlad wriggled until his flailing feet hammered into fourteen year old David, brooding sullenly by the window.

David shoved the small sandals away. "Yo! What the hell you kicking me for? Kick Val, not me! You got a death wish or

11

something?"

"You helped them, you bastard!" Vlad spat, swearing for the first time in his life. "You said you were their friend! You didn't even try to stop Val! None of you did! You let Val leave them there to die! Traitors!"

David raised a powerful fist high. "You shut your damn mouth, you undersized bag of bird shit! I'll pound you to a pancake so thin we'll have to hold you up to the sun to find your face!"

"Fuck you!" Vlad screamed back, trying to remember every bad word he'd ever heard David use. "Fuck you and your mother and everyone you ever knew, twice backwards in a sandstorm! You didn't have the nerve to save Dimi and Sarah, where you gonna get the nerve to flatten me?"

Galina wrestled Vladimir to her other side. "BOYS! Vlad, stop that language! David, sit back and let him be!"

"Val?" Little Nikky, youngest of the boys, spoke up from the front row. "If I be bad like Sarah, will you make me be deaded in the sand, too?" His lower lip pressed tight against the upper, and it shivered. Sarah was his friend, too.

"Oh no, Nikky! No!" Val glanced back with a sorrowful expression. Nikky was so much younger he tended to be forgotten in the chaos. The twins were old enough to be his mother – indeed, five years older than their mother when Val and Galina were born. "No one is going to die. Sarah and Dmitri are taking a different ship, that's all. We'll meet up with them when we land on Earth. You'll see."

To the back row she said, "Enough, Vlad. You know better than to use those words. You're upsetting Nikky."

"I don't give a damn!" Vlad shouted rabidly. "Murderer! I hate you! I won't get on that ship! Not without Sarah! Prick fuck bastard!" He arched against Galina and kicked the front seat as hard as he could. Sergei leaned forward to avoid being kicked in the head.

David sneered. "Cool it, Fork Man! You're gonna mess yourself. Your brain's not big enough to handle words like that. See what you've done to him, Val? You made him snap his tiny little mind."

"Val?" Nikky asked. "What's a bassard?"

Eating breakfast at the spaceport proved pointless. Only Nikky had any appetite. Galina couldn't enter the crowded eatery with her charge. She sat instead in the open waiting area, holding Vlad, whose exhaustive struggles had been replaced by tears.

The call to board came on time. The orbital shuttle would take them up to the interstellar cruiser circling the planet, then a fifty-four hour flight to Earth. Home. Most of them hadn't been there in four years, and baby Marina had been born on Navara.

Valeria held the baby, counting heads. Sergei, David, Katya

12

holding Nikky's hand, Galina dragging Vladimir. All there. They were almost to the boarding ramp, ID in hand, when Vlad broke free and took off as fast as he could run, ducking into the one place he knew the twins couldn't touch him: the men's restroom.

He glanced about, heart fluttering from flight and not a little fear. Vladimir had never deliberately misbehaved; this was a first. He wasn't allowed in public restrooms without one of the older boys; this was a first, too. That pressure added to his overloaded nerves, and he swallowed hard against the earthquakes in his fragile stomach. A red-skinned alien of a species Vlad didn't recognize turned a harsh yellow eyestalk toward him and grumbled something guttural. Vlad bolted across the room and locked himself in a private stall.

Galina hadn't been far behind, her long legs making up for Vlad's speed, but her shoulders sagged as the door shut. Three days as Vlad's guardian, and already he'd run away.

"Vladimir?" she called in the doorway. "Vlad, make it quick. We're boarding. You can go on the shuttle."

Valeria approached with David. Katya and Sergei went ahead with Nikky and the baby, but she wouldn't let David out of her sight.

"What do I do?" Galina said. "It's busy in there. I can't exactly go in, and I hate to call Security. He's already so upset as it is."

David was tall and muscular. Valeria shot him an inquiring look.

David's lip curled. "Oh no. No way! It's bad enough I got drafted onto the baby side of the family. Don't expect me to become your lead henchman. Did it ever occur to you maybe I'm on his side?"

Val closed her eyes and counted to ten. "David, please. I'm asking nicely. Could you please get your brother for Galina? Carry him if you have to."

David stalled a few more precious seconds. "Maybe he has a legitimate reason for being in there. You know his rotten stomach. What am I supposed to do, yank him off the sanitary? I'm not getting pissed or puked on."

Valeria sighed. "David…"

Galina took a deep breath. "I'll get him."

David's hand landed heavy on her shoulder. "I'll do it. For your sake, Gal. You don't need any more embarrassment."

"Yo, Fork Man! Where are you?" Fork Man, for the time not very long ago that Vladimir tried to protect Sarah from bossy Val with a carving fork. David wandered down the row of humanoid privacy stalls, perhaps a dozen having opaque occupancy screens activated across the doorways. All he could see were vague shadows. "You can't hide from me forever. I'll call Security."

Here it was. Had to be him. The dark outline was too small to be anything else. " … And they'll come in here, and turn off the screen,

13

and catch you standing there with your pants around your ankles and your hand on your sorry little excuse of a …"

"I'm not going you can't make me!" Vlad shouted from the stall. "Fuck you! Fuck Valeria! You don't give a damn about them at all, or you woulda done something! You told Dimi you would! All you are is talk! You aren't so big and tough! Someone's gotta help them!"

"You better watch what you say, rodent! I'll give you to the count of three to drop that screen or I get Security. *Ahdin! … Dva! … **Tri!***"

"All right!" Vlad kicked the switch with his foot and the energy field disappeared. He stood on the sanitary unit, braced defiantly, face streaked with tears. David dragged him by the hair and slammed him against the restroom wall.

Vlad's head bounced against the bright tile and he cried anew, arms raised in a futile attempt to protect himself.

David towered over Vlad by four and a half years, fifty centimeters, and more than sixty-five kilos. He grabbed his brother by the shirtfront, twisting the fabric like Father used to do, until Vlad stood on his tiptoes.

"You runty little turd! Who the hell you think you are? I ought to rip your tongue out and shove it up your ass, saying shit like that! I could punch you in the jaw so hard they'll have to fuse the pieces back together and it'll be months before you can even hope to tell Sarah what happened. At least you got Galina on your side! I gotta answer to the Tsaritsa herself, and you going off like this makes me have to kiss up or dig my own grave right at the start. Knock your shit off!" He banged Vlad against the wall again. "Like me and Sergei aren't pissed! You think Kat's cryin' because she's happy?"

Vlad whimpered. "I don't care."

"Like shit you don't! You think I wanted to leave them? You don't think I want to head back there right now? I even thought about taking your whiney little snot-covered ass with me if I had a way, but they're right behind us! By the time we got back home, they'd be here boarding, so knock it off already! Two days! You can live without holding Miss Brainiac's hand for two fucking days." He released Vlad with a stumbling shove. "Now drag it! Because I sure as shit don't feel like carrying you, and if you don't get out there, Val's gonna come in here after us. Galina has enough shit to deal with without you going mental on her. Go!" He pushed Vlad roughly to the exit.

"I'll give you credit, Fork Man," David said with some admiration. "I never, ever, would have bet money you had any of this in you. There is definitely hope for you, Rodent. Definitely some hope. You won't be able to get away with it for long, though. Trust me!"

Valeria opened the door to one of their adjoining cabins on the *Moondancer,* and the parade followed. Destination reached, Galina let go of Vladimir, and he collapsed in a ball on the floor. Katya set baby Marina down and let her run.

"Not bad," Val said, looking around. "How do you want to divide up?" There were two narrow doubles in one room, and four single bunks in the other.

"Boys in one, girls in the other?" Galina suggested.

David dropped his load of carry bags in the middle of the room. He kept his, stepped over Vlad, stalked to the other cabin, and hoisted himself onto an upper bunk. He dug in a pocket, plugged the earpieces to his music player into his ears, and lay down with his back to everyone.

"David!" Galina objected, gazing at the mountain of bags on the floor.

"Let him go," Val said. "He's quiet. Let's not push it." She picked the baby's bag and her own out of the pile and placed them on a bed. "Why don't you take the boys in there, and I'll keep the little ones here with me and Kat."

Sergei didn't need direction. He shoved past Valeria and claimed the bed under David's. He ripped his notebook and scribe from his bag and locked himself in the tiny lavatory.

"Come on, Vlad," Galina said gently. "Let's get you settled. You'll feel better once you lie down." She bent down to help him, but Vlad gagged and retched, his stomach too empty to vomit more than a mouthful of bile onto the front of his shirt.

Valeria lost patience. "Now go change! You're old enough to make it to the sanitary!" Vlad hugged his stomach and began to wail.

Val gave up. "Just put him on the bed here. He can sleep with Nik. Take Kat with you."

Nikky bounced energetically on a bed. "'Leria? Val? Is my birfday now?"

"Seven days, Nik." Valeria swung him down, and she and Galina lifted Vladimir onto the bed. Galina located his carry-on and proceeded to change his shirt as if he were two, not ten.

The girls sorted the luggage and matched it to beds. Fifty-four hours and they would be back to Earth. A strange city, no parents, no jobs, no money, and an uncle to meet they'd never known existed, but at least it was Earth. Sergei banged his way out of the lavatory and slammed himself onto his bed, scribbling in his notebook with explosive fury.

Running the length of both rooms, Nikky sang at the top of his lungs, "Birfday, my birfday! Seven days, I be four! Seven days, I be four! Val? How manys is seven?"

Katya stopped him. "Shah, Nik. This many," and she helped him count seven fingers.

"Have you seen the emergency bag?" Val asked. "We might as well start Vlad on his stomach medicine before he damages something. Maybe it will calm him down."

Gal rummaged until she found it. Vlad kicked his feet and shook his head until Valeria held him and Galina poured. He spat it back in a fountain of pink.

"God damn it, Vladimir!" Val shoved him away while Galina wiped her hands and shirt. "Enough's enough! I understand you're upset, but you're taking this too far! It's only two days!"

Vlad shook between sobs. "No I'm not! YOU took it too far! YOU did this to us! YOU'RE the reason they're not here right now! I HATE you! I want SARAH! MURDERER!"

"Calm down, Vlad," Galina soothed, but David's shadow blocked the doorway. The twins stepped back.

David glared at his brother; Vlad seemed to shrink even smaller. "Shut the fuck up! I can hear your snot-faced screaming over there through my receivers." He stormed over to the bed. Vlad braced for pain, but David merely lifted him with one hand. The smaller boy shrieked as his pants were yanked to his knees.

"David!" Valeria said sharply. "What are you …?"

David grabbed the self-dispensing bottle and held it before Vlad. "I am not listening to you puke for the next two days. You either drink this shit or I'm pouring it in your ass and holding you upside down until it reaches your stomach. Pick one!"

Vlad swallowed as fast as he could.

David released his brother and returned to his bunk in a torrent of curses. Vlad fixed his pants and pulled the tiny fourth-class starliner pillow over his head to cry in privacy.

Valeria forced herself out of self-pity. "This is no way to begin a trip. Come on, everyone. Let's pull it together and see what the ship's got going for it. Get your shoes."

"I want to go! I want to go! I want to go!" Nikky screeched on the run. "Is it my birfday now?"

Katya wiped her eyes and reached for her shoulderbag.

David didn't move.

Vlad didn't move.

Sergei didn't turn his head, but one dark eye twisted to glare at his sisters.

Stalemate.

"Come on, guys," Galina said without enthusiasm. "It'll be fun."

"I don't feel like moving much," Sergei said. "The lighter gravity and deep space and all. I need time to get used to it."

"You go ahead," Galina said. "I'll stay here with the boys."

Val's eyes flicked toward David. "Is that such a good idea?"

"We'll be fine."

When Val returned, Vlad had fallen into an exhausted sleep, lulled by the relaxants in the stomach medicine. David hadn't twitched. Sergei's face stayed buried in his pillow, whether ill or tearful or angry no one would ever know. The twins got everyone up for dinner, though the smothering tension left empty stomachs hungerless. David's jaw locked in a fierce scowl. Sergei said nothing beyond his order. Vlad sat emptily, refusing so much as water. Katya tried to hold his hand as Sarah would have done, but the cold little hand was limp and lifeless.

On returning to the room, Galina picked up Sergei's notebook, half under her bunk. Her eyes fell on the open page, and she handed it to Valeria in tears.

I HATE THEM had been written over and over, perhaps a hundred times, each line punctuated by a tiny hole where the endlessly sharp fabricated pencil had been stabbed through the paper.

> *Loyalty was the string that bound everyone together. Loyalty to each other, to know that no matter how bad things got, we would pull through if we all stuck together, if we helped drag each other along no one would be left to weather the storm alone. Now that string has been cut, deliberately, when we weren't looking, and the very fabric of life has begun to unravel with amazing speed. I wish I had wings, for I would soar back through time with the speed of a dragon and stand my ground, let the flames of anger belch forth from my jaws and not allow the ties to be broken. Now wings aren't enough, for in this cold emptiness of space in which we are suspended even Angels cannot fly, and in her absence I am engulfed by hatred.*

Val threw her hands up in futility. "Why not? Why shouldn't he hate me, too? I've broken the Fearsome Four. God! Speed us home and get this over with! You'd think I killed and buried them! All I freakin' want is Dmitri to realize a little of what I'm going through. Is that so wrong? To understand that taking care of Sarah – or any of them – is no great picnic in the park. It's hard work, Gal! You know it, I know it, Kat knows it, but I can't get Dimi to see that. By the time we land, he should have gotten the message. That's all I want."

"I know," Galina agreed. "I just think we should have found a different way. You promised Vlad and Sarah you wouldn't split them up. I think it's the broken promise that hurts more than the separation." She left Val to stew, and presented the notebook to Sergei.

"I think Nik got hold of this," she apologized. "I found it over there. I know things are kind of tough right now. Is there anything you want to talk about? Anything I can help with? Even just a hug?"

Sergei, so possessive about his writings, accepted the notebook with unusual apathy. He tucked it under his pillow. "I think I said it all already," he said with a scowl, and buried his nose in the book Sarah had given him to read.

Day two. David watched the clock, materializing on the dot for Vlad's stomach medicine. No words were exchanged, but Vlad drained every drop. David waited until no one was looking, then swallowed a double-dose himself.

"What are you looking at, Rodent? You think you're the only one whose stomach's in knots?"

Vlad burrowed back under his covers. The liquid didn't have nearly as much narcotic as David hoped, and he paid for his gamble with two days' constipation. If anyone needed the medication without prescription, it was Nikky.

Valeria readied the baby so they could walk the ship. Having the two rooms for Nikky and Marina to bounce in helped, but walking the corridors and playing in the videotheaters did a lot more to wear them out.

Nikky wandered into the adjoining room. "My tummy hurts."

Galina brushed her hair. "It's probably the change in gravity."

Val peered across the room. "What's on his face, Gal?"

Galina looked closer. She rubbed a thumb on his pink-stained chin. "Fruit juice. I think it's the nimbura fruit we packed. Oh, Nik! Look at your clothes. Let's go change you."

"My tummy hurts."

"Nikky! No wonder! You must have eaten half the bag," Galina said from the other room. A dozen sticky fruit pits lay scattered across the bedcover. Val entered the room just in time to hear the sputtering wet gurgle.

Nikky stared in shock, then started to cry. Val's nose twitched, then Galina's. Vlad gave a soft gag and pulled the covers over his nose.

"Nikky!"

"It was an accident!" Nikky howled. "I saided my tummy hurt!"

"Run – no, don't move, Nik." Val bent down to take off his shoes. "Oh, Lord! It's in his socks. Do you think they have laundry facilities

18

on board?"

"They must, somewhere." Galina lifted the boy by his elbows and carried him to the lavatory.

Valeria dug hygienic wipes from the baby's bag and cleaned the floor. "You must have seen him over there, Vlad. Why didn't you stop him?"

Vladimir sat up fast. "Because watching him is SARAH'S job! SARAH watches him, and she's not here! SHE would have stopped him! You get what you deserve, Val!" He took a deep breath and began to wail.

"Don't think I'm cleaning anything!" David bellowed from his bed fortress. "That was DIMI's job. If he was here, he could do it, but for some ugly reason he's NOT, so YOU'RE stuck with it, NOT ME!"

"So you let your baby brother eat himself sick to get back at me?" Val started, but Sergei stepped between her and Vlad.

"Come on. You belong over there with us." He half-carried Vlad to his own bed and flopped down next to him to read. "Don't you dare throw up on my bed," Sergei threatened, "and if you pee on it, I'll turn you over to David."

Vlad promised, and crawled between Sergei and the wall, snuffling. Every so often, when no one could see, Sergei ruffled his brother's hair, or gave his back a rub. He was twelve now; hugging a boy, even a little brother, wasn't about to happen.

Val tucked a clean Nikky into bed and gave him a different medication. "Well, there goes the morning. I guess we're stuck here."

"I'll stay, if you want," Katya volunteered.

"And leave you with everything? I wouldn't do that to you."

David rolled over. "You mean leave her with *me*, because you know damned well I'm not leaving the room, and you don't trust me to take a piss alone. 'Don't leave Kat with him! He'll beat her up and run off somewheres!' I know I can't win your respect, but why the hell are you pissing on Kat? You used to trust her. Or maybe not," he reconsidered. "You never think she's able to be in charge, ever, and she's an adult now. You hate us so much you won't take a walk and leave her in charge of two invalids and a ghost writer? What's Sergei going to do? Throw papers at her? You people make me sick." He flopped back to face the wall.

"I don't hate anyone!" Val declared. "You people want to be treated like adults, then you have to act like them! This isn't a funeral! There are plenty of fun things to do on this ship, and if you want to spend your time reveling in misery and self-pity just because Sarah's on a different ship, then every one of you deserves to be miserable. Fine. Katya, you're in charge. Gal and I will take the baby for a walk. If David so much as moves from that bed, call ship's security." She took Marina and left. Galina shook her head and followed.

David swung off the bed in a flash.

"What are you up to?" Katya said.

He parked himself on the end of Sergei's bunk. "How're you guys holding up?"

Sergei sat up and closed Sarah's book. "Lousy!" he replied with a scowl. "I can't believe you, though. You're never this quiet. I figured you'd have thrown her out an airlock or something by now."

"Just waiting for the right moment."

"What are you talking about?" Katya demanded.

"What about you, Rodent? You haven't pissed yourself, have you?"

Vlad wiped his nose on his hand and shook his head.

David punched the boy on the arm hard enough to leave a bruise. "Hey! That was really good, reminding her about Sarah like that. Keep it up."

"You better not dare plot anything!" Kat warned.

"Cryin' out loud, will you lay off the paranoia?" David snarled. "I get enough of that shit from Val. We're only relaxing, now that we're out of the Evil Eye. We're all that's left, and we got to stick together. She's not going to get another of us without real bloodshed. You tell her to leave us alone, or they'll need a military escort to get us off this ship, and that's a promise. Dimi said I'm in charge until he gets here, and I sure as shit will be. Val has managed to destroy everything this family ever believed in. Not even Father was able to do that, but Val did it in less than a week. You've always been one of us, Kat, but where are your loyalties right now? With the Tsaritsa, or with your family?"

"I will not be a part of any plot against Val," Kat insisted, "but I really miss them, too."

"Then so be it. Go take care of Nikky, before you have to clean him again. We're just happy to have Val stop suffocating us for a while, okay? Cards, Kat?"

Katya checked on Nikky, found a program on the cinetron for him to watch. "Sure. I'm not Sarah, but I'll play."

One

Russian Federation of States
Earth
United Planetary Alliance
Earthdate: 10 February, 2264

*V*aleria Kirushenko paused a moment to breathe. Air. Real, sweet air. Heavy, damp, cool Earth air, weighing richly in every crevice of her lungs. Fifty weeks since she'd last breathed the freshness, and it lifted her dragging spirits. She'd spent the last year taking care of her family in the thin burning dust of the desert world Navara. They needed this change, needed to leave the past far behind on that rotten planet where life never got better, only worse. The air at Moscow Interstellar Spaceport smelled slightly off, of sweaty people and food and new carpeting and luggage, but it was *home.*

Two and a half days they'd spent in transit; herself, her identical twin Galina, and six of their eleven younger brothers and sisters. Two days that seemed more like two years. The mood in their cramped quarters had been explosive, but Valeria stood by her decision. She had deliberately, vindictively left two of their own behind.

Sixteen-year-old Dmitri was a good kid at heart – more even-tempered and practical than David, but not nearly as wise and responsible as their brother Viktor. When young Sarah, pushed to her limits by a string of family tragedies, suffered a mental collapse, Dmitri got an idea that he could handle the intense moods better than Val, and challenged her on it.

Valeria had to admit, Dimi *was* good with Sarah. He had the insight and patience to reach her when Val herself couldn't. But Dmitri never thought past his next meal or his next girlfriend, whichever came first. He opposed Sarah's treatment from the start, and in a bold affront to Val's authority, forged his birth records and convinced a court to appoint him Sarah's legal guardian before Val had a chance. How could she let Dmitri get away with that and ever hope to keep control over David? Or Sergei, Vlad, and Nikky? Mother was dead, Father in prison for the next seven to fifteen years.

In the hardest decision of her life, she left the two behind. Dmitri had never been responsible for anything in his life. After two days caring for his sister all on his own – from planning the trip to Earth to minding her medications and fears and her own stubborn streaks, he would gain some badly needed wisdom. He would turn Sarah's custody over to Galina, and life would resume some semblance of sanity. Dmitri would learn a lesson, and David would see Val as a serious player in the game of leadership.

Leaving Sarah, though.... The child was brilliant, so academically advanced at the age of nine she would have started university classes the following school year, but the distresses of home had broken her emotionally. In one dreadful year, their youngest sister was born, their mother died, and the two eldest boys, Alexei and Viktor, left home under strained circumstances. Six-year-old Elizabyeta died in an accident, and Father stood trial on charges of murder. It was more strain than any of them could bear, but Sarah, an eyewitness to each and every event, took it worst of all, spending three months in a psychiatric hospital. Sarah's absence weighed heavy on Val's heart.

Sarah and Vladimir, just nine months apart in age, were inseparable best friends. Valeria swore they even breathed at the same time. For each of them, the greatest fear was to be without the other, and now Val had done just that. Vladimir was on the edge of a breakdown himself; Valeria felt ill to think how Sarah might be faring.

Landing in Moscow was the first step in putting the pieces back together. Valeria carried the baby, Galina held onto Nikky, and Katya supported Vlad. David and Sergei bore the brunt of the carry-bags. They parked themselves near the cargo claim to await thirty more cases.

Valeria scanned the bustling crowds. She expected to rendezvous with Uncle Tomas – Mother's older brother – but she'd never met him. They'd been in contact, but not via a video channel. All she had was a photo, twenty-five years old.

Fifteen travel cases had come through customs when a man approached. He appeared fortyish, with hazel eyes and sable hair combed to the side. His long coat and gripper boots were impeccably stylish for the Moscow winter. He looked startlingly like an older version of their brother Viktor, but with Dmitri's slighter build.

"*Izvenitye, pazhal'sta,*" he said to Valeria. "*Valeria Kirushenko?*"

"*Da, Valeria Kirushenko.*"

"Tómas Fedorovitch Ivanov."

"Uncle Tomas! Pleased to meet you!" She shifted the baby to shake his hand. He pulled her in instead and kissed her on both cheeks. Val caught the cue and returned the greeting. "We can't thank you enough for your offer. You've really helped us out of a bind."

"Think nothing of it," Ivanov said, playing a peeking game with baby Marina, two weeks shy of her first birthday. "I'm glad to help. There's been unnecessary bad blood between our families for far too long. How was your flight?"

"Very well, all told." She introduced the family. "There's two more coming on another flight."

"Why don't I run and check the schedule?" Galina offered. "I'll find out when they're arriving."

The rest of the luggage arrived, but Galina hadn't returned. The boys loaded the bags onto a courtesy carrier and moved the group to the flight desk. Galina leaned over the counter on tiptoe, eyeing the coordinator's viewscreen.

"Did you find it?" Val asked.

Galina frowned. "No. Eight flights left for Earth in the past two days. Their names aren't on the passenger list for any of them."

"What do you mean? Could they have boarded something that

made an unplanned stop at Navara? Maybe they weren't disembarking in Moscow. Could they have a connecting flight from somewhere else?"

"That's what they're checking now."

A chill prickled down Valeria's neck. "You don't think they ran into trouble, do you? What if they wouldn't accept Dmitri's paperwork? You don't think Sarah might have had a problem?"

"Of course not. Even if she did, Dmitri could handle it."

"I'm sorry," said the woman behind the flight desk. "There are no passengers registered under those names on any incoming flight. Please try again later; we update hourly."

"Thank you. I will do that." Galina turned away from the desk.

"When are they coming?" David demanded.

Galina braced for an outburst. "They're not on today's flights. I'll call back first thing in the morning and try again."

"Why? Why aren't they? Where…?"

"We'll know tomorrow when they tell us themselves, won't we."

Mother never discussed her family. She was seventeen when she eloped with Father, six years her elder. That much the children knew, and the fact that Mother's family strongly opposed the match. They knew Mother was well-educated, though she never graduated a university. Mother – always gentle, always soft-spoken, always preoccupied with Father or a baby – insisted her children grow up with the same aristocratic mindset no matter where they might live. She insisted on manners at all times, that her children be fluent in both the language of their Russian ancestry and the Standard Interstellar English that ruled the business world, made sure they could appreciate fine art, and that every one of them knew the performance end of a piano.

Such graces eluded Father. Two doctoral degrees to his name, a wall's worth of honors, his civilization disappeared the moment he entered the house. He had acceptable manners in public, but at home he'd grown increasingly rude and drunken and violent, beating them without mercy. His foul mouth had been Mother's vexation. Nothing their parents did, however, ever hinted at what the children discovered.

The spaceport shuttle took them on the high-altitude flight to Minsk. In accordance with city law, they dropped speed and flew past the industrial heart at low altitude, past the sprawling suburban developments to the far edge of the city, where snow-covered lawns stretched before some of the largest homes they'd ever seen. Trees! Real trees, so unlike the sparse needle-scrub of the Navaran desert. Nikky had never seen trees or snow, and stared at the bare trunks as if grotesque alien sculptures. Nothing in memory was as grand as this, not even the years they'd lived in their big *pomyest* in Kiev.

A long expanse of property approached on the left, coated with a flawless layer of winter snow. The land sloped gently more than a hectare up a low rise, and ended in the largest private home they'd ever seen. The creamy color of modern masonry, built in a style at least a hundred years old, its high-peaked, solar-tiled roof towered four stories and seemed to fill the horizon. Enormous laser-carved doors highlighted a two-level veranda. The architecture screamed of the baroque, post-World-War-III-recovery Era of Extravagance, dripping with artistically contrived details that seemed to shout, *We have survived! We have it all!*

The shuttle slowed, then stopped. Tomas handed the driver a tag; the driver waved it at a security eye, then banked and cornered the long shuttle. It crawled up a marked flyway to the side of that magnificent structure, settling under a covered fly-through.

"Tell me I'm dreaming," Kat whispered as they climbed out.

"This is your house?" Galina murmured.

Uncle Tomas looked amused. "You don't know about the Velikaya Estate? This is where your mother and I grew up."

He led them through the side entrance, no less opulent for the location of the door. Inside had a more familiar feel; the decoration mirrored Mother's tastes. Paintings hung on quilted walls. Cut-crystal lamps dangled from the high embossed ceiling. Flowering plants flourished under spotlights in dark corners, and pedestals and carved nooks highlighted large statuary. The house echoed with the profound silence of a deep sleep.

An older woman in dark livery hurried down the hall. "Welcome home, Master Ivanov."

Tomas handed her his coat. "*Spasiba*, Olga. Please see to it that the children's luggage is delivered upstairs, and send someone for their outerwear."

"Immediately, sir." She disappeared down the long corridor as silently as she'd arrived.

Uncle Tomas disturbed the slumbering perfection. "Mamá? We're here."

"In the lounge, Tomas," came a woman's distant reply.

He led the parade to a room so huge it had two entrances on the same wall. An immense fireplace took up much of the space between the doors, though the brightly burning fire came from artificial logs. Three separate sitting areas huddled about the room, the largest consisting of three fat sofas and two equally overstuffed armchairs in a horseshoe before the fireplace. Above the mantle hung a stylized painting nearly two meters tall. A concert grand piano – dark blue, not black – spread across the front corner; a well-stocked wet bar hugged the back. Glass doors led outside, framed, as were the tall windows, in heavy winter drapes. The entire room sported soft dusty-greens and blues, as peaceful as a calm sea.

In the center stood a petite woman, perhaps seventy, elegant in a lilac suit. Her chin-length hair was dyed lightest blonde; the face it framed was creased but not yet enough to be called wrinkled. It didn't take much imagination to see her as an older version of Mother.

Nikky hugged Katya's legs, peeking at the stranger with a single, wary eye. Vlad's cold hand snaked its way into Sergei's; Sergei gripped it tightly. Still dressed in Navaran clothes and insulating desert robes, they no doubt presented an odd picture. The woman stared with a chilling sense of arrogance.

Uncle Tomas took over as if he'd known them all his life. "Mamá, may I present eight of Maryana's children." To the children, he said, "This is your mother's mother, Andrea Maximovna Ivanova."

Valeria broke out of the pack, misleadingly confident. She took the woman by the hand and kissed her on both cheeks. "Grandmother? Thank you so much for allowing us to stay here. We are most grateful."

The cool features broke into a soft smile. "You are welcome, my dear. I've been eager to meet you. Can it really be that long? You are the eldest? What's your name, dear?"

"I'm Valeria. My sister Galina and I are the oldest. We're twenty-three." She gestured back to Gal, struggling to hold the baby, who, after hours of sitting in shuttles, wanted very much to get down.

"Twins!" Mrs. Ivanov said with surprise. "I didn't know. The last time I saw my daughter, she told us she was expecting. She was seventeen. Fyodor was so angry he refused to acknowledge her existence. He felt she had thrown her life away. You must have been that baby. I guess, in a way, we've met before."

"I can't imagine having to raise a child at that age, let alone twins." Val smiled, unsure the insinuation that she and Gal had been the ruination of their mother's life had been unintentional. Of course she knew what twins would have been like; she'd been raising siblings all her life. Katya and Dmitri, like Vlad and Sarah, were less than a year apart in age; as close to twins as one could get. And at twenty-three, Mother had only four children to worry about.

Grandmother Ivanova inspected the group. She nodded at Katya, tipping the girl's chin as if looking for the pedigree of a well-bred animal. "I can see your mother in you, child. The face, the eyes, the carriage."

Katya gave an anxious curtsey. "Ekaterina, Ma'am. Thank you. My mother was a beautiful woman."

Mrs. Ivanov gazed down the row, took a few steps, and did the same to Vlad, pulling him from his hiding place behind Sergei. "Here, too, Tomas. Look at the eyes. They're dark, but those are

Maryana's eyes. How old are you, little boy?"

Vlad glared at the word 'little.' He shook her hand lightly. "My name is Vladimir, and I'm *ten*." If he stood straight, he looked like a skinny seven.

"You have your Mother's build. The rest of you ...." Madame Ivanova rubbed her amethyst necklace with long, bony fingers. She stared critically at Sergeí, who overlooked her by more than fifteen centimeters, with his Father's piercing eyes, the stubborn curls of his father's mother, and his own mother's blond coloring. "I don't know."

"Sergei, Ma'am." He stepped forward and gave a deep bow. As he'd seen his father do so often to his mother, he lifted his grandmother's hand and kissed the back of it with flair. "It's a pleasure to meet you."

The woman stared at David last, clutching her necklace as though he might steal it.

Much to Valeria's horror, David, just the week before, had chopped his thick black hair into a wild cut, spiking all over his head with several long strands left hanging in his eyes. He wore a cord choker around his neck, a single row of stone beads woven through it. Two gold earrings pierced his left ear, one at the top and one at the bottom. His chocolate-brown desert robe blended in on Navara, but would be a suicidal fashion statement on Earth. Though it had been the style among his rowdy friends, this time he didn't wear a line of black eyeliner on his lower lashes.

David forced a smile. He still had one advantage Sergei had overlooked. He kissed Grandmother's hand. "David *Fyodor* Kirushenko, Ma'am."

The ace up David's sleeve worked. Grandmother seemed to relax. "You were named after your grandfather? My late husband Fyodor? Maryana gave you all the double names as well?"

"Yes, Ma'am."

Grandmother looked him over again, not quite as hard. "You have your mother's eyes," she said at last. "The shape isn't right, but the color is."

"Yes, Ma'am."

The crown of the massive foyer, the grand central staircase curved wide and graceful to the second floor, the dark wood gleaming with a mirror-like finish. Uncle Tomas showed them to their rooms. Upstairs lay another sitting area, grandmother's suite, two more staircases, a lift, and a huge foyer out to the balcony over the veranda. Five of the eight guest bedrooms had been made up; their luggage had been brought to their assigned rooms and unpacked while they lunched, as if by elves. The twins were paired together, Katya with Sarah when she arrived, Vlad and Sergei, David and a waiting bed for

Dmitri, and Nikky and Marina in a room already set as a nursery. And bathrooms! Every room had its own bath! At home, fourteen people had fought over just two. This fact impressed them more than anything else.

Dinner proved extraordinary, held in the dining room whose table could stretch to hold as many as thirty. An immense ham was carved and served by the kitchen staff as bowl after bowl of side dishes and breads were passed. Tired from their journey, made sleepy by overindulgence at dinner, Valeria suggested they might retire early.

"A wonderful job, everybody," she praised once they were upstairs. She hugged David. "You were perfect! Thank you."

David knew the compliments were for keeping his mouth shut and not doing anything shocking, but it did nothing to ease his anger over the fact Dmitri had missed out on a dinner like that.

Two

Tired and long past ready for bed, Sergei couldn't help laughing as David preened shirtless in the large mirror. David looked this way and that, checking out his muscles and playing with his upper lip.

"You're really going to do it?" Sergei said. "How long do you think it'll take 'til she notices? It's been four days. It still looks like dirt."

David caressed the thin dark hairs on the edge of his lip. If skin massage were any help to growing hair, he'd have a mustache to rival Stalin's by the end of the week. "More than you can grow!"

"I'm not trying to piss off Val. Once she realizes it, she'll rip it out with her fingers."

"Let her try. She won't make a scene here. She's kissing ass so hard she doesn't know which direction to pucker next. Now's the time to ask her for anything you ever wanted. She'd do anything right now to keep us quiet." David flapped open a shirt and put it on.

A mousy knock tapped the door. Sergei let Vladimir in.

"What the Hell do you want?" David demanded. "Until Dimi gets back, this room's mine alone. No babies allowed."

Vlad's thin shoulders slumped. Exhaustion weighed heavy on him, but never in his life had he slept in a room by himself. If Sarah had been there, she would have climbed in bed next to him, holding his hand until they fell asleep. But Sarah wasn't there.

"Nichevo," he mumbled. "Serg, you comin' to bed?"

"Yeah, soon."

Vlad turned to leave, but David blocked his path. "What'd you want, Rodent?" he said less gruffly.

Vlad hesitated.

David looked down at the sad face braced for the next rebuff, and the idea of *responsibility* slammed into him with the force of an asteroid. For the first time he realized that, at least for another day, *he* was the oldest boy. *He* was the leader of the diminished pack. Vlad came to *him* to ask a question because Vlad was looking to *him* for life's answers, and all he'd ever done was make fun of the little rat. David had never been in charge of anything; never, ever responsible at all. Even when he acted as leader of the Fearsome Four – the name he, Sergei, Sarah and Vlad had given themselves – he'd just been the oldest of the group. No accountability had ever been associated with the position. David wasn't sure he liked this new feeling, wasn't sure what to do with it.

He dropped his Attitude. "I mean, don't tell me you came in here just to tell Sergei it was time for bed. I guess you can hang out if you want."

Vlad shrugged. He perched on the edge of a bed.

David dropped on the opposite bed. Vlad watched him through submissive little glances. David couldn't remember a single time he'd ever really *tried* to talk to Vlad. Outside of parentage, they had nothing in common.

"So, what'd you want?"

Still Vlad hesitated. "Do you think they're okay? Galina told Dimi two hours. Where are they?"

A knife twisted in the wound of David's own worries. "'Course they're all right! You think Dimi can't catch a flight on his own? The flight could have been filled – it could have been delayed, or canceled. Maybe they had to stop for some reason. Galina will find out tomorrow. Don't you go all cry-babied on me."

"I'm not. David? You don't think maybe Sarah... ?" Vlad had seen his sister at her worst, talking to imaginary voices and harming herself.

"No! She was over that stuff. She knows it's just a couple days. She's fine."

"But *Dave!*" Vlad fell into his about-to-cry look. "You didn't see her when Galina pulled me out of there! She ..."

David lost patience. "She's *fine*, Vlad! Enough already! Dimi knows what he's doing. He had it all planned. Serg, grab my cards over there."

"You're worried, too!" Vlad realized. "That's why you won't talk about it!"

David slid to the floor and dealt out cards. "Shut *up*, Vlad. Or you want me to do it for you? I let you stay in here, didn't I? Play!"

Three

mitri struggled down the corridor of the cruise ship with his carryall over his shoulder, one of his travel cases and one of his sister's in one arm, boarding pass clenched in his other hand. He searched the room numbers for their cabin, all the while with Sarah, her huge backpack dragging behind her, clutching the waistband of his pants.

"This is it." He slid the boarding pass into a scanner to unlock the door. It opened, and he nearly threw the cases in to get rid of them. Dmitri wasn't particularly tall, slim as a new blade of grass, and the cases were heavy. The economy room wasn't much bigger than his closet of a bedroom at home.

"Any preference?"

Sarah glanced side to side, stiff with tension. She hiked her bag onto the left bed and sat down, still holding the straps. She stared at the floor while Dmitri piled the cases on the small table.

Her brother noticed the blank look. He brushed his dark bangs back with his fingers and smoothed them into place. "You okay?"

"Yeah. It's just the gravity change."

He snapped open a case and dug around. "I feel it in my stomach, too. It shouldn't take long to adjust. It's only a tenth of a G. Lie down if you feel dizzy. And it's easier to breathe with the heavier air."

Sarah hugged her lumpy bag. "What time is it, back on Earth?"

Dmitri stuffed tomorrow's clothes into the tiny courtesy drawers in the wall. "I can't do that stuff in my head. Find out the Unified time, convert it to Earth time, then add two hours to Greenwich Mean. You're so smart, figure it out yourself."

"Just wondering."

"I'll check it when I'm done." Sarah had become fragile when it came to things that upset her – so fragile, in fact, she needed heavy medications to help her keep her wits, and the threat of trouble was very real. He knelt in front of her, his hand over hers. "Hey. You sure you're okay? I swear, it's just for a little while. Understand? It's not like Val's just screwing me over. She's screwing you, too. Doesn't that make you even a *little* mad?"

Sarah's curtain of platinum hair hid her face. "I'm mad at her. She broke her promise to me and Vlad. She swore she'd never split us up. With six witnesses she swore, but she did it anyway. Did you hear Vlad crying? He's just not strong, Dimi."

"Shh. I know. Then you see what I'm trying to do?" He rubbed her arm in sympathy. "Don't you wish you could make Val even half as mad as you? Don't you want to get even with her for what she's done to us? Or what she's doing to Vlad? Trust me. We'll go home, but in our own sweet time, under our own terms. She'll have to play our way this time. Can you hang in here with me?"

She gazed into his eyes, dark like Vlad's but not as large. His hair was darker than Vlad's, nearly black. Vlad's was softer, though, and not as thick. Sarah didn't like sudden changes, and this was certainly a last-minute impulse, but Dimi was older and he was in charge. She had to be thankful for that, because if it weren't for him, Valeria would have locked her up in a hospital instead. She had to do what he said. That was part of the deal, and she'd agreed to it before a judge.

"I don't have a choice, do I."

"Well, if you really, really, *really* insist ..."

"Just make it quick." Sarah lay down, unsure if she was sicker from the change in gravity or the heartache crushing her.

He dragged her up for a late dinner, though she ate little and asked to return before he'd finished. Morbidly tired, Sarah corralled herself in her bed with the knapsack and closed her eyes.

"You're going to sleep?" Dmitri said.

"Yes. Aren't you?"

"I guess I could. You don't expect me to kiss you goodnight, do you?"

"No." Their brother Viktor would have. Viktor always had a kiss for her. She was his best girlfriend. He'd said so himself, dozens of times.

Dmitri flipped back his own sheet and ordered the room to kill the lights. "Good night, then."

Sarah sat up fast. "Dimi!"

"What?"

"Put the lights back on a little."

"Lights, ten percent," he ordered the room, and the overheads glowed dimly. "What's the matter? We always sleep in the dark."

"It's a strange room. What if I need the lavatory?"

"Whatever." Dmitri lay down and waited for his thoughts to clear enough for sleep.

* * *

Auburn hair draped in a feathery sheet over the girl's naked breasts. Her long-lashed eyes looked deep into Dmitri's as she slid her body across his bare chest. His young body convulsed with pleasure as she pressed her lips into the hollow between his ear and jaw, her soft breath blowing gently in his ear. He'd been waiting for this moment his entire life. He twisted to roll over and return her kisses with animal passion, caressing a round breast, but he tangled in the blanket. He couldn't turn over. She was lying on the blanket. She wouldn't get off the blanket. She wouldn't move off the damned blanket. She was ... fading away ...

Dmitri could have cried to see the dream disappear. The girl seemed so real! He could smell her spicy perfume, still feel the creamy softness of her bronzed skin, feel his groin ache with need for her. He rolled over, still mostly asleep, but she was lying on the blanket and he couldn't move.

She what?

Dmitri bolted upright to find Sarah curled next to him, asleep on the blanket.

"What the Hell are you doing!" he shouted, stabbing her with his elbow. "You can't sleep here!"

Sarah fell off the narrow bed with a thump. "I had a nightmare," she explained in a small voice. Her violet-blue eyes looked bigger and darker in the dim light. "Kat hugs me when I can't sleep."

He clutched the blanket to his chest. "That's because she's a *girl*! Nine-year-old girls do not crawl in bed with sixteen-year-old boys! Especially their brothers! The least you could have done was warn me!"

Sarah scrambled onto her bed. "You were sleeping. I was afraid to wake you. I thought it would be okay. I always climb in bed with Vlad when I can't sleep. I'm sorry." She leaned her back against the wall and pulled her knees up to her chest, rocking in self-consolation.

"Lights up," Dmitri ordered. He ran a hand through his sleep-messed hair. He knew for a fact Sarah suffered brutal nightmares, trapped still asleep but part awake, screaming and fighting invisible demons that seemed so real to her. Her medications were supposed to help, but the day had been unusually stressful.

He climbed out of bed and sat next to her, bare feet sticking out over the side of her bed. "I'm sorry for yelling. I was dreaming, too, and I think you kind of got worked into the dream. I didn't expect you to be there."

Sarah nodded. Two tears slid onto her cheeks. She tipped her head back and blinked, keeping the rest contained.

Dimi noticed. "Hey! Hey!" He put a guilty arm around her shoulders. "I'm *sorry*. We'll work something out about your dreams, okay?"

Sarah scrubbed her eyes with the heels of her hands. "It's like I don't even know you, Dimi. I've lived with you all my life, but... This isn't the same. I agreed to this because I liked you. You were nice to me, and you were funny and made me laugh inside. This is different. I've never been alone with just *you*. I'm trying to be good, but it's going to take time to get used to you like this." She hugged her knees and rested her head on them.

"I know. I feel it, too. It'll get easier, I promise. We'll work it all out." He slid up to the top of her bed, pushed the pillow next to the wall, and slouched against it.

"Come on," he said, patting the space next to him. "I guess I can sleep like this for half a night. You're not Vlad. You're housebroken."

The strain on Sarah's face eased. She crawled up the bed and nestled in his arm. "Viktor used to sit up like this with me."

"Yeah, he did, didn't he. Well, if he did it, I guess that means I'm doing something right."

Four

A loud knock woke David too early the next morning. He sat up, needing a second to remember where he was. Sergei and Vlad, asleep in the other bed, sat up as well.

"Come in."

Uncle Tomas opened the door. "Breakfast is at seven." He noticed the bedmates. "I wondered where you went. If you'd rather, I can have the rooms rearranged, have three beds put in here."

"No, thanks," David said. "We were all up kind of late, so they burned out here. Dimi will be here today, anyway." *Late?* It had been after two. It was easier to stuff Vlad in the empty bed than drag him back to the other room asleep, and David figured Sergei would keep the little wretch from falling out of bed.

"That's fine. David, isn't it?" Uncle Tomas remembered. "May I speak to you for a minute, please? Out here, alone?"

"I guess." David followed him out.

Uncle Tomas shut the door. "I had a long talk with Mamá last night, and I'm afraid I've got good news and bad news, whichever is which."

"About what?" David hadn't been here long enough or said enough to mess things up – yet.

"I don't know what you are used to, but no doubt things will run differently here. You can keep the hair and earrings, but the mustache has to go. I'm sorry. I know what it can mean to a boy your age, but it's the best I can do. Mamá doesn't care for facial hair, especially on young men. If you need remover or growth inhibitor, I can have some brought up unobtrusively."

Annoyance settled on David's face, and he didn't do much to hide it. "No thank you, sir. I have some." Experience made him suspicious. "Did Val ask you to say that?"

"The decree came from Mamá herself. Should I have asked Valeria to tell you instead?"

"No! No, that's fine. It's probably better you don't. I'll take care of it." He put his hand on the door, hoping he'd be excused.

"And, David? Keep the earrings small. It wasn't easy to get them approved."

"Yes sir. Thank you, sir. I'm sure it wasn't." David tried to seem grateful, amazed that his uncle had had the courtesy to confront him directly, rather than filter the message through Valeria. Obviously Val hadn't had time to poison Tomas against him yet. "That old woman doesn't like us much, does she."

Tomas chuckled. "Give her some time. I'm afraid your grandmother doesn't know what's popular – not that I really do, either. It's not that she doesn't want you here, she's just a little overwhelmed. She'll settle down once she's learned your names. She's not as bad as you think."

* * *

Uncle Tomas had six channels to his comm system, linked to nearly every room in the house. David, lip reddened but hairless, hoped to try some investigation of his own. No doubt he and Sergei could find them. They knew Dmitri better than Val.

Their uncle, however, had other ideas, including a tour of the city. The twins declined, leaving Katya and the four boys to take up the offer.

David balked. "You can't fool me. You want him to get us out of here and keep us busy. Well, I'm not going! I can navigate a commlink, too, you know."

"Please, David," Katya begged. "There's nothing you can do here. Chances are they'll be waiting when we get back. Uncle Tomas has already cleared his schedule. You can't insult him like that after he's been so kind."

David went, but not happily. He rode through Minsk in the back of his uncle's Copernicus 565 Super Cell J low-altitude luxury cruiser, seated with Nikky and Vlad. The pearl-gray cruiser was of a class David had only dreamed of: the cloud-like interior, the smooth deceleration, the vibrationless ride so unlike the jittery, twelve-passenger workhorse they'd had on Navara. Any other day he would have asked to see the power arrays and tech schematics, pried off an access panel or two, but today his thoughts were elsewhere. Cities were all the same. They all had markets, schools and civic buildings, restaurants, hotels and tourist attractions. A little luck and he'd never have to set foot in the overgrown marble library Sergei sighed at longingly. Who cared about monuments to centuries-old wars towering in snow-covered parks? The people were dead and out of their misery. The sky mirrored his mood – sunless, cold steel gray.

He spoke for the first time in an hour. "Did Father live in Minsk, too?"

Tomas adjusted a forward climate control. "I believe he did, but I'm not sure exactly where. I could find out for you, if you'd like."

"No need. Just wondering." He flicked his thumbnail against his teeth, thinking. He knew nothing about his father's family, nothing at all, except that Katya was named for a sister. Wherever Father grew up, it couldn't have been as nice as Uncle Tomas' place. There was no way such class could breed such abomination. Outside, fat flakes of snow started to fall.

Nikky twisted until he squirmed out of the seat restraints. "Look! Look! What's that?"

"It's snowing, Nik," Katya said as he crawled over David to press his nose to the window. "That's how the snow gets on the ground."

"It's comin' from the sky!" Nikky shouted. "Sarah tolded me about snow! Look, Vladdy! Look! It's comin' out everywheres!"

David sat Nikky on his lap, saving himself from the sharp knees gouging his groin. He caught sight of Vlad's chin quivering. "Knock it off," he warned in a low voice.

"It's the one thing she wanted to see …."

"It's February! It's not about to melt! Stop acting like they're dead. So you didn't get to share the first snowflake you saw. Turn it off!" *Goddamned fucking little crybaby.*

Vlad swallowed and ran a finger over his eyes.

Uncle Tomas found a place to settle the cruiser. "Close enough. Come! We'll get some lunch and look in the shops. Valeria said you boys need snowgear."

Nikky spun in circles, trying to see all the snow fall at once. Sergei showed him how to catch snowflakes on his tongue, and that put an end to any forward progress until Uncle Tomas picked Nikky up and carried him. He snapped joyfully at flakes over Tomas's shoulder.

After lunch, they walked the busy commercial streets of the city's grand center, until Tomas entered a clothing boutique. "I have four desert boys who need to be outfitted for snow," he told the assistant. "What do you recommend?" The woman showed him various items.

Katya examined an advertised price. She had Valeria's bankcard to pay for the purchases, but the arctic suit Uncle Tomas was stuffing Nikky into cost almost half of what Val wanted to spend on everything. "These are average prices?" she asked casually.

"I have no idea," Tomas admitted. "It's a quality brand; I never bother to compare. Is that warmer, Snowtiger?" He pulled the fasteners to the suit's hood tight around the child's face. "Now wait for everyone else before you run outside."

David waved from a distant corner. "Sergei! Get a look at this!" He whistled softly at a display of black jackets. "Nice or what!"

Sergei came to admire. "Whoa! They real?"

David searched for a content label. "Yeah! It's an actual cow skin! Look at the *price*! Feel that, though! There's nothing like *that* on all of Navara."

Sergei stroked the buttery-soft suede. "Keep dreaming. Maybe in ten years, if we're lucky."

"Tell me you don't see anything here you like," Katya whispered behind the boys while Uncle Tomas outfitted a somber Vladimir. "Val will kill me if I spend even half as much as he's picked out. What am I going to do?"

"Relax, Kat. You don't think Serg and I would be caught dead in arctic suits, do you? Look at this, though." David showed her the jacket.

She brushed the leather with her fingers. "I won't even ask… "

"You don't want to know. It's real."

Katya jerked her hand back. "Real? *Real* real? Ick!"

Tomas joined the group with Vlad and Nikky, overhearing. "You're right, Katerina. It's controversial to wear leather, but I admit, I've indulged in it once or twice myself. Try it on, David."

David shook his head. Even Father didn't wear animal. "Nah. We were just looking."

"Try it on," his uncle insisted.

David ran a finger along the jacket's collar.

"Go on! They take the teeth out before they sew it. It can't bite you."

David glanced at Sergei.

Sergei shrugged back.

David chose one and slipped his arms in. The silvery lining was imitation silk, slippery and cool to the touch. Invisible fasteners closed five centimeters to the left of center, and silver chains adjusted the fit at the hips. David caught sight of himself in the store's compufit mirror.

Katya saw the gleam in his eye. The jacket matched his style, made even the silly haircut seem right. "It's not a winter coat, though," she said tactfully. "One day in the snow and it would be ruined forever. That's the beauty of imitation fabrics."

David took one last look. "You're right. It is nice, though."

"So wear it on dry days," Uncle Tomas suggested.

"I'd get pretty cold on the wet ones." David returned the planet's most wonderful jacket to the display.

Tomas gestured toward a life-size video display of models in high-style winter wear. "So get something else for the snow."

David choked. "No, sir. Val's got eight of us to keep in clothes. I need something more multipurpose."

"Nonsense! It's nice, you want it, put it on the pile. It's my bill."

Katya paled. "That's very generous of you, Uncle Tomas, but we couldn't possibly allow you to buy all this. We appreciate the offer, but we must refuse."

"I won't hear another word about it. Every year I sent your Mother a cash transfer for her birthday. I can't do that anymore; consider it a birthday gift from your mother."

The mention of Mother and birthdays, days before Nikky's birthday and a week or so before the first anniversary of Marina's birth and Mother's death, added to Katya's guilt. "I can't allow it," she insisted. "Not without Val's approval."

Uncle Tomas held up a hand. "Leave it to me. David, give me the jacket."

David knew better than to hope, but his uncle didn't sound like 'no' was an acceptable answer. Katya's look of panic didn't help at all. "Thank you, sir, but I couldn't ask you for something like that."

Uncle Tomas looked from David to Katya several times. "Will you stop trying to outpolite each other? I'm starting to feel insulted." He grabbed a random jacket. "Is it this one?"

"No sir," David said, retrieving the correct size.

Katya winced. "Go up a measure. You're still growing."

"How about you, Sergei?" Tomas asked, hand poised to take a second jacket. "Do you like this style, too?"

Sergei shook his head. "No thank you, sir. I'll stick to the artificials. I'm on the cow's side."

They tore into the house, wearing new outerwear and carrying their old desert robes. Over his shoulder, David carried a warmer, weatherproof coat wrapped in store plastic. After a brief search, they found their sisters in a media-entertainment room off the back hallway. The grand house had no holovision platform, but the videoscreen took up the better part of an entire wall, four by five meters in size. Angled ceiling panels and more than a dozen powerful audio units achieved acoustic perfection. Even the commlink tied into the giant screen. For a room seldom used by anyone but guests, it was terribly impressive.

Nikky and Vlad recounted their excursion, each to a different twin. Valeria balanced Nikky on her knees, laughing as he chattered about the snow. Her eyes caught sight of David, regal in the black suede, and her smile faded. She slid Nikky to the sofa and stood up.

Katya intervened. "Before you say anything, you need to know he did his very best to refuse. You would have been proud of him, Val. He's got something for the snow as well."

Val examined the parkas and hats and insulated gloves with a critical eye. She cringed at the fact they had worn the new thermal boots through the house. She ran a hand down the front of David's jacket, locking her eyes on his with an accusatory gaze. David pulled himself up taller – still six centimeters shy of his sister – and met the inquisition fearlessly, knowing he'd done nothing wrong this time.

Val kept her anguish to a whisper. "Katya! I *trusted* you with the bank card! There's no way …"

"Val, I can explain. *Please* don't be upset with David… "

Uncle Tomas entered, having shed his coat. He stood behind the group and clapped his hands on David's strong shoulders. "What do you think, Valeria?" he asked proudly. "Does this coat make the boy? He drives a hard bargain, I'll give him that. I nearly had to seal him in it to get him to agree."

"It's very nice, but David knows full well that's not the kind of coat he was supposed to buy. He'll have ruined it a month from now." Valeria touched the fabric again. "Is that *real*?"

David nodded, brushing her fingerprints from the leather.

"I only buy the best." Tomas pushed Sergei's hat forward over his eyes. He winked when the boy turned around glaring, expecting to be mad at David.

Val frowned. "What do you mean *you*? I gave Katya our banking card… "

"*That's* what I tried to tell you," Katya sighed under her breath. "I tried, Val. I really, really wish *you'd* been there… "

Tomas waved everything away. "It was entirely my pleasure. You do need to teach your brothers and sisters to accept gifts more graciously though. I'm not used to hearing refusals to my offers, especially three or four times in a row. You must run a tight ship."

Val adjusted the cuffs on Nikky's arctic suit as he hugged her leg. "Uncle Tomas… That was a most kind and thoughtful thing to do, but, really, I can't expect you to clothe everyone as well. We're extremely grateful for your hospitality, but… "

"Not another word about it. I've missed out on twenty-something years' worth of nieces and nephews. I don't see where I can't give a gift or two to help make up for that." Tomas held his smile, but his eyes had lost their amusement.

"I don't wish to cause offense, sir, but perhaps we should discuss this further in private."

Tomas lost the smile. "If you insist. I must attend to some missed calls; shall we say in a half hour, in my study?"

"Thank you, sir. I appreciate it."

Tomas regained his energy. "Well, boys! You won't freeze now. Why don't you take our Snowtiger here outside and enjoy the snow? When I was your age and the snow was right, we would build great snowcastles between the trees. Go out through the door in the kitchen. Marya won't mind."

Nikky let out a shriek of delight. Sergei looked at Vladimir, and a wild grin curled across his face. "Snowball fight!" Vlad gave a whoop and raced him out of the room, Nikky running hard just to keep them in sight.

"Walk!" Galina called after them.

Tomas excused himself. "I'll see you in a bit."

David unfastened the jacket. "You can stop staring at me. I never asked to own it; I only stopped to look. I could only refuse so many times before he got pissed."

Valeria's hands dropped to her sides with a soft slap. "I believe you. I just wish it hadn't been something so extravagant."

"I take it you found them, since you're not searching. What time are they coming in? Vlad and I are going with you to get them."

Val paused. "No, David. Their names aren't on any of the incoming passenger lists, not from anywhere. I don't know what's going on."

"What do you mean?" he demanded. "They have to be on today's lists! Why did you stop? Why aren't you working on it? What did you *do* to them?" His voice rose like a thundercloud. "*Damn* you!"

He stormed to the room's interface, pitching the extra coat on a sofa and ordering the display on. The huge screen glowed to life and flashed an options menu. He chose an outside comm line and ordered a search of his own. The screen narrowed the parameters in thirty-centimeter letters.

Galina rose from the sofa. "There's nothing more we can do right now. The next passenger update is posted at 1800 hours. Val and I contacted City Security at Kar Ku'umi and filed a missing persons report. They'll work on it from their end."

"I knew it! I *knew* it!" His fist pounded the control panel, impatient at the lack of answers. "I knew I should have been here finding them instead of dragging around some goddamned city! I never should have left without them."

He whirled on Valeria. "Goddamn you, Val! This is all your fault! If you weren't so freakin' high and mighty, they'd have been with us all along!"

"Shhh, David! I feel just as bad about this as you do." Val put her hand on his arm. "We'll – "

David wrenched away. "*Don't you touch me!*" His blue eyes glared cold and sinister as he pointed at her.

"*You lost them, you find them, Val!* You *find* them! You find them or else!" He dropped his arm to his side, hands clenched into meaty fists that ached to lash out and disprove his impotence through the destruction of matter, but he didn't dare here. Not yet. He breathed hard for several seconds, let the danger pass, then shook his head in disgust. He grabbed his other coat.

"I'm outta here." He headed for the door.

"David!" Galina called in a strained voice. He stopped.

"David, please! Don't say anything to Vlad yet. Don't upset him unnecessarily."

The back of David's dark head swung side to side. He stalked back into the room.

"You don't get it, do you? Do you *really* think I could upset Vlad any more than he is? I've tortured that kid so much his bony ass rattles in his skin when I so much as walk near him! So I know when that kid comes to me," he took a step forward, stabbing himself in the chest with his thumb, "to *me*!" He swallowed, eyes burning with an unfamiliar emotion. "He comes to *me* looking for some kind of break from what's going through his undersized head, that's when I know just how bad off that kid is without Sarah here to take care of him. There's nothing I could possibly do to make him feel any worse than he does already. I'm the one keeping that kid together! I know you don't think shit about me, but give me *some* credit.

"Screw all of you," he spat, and stalked out.

* * *

Tomas answered the knock at his study door. Juggling business on both sides of the Atlantic, as well as off-planet trips, his dealings ran on a clock of their own, and a home office kept him in touch. "Come in, Valeria. Please, sit."

"Thank you." Valeria chose one of several heavy chairs before Tomas's desk. Compared to the rest of the house, the office seemed spartan, lacking the ornamentation that proliferated like fungus in the main rooms. The grand L-shaped desk anchored the center of the room. Cabinets of more modern design lined the wall behind it, all bearing flashing security locks.

Tomas studied her with piercing eyes, chin on his thumb. He didn't smile. The silence was uncomfortable, but Val said nothing.

He dropped his hand into his lap. "Well, Valeria, I understand you're not happy with me. I hope this once, at least, you'll let the children keep the gifts."

Val blushed. Once again she was bulldozing when all she needed was a hand trowel. "I'm sorry if I seemed rude, but I never intended for you to purchase those things. I hope that's not what you were led to believe. We are perfectly able to pay our way."

"The idea was mine. I was the one enjoying myself. Katerina all but wrestled me for the right to purchase the items, and I told David I would buy the jacket with or without his permission. He was calm and polite on the outside, but you could see the excitement in his eyes," Tomas said, remembering. "I don't often see that kind of frank appreciation. I found it refreshing. I'm sorry if it upset you."

Val coughed on her chagrin. "I'm sorry, sir." She stared for a moment at the carved edge of the desk, then lifted her head to run her eyes once more around the room. So different, yet in a way strangely reminiscent of several of the homes her family had lived in.

"I'm afraid we're all a bit - stunned - by everything here. Two months ago, I knew Mother had a brother, but I didn't know your name. I knew Mother was estranged from her family, but no one ever spoke of it. After his trial, I asked Father if there was anyone who could help us. He gave me his sister's name, and a guess where I might find her. I asked about Mother's alleged brother. He told me Mother's family wouldn't give us the time of day, that they'd refused her efforts to patch things up. Eventually he told me, but he wouldn't tell me the address. I searched every type of database; you were my thirty-seventh response. Five years I was at university right there in Moscow; we lived there seven years before that. I must have walked past the Ivanov building hundreds of times, and I never knew.

"As I said in my letter to you," Val continued, sometimes looking at him, sometimes at her hands fumbling in her lap, "all I wanted was for someone to find us an apartment, or perhaps lend a floor to sleep on while we found one ourselves. We know we're a crowd; we didn't want anyone put out by the commotion. I had no idea Mother came from a house so... *palatial* as this. Father made a good living," Val explained with apology. "He just had to stretch it among fourteen of us. Our house in Kiev was similar. We had twelve rooms on the edge of the city. Mother had her piano and her art and fancy carpets and the hired help, just like here. She was very proud of that house, and Father was proud he could buy it for her." Those were good times, in that beautiful house. When Val thought of home, of her parents together, she remembered that house.

"Mamá will be glad to hear that," Tomas said. "My father had this vision of my sister starving to death in some freezing apartment somewhere."

Valeria laughed. "No, sir! Father would never have allowed that." She grew serious again. "We aren't poor relatives looking for a handout. That's not why we're here. Father never owed a credit to anyone, and I'm not about to change that precept. I mean it when I say we had no idea how you lived. I'm sorry if I was tactless, but I don't want everyone to get used to having luxuries Galina and I won't be able to provide, at least not at the start."

"I see."

Uncle Tomas certainly didn't like anyone to know his mind until he was ready. "I'm sorry, sir. That didn't come out right. I'm most grateful for everything you've done for us. If you threw us out tonight, I'd still be thankful. You and Grandmother have been most gracious hosts."

"Valeria," Tomas said, annoyingly bland, "if I had any doubt of your intent, I would not have invited you here. I research my endeavors well. Resemblances aside, I have no doubt you are my sister's children. A blood test proved it. Yes, I kept in private contact with my sister, but I rarely knew her location. I know at one point she lived in Tbilisi, I knew at some point she was in Moscow, but she didn't think direct contact would be a good idea. She kept details to herself, afraid Papa might make trouble. No one had been murdered on Navara in at least two centuries; your father's trial made galactic headlines. I heard the name, called up a biography from the news agency, and realized I'd uncovered my sister's family. I wish I had known earlier of your family's difficulties. I would have helped in any way possible. I sent an anonymous staff to observe at the trial. I wanted to contact you directly then, but I didn't know if it might complicate matters even more."

"I'm sure it would have. Mother was well aware of what was going on. She was quite skilled at handling Father's moods. I think she was very wise not to get anyone else involved. Father relied on her for everything; if he thought she had lost faith in him, it could only have made things worse. Hence, everything fell apart after she died."

Valeria could discuss her parents in vague terms, or at least in happy ones, but the wounds of Father's trial were too new, too raw, and she had too many worries to waste energy digging up the more sordid details of Father's alcoholism. Home hadn't been bad when she'd left for university. It had taken months for her to believe the stories of her siblings, to believe her own eyes.

"Perhaps. I've enjoyed these two days with your family, Valeria. They're great kids, full of fun. I was married for fourteen years." Pain pinched his face, gaze traveling across the room to a framed holoportrait of a pretty woman. "Lora was five months pregnant with our first child, a little boy, when she died in a commuter wreck. We hadn't even picked out a name. I'd like to think my son would have been a lot like your Nikky. He's a wonderful little boy. He certainly loves the snow."

"I'm so sorry. I had no idea..."

Her uncle brightened. "Of course you didn't. Anyway... My father was the one who kept our families apart. He forbade Mamá from displaying photos, even speaking Maryana's name. He erased her very existence. I begged them to tell me where she was, but I got nowhere until Maryana contacted me, trying to make peace. I kept up that contact, not as frequently as I could have, I'm ashamed to say. When Papa died, the anger died with him.

"Family is family, Valeria. As far as I'm concerned, half this house would have belonged to your mother. If you want to live elsewhere, pursue a career, that's your business, but the house is open to you. You're welcome to stay, be it one day or the next ten years. I understand your protectiveness of your brothers and sisters. They're an exuberant bunch, and I'm afraid I may have gotten carried away. I apologize for that.

"I'm asking you to stay, Valeria," Tomas pleaded, "if not for any reason of your own, then to help me ease my guilt over not being there for your mother for the last twenty-four years. I promise to back off and let you parent everyone as you've been doing. It looks to me like you've been doing a wonderful job."

Valeria couldn't help but laugh, blinking back tears. Her uncle's manner was soft and soothing, even wistful, so very much like her mother's. He sounded honest and heartfelt, dangling this lifeline before her. Guilt interrupted her relief.

What would her father think of the arrangement?

Begging a favor was one thing, but... Father had never been welcome here. He'd been hated, denounced, spat on, threatened, and here she sat in the lion's den, suckling on the grace of his slanderers. On the other hand, how could she insult Tomas by saying 'no?' She'd have to work that out in another conversation. At the moment, she didn't have much choice.

"Thank you, sir. You are most kind, but if I were any good at parenting, we wouldn't be in the messes we're in right now," she confided. "If you're really sincere, I'd like to accept your offer – at least temporarily. I'm afraid I've got to head back to Navara ..."

* * *

David changed coats and ran outside with his brothers. He wanted desperately to get away, away from Val, away from the big strange house, away from the turmoil inside him. On Navara he would have dropped with his friends, taken his share of mood-altering substances, maybe raised a little hell and returned feeling vindicated. Here, he had no friends, no contraband yet, and nowhere to run. He burned off anger slogging through the snow, building walls for battlements and whipping snowballs at Vlad and Sergei as fast and hard as he could.

He fled to his room after dinner, the first chance he had to be alone. He kicked off his shoes and started the room's computer on a trail. He wouldn't stand by and watch Val fumble everything. While the computer ran a search, he ran one of his own, ransacking the

42

shoulder pack he'd carried on their flight.

Was it still there?

He dumped the contents across the bed, poking. In a pocket sat a voucher with the small amount of spending money Val had given each of them at the start of the trip. David still had most of his, hoarding it in case he had to help Dmitri. *There.* He picked out a crumpled scrap of plastic paper and smoothed it. On it was an eighteen-digit code in Dmitri's scraggly handwriting.

Before they left Navara, Dmitri and Valeria were at each other's throats. Valeria had had legal custody of David for 30 minutes; he was torn between support of his brother and not wanting to start a full-fledged war with Val from the word go. He had honestly meant to try and make the arrangement work, but hell erupted almost immediately. Val would antagonize Dimi, and he'd grab or shove her in response. Each time, Val would threaten to call City Security, and Dmitri feared she would. He'd slipped David the access numbers for his bank card.

"I'm trusting you," Dmitri'd warned him. "Don't look at it except to get me out of holding. Just because I put you down as an alternate, don't think you can snitch money to have fun with your friends. I know every credit in there on a first-name basis, and you're the only other person with the numbers."

The honor stunned him. Everyone considered him the waste in the family, the one that went bad, never to be trusted; no one had ever shown any faith in him. He kept a tight hold on the paper, afraid he'd lose it, afraid he might have to use it, afraid of disappointing the one person who seemed to think he was capable of responsibility. Val never did call the authorities, but David hadn't destroyed the paper. He ran the numbers through the computer.

He couldn't access the credits from here; he'd need a secured finance server, but he could check the account's status. The screen clicked off menu after menu.

There. A 938 credit debit authorized at Shir P'an, the day *after* they should have left for Earth. So they'd made it to Shir P'an. Now, where'd they go?

Nothing Earthbound, Val had insisted.

David tried to think. "Computer, access: spaceport, Shir P'an, Navara II; flight schedules, Earthdate eight February, 2264." His shoulders sagged as more than four hundred entries scrolled rapidly.

"Computer: refine, outbound ships only." Half the list disappeared. "Computer: same list, eliminate all Earth-bound flights." Seven flights vanished from the directory screen.

David was on a roll now. "Computer: cross-reference flight schedule eight February with flight booking. List all destinations originating Shir P'an, Navara, costing 400 to 500 interstellar credits." He hunched close to the screen as the list disappeared. Six destinations remained; thirteen flights. *Almost there!*

He took a deep breath. "Computer: present screen, list passengers for eight February, 2264."

INFORMATION UNAVAILABLE

The flights had landed; the information had been superseded.

David's hopes sank.

What are you up to, Dimi? You promised you'd be right behind us. You promised me!

David rested his mouth on his knuckles. If Val had done something like that to him, he'd be out for murder. Dmitri wasn't the type for blood; he was more creative than that.

What kind of retaliation are you plotting, Dim? Why wouldn't you tell me? *You know I would have helped.*

David needed more capable brain power.

He walked in next door without a knock. Sergei looked up from his room's interface, trying his own hand at following the invisible trail, for Vlad's sake. Vladimir gazed out the tall windows, his back to the room, pretending to watch the running lights of high-altitude globe-hoppers crossing the starry sky. He didn't turn at the sound of the door.

"Hey," Sergei acknowledged.

David saw the screen. "Forget it. You're on the wrong track."

"You find something?!"

"Maybe." David motioned toward Vlad. Sergei shook his head grimly. Vlad's shoulders heaved with silent sobs, and David felt that strange twinge again.

"Listen," he whispered, hoping Vlad couldn't hear. "I don't know what Dimi's doing, but he's not coming back. He bought two tickets to one of six possible destinations, none of them Earth."

"How do you know?"

David wagged a finger. "You didn't believe me when I told you I know more than Val, did you. Computer, overlay commlink five," he ordered, and the screen from his room transferred to Sergei's. He explained his logic.

"*Why?*" Sergei said. "Why would he do that? He's *got* to come back! What about Sarah?"

"Shah! *Shh!*" David motioned toward Vlad. He kept his voice low. "That's what scares me. He doesn't have to. He's got a fat load of cash, the world thinks he's an adult, and he's got papers on Sarah. But he told me absolutely, positively he was following us."

"He wouldn't do that to Sarah," Sergei agreed. "He was all set to give her over to Galina, even if he couldn't make the flight."

"Think on it for me." David watched Vladimir rub a hand across his face. He left the computer and sat on Sergei's bed.

"Hey, Vlad."

44

Vlad gave a long sniff and turned around. His smile pressed too tight, eyes bloodshot. "I'm okay, Dave! I'm not bein' a crybaby!"

The boy was so pathetic David didn't know whether to laugh or cry. "Come here, Vlad," he beckoned. "We need to talk. Man to Man." Someone had to break the news. Valeria would drag hope out forever, making it worse.

Vlad's eyes grew round with fear. He looked to Sergei for direction; Sergei hesitated, then gave a nod. Vladimir slunk over, braced for punishment.

David reeled him in until the boy sat on his knee. "Look, Forkman, you're still doing this all wrong. There's a time and a place for everything. Remember when Father used to whip the skin off us?"

Vlad rubbed his nose wetly across the back of his hand. "Nobody could forget that."

" 'Course not. It hurt like Hell. There wasn't one of us who didn't cry after getting hit with that a couple times. I did, Dimi did, Vik, too …"

"Not Sarah!" Vlad reminded him with pride. "She didn't always cry."

David flashed a look of annoyance. "Because Sarah's wacked in the head! She blew a couple of those super-smart circuits of hers not crying. The point is, it was okay to cry then, you had a damned good reason. Remember Mother's funeral? Every one of us cried our eyes out …"

"Sarah didn't."

David clenched his teeth. "Because Sarah's *wacked*, you idiot! You know it! You've seen it! Enough about her! We could cry then because you're supposed to cry at a funeral. You're expected to. What I'm saying is …."

David faltered. He looked at the floor, then at Vlad, wishing there was still somebody he could look up to like this, who could give him the same advice. "I think this is getting to be one of those times. I'm … giving you my permission. I'm officially … giving up hope."

Vlad gave a distrustful sniff. "On me, or on …?"

David sighed sourly. "No. There may still be hope for you, Vlad. I'm officially giving up hope on the … situation."

Vlad slid off his brother's knee. "You can't give up! You're all they've *got*! Valeria doesn't *want* to find them! She *hates* them!"

"I know they're not dead, but I don't know what Dimi's doing and I have no way to find out. But I can't sit around the rest of my life, waiting." He swallowed hard against a sob of his own.

"I'm too goddamned freakin' miserable this way. I got to stop thinking about it, and I can't with you walking around bawling all the time. So let's have our little funeral now, get this over with, and when they do turn up, we'll be twice as glad to see them. You have my official permission to cry until sunrise without penalty, and then you're not going to do it again unless another good reason comes along. Got it?"

Dimi promised he would be here!

Vlad's face screwed itself up as he collapsed against his brother's neck.

"Why?" he wailed on David's broad shoulder. "Why aren't they here? Where is she? I want her here! Val promised! It's - not - fair!"

Caring had never part of David's vocabulary, unless preceded by *not*. He expected Vlad to go back to his window or throw himself on the bed or something, not start wiping snot on him. His first instinct was to shove the kid away, but after two aborted tries, David put his arms around his little brother, holding him tighter and tighter as he fought for control of his own. He put his head down, biting his lip, refusing to give in. *A reputation was a reputation, dammit.*

Sergei slid next to David, a hand of concern on Vlad's back. David pulled him into the cluster.

"Get it all out now, Vlad," he said in a strained voice, "'cause if I catch you doing it tomorrow, I'm going to kick your ass."

Five

Alpha Centauri V
Earthdate: 12 February, 2264

Dmitri stretched backwards on the mat in the sunshine that radiated delightfully *warm,* not fiery hot. The sky was greener than Earth's, more teal than blue, and clouds – white, fluffy *moisture* clouds – drifted lazily high in the sky. A refreshing salty breeze blew in off the bay, nothing like the hot, gritty, desiccating winds that blasted the Navaran landscape. He lounged on the beach in his swims, blissfully content.

"Now isn't this better?"

"If you say so." Sarah sighed, sitting on the damp sand a few meters closer to the water, one of his shirts hanging loosely over her swimsuit. It wasn't until Father's trial two months ago that she'd learned just how terribly her back had been scarred during a brutal beating. She kept covered. Her fingers dug a pebble out of the sand and threw it at the low surf at her toes. "You promised we could see snow. We had more than enough sun and sand on Navara. I hoped to at least see *trees.*"

Three days, and Dmitri would be the first to admit, he was in over his head. Being in charge alone wasn't anything like babysitting at home. Sarah moped and sighed every time he wanted to do something – something that didn't take them in the immediate direction of home. The weight of his new responsibility hung like a stone around his neck.

"So go sit on the grass," he said, knowing full well she wouldn't walk back across the dune breaks and boardwalk to the lawns. Sarah was never more than an arm's length away, holding his hand or grabbing onto his clothes, waiting anxiously by lavatory doors. Dmitri didn't remember Sarah as being this fearful. She'd always been the brave one, Vlad's nervous hand perpetually locked in hers, unafraid to fight someone even twice her size.

He worked out a temporary measure on the night fears. She could sleep on his bed, but only if she woke him first and he agreed, and she wasn't allowed under his blankets. At home, there had been safety in numbers. He had to admit, being separated from their litter *was* a bit strange, but he enjoyed the freedom.

If only she would.

Sarah squinted at him, hand shading her eyes. "When can I call Earth? I promised I would call every day, and you haven't let me yet."

"When we get back to the room," Dmitri swore, and rolled over to toast his back.

"Is that on real time, or the unknown-distant-future-time in your head we've been living on?"

"Before dinner! If it's gonna be such a big deal all the time, I can always stick you on a transport and hope someone meets you when you land," he threatened. "Of course, you better hope Galina gets the message, because you know Val won't do it."

Sarah hung her head in contrition, the waterfall of hair over her face. "It's not a problem."

A shadow blocked the sun as another beachgoer spread out a mat near Dmitri. He opened his eyes to see an exquisite pair of human feet. He followed them upwards with his eyes, past the slender ankles, up the long, long shapely legs that seemed to stretch to the sun, to short dark hair and a heart-shaped face. Her yellow beachwear was impolitely brief. The two-piece top must have been glued on, for Dimi didn't see any type of string holding it in place.

She leaned over in the swimsuit that wasn't. "I'm sorry. Did I get sand on your mat?"

Dmitri propped himself on an elbow and gave her his best inviting smile, the one his girlfriend Sharinna said made him irresistible. "Not at all!"

Sarah watched the exchange with disgust. A shell washed up, banging against her foot. She picked it up and examined it without much interest until she saw it contained a tiny creature. Here was someone who never went too far from home.

Six

If Vlad was still upset, he didn't show it the next day. David was impressed, except that Vlad now transferred all that nervous clinging over to him. What started out as a simple compliment a few weeks before had turned into a prison sentence. Vlad didn't hang on him the way he hung on Sarah – Vlad knew better than to touch him – but the boy followed him like a shadow. David couldn't take a piss without Vlad waiting by the door. At least he'd stopped sniveling.

David sat through breakfast, pretending to be absorbed in his food, Vlad and Sergei flanking him like trusted advisors.

Val tried to connect. "David, I said I'm *leaving* for a week. I'm going back to Navara tonight, and I'm taking Katya with me. I'm depending on you to help Galina with the boys, not get them wild. Please."

David stayed perfectly pleasant. "Sure, Gal. Whatever you need. No problem. Even if Val is wasting her time."

"What do you mean?" Galina and Val said at the same time.

"David, if you know something I don't, I would appreciate you sharing it with me," Val said.

David made sure he took time to chew his food and follow it with an entire glass of juice.

Sergei answered for him. "David thinks they've left Navara."

"Why didn't you tell me? What did Dmitri tell you? Where are they?"

David stomped Sergei's foot under the table. "I don't know where they are, Val. It's just a feeling I've got. I offered to help you search, but you said you had everything under control. They aren't en route to Earth, and the passenger lists I found had been superseded, so I don't know. But I'd stake an extra year in school they're not on Navara."

"David," Uncle Tomas said uncomfortably, "if you can shed some light on this, you'd save everyone a lot of aggravation."

"I'm sorry, sir. If I knew more, I wouldn't be sitting here right now."

Galina took the boys into the city, to examine the schools and pursue a couple of employment leads. The thought of starting over in another new school sent acid pouring into Vlad's stomach. Sergei wasn't entirely impressed, either. He'd always been a form ahead; he didn't want to be held back by an arbitrary rule in a policy manual about ages and levels. David wanted no part of any school, ever. Schools were interchangeable, one as boring as the next. Galina indulged Sergei's pleadings and allowed him a half hour to explore the ancient downtown library.

Val pulled them together after lunch, deliberating if she should go to Navara or not, and what to do if she didn't. David kept his eye on Vlad, but the boy stayed composed. He had to give the Rodent credit; while Valeria blathered on about Dmitri and Sarah, Vlad played cards on the carpet with Sergei. Vlad still looked as if his dog had just died, but he'd made a bargain and was trying his small damnedest to keep it.

David dozed in an overstuffed armchair, ignoring the conversations. He'd stayed with Vlad last night until the kid ran dry. At times it had been all David could do to keep from crying with him. Sergei's face had been wet once or twice; he pretended it wasn't, and David pretended not to notice. Sergei was intensely private, not given to loud displays of anger or despair. He poured his frustrations onto paper, not people, and this time something inside David told him not to poke fun.

His mind drifted. Three late nights in a row were taking their toll. There'd been talk of some party next weekend, to introduce them to Grandmother's friends and acquaintances, a whole night of over-dressed strangers whose names he'd never remember, pinching his cheeks and asking questions about where they'd been, what they'd done, where their parents were. He sure as shit wasn't about to change his hair. Let 'em stare! Maybe he'd dye the tips – blond, maybe, or a sizzling puke green. It would probably give the Old Lady a heart attack. Val would stroke out, and he'd probably piss off Uncle Tomas, too. Too bad, 'cause Uncle Tomas seemed like he might be kind of electric under it all...

One of the house staff spoke from the doorway, breaking his reverie. "Excuse me, Miss Valeria, but there's an incoming call for you; the closest comm is the library."

David's eyes flew open, and he saw Vladimir's heart practically burst through his chest. Vlad moved so fast he trampled Sergei in his rush to get out.

"IT'S THEM! IT'S THEM!" he screeched, racing five steps ahead of the pack.

Vlad threw himself onto the library's desk chair as everyone jockeyed for a view of the screen. "SARAH! I *knew* it was you! I knew it! I knew you weren't lost!"

It *was* Sarah on the library monitor, nose lightly sunburned.

Valeria pushed Vlad to the side as she leaned into the screen. "Sarah! Where *are* you! Is everything okay? Are you all right? We've been so worried about you!"

Sarah forced a smile. "I'm okay."

"Where are you? Where's Dimi? What's happened?"

"We're … on Centauri V."

"*Centauri?*" Val's anguish rang loud and clear. "Sarah, what are you doing on Centauri? We've been waiting for you for two days! Where's Dmitri?"

Sarah turned, as if listening to instructions. "He's here."

"Put him on. Let me talk to him."

Sarah made pleading faces, at last stomping her foot, her warning sign of anger, glowering by the time Dmitri appeared next to her on the screen. Seeing Valeria, his features clouded into a cold look of hate.

"Dimi! We've been waiting for you," Val said in her most forgiving voice. "We've been out of our heads with worry about…"

"If you were that worried about us, you wouldn't have left us on Navara," he said. "It's hard to go somewhere you know you're not wanted, and you made it perfectly clear we weren't supposed to come with you. You abandoned us without so much as breakfast. Like you kept reminding me, I'm an adult now; I'm supposed to do things myself. We're traveling a while until things cool down. Maybe we'll catch up with you, maybe we won't. We'll be in touch eventually."

Val's voice shook. "What do you mean, travel? What about Sarah? You can't keep Sarah like that! You belong *here*, Dimi! I'm sorry if I upset you, but we *do* want you here! Sarah, is this what you want, too?"

Sarah waited, pale and strained, at the edge of the picture. "I want to be with Vlad."

"Stay right where you are!" Valeria ordered in a rush, trying to pinpoint the call before Dmitri could cut transmission. "I'm coming to get you. I'll be on a flight within an hour. Wait for me!"

Dmitri pushed Sarah off screen, struggled to keep her there. "*You* can't do that, Val, remember? You kept beating me over the head with the fact *I* am her guardian. You can't touch her."

"Be reasonable! You know that document isn't legal …"

"Prove it."

"*Sarah!*" Val shouted. "Put Sarah back on! Sarah, are you okay? He's not hurting you, is he?"

Sarah pushed onto the screen. "No, Val. Honest! I'm okay. 'Mitri's being really good to me, but I want to come home now. Vlad?"

"Sar?" Vlad wormed under Valeria's arm. The fingers from one hand snaked onto the videopickup, his other hand crawled over to the viewer. Sarah pressed hers against her pickup until, on the screens, the fingers appeared to touch, the closest they could come to holding hands four light-years away. Vladimir's courage fell away, and his lip began its familiar shiver.

"We'll keep in touch when we can, but we're not coming back," Dmitri decided. "Not now, anyway. Maybe after I'm eighteen, and you can't pull shit. We've had enough of your games." His anger slipped as he added, "Tell David... Tell David I'm sorry. I never planned on this. I'm trusting him to take my place. You invented the game, Val, but you won't win it. Check mate."

The screen went black, except for the glowing yellow **END TRANSMISSION** message. Vlad's fingers slid down the screen.

"What the hell is he doing?!" Val whispered.

"*YOU!*" David shouted suddenly, making everyone jump. He spun Valeria away from the viewscreen and seized her throat.

"It's your goddamned fault, you son of a bitch!" He forced her backward across the room, squeezing, squeezing her neck with his strong fingers, ramming her into the wall of shelves on the far side of the room two, three, four times, until several data cases rained down on them. *"It's all your fault!"*

Katya shrieked. *"David! Stop!"*

David hammered a fury-driven fist onto his sister's face. Another followed seconds after, plowing into her unprotected middle and knocking away any air she'd been able to gasp. A third blow, a fourth, now more difficult with Katya and Sergei each trying desperately to hold back a muscular arm, and Galina squeezing between. He landed seven hard blows, blind with rage, before Uncle Tomas came running. Tomas wrapped his arms around David and pulled him back.

"Get her!" someone shouted hysterically. "Hit 'er! *Harder!* Hit 'er again!"

Valeria slid sideways to the floor, face dark, until she began to crow and gasp. Galina knelt, cradling her twin.

"... *deserve* it! And he's right! He's *right!*" Vladimir shrieked. "And now she's *never* coming back! It *IS* all your fault!" He bolted from the room, his footsteps soft thumps on the carpeting but hammers up the grand staircase that wasn't used to such abuse.

David stopped fighting his uncle's hold. Rage abated, his senses returned. He shook as he realized what he'd done. Not Father this time, but *him*.

"Oh. My. God," he whispered, emphasizing each syllable. His knees failed, and he sank to the floor.

"What did I do? *Val?* Oh my God, Val! I'm *sorry!* I'm so sorry, Val! *Oh my God. Ohhh my God!*" David crawled to her feet as the color returned to her face. Galina supported her on one side,

Katya held her hand on the other.

"Val? I'm sorry!" he begged from all fours. "I can't believe I did that! Oh my God, Val! Shit! *Shit!* Val, I'm sorry! I didn't mean to do it! You've got to believe me! Oh God! Please, Val! *Please* be okay!"

Uncle Tomas pulled him up; a hand stayed firm on his shoulder.

"How bad is she hurt?" Tomas asked.

Galina shook her head. "I don't know. She's bruising fast."

Valeria held up a weak hand. "I'm okay. My fault," she rasped, one eye seeming to swell as they watched. "Not his. Don't blame…"

Grandmother Ivanov strode into the room. "What's going on in here? Tomas! Who was running on the stairs? I will not have shouting and running through this house – Lord Gracious, what's happened?"

"I didn't mean to do it!" David blubbered. "When Dimi said he wasn't coming back – *Oh God*, Val! You gotta believe me! I didn't mean it!"

Tomas glossed it over with a wave of his hand. "Just a little dispute, Mamá. It's done now."

"Darling, you're hurt," Andrea said as Valeria struggled to her feet with Galina and Katya's help. "Take her to the kitchen; ask Marya for something cold. I'll call Doctor Masarsky and see if he'll come by. He owes me a favor."

"I'll be fine," Valeria insisted hoarsely. The sad look of concern she gave her brother only made him cry harder. She reached out to him, but Galina steered her toward the door.

Once the immediate crisis passed, Sergei turned his back to the room, staring out the tall, narrow library windows. He focused on the peaceful expanse of estate, where, far back on the property, by the huge outbuilding where Uncle Tomas kept his cruiser and other vehicles, Nikky rolled in the snow that fell all the night before. Kiev born, desert raised, Nikky was enchanted by the snow. Uncle Tomas located an old pair of skis and spent the morning shuffling around the yard in them, Nikky standing on his toes.

Snow.

Sergei turned to Val as she left the room.

"I feel bad for you, Val," he said in a husky voice, "and maybe David shouldn't have done that, but would it really have been so hard to take them with us? You couldn't find it *anywhere* inside you to keep us together? She only wanted to stay with Vlad and see snow again, but you wouldn't let her do either. I'll never be able to look at snow again without thinking about that."

Valeria began to cry herself. "I'm sorry," she whispered. "I really am." But Sergei had turned away.

Grandmother waited until Valeria left the room. "Tomas, I *will not* tolerate violence! We do not need the law here, crawling through our affairs and reporting them to the press. You will put an end to this, or they will have to leave. Honestly, Tomas! Did you really expect the good of the mother to counteract the base heredity of the father?" She glared sharply at David, then hurried after Valeria.

"Come with me, David," Uncle Tomas said, guiding the boy by his shoulder. Sergei watched them go, crushed with sympathy, but David never looked back.

Seven

Uncle Tomas motioned David through a door in a back hall and down a flight of service stairs. "Down here. All the way to the end."

David's stomach tightened to the density of a black hole. He deserved the whipping of his life, and he accepted that. Father had strict rules about not beating on the girls. But down here, in a basement, alone, where no one could help him if he truly feared for his life? He wasn't used to being *alone*. Father's violence he knew well, but what was Uncle Tomas' style? Cruel or quick? Hands or objects? Head, body, or backside?

Tomas placed his hand on a palmgrid to unlock the door. "This is the service entrance, but I didn't feel like walking around."

David found himself in a pleasant room for entertaining, smaller than anything upstairs, though anything short of a launch pad seemed smaller. Three short sofas formed a circle around a low table. A large recess took up half of the back of the room; the length of the inside wall was a stocked liquor bar. Father could have stayed drunk for weeks.

Uncle Tomas walked behind the bar. "This is my apartment. I moved down here six years ago when my wife died. I don't need a whole house to myself for the short times I'm here."

Sweat ran cold down David's back as Tomas looked around the bar, chose a large container, and filled it with ice from a bin. Anticipation gripped his innards with diabolical strength, but his uncle seemed in no hurry. David wiped his face on his sleeve and took a deep breath in preparation.

Tomas dug behind the bar and offered a cloth napkin. "Please, no sleeves."

"*Spasiba.*" David accepted it, used it, hoped his hand didn't shake too obviously. He didn't want to be sick, not on all that nice carpet. No doubt that would make things even worse.

Tomas searched cabinets, then hit a switch on the wall.

"Kitchen," he directed the intercom. "Marya? Please have dinner for two brought to the apartment. *Spasiba.*"

David's stomach rolled with a lifeless thump. *I'm not going to be walking out of here*, he realized. *Shit, man! He's gonna pound me!*

He could bear the suspense no longer. "Where do you want me to stand?"

"I'm sorry, David. Pick a seat, anywhere."

That made no sense at all. "Where do you want me to *stand?*" he repeated. "Or should I just bend over the bar? Clothes or skin? Or do you go for the face?"

Tomas watched him with bewilderment. "I'm afraid I must have missed something. What are you talking about?"

"You're gonna belt me, aren't you? Peel me a new ass? I just – wanted to know what your routine was."

"*What?* Good Lord! You're serious, aren't you. You think I'm – David, I haven't hit anybody since I was twelve! I couldn't hit you!"

"It's okay. I know I deserve it. I won't fight you. Just, please, sir, hit fair." He squirmed, looking at his feet. He was in no position to ask favors.

"David, I'm *not* going to hit you! Is that what you think I brought you down here for?"

"Isn't it? Isn't that what the ice is for? After?"

"Great Lord, *no!*" Tomas stared at the bowl of ice as if it had become an instrument of torture. He put it on the bar and took a step away. "I brought you down here to *talk* to you, to get you away from the situation and let you calm down. I'm not going to hit you."

Kindness didn't add up in David's book. "Why not? I deserve it."

"That may be, but I just don't do that," Tomas insisted. "The ice is to keep things cold. I was about to ask what you drink."

It was David's turn to be confused. "I'm too young to drink," he said, listening for the trap. "If you don't hit, then what do you do?"

"I don't *do* anything, David. I didn't bring you down here to punish you; you must believe me on that. I don't know why you hurt your sister, but I do intend to find out.

"Another thing – just a point of etiquette – never mention your age unless someone asks. I haven't met a teenaged boy yet who hasn't nipped at least once from his parent's stock. Let's start over. What do you drink?"

David didn't know whether to relax or stay nervous. Adults were never this nice – not parents, not teachers, not law enforcement. Adults had ulterior motives.

"Uh, beer, I guess." He was pretty sure Uncle Tomas wouldn't believe he didn't drink, and to answer honestly would incriminate himself. He could use a hard drink right now, but David wasn't familiar with a lot of names. Liquor had to be imported on Navara, and the import surcharges put it far out of reach of his crowd. He stuck to Father's vices. "Beer or vodka."

"Good choice." The older man pushed four bottles and a bottle of vodka into the ice, and grabbed glasses from the bar.

Tomas gestured to the sofas. "Please, sit. I swear, David, I am *not* out to hurt you." He placed everything on the table. Taking a foil-wrapped bottle from the ice, he opened it and handed it to his nephew, taking one for himself.

David perched on an adjacent sofa. He took a polite taste. The beer ran down his throat icy and smooth, far better than the cheap, warm, bitter stuff his friends drank on Navara. *Lizard-piss*, they'd called it. He took a longer swallow, hoping it would calm his nerves. He had no idea what to expect now.

Tomas was about to hand the boy a glass, but put it down and picked up his bottle instead. He skipped the sofa and sat on the floor in front of it, crossing his legs in a manner David didn't think people his uncle's age could do. He sipped his beer, waiting.

"So, your father used to beat you, I take it."

David straightened up quickly. "Yes, sir."

"Just you, or everybody?"

"Everybody, more or less. Only when he was drinking, though." David clung to the beer. They'd never discussed Father's temper outside of themselves, not with anybody, not even Mother. An unspoken code arose among the seven that bore the brunt during those worst years. You never watched, but you stayed near in case things got out of hand – because a couple of times they did. You helped each other afterwards, because you could be next. You never, ever, made fun of anybody during or after. There were certain incidents you never talked about. And you never, ever, *ever* told anybody, because if Father found out, there'd be twice as much misery. Even with Father locked up, it was hard to break those rules, but David felt oddly compelled to tell Tomas the truth.

"Which was often?"

"Sometimes, sir, yes."

Tomas closed his eyes. "Tell me one thing, David, no matter how awful the truth. Did your father ever hit my sister – your mother?"

"No sir! Not ever! They never even fought. He really loved her."

Uncle Tomas broke into a heartwarming smile, not unlike that of his sister. "Thank you, David. That's good to know. I wouldn't be able to live with myself if he had. I've never met your father, and I won't dislike a person without a good reason. Now," Tomas nursed his beer and settled deeper against the sofa, "start at the beginning and tell me what happened upstairs."

David finished his beer before he finished the story. Tomas

opened another and handed it to him. Halfway through that, David caught up with the story, nerves steadier, his tongue looser.

He rubbed his thumb gloomily around the rim of the bottle. "I can't believe I did that. Val's gonna have me cremated. She threw Dimi out for a hell of a lot less."

"I wouldn't worry yet," Tomas said, opening his second beer. "It's my house; she can't throw you out. The one you have to work on is Mamá. She has a harsh stance on physical violence. She feels that sort of thing is beneath our class."

David's hair stood up higher. He downed the rest of his beer in one long swallow, to give his brain time to catch his tongue.

"My family may not have lived like this, but we're not galactic trash. No disrespect intended, *sir*."

"I'm sorry, David. Of course not. I didn't mean it as an insult," Tomas corrected. "I certainly don't view your family that way. I fully intended to include you and your family in my global 'our'."

He sighed and took a half-hearted swallow. "You asked me before what I 'do.' I'm a business man, David. I'm a relations specialist. I'm used to entertaining clients from every possible type of culture and background, swaying their business to my companies. To make my deals, I rely on a team of research staff. I need to know everything I possibly can about my clients, where they're coming from, their tastes, their experiences, what their long-term objectives are, what they expect from me. Right now, David, *you* are my client. I want to know everything about you and your family, no details spared. Nothing off-limits. Feel free to ask the same of me; I'll answer anything you ask, no matter how intimate, no offense taken. When I feel I know everything I possibly can about you, I'll know what to do. I like you, David, despite your faults. I want to help, but first I need to know *you*."

David filled with trepidation. Nobody just *talked*. What would the man do if he didn't? How far could you push nicey-nice Uncle Tomas before he'd break? What would happen when he did? A simple beating would have been a hell of a lot quicker, a lot easier to handle, but he was stuck here all alone, and freakin' Viktor or Dimi wasn't going to rescue him this time. Hell, he'd already cried like Vlad in front of his uncle. Who was he fooling?

He gazed at the bottle in his hand. What a shame it was empty. It was very good beer.

"You won't like what you find," he warned.

Dinner was no less grand when served on trays. Uncle Tomas certainly knew how to entertain. He knew how to drink as well. David watched with a well-trained eye, waiting for the moment when the accumulation of beer would tip the pleasant manner toward a foul, reckless one. It never came. Uncle Tomas was a slow, calculating drinker. He never took a bottle for himself unless his guest did, never succumbed to the dishonor of inebriation. He kept David on the edge, relaxed and talkative, but never let him lose control.

David sat in amazement. The goal among his friends had been to get as drunk as you could as quickly as possible. Half the time they wasted their money puking the sour stuff into the sand. Slow and steady seemed a much better way.

They slouched around the low table in the sitting area. A thick slice of raspberry-lemon torte lay on a plate before him, but David only picked at it despite the temptation. The glass in his hand held ice water this time, his stomach bursting with food and alcohol. The overindulgence left him sleepy, and he wondered what was happening upstairs. No reason for Val to go to Navara now.

Freakin' Dimi.

He understood why, but he didn't have to like it.

Tomas switched directions yet again. "David, have you thought about your education?"

"Not if I've been able to help it?" David said, wishing there was room in his stomach for just one more quality beer. "Valeria wanted to find a place to live first."

"Not schooling, David. *Education.* What learning goals do you have, what skills are you trying to develop for the future? What are your interests? How are your grades?"

David raised a shoulder. "Could be better."

"Failing?"

"No sir! Father insisted we do well in school. I just – slipped a little this year."

"I went to one of the finest schools in Russia, up in Moscow," Tomas said fondly. "It's extremely prestigious, quite difficult to be accepted into. I'm on the Board of Trustees. If you would like, I'd be willing to send you there as well."

"Like a private academy?" State schools didn't have Trustees. David hated anything to do with school; good education would be twice the waste. "Isn't Moscow kind of far?"

"You would board there," Tomas acknowledged. "You'd come home on the weekends and such, and if necessary I could send someone for you during the week. I don't mean *just* you, of course. The offer is open to your brothers as well."

"That's one way to get rid of us."

"That's not what I meant to imply. If you'd rather not, that's perfectly fine, but I'm offering you the chance of a lifetime, David. Few people get such an opportunity."

David watched a melting ice cube lose its balance and roll over with a crackle in his glass. "I don't mean to sound ungrateful, sir, but I need time to think about something like that. Val doesn't like me out of her sight."

Val. Stuck up, smothering, overbearing, suspicious Valeria. Val, who had fought long and hard not to have him expelled from his last school. Val, who hounded him to make sure his grades didn't plummet. Val, who by some miracle said yes when he asked to be included with the older kids on the two-day trip to visit Sarah in the psychiatric hospital.

Val, whom he'd beat the living shit out of.

David fell silent, lost in thought. *How should he word it?* "Could we go back upstairs? This has all been – out of orbit, but, I'd really like to know if Val's okay."

Uncle Tomas smiled. "Are you ready for that now?"

David nodded with relief. "Yes, sir."

He tiptoed down the dimly lit hall, past his room, the room that now belonged to him alone; past the boys', and Katya's, and the nursery on the opposite side; down to the very end to what had once been his mother's room, where the twins were. David stood in the hall, starting toward the door and turning away a half-dozen times. His stomach fluttered, his heart flopped, his fearsome reputation not enough to give him nerve. He nearly hit the ceiling when the door next to him opened.

Katerina emerged from the nursery. "David!" She threw her arms around him and kissed his cheek. "Are you all right? Where have you *been*? We were worried…"

Of any of them, Katya was the most forgiving. She'd always done right by him, no matter how bad he'd been. "You're still speaking to me?"

"Of course! We were all torn up by the call. It shattered everybody." She gave him a fragile smile that threatened to turn to tears. "We were so worried. You were gone so long."

"Uncle Tomas hid me in his apartment. Is she okay? You gotta believe me, I never meant to do that. It just … happened."

Katya couldn't hide the truth. "Grandmother had a doctor come to the house. She's got a cracked cheekbone and a broken rib, but she'll be fine. The doctor took care of it, no questions asked."

David fought the urge to drop to his knees. *Doctors.* In all the years of Father being on the rampage, he could probably count on his fingers the number of times they'd seen a doctor for an injury. His own three broken ribs, Vlad's broken hand, a few others. They took care of their own, no matter how bad things looked. David snapped once, just *once,* and he'd done as much damage as Father ever did.

At fourteen.

And sober.

58

Too much beer, David realized as tears forced upwards again. "*Fuck!* I'm just as bad as freakin' Father. Worse!"

Kat put her arms around him. "Shh! No you're not! Come on. She wants to talk to you. She's been going crazy, not knowing where you were."

"*No!* I can't!" he pleaded, pulling back. "I can't go in there!"

"Of course you can." Katya tapped on the door, then opened it. "I have someone to see you," she said, and dragged a reluctant David in.

Valeria sat up on the carved bed. "David!"

Katya pushed him into the room, then backed out, closing the door.

David shook. Galina rose from her chair as if to protect her twin, but Val waved her away.

"Go. Let me talk to him alone."

"You sure?" Galina looked weary, as if she'd already been up all night. She stared hard at David. "I'll be right outside."

"Come here, David," Val said softly, patting the bed. "I was worried about you. We had no idea where you disappeared to. Come tell me where you've been." She spoke as if her throat hurt.

David lifted his eyes, then wished he hadn't. One side of Val's face puffed out, a grotesque purple blushing the cheek. Around her throat were dark marks, the size and shape of fingers.

His fingers.

He couldn't hide the evidence, lie his way out of it, blame anyone else or pretend it didn't happen. *He* did that.

"Come here," Val repeated, and he went, dragging shoes that weighed a half ton each. He balanced on the edge of the bed near her. She picked up his hand and squeezed it.

"I'm sorry, David. I am so sorry. You tried to tell me I was pushing Dimi too hard, and I blew you off. I was so intent on getting even, on teaching a rotten lesson, I let everything go too far. It was horrible of me to do that. I am so sorry it had to come to this for me to realize it. I don't blame you for hitting me. I hadn't realized how much I hurt everyone. I wish someone had knocked sense into me a week ago."

David gave a hard shake. "Don't say that. Kick the shit out of me, break a chair over my head, slap me around, but don't make nice to me after what I did. I can't take it! I don't know what happened, I just cracked, and I am very sorry for doing that. *Please!* I can't take anyone else being nice to me when I don't deserve it!"

The exhaustion, the alcohol, the disappointment caught up with him. Val putting a forgiving arm around him pushed him over the edge. David would always remember the gasping little squeal as the stupidest noise he ever made in his life, as he fell over, put his head in his sister's lap, and bawled like a baby.

Tail tucked tight between his legs, David slunk back to his room some time later. At the very least, he'd expected to be chewed up and spit out, lectured to death, impounded, imprisoned, and shipped off to a counseling camp for youthful offenders. He never expected to be *forgiven*. Val just wasn't like that. Being in this big house made everyone *weird.*

He wasn't alone. As he entered his room, Sergei and Vlad sat up in the now-ownerless bed.

Sergei crawled to the end. "Where you *been*? What happened? What'd he do to you? You hurt bad? You need anything?" Vlad clutched the bed sheet, eyes puffy and red in his frightened face.

The last thing David wanted was company, but his brothers' concern was a comfort nonetheless, nothing they wouldn't have done at home. He sat on his bed and kicked off his shoes, then stripped his shirt.

"It's so unreal I could almost believe it was a dream. He didn't touch me. He didn't lay a damned *finger* on me. Can you believe that? I even asked him when he was gonna hit me, and I swear he turned green. We sat in his apartment, drinking beer and vodka and talking the whole time. Is that unreal?" David played with his shirt, mystified. "He drank, and he drank, and he never once stopped being nice. I don't get it."

"Wow!" Sergei breathed. "He gave you *beer*? And you busted her up good!"

David grimaced. "I'm not proud of that, so don't talk about it. How you doing over there, Vlad?"

The younger boy shrugged, sniffing, his thin fingers worrying the blanket.

"What's with him?"

"He says he'd rather die than be without Sarah," Sergei replied, "but he doesn't know how to do it, and I wouldn't tell him, so now he's not talking to anybody. I figured I'd better stay with him, just in case."

David closed his eyes and shook his head. *Vlad, Vlad, Vlad. Such a damned baby you ask permission for suicide.*

"Knock it off, Vlad!" he ordered with a more characteristic growl. "You're stuck living with all this shit just like the rest of us. What if they come back next month and Sarah runs in here looking for you, and Sergei's gotta tell her you had a fit and killed yourself? You think that'd make her happy?"

Vlad's face scrunched as new tears fell.

"Sure as shit not! She'd dig you up, rip your arms off, and kick your bony ass from here to Siberia. Don't let me hear stupid shit like that out of you again, or I'll kick your ass for her," David threatened with more humor than vehemence. He certainly wasn't the one to be jumping on anybody, not after today. "I can't blame you on the other, though. I sure as shit don't feel much like talking right now, either."

He stood up, turned his back and stripped off his pants, assuring his brothers there wasn't a new mark on him. The old ones were slowly fading. Cold Russian winters or no, he collapsed into bed in his underwear, leaving the boys to turn off the lights.

Eight

Sarah'd wanted that video call, pestered him for days, but to see Vladimir, to talk to him, to almost but not really touch him – and not know when she might – proved too much of a strain. When the transmission ended, so did Sarah's brave façade. She dropped where she stood, curled over her knees, and began to wail. Dmitri felt bad for her, missing whiny little Vlad as much as she did.

Sarah banged her head on the hotel carpeting with increasing strength. Her scalp had required surgical repair once already, and her arms and legs bore the scars of six months' of self-torture.

"Stop that!" Dmitri said. Sarah gave a louder cry, wrapped her fingers in her hair and yanked strands from her head. As he wrestled for her hands, she smashed her head on his and leapt away.

Sarah was determined to hurt herself, banging off the walls and furniture and anything she could grab, anything to create a physical pain severe enough to override the emotional pain inside. Dmitri couldn't let her in the bathroom – if she locked the door, there was no telling what she'd do before he could override it. He'd been trying to stop her from gouging herself with a hair comb when she pulled away and darted for the balcony.

Dmitri realized her goal a split-second later. *Escape or harm?* She'd never outright tried to kill herself, but... He couldn't take that risk. While she ran around the bed, he ran over it, tackling her as she reached the balcony door.

Sarah kicked and clawed, but she couldn't move. He lay across her back with her arms caught crossed under her, his arm preventing the stubborn head from hitting the floor.

He wiped the sweat from his eyes on her shirt. "Stop, Sar. I know you're upset. I know you're probably mad at me, but I'm not about to let you hurt yourself, so stop." He slid the door closed with his foot. When he thought she'd calmed, he sat up, held her by the wrist and locked the balcony, then pulled a table over to block it. Sarah kicked him in the elbow when he wasn't looking. He let go with a curse.

She bolted for the door. Again he tackled her. "Knock it off! I said I won't let you, and I mean it!"

It was the first emotional storm he'd ever been in charge of, and there was no one to help, no time to look things up in her files, nothing to go on but his memory and his wits. Sarah retreated to a corner on her hands and knees, and there they waited, each watching for the other to make the first move.

"Enough now!" Dmitri ordered. "I'm coming over there and I'm going to comb your hair. Then we're going down to dinner. If you fight me, I will carry you down there just as you are, kicking and screaming. The hotel will call security on you for disturbing the guests, and they can take it from there. You decide. After dinner we'll come back, and you can hide under the bed all night for all I care."

Choices, the hospital had taught him. *Tell her what's happening, give her the choices, and let her pull herself together.* He rose to his feet and waited. She rubbed her eyes with the back of her hand, but stayed sitting. Picking up the confiscated comb, he moved toward her.

Dmitri kept her by his side at the restaurant. Long hair combed and pulled back clumsily, she crunched into herself, not speaking. He hadn't figured out yet if it was just to be nasty, or if she had retreated mentally. One he could ignore, the other could be trouble. He had so much to think about now, so much to remember.

Dmitri was reading the menu to her when a passing voice caught his attention. It was Lalla, the long-legged girl from the beach, now clad in a champagne-colored dress that began in a strap around her neck and plunged open to her navel, her jet-black hair brushing her jaw. Two strips of fabric attached to the choker band were all that held up that clingy dress. Dmitri's eyes followed the dress ...*the dress ...the beeeauuutiful dress with those anti-grav titki...* up to her inquiring face.

"Hello again!" she said. "Fancy meeting you here."

Dmitri smiled and stood up. "Hello! Have you eaten yet? Won't you join us?" He gestured to the table.

"I'd love to!"

Dmitri nearly tripped himself pulling out a chair. Sarah didn't move her head, but her eyes followed the activity.

Lalla bent to the side, peering at Sarah, but the younger girl bowed face-down to the table. "I'm not interrupting anything, am I?"

Dmitri stared brainlessly at the girl? *Woman?* She had to be older, traveling alone and so self–assured. With a start, Dmitri realized she was talking about Sarah. "Huh? No! No, not at all! She doesn't feel very well. I brought her with me to make sure she's okay."

"Wouldn't she be better off in bed?"

The top of the dress relaxed when she sat; if she moved exactly the right way, the plunging neckline might gap so loose Dmitri was certain he'd be able to see an entire bare breast. Sweat rolled down his back. "Huh?"

The girl leaned forward to pick up her water glass. "If she doesn't feel well. Shouldn't she be resting or something?"

Lean right, dress pulls tight; sit back, see the slack. Dmitri blushed. "No, no, it's not that kind of sick. She spoke to family this afternoon, and now she's homesick."

"Oh."

Sarah put her head down on her crossed arms and looked the other way. A waiter came to take their requests; the word *cocktail* caught her attention.

Dmitri cast lovesick gazes at the girl. "That sounds interesting. Make that two."

Sarah's stare burned into his cheek. A minute passed before he realized it.

"What's the matter with you?" he whispered.

"Dimi! You don't drink!" It wasn't a request, but a revelation.

How would he ever impress a girl – a grown *woman!* – with a kid hanging around? "Yeah, I do," he said, shattering her faith. "Why do you think I threw myself a party before we left? Just to have some friends over to listen to music? So what? Relax! Go back into your little trance. I'm fine." He turned back to his new friend.

Lalla accompanied them back to their room, arm linked with Dmitri's, smiling and laughing. Sarah grabbed his other hand, but he pushed her away.

"Knock it off!" Dmitri unlocked the door, and she fled inside.

In the hall, Lalla dragged a long-nailed finger down his neck and onto his chest. "Tonight's my last night here. I leave in the morning. Why don't you tuck babykins in for the night, and keep me from being lonely?" She left no doubt of her intentions on his lips.

A shiver started at Dmitri's head and finished somewhere in the floor, taking his breath with it. He wrestled his lip free.

"I – I don' know. She's never ... left alone before..."

"She's a big girl. She can sleep by herself. Or do you have to tell her a story first? Are you sure you're as old as you say? Do you even know what I'm offering?"

Dmitri took offense. He was only a *month* from seventeen, even if his ID said a year older. "How would you like me to prove myself?" He pulled the girl hard against him and answered her lips, his other hand sliding down that slippery-smooth dress to squeeze the curves of her perfect backside. She melted her silky softness against him.

She couldn't. No way. There was no way *she was wearing* anything *under that dress.* "Is – *dat* what you were asking about? I'll – I'll see what I can do."

"Six–one–seven–five," she purred, trailing a pink nail under his chin. "I'll be waiting."

Dmitri hyperventilated, watching the back of the dress swing side to side as she walked toward the lift.

This was It! The Big One! And she suggested it! He spun to fly into the room, only to turn wrong and crash head-on into the wall. The pain calmed him. Holding his nose and cursing, he rushed through the door.

Sarah lay face down on her bed. Dmitri threw himself on his knees next to her.

"Sar? Hey, come on. Take the fingers out of your ears. I want to ask you something."

Sarah unfolded. She looked for the girl.

"Sar?" He tried not to seem in a hurry despite the fact he was sweating and shaking and his clothes were uncomfortably tight. "Would you mind staying in the room for a little while? Just a little bit? I just want to talk with Lalla for a few minutes … "

Sarah sat up fast. "By yourself? Dimi, there's nobody else here! It's not safe alone!"

"Shh! Calm down! Please? Just for an hour? Look, I'll even set the clock." Dmitri ran to the room's general-purpose computer and set the chronometer to sound a chime. "Just an hour, Sar! Take a long bath, hide in my bed - just tell me you can stay alone for an hour without hurting yourself. I'll be right here in the hotel. I'm not going anywhere. I'll be *right back*."

"I don't have a choice, do I?"

His face fell. She looked so damned little and scared. Guilt rose up, dulling his eagerness. "Well, I am *asking,* not telling …"

"Just an hour?"

"Just one," Dmitri swore.

"Yeah," Sarah whispered in defeat. "What if something happens?"

Dmitri planted a kiss on her forehead. "Nothing's going to happen! You're okay." In less than a minute he doused himself in cologne, raked his fingers through his hair, and ran out the door.

Dmitri lay on his side, holding her athletic warmth to him, unable to believe he wasn't dreaming. Twice – *twice!* in a row, and she licked at his ear *again,* nuzzling and kneading like a cat. This wasn't reality! It was more like the unmarked computer card that had been passed around secretly at school, to be viewed in supreme privacy. Oh, what he'd be able to brag to David!

Dmitri returned her ravenous kisses. Over her cheek, he glimpsed the room's chronometer. Something about time itched in the back of his mind.

"Shit!"

Twenty minutes. He was twenty minutes late already. He leapt up and grabbed for his pants.

"What? What's wrong?" Lalla demanded. "Where are you going?"

"I've got to check on Sarah." He rushed, sliding his feet into his shoes.

"What?! You're kidding me! You're leaving me to go check on some *brat*? What is she, eleven? Twelve? She can take care of herself. I thought we had something here?"

"Nine!" Dmitri said, yanking on his shirt. "She's only *nine*, and she's not right in the head. She gets these ... moods. She could kill herself. We *do* have something going, and we'll *keep* it going! I just have to make sure she's okay. I'll be *right back.*" He knelt on the bed and stabbed her lips with his.

"You're standing me up for some deranged kid*?* What kind of a man are you?! You walk out that door, don't you dare come back!"

"Five minutes!" Dimi pleaded, backing out as he fastened his pants. "I'll be right back!"

"No you won't, you goddamned ...!"

He didn't hear the rest of her shout as he sprinted down the hall.

Dmitri hit the lock code on his door and burst into the room, breathless.

Empty.

He checked the bathroom.

No one.

"Sarah!" The balcony was locked. She couldn't have done that from the outside. "Sarah, come out, it's not funny."

Nothing.

Not in the beds. Not under them.

The closet. She and Vlad always hid in closets. His dream of returning to the Pleasure Palace of 6175 faded into mist.

Sarah scrunched inside, penned in by their travel cases, wearing the white gauzy nightshirt that technically belonged to their sister Katya. She clutched something to her chest, crying to end the world. Faint scratches reddened her cheeks where she'd tried to gouge them, but this week her nails were chewed too short to do any damage.

Dmitri sat at the door of the closet, repentant, but he felt too damned good inside to feel sorry. He hung his head.

"I'm back, just like I said. I know, I'm twenty minutes late. I rushed back as soon as I saw the time. I'm sorry."

"The timer... went off," Sarah sobbed, "and *you... didn't... come... back!*" She rubbed her nose with the hem of the nightshirt, gasping.

"Come out here and sit." Dmitri patted the floor next to him, and she dragged herself over to hunch at his side.

"I'm sorry. I'm not Val; you know I'd never ditch you. I ran all the way." He put a conciliatory arm around her. One of his socks was inside out; he folded the foot under his other leg, but he couldn't suppress his grin.

Sarah wiped her face on his shirt, catching the look. The sharp vapors of the girl's perfume pierced her nose, even through her tears. "She kissed you, didn't she?"

Dimi choked and eyed the ceiling. "Yeah, she did," he exhaled. "You got me there." He reached for what she clutched to her chest. "What have you got? Gimme."

Reluctantly, Sarah gave up the paper. It was a large photo of their entire family at the time, taken by a journal photographer. Mother was newly pregnant with Nikky, Elizabyeta was still the spoiled baby, and Father was all the talk of the archaeology circles. He'd made an important accidental find, unraveling some major mysteries in the history of a alien culture. There had been awards and parties, lectures and interviews. The year that followed had been a year of incredible happiness. Father wasn't angry, he wasn't drinking, he wasn't hitting. It was a very good year.

"Cryin' out loud. Remember this? Where'd you get it?"

"In Mother's room, before Val packed them."

Dmitri had been eleven or so. Vlad and Sarah held hands tightly even then. What were they, four? Five? "Man, everything was good back then, wasn't it? Why don't we put it up on the mirror, where we can see it. It'll kind of be like we're home." Before he could stand, an angry fist pounded their door. Sarah launched herself onto her bed, out of the way.

"I know you're in there! Open up!"

Dmitri pushed the door release. Lalla stormed in, once again wearing the slinky dress.

"How *dare* you!" she raged. She flew up to Dmitri, matching every step he retreated. "How dare you treat me like that! Of all the conceited tricks! I have never been so degraded and ... humiliated! Who do you think you are?"

Dmitri leaned backwards. "I-I-I told you, Lalla! I just had to check in. I was coming right back. Look at her! She was already falling apart..."

"I don't give a damn! When I make an offer like that, I expect to be satisfied, and I am *far* from satisfied!"

Dmitri's face clouded over. She certainly seemed satisfied half

66

an hour ago. "Now wait a minute!"

"No, *you* wait, you bastard!" Without warning, she slapped his cheek. The slap was followed by her heel planting itself on the top of his foot, the pain of which distracted him from noticing her hoist the long skirt and deliver the pointed toe of her shoe into his groin. Dmitri's protest turned into a breathless silence of pain.

"*Now* I'm satisfied, you miserable *shit!*" Lalla cried. "Nobody walks out on me unless I tell them to!" She noticed Sarah cringing on the bed.

Sarah slid from the bed into the gap against the wall, cowering. Her brother twitched soundlessly on the floor, incapacitated. She was on her own, after all.

"And you, you little baby! You sure as Hell know how to kill a perfectly good evening! If you're such a goddamned nutcase, why aren't you locked up?" In the hiss of the sliding door, Lalla disappeared.

It took a long moan from her brother to spur Sarah into motion. She crept from the corner, making sure the mad woman had really gone, then locked the door. She dropped to her knees next to him. Hanging out with five older brothers, she knew damned well not ever to do what that woman did, not even as a joke.

"Want me to get an ice block or something?"

Dmitri rocked on the floor, hands between his thighs. "No," he gasped. "Just kill me now." This was more his luck. Keep a promise to one female, and get ripped apart by another. At least Sarah wasn't laughing.

Sarah shifted and rested her back against the end of the bed, hugging her knees. She sat for several minutes, watching.

"You tried to touch her chest, didn't you?"

"*What*? What the hell are you talking about?"

"That's what David told Sergei and Vlad. If you touch a girl's chest, you'll get hit. That's what he told me I should do when I get older. Is that what you did?"

Dmitri shook his head. Leave it to David to feed her twisted half-truths. He managed to roll onto his back. "Yeah," he sighed. "Something like that."

The noise hit Dmitri like a cold knife, waking him from a dead sleep and shaking him to his soul. He sat straight up in the bed. A second scream stabbed the dark, almost in his ear, a girl's high-pitched wail.

Sarah!

He kicked back the blanket and activated the room lights. Sarah stood in the corner on tiptoe, unable to shake a demon dream. She pressed backward into the wall, hands out, reaching slowly for or pushing away something invisible. Dmitri and Val had undergone intensive training at the psychiatric hospital to learn how to help Sarah, and they'd been shown how to handle the dreams. He'd seen her have two or three nightmares, but Valeria had been the one to work through them, coaxing the girl awake while Dmitri stood by, useless.

Dmitri climbed over her bed. "Sar? Wake up! You're dreaming! Wake up."

Sarah continued to shriek, seized by a look of something too horrible to comprehend.

He tried to remember what Val said and did. "Come on, Kid, wake up. It's okay. I'm right here. It's just me."

They'd called each other all kinds of names growing up – the house was forever full of Brains and Idiots, Crybabies and Romeos, Brats and Traitors to the cause of the day. Mother would slur Dmitri-Mikhail to D'misha, or Sar'ina for Sarah Irina – but almost never cutesy things. Val tried it now and then, and it never sounded right. Besides, calling Sarah *sweetheart* or *darling* or *honey* – if he could bring himself to say something like that – would more likely get him a fist in the mouth. Sarah counted herself as one of the boys, and would beat the spit out of anyone who treated her otherwise.

Dmitri made the mistake of touching her too soon. She attacked him, screaming and shrieking.

"*Shah! Sarah! Stoi!* Sarah, *stop*! You're going to get us in trouble!" She slid to the floor, kicking.

A chime sounded. Dmitri glanced at the door, then at Sarah struggling.

The door chimed again. "Hotel Security! Open the door, please."
Shit!

"Come on, Sar! It's now or never!" Dmitri pleaded. "You don't want them seeing you like this, do you?" He made a fast grab and caught a wrist.

A bang on the door this time. "Hotel Security! If you don't release the door, we will be forced to override it."

Dmitri fought the heels pummeling his knees. "Then do it! I'm kind of busy here!"

Two hotel security officers entered, voiding the lock with an emergency code. They surveyed the scene: a male clad only in sleep shorts, a rumpled bed, a younger female screaming and fighting the male.

"Assault in progress, send backup," one of the men said to a wristcom. The other grabbed Dmitri from behind, wrenching him onto the bed. A knee planted itself between Dmitri's shoulder blades; his arms were yanked and crossed over his head. The first man squatted before Sarah, speaking to her.

"What the hell are you doing?" mattress-muffled Dmitri demanded. "Let me go! I'm trying to help her!"

"Sure you are," his captor said, crushing Dmitri under his knee. "Explain it in court."

Fate chose that moment for Sarah to awaken. The blankness in her eyes disappeared, and she focused on the man before her. The man was not Dmitri, nor anyone she recognized. She saw the second man fighting to hold down what appeared to be her brother, while three other people rushed in.

The new, sharp shriek had a different tone than the wail of the nightmare. Sarah let loose a strong kick, feet together, knocking the man backwards. She launched herself at the man holding her brother, smashing his head and ears with her fists, gouging at his eyes. She grabbed two handfuls of hair and yanked with all her weight, jerking the man's head back, pulling him off her brother. Dmitri leapt up. All kinds of hands came at them now.

"Let go of her!" Dmitri fought to get to her, but two men grabbed his arms and twisted them behind. "Will you please tell me what you're doing? Sarah, stop! It's okay!"

"Get him out of here," the first security man said.

"NO!" Dmitri braced himself, but fifty-five kilos were nothing against two large men. "Stop! You don't know what you're doing! *Sarah!*"

Sarah broke off to see him being hauled out. She sprinted after him, but people blocked her way.

An unknown woman knelt in Sarah's path. "Relax, honey, we just want to talk to you. You're safe now. We just want to ask you some questions, make sure you're all right. No one here is going to hurt you."

Dmitri cursed distantly down the hall. Sarah made one more wild attempt to run, but there were too many hands. Unfamiliar hands in front of her, strange hands touching her, other hands restraining her, separating her from Dmitri.

Sarah ran to the farthest corner of the room, curling tightly on her knees. She covered her head with her arms and burrowed her mind deep, deep inside itself, safe in the darkness.

Dmitri sat in a hotel office, glaring at the man interrogating him. Two security personnel stood near, as well as the hotel manager and two City Patrol officers. "I've told you five times now. S*he had a nightmare.* Will you please tell me where she is?"

"That's not what it looked like to me. Tell me again why you came here."

"I *told* you, dammit! We're on holiday before we join our family on Earth. Now *I want – to see – my sister!*"

He twisted around, but a hand on his shoulder pushed him back. "Look, if you don't believe me, then call her psychiatrist, for crying out loud! Dr. John Carver at Rangler Psychiatric, on Starbase 4! He'll tell you the same thing."

The officer weighed the idea. He tipped his head toward the office commlink, and one of the men placed a hyperspace call.

"John Carver at Starbase 4," Dmitri over-enunciated. He couldn't imagine how Sarah was doing. *How freakin' long would it take her to calm down after this? Days? Weeks? A year? Ever?*

"I want to see my sister," he repeated stubbornly.

An officer gestured to another man by the door. "If she is your sister. We'll see what she had to say."

A lengthy time passed before the door opened again. The man retrieving Sarah entered first, disheveled. His fingers wrapped a bleeding bite on his hand, and a sizable tear flapped on his shirt. He gave wide berth to the door.

"They couldn't get a word out of her. Who knows where she's from."

Wary, Sarah tiptoed to the doorway, face as white as her nightshirt, tensed and ready for the first sign of deceit. Two more staff, women, followed. Sarah sniffed at the room, distrustful.

"Sarah!" Dmitri called with relief. "It's okay."

She threw herself on him with a squeal and burst into tears.

Dmitri pulled her onto his knee and kissed the top of her head. Never in his whole life had he been so glad to see someone.

"Sarah, baby." The endearment sounded as if it were the most natural thing in the world. "You okay? They didn't hurt you, did they? Shh. I've got you now." Nobody messed with a Kirushenko like this. Dmitri didn't care about odds now. He was ready to fight.

"What'd he say?" the officer asked the man by the commlink.

"The stories match. She's in the care of a psychiatrist, she has a history of severe nightmares, and her older brother's in charge of her. The Doc wants to talk to him." The lead officer gave consent, and the second man pivoted the viewscreen.

Dr. Carver, the one and only doctor in the universe Sarah trusted. Officially, he wasn't even her doctor anymore, but he'd let himself get over-involved with his young patient, and was now more of a family friend.

Dr. Carver's youthful face filled the screen. "Dmitri, what the hell's going on? You didn't throw another party, did you?"

"No sir!" Dmitri said above Sarah's weeping. "I'm sorry to have bothered you at all, but I couldn't think of anyone else they might believe."

"That's okay. You rescued me from a very dull pharmaceutical review. What's happened?"

Dmitri ran down the last hour. "Until now, everything's gone really well. She got upset after talking to Vlad, but I handled it like you said, and it worked out fine. I'm sure it was just the stress of the day. Now she's scared out of her mind."

"Stress could do it," Carver agreed. He sat down at the viewscreen. "Sarah?" he called. "It's John, Sar. Can you look at me?"

Dmitri urged her to turn around.

"You had another dream?"

"Yeah."

"Old or new?"

"New!"

"But you're awake now, and you're okay," Carver reminded her. "And you're going to tell Dmitri all about it, aren't you?" Sarah didn't look at him, but she nodded.

Carver turned serious. "Dmitri, you may be doing a good job, but take my advice: get her *home*, before something happens that you can't handle. You won't be helping her at that point. I'll keep that promise I made, Sar. I'll call Valeria in three weeks, and I'd better see you answering the call. I mean it, Dmitri! No more playing around! This isn't a game. You did your thing, you made your point, now *get her home*. Get her in school. She needs stability."

"I'll take it into consideration, sir," Dmitri said. "Thank you."

"Home!" the doctor repeated. "Carver out." The screen went black.

The hotel manager cleared his throat. "Mr. Kirushenko, we owe you an apology. Please try to see it from our viewpoint."

Dmitri's fury boiled anew. He rose and faced his captors, holding a trembling Sarah close. He had to look up to stare the man in the eye, but no one shorter than Father would ever intimidate him.

"Fuck you and your apology! How dare you terrorize us like that! Do you think I would have asked you to come in if I was trying to hurt her? You never asked what was going on; you never let me explain when I tried. I wanted your help, but you attacked me before I could ask. Do you have any idea how far you may have set her back? *Fuck you!* Apologize to someone else, because it won't do you any good here. Stand up, Sar," he said to her. "You're too big; I can't carry you."

Sarah stared with awe, hiccupping.

"Maybe I can." He twisted until she stood behind him. "Up!" he ordered, and Sarah understood. With a jump, she climbed up him, piggy-back. Dimi carried her back to the room.

He released her on her bed and threw himself next to her, face in the pillow. He dropped his arm over her.

"Does anything *ever* go right in the universe?" he asked.

Sarah gave a hard cough and wiped her face on the bed sheet. "No," she said with certainty.

Nine

David glanced at his brothers, but they stared expectantly at him. Being the oldest really chewed sand. He sighed and knocked on the study door.

"Come."

Tomas sat at his computer, setting up the next week's schedules. He'd be flying back to New York in a few days.

"Boys! What can I do for you?" he said warmly. "Sit down. Staying out of trouble today, I hope?"

"Yes, sir," David replied. Today he didn't have the nerve to hit a fly. Val hadn't shown up for breakfast or lunch. "Sir – Uncle Tomas, sir – We've been doing a lot of talking, and... If you were serious, we'd like to take you up on your offer about that school in Moscow. We'd like to give it a try."

Tomas leaned back in his chair. "I didn't think you cared about school, David."

"I don't, sir, but... Everything here is so different. It's hard to figure out what we're supposed to be doing, and when, and who we're supposed to listen to. I have to go to school *somewhere,* and I figured, maybe it would be good to make a clean break. I need to be somewhere Dmitri *isn't* supposed to be, somewhere I'm not thinking about him all the time. You said we'd come back on the weekends, right?"

"Absolutely. Someone would meet you, even if it's only the cook. Your reasoning sounds more mature today, David. You've put some thought into this."

"Yessir." Some thought, yes, but probably not the kind his uncle hoped. He had to be at school whether he wanted to or not, but it seemed a good reason not to have to face Valeria every day. Uncle Tomas still had to get the idea past Val. Galina would say yes for Sergei and Vlad, but Val... Val didn't like giving up control.

"How about you, Sergei?" Tomas asked. "You understand what you'd be getting into?"

Sergei had the nerve to look eager. "Yes, sir! I read all their info on the 'link. It sounds orbital! I skipped first form back in Kiev. I did well in eighth form on Navara, but the local school here has a rule about staying with your age group. I'd have to go to an advanced seventh form class. It sets me back a whole year. If your school

72

will keep me in eighth form, I'd much rather be there, sir."

"That shouldn't be a problem. How about you, Vladimir? What form are you in?"

Vlad perched on the edge of his chair, silent and sad. If he sat back, his toes didn't touch the ground. He held up four fingers.

Tomas made a pained face. "I'm sorry, Vladimir, but Northern Hall starts at sixth form. Do you do well in school?"

Vlad looked at his knees and shook his head, too close to tears.

Sergei gave him a rallying jab to the arm. "He does okay. He just freezes on tests."

"That can happen. We'll see how you do the rest of the year, and next year we can make plans for sixth. That's the best I can do, I'm afraid. Let me set up an appointment for tomorrow. You're welcome to come along, Vladimir."

Vlad nodded, but he didn't look any happier.

David had barely dressed in the morning when Uncle Tomas knocked on his door.

"A word to the wise, David," Tomas told him. "Comb the hair *down*. Are you absolutely sure this is what you want?"

"Yes, sir," David swore.

"Then, if I may be so bold as to save you trouble later… "

Tomas produced a pair of scissors, and David stood still as his uncle snipped the three long strands of hair on his forehead, evening the hairline. Now he looked like some fly-boy know-it-all Space Fleet recruit.

It's only hair, he consoled himself. *It'll grow back.* But he wondered if he would be able to handle a boarding school, even five days a week.

He sat in the director's office with his brothers and his uncle. The placement test had been difficult, David wracking his brain for faint memories. *Why hadn't he paid more attention!* He almost chickened out of the deal. Boarding school went against everything he'd ever done in his life. It just wasn't … *him.*

"Sergei, your performance on the placement exam was excellent," the director said. "Combined with your transcript from your previous school, I have no hesitation placing you in the eighth form class. If you continue to apply yourself, you'll be a great asset to Northern."

"Thank you, sir," Sergei grinned. "I'm looking forward to coming here."

David gagged. *Kiss ass!* But he knew Sergei meant it.

The director changed screens on his computer. "David… "

David clenched his thumbs and tried to look intelligent.

"Your score for ninth form just meets our minimum. That's a bit low for most of our students. It's your transcript, however, that worries me more. Just three months ago it was recommended you be expelled from your last school for ongoing disruptive behavior. I understand your family experienced several tragedies recently, but we are a school for serious scholars, not a correctional facility for troubled youth."

Not a muscle changed in Uncle Tomas' face, but he did turn his head ever so slightly to watch David from the corner of his eye.

Shit! "I understand that, sir. That incident involved myself and an older brother, and it was a misunderstanding based on circumstantial evidence. It wouldn't happen again."

The director didn't seem impressed. "There are two hundred and fifty boys in residence here, with a waiting list twice as long. We have a hard-line policy on fighting. There are no second chances, no excuses whatsoever. No one gets special treatment here."

David wasn't sure how to meet the cold look without turning it into a challenge. "I'm not asking for any, sir. I only want a chance to prove myself."

Uncle Tomas chewed him up and spat him out bloody, but at least he had the courtesy to wait until they returned to Minsk. David found himself escorted directly to his uncle's office.

"Who the hell do you think you're screwing with?" Tomas exploded. He stabbed a finger at David, forcing him up against the window on his toes. *"Where do you get the nerve to make that kind of* fool *out of me?* To ask me to get you into one of the top two schools in the country on lousy grades, three-quarters of the way into the school year, and fail to mention you were almost *expelled* three months ago? You should count your blessings I'm not a violent man, David, because right now I wouldn't be talking to you!"

Old fears flooded back in half a heartbeat. "I'm sorry, sir! I'd forgotten all about that! Please! I swear, I didn't set out to fool you. I'm sorry!" The flinching came naturally.

A vein on Uncle Tomas' temple showed blue and throbbing through his skin. *"Don't screw with me, David.* This is the only time I'm going to warn you. Don't *ever* fail to mention that kind of detail to me again." He dug the point of his finger into the boy's breastbone, nose to nose. "Don't *ever* screw with my business dealings. I'm ultimately at fault for not checking first, but remember this: without lifting a hand, I can make you miserable in ways your father never *dreamed.* Give me your transcript. *I* own it now."

David handed the card over wordlessly.

"Now get out of my office!" Tomas ordered. "Tell your brothers I want their transcripts, too."

David ran.

Galina and Tomas brought them to the school, and with a lot of prodding, Valeria came along, too. The ease with which Valeria agreed to the idea unnerved David, a short, "If you think you'll be happy there," and nothing else – no questions, no penetrating looks, no lectures about behavior and expectations. It just wasn't, *Val*. The boys had hoped to room together, but students were divided by levels among three residence halls. They could be together the following year.

David knew there would be adjustments, but some of them... were going to take time. His roommate, Erik, seemed okay, an easy-going Norwegian kid who didn't seem to resent an intrusion so late in the year. David's hair stuck out among the conservative styles of the other boys, too long to be close-cropped, too short to be combed anything but up or down. It would grow. Clothing styles were irrelevant: students wore uniforms, of all ghastly things. Gray pants, black sweaters, seamless white shirts. He felt like a clone, sitting in a classroom with fifteen other boys all dressed alike, at the same desks, doing the same difficult work. There weren't even any girls to distract him. And discipline! There was no chance of daydreaming: students were expected to stand when they spoke, making not knowing the answer twice as bad.

Georgi, the Ivanov mechanic, flew Galina up to fetch them 'home' for the weekend. The huge house seemed more comfortable now. Vlad followed him like a puppy and never stopped talking. Grandmother chose his school, right there in Minsk, but he didn't have to live there. He had uniforms too, but his were plum and gray. There were only thirteen kids in his class, counting him, and only twenty-three in the entire *form*! He almost *died* the first day when they served stuffed cabbage for lunch because *everyone* knew how much he *hated* cabbage, and everyone laughed at him on Thursday when he played soccer and missed the ball and his shoe flew off and hit another kid *right* in the *butt* ...

David had never realized Vlad could be kind of entertaining.

Valeria left her room only once the entire weekend. She greeted him with a weak smile and a light hug, too quiet for comfort. The bruises on her throat were almost gone. She had the haunted look Sarah used to get.

Nine days, and just when David thought he might be able to survive, *gavno* hit the floor. He returned to his room after classes, only to find the building littered with copies of a news clipping called up from the archives. Posters plastered the walls every few meters, in halls, on doors, the lavatories, the slow-scrolling memo board in the dorm entryway. Copies popped up on every computer screen.

Someone had done a damned good job.

UNIVERSITY PROFESSOR
GUILTY AS CHARGED

screamed the headline, highlighted in blinding orange ink. At the bottom was a photograph of the professor's family leaving the Kar Ku'umi court building, mobbed by reporters, and a very clear enhanced image of David and Sergei's faces in the crowd, circled in red.

Whispers and laughter followed him down the halls; eyes glinted from cracks in doors. He ripped the page from his door and crumpled it before entering.

"I didn't do it!" Erik said immediately. "But I know who did. If they ask, I'm willing to tell. That's a real shitter, man."

David buried his face on his bed, his brief shot at life over.

He called home. "I need to talk to Valeria."

"I'm sorry, Master David, but Miss Valeria isn't answering calls," the house manager informed him.

"Can I talk to Uncle Tomas?"

"Mr. Ivanov is at a conference in Djakarta. Would you like to leave him a message on his board?"

"Galina?"

"I can't get you right now, David," Galina insisted, looking unusually harried on the screen. "I know it's hard, but tough it out. You've lived through worse. You'll be home in two days."

David broke the shelf in the commlink booth with one blow of his fist.

They'd papered Sergei, too. The resident teacher made the students dispose of all printouts, but it was too late. The conversational noise at dinner disappeared, replaced by sniggers, elbows, and dozens of eyes burning into David's back.

David tried. He *tried*, but after twenty minutes of overhearing rumors swelling and twisting, he couldn't take any more. He shoved his chair back from the table and stood on it.

"For your information," he addressed the suddenly silent room, "if any of you illiterates bothered to read the article, the charge was negligent homicide, not murder. The sentence is seven to fifteen years in a rehab facility. That's what you're charged with when you're 207 centimeters and you're drunk and you hit a whiney six-year-old with a thirty-nine centimeter fist and accidentally break her neck. *Yes*, I was there when it happened, *yes*, I saw the corpse, and I'm already aware of the fact I was at the trial and had to rat on my father. Any of you spineless pricks want the truth, have the balls to ask my face. You want to talk about it behind my back, go ahead, but get the facts right."

He stalked out of the dining room without permission, and without giving a damn about it, either.

Ten

Dmitri awoke just before noon, Sarah huddled against him. They hadn't fallen asleep until after sun-up, Sarah choking out some of the horror of her dream, Dmitri's thoughts restless in his head.

After breakfast, he patted the corner of her bed. "Sit." Sarah sat obediently.

"I... did a lot of thinking... about last night, you know? I'm sure it was partly my fault. I never should have made you stay alone like that. I knew better, and... I'm sorry. She was just so... I've never had anyone say those things to me before." Dmitri couldn't explain it. Not politely. Not to a nine-year-old. "I just really, really wanted to stay with her, and I got mad because I had to take care of you instead. I should have told her no to start with. I'll try not to do something that stupid again."

Sarah nodded. "It's not your fault. She needed to wear more clothes."

Dmitri gave a laugh, remembering what had started out as the best night of his life. "Yeah, well... Last night, I realized I've kind of been doing whatever the hell I wanted, and not caring about what you might want, and that we're really more in this together. Partners. I mean, I'm still in charge and all," he corrected, and Sarah nodded agreement, "but it hasn't been very fair to you. So," he said, activating the computer, "it's your turn."

Choices...

He called up a travel guide. The hotel canceled their bill in apology, but wouldn't extend the gratuity. "We're not staying here another night, that's for sure. Pick somewhere you want to go, except – you know." Home was still off-limits. "Try to keep the flightfares low, okay? And stick to less fancy hotels. Let's start stretching our money.

He motioned to the viewscreen. "Go ahead. Anything you want. Your turn."

* * * 2 * * *

Safari. Dmitri couldn't believe he agreed to a goddamned *safari*, but here he was, sweating his ass off on the vast grasslands of Lexan

III; watching a colony of flat animals frolic and glide on the open plain. Outside of the four beady eyes and the sharp tail, they reminded him of little gray pancakes slithering over the grass. They'd scamper about, dancing a flappy happy dance, then suddenly freeze, sniffing the air with their tails. Amusing for the first three minutes, and painfully dull after that. Except to Sarah.

Dimi would have enjoyed it as a science holo, with editing and narration, but Sarah would have run with them if she could. She'd picked the trip, planned it, so gosh-darned excited she couldn't sleep at night, afraid she might miss something.

Camping on a wild savanna, he'd had to institute some rules. If she couldn't sleep, Sarah wasn't allowed past the dome flaps, or he threatened to tie her up at night. Dmitri woke the first night to find himself the only occupant of their isodome. Visions of Sarah being eaten by some tiger-like thing she'd chased after flashed through his head. He found her in the center of the dark camp, too restless to sleep, enthralled by a night sky glowing with a million visible stars and a setting blue moon.

He sat next to her in the long grass. "Looking for Earth?"

"No. I have no idea where it is from here. It's just a beautiful sky. I've counted eight meteors so far." She hugged him tightly.

"Happy?"

"Oh yes! Isn't this just the *best*! There's so much to see, so much to learn! Thank you for letting me pick."

Four days on the open plains, and they came to the city where the safari ended. Enough new ideas spinning in her head, Sarah wanted only one thing: to tell Vlad about it, and she pestered Dmitri until he gave in.

"Call him, then. But I don't care if you stomp your foot until it breaks, I'm not talking to Valeria. Got it? And no falling apart when it's over." Sarah promised.

"*Dohm Ivanova, Ekaterina,*" Katya answered. Her eyes grew wide. "*Sarah!*"

Sarah smiled shyly. "Hi, Katya. Can I talk to Vlad?"

"Sarah! Where are you? Are you all right? Hang on, he's here…" Katya hit the intercom switch on the control board. "Vlad! I need you in the library, *right now!*"

Sarah glanced off screen. "Dimi wants to talk to David, too."

"Dimi, please come to the screen," Kat begged. "It's okay, I'm alone."

Dmitri tapped Sarah's bottom until she shared the chair. He and Katya had always been close – close in age, close in friendship. He owed her at least a hello.

"Hi, Kat."

Katya lost her smile. "Please come home, Dimi! *Please!* I swear I'm the only sane one left. David and Sergei are at a boarding school in Moscow. He's only here on the weekends. He was supposed to share a room with you, but he couldn't bear to look at the empty bed every day. Vlad's still crying himself to sleep. Valeria won't leave her room anymore. She's dying inside, Dimi! She blames herself for the whole mess. Galina's been running everything alone."

"Val brought this on herself. She won't get sympathy from me," Dmitri said coldly.

"Dimi, *please!* You're *forgiven*, you're off the hook... "

"What, Kat?" came Vlad's voice in the distance.

"Hurry! A call for you!"

Vlad expected one of the boys. He sat down hard when he saw the image.

"Vlad!" Sarah shouted. "You should have been with us! We went on safari! I saw sixty-three Lexan harpbirds with my *own eyes*! We rode on garrods – even *me!* – and our camp got attacked by bats and Dmitri got bit by something and his whole arm swelled up! It was incredible!" Rare was the day when Vlad couldn't get a word in edgewise around Sarah.

"Too radical!" Vlad breathed. "I had go back to school. So far I'm doing okay. And Sar! David's been so nice! You'd never believe it! He hasn't called me a name in so long! He even lets me kick with him and Sergei, as long as I don't talk too much – I mean, like really *hang!*"

It was Sarah's turn to be amazed. "Nova! What's it like there? Is it like Kiev?"

"You'd like Uncle Tomas. He's really nice, and he never gets mad, even when I hit a table last week and knocked over some flowers and the water went everywhere. He didn't even yell! He just told me to slow down and be more careful. We're not supposed to run in the house, but *gosh*! The halls are so big you just have to have races down them. And when David beat up Val, Uncle Tomas didn't even whip him for it! Can you believe that?"

"David beat up... ?" Sarah started, but Dmitri cut her off.

"Look, I'm glad to see you two happy again, but the live feed costs a fortune. Kat, can you set up a mailbox for us, my name and Sarah's, text only? They can send each other messages until their fingers cramp. I'll transfer you the money to pay for it."

"That's not fair!" Vlad wailed. "I hate writing!"

"I'll pay for it," Katya offered. "We have more money here than you can imagine. Save yours for tickets home. And soon, Dimi! We miss you, and we want you back."

Dmitri dropped his gaze. "Someday. Tell David I miss him, and I really, really wish I could talk to him. Be good, Vlad. Write Sarah so she'll stay off my back. We'll be in touch."

"We love you!" Katya squeezed in before the call disconnected.

Dear Sarah (and Dimi, too),

You know I'm no good at writing, so Sergei's doing this for me and I'm just telling him what to say.

School's okay. I passed my second test all on my own.

Sergei and David go to a fancy school in Moscow, Northern Hall. It's really nice. They come home for the weekends. David went because he can't stand being around Valeria any more after he beat her up. He feels bad about it now, but Val blames herself, and they just kind of avoid each other. I don't think he was wrong at all. I'm glad he did it, and I wish I'd helped. Did I tell you about that? [Vlad's not supposed to be talking about this, and if David finds out he'll kill him, but I'm printing it anyway – Sergei] After you called and Dimi said he wasn't coming back, David freaked and really clobbered Val – I mean, like broke her face and tried to choke her to death and stuff. And Uncle Tomas never even whomped him for it! David says Uncle Tomas doesn't hit people, but I still wonder if it's because he doesn't like Val.

Hey Sarah – it's Sergei. I'm glad you're having fun, but I wish you were here. We really miss you (and Dimi too). We're reading a really good novel in school I know you'd like. It's called March of the Dragonfly *by Azarael Kingsford. If you can, read it. Tell Dmitri, David said that – and I quote – "If that Bastard wants to talk to me, he can just get his goddamned ass home and say it to my fucking face, because I got nothing to say to him." I'm just reporting, not approving. If we don't write again in time, tell Dmitri Happy Seventeenth/Eighteenth Birthday, whichever way he's celebrating it.*

Write us soon.

Vlad

and Sergei

Dear Vlad (and Sergei and David and Katya and Nikky and Marina and Galina and Val, too, I guess),

I'm doing really really well. Dmitri's trying hard to do everything right by me. Val should be impressed. And yes, Galina, I am washing my hair. We finished our safari, and Dmitri took me to a huge amusement park in the Geminid system. I got sick on a simulator.

I'll try to read that book as soon as I can, Serg. Thanks. I won't tell you Dmitri's reply to David, because I'm not allowed to write those words, and I know deep down he doesn't mean it. He misses David a lot. You don't need to be in school to figure that out.

It's my turn again. I'll write again after our next trip.

Having fun, I guess, but wishing I was home,

S.I.K

* * * 3 * * *

Earthdate: 11 March, 2264

Katya lounged in her room, watching a teen program on a vid channel, when the answering service let a personal call through. She waited another three chirps, hoping someone else would get it, but Vlad was asleep, Val wouldn't, and Galina was probably busy. Katya sighed, walked to the desk, and hit the receive switch.

"*Dohm Ivanova*. Dr. Carver! How did you know we were here?"

"Katerina," John Carver remembered. He'd met her when she'd come with her family to visit Sarah at the hospital, talked with her socially at her father's murder trial.

"How are you? How is everyone? I promised Sarah I would call a month after the move to see how she was."

Katya evaded the remark with a cheerful smile. "I'm doing fine, thank you. My birthday's coming up and I'll be officially eighteen. I'm trying to decide on a university for fall."

"Congratulations! That's wonderful! It's about time something went right for your family. How's Sarah doing? Can I talk to her?"

Katya's smile faded. "She's not here. It's a long story, but Dmitri and Sarah didn't come with us. I have no idea where they are. They called the other week. She and Vlad have been sending each other letters, and she sounds terrific. We miss her something terrible, though."

Carver nodded. "I know what happened. I called the day after you left. Sarah was so upset I flew out there myself. She gave me this number and told me to call in a month. I talked to them again about a week later. I told Dmitri to get her home back *then*! I can't believe he hasn't returned. What's he waiting for? A disaster? Did he give any idea when he might come back?" John did little to disguise his outrage.

"At one point he said not for a year. I know Sarah's not happy about that. She'd never leave Vlad voluntarily. I worry about her."

"Dammit all! If I'd known he would take it this far, I would have stopped them back on Navara. I could have, but Dmitri was so defensive I didn't want to scare him off, for Sarah's sake. What does Valeria say about it?"

Katya's shoulders drooped further, and she looked ill. "Doctor Carver? Please tell me what to do! We don't know *what* to do with Val anymore…"

Eleven

Earthdate: 18 March, 2264

"Aren't you getting up? We're supposed to be celebrating. Come on! It's almost lunch."

Sarah pulled her blankets tighter. "No."

"Don't go bratty on me today. You can do whatever you want on your birthday, and I promise not to complain."

Dmitri checked the mirror one last time, licking his finger to smooth out a lone stray hair. *Perfect.* Today he could tear up his liberation papers. As far as his ID claimed, he was now a full-fledged adult.

Sarah dragged herself up. She stood by the bed, twitching. A finger jerked, then a shoulder, then her head tilted a little to the side as the other shoulder came up, then an eyelid – a quiver here, a tremor there, all over. She rubbed her arms as if chilled.

Dmitri saw it all in the mirror. "What's the matter?"

"I don't feel good. I'm twitchy and my stomach hurts. I'm so tired I can't move."

He didn't like the way she looked. He'd seen that look before, at home, but what did it mean?

"Another dream?"

Sarah shook her head. Her restlessness grew as he watched.

"You're still taking that orangy stuff, right? The Antivox? You don't have voices, do you?" *Please, no!* He had no idea what psychiatric treatments were available on this planet. "You have enough of that stuff?"

Sarah paused, searching for a hint of the irrational voices that once tormented her. "No, no voices. I've got a month or so left before I need a refill. Dimi, I really don't feel good."

"Relax. You're okay. Lie down 'til I figure this out. Let me think." Dmitri tried to sound positive, as if he knew what he was doing. If he didn't panic, maybe she wouldn't.

Sarah sat for three seconds, then bounced up again. "I can't." She rubbed her arms and paced, twitching.

Dmitri ran through the possibilities in his head. *It wasn't a dream, it wasn't the voices, she was still taking her meds, she...*

"Sar, how long have you felt sick? How long have we been away?"

Sarah grimaced through a particularly hard eyeblink. "It started three days ago. We left 8 February. Today's 18 March. Six or seven weeks."

Shit! "The meds! The stuff in your arm! We forgot about it. You need the pack replaced. Where did I put the pills?" One of her drugs was implanted in her shoulder every six weeks, to keep the levels steady.

Think, you idiot! Dmitri'd hidden the bottles of spare pills, afraid she'd throw them away, or perhaps OD on them in a moment of grief. She hadn't needed them with the med pack in place.

Sarah nodded, hugging herself. "I wasn't twitchy last time."

"You weren't on as high a dose last time." Dmitri tore through the bags of luggage until he came up with the proper pills. *How many?* He should know all this stuff! He was in charge! Dr. Carver raised the dose last time. *Five or six pills*, he said. Dimi was pretty sure. He dumped them into his hand and grabbed a glass of water. "Take these."

Sarah twisted away as if he held a foul substance. "I can't take them like that, Dimi. I *can't*! I'll choke!"

He'd forgotten that detail, too. The little yellow triangles were no bigger than a raisin, but Mother had always crushed Sarah's pills and mixed them with a sugary fruit syrup. Lacking any of that, Dmitri dropped the pills on the clothing cabinet and crunched them under the bottom of the water glass. He poured out all but two centimeters of water and scraped the crushed tablets into the glass. He held it out to her. "Here. Drink it down."

"I can't drink that! They taste horrible! I need fruit juice or something."

"I don't have any fruit juice." He swished the liquid around to help dissolve the bigger crumbs. "I already put them in the water. Just hold your breath. After you get dressed, we'll get a lemon fizzy. Come on." He held the glass up to her twitching head.

Sarah gagged most of it back. "They're not crushed enough. Katya makes them powdery."

"Tomorrow I'll do better, but right now you have to drink this. Just *do* it!" Dmitri grew stern for the first time. He'd seen her in real crisis. He couldn't handle that. *Hospitals* couldn't handle that. Dmitri tipped the water into her mouth with one hand and grabbed her nose with the other. Sarah spluttered, but most of the mouthful went down.

"Don't do that to me! I feel bad enough without you being mean."

"I'm not being mean. You have to take them. Now, you can do it in two big swallows, or a lot of little ones, but if you spill it, I'll get more and we'll start over. Understand? There you go," he soothed as she took the glass and tried a smaller gulp on her own. "You'll feel better in a little while."

Twelve

David lost track of the number of weekends he'd come home. He hated to admit it, but he almost liked this school. Most of his fears came to naught. He addressed his problems head on, proved he couldn't be intimidated, and by the following week most of the nonsense had died off, just as Galina promised. The unrelenting workload at Northern floored him, but he liked being able to kick back with his friends whenever he felt like it. There'd been a big sports meet at school on Thursday against St. Basil's, and Northern's affiliate girl's school, Villovsky, came to cheer them on. David hadn't had the nerve to talk to any of the girls, but he put serious time into scouting out potential conquests.

He was happier than he'd expected, but he couldn't shake the feeling he was living a lie. *Boarding school?* His old friends would tell him he'd sold out, bent over, puckered to the Establishment. Jeff would never have understood this move. Hell, six months ago David would have been the first to pick a fight with someone who looked like he did now. He was letting someone else tell him what he could wear, how to cut his hair and what type of jewelry he could sport. Father was one thing, but this – this willing – *subservience!* What was he doing to himself?

Katya relayed Dmitri's message. David was pissed at his brother for having the guts to disappear, but he missed him, too. Being the oldest was a drag, and he'd gladly give up one of his earrings to be second in line again. Wouldn't school be a blast with Dimi there! Sergei was okay, but he wasn't Dimi. The most rebellious thing Sergei ever did was cross the street without asking. He didn't fight, didn't drink, rarely swore, never handed in schoolwork late, he wasn't even old enough to mess with girls yet. How could you spill your guts to someone who couldn't possibly understand? Yeah, they were brothers to the core, a bond forged long ago through blood and tears, only death could tear them asunder (*what the hell did ass–under mean, anyway?)*, but they weren't really… *friends.*

Thoughts bounced off each other in David's head.

He was still himself.

Wasn't he?

Could he have lost his spirit in only three months? Hell, the other week he'd walked away from what could have been a glorious fight. A strong reputation for not putting up with shit was better than respectability any day.

Wasn't it? Didn't a firm reputation *earn* you respect?

David stared hard in the mirror, wanting to understand the person he saw. His black hair had grown in, mainstream and conforming. He pulled it back with his fingers, remembering what it looked like wild.

Screw everything. He dug into his closet and changed into old clothes: black pants, a bright shirt, and his ankle-high desert boots. The boots were tight, but he wrestled them on anyway. Maybe he'd get a new pair today, as good an excuse as any to get out. He slicked his longer hair back as best he could, leaving a shag down the front, and lacquered it in place.

Better. He felt more like himself, a tough kid with no worries except for staying out of Father's way. If only he had somewhere to hang. He didn't know any of the local youth, just his friends in Moscow, who came from all over anyway.

He pulled his suede jacket on with ceremony and checked the mirror. The hair would have to do, but the rest looked good. As an afterthought, David pocketed a small black pencil. If he felt like Attitude today, then dammit, he was going to *be* Attitude.

He leaned in the younger boys' doorway. "Comin' with me?" he asked Sergei. "I need your help at the library."

"You're going inside a *library*?" Sergei hooted. "Is the sun going nova or something? This I gotta see! Coming, Vlad?"

Vladimir dove for his shoes. He hadn't heard where they were going, but it didn't matter. He'd been invited to go.

They followed the walk to the streetpath. David stopped at the edge of the property. Two stone pillars marked the start of the flyway, one bearing a polished metal plaque with the address engraved on it. He bent down, checked the clarity of the reflection, then pulled the black eyeliner out of his pocket and drew a line along the lashes under each eye, using the plaque as a mirror. He'd have to wear the cosmetics back into the house, but he didn't care. So he'd darkened his eyes down. So what.

Sergei noticed. "What're you doing? You have no intention of going to a library, do you. We're just alibis to cover you."

"I thought paranoia was Vlad's trademark? Cryin' out loud! When was the last time I got you in trouble? Can't I bring a little style to this crappy city without being accused of something? Saturn's rings, you sound like Val. If you're gonna give me shit like that, don't come. Vlad and I can figure out the library by ourselves." David walked toward the tram stop.

Vlad glanced at Sergei with nervous eyes, then ran after David.

Sergei shook his head in disgust and followed. Someone had to look out for Vlad.

The first stop off the tram brought new boots. What seemed tight in David's room was unbearable a half-hour later. Uncle Tomas preferred to have all of his clothing, especially shoes, custom-made, but David wasn't waiting twenty-four hours for delivery.

They walked the twelve blocks from the shoe shop to the old gray hulk of a library. Snow lingered deep only in the shady places, real spring warmth hinting in the air at last. As the boys reached the rise of worn stone steps, they passed two older youths coming down. One smoked a tobacco cigarette.

Vlad wrinkled his nose and moved behind Sergei. Not even Father had that nasty habit. When they reached the top, David wasn't behind them. Below, David handed the smoking boy hard currency. The boy gave him a cigarette and lit it for him.

Sergei and Vlad walked back down as David vaulted onto the wall at the edge of the steps and sat. Sergei glared at him.

"You're really out to get your ass kicked today, aren't you. What the hell are you doing? At least don't do that out here. Someone will report you for being underage, and Vlad and I will get in trouble, too."

"David!" Vlad cried in disbelief. "That will *kill* you!"

"Vlad, so help me, if you don't put those eyes back in your head, I'll poke 'em in myself." David held his hand up with two fingers extended. Vlad jumped three steps back and hung his head.

"When are you gonna grow up? One a month won't kill me, but I might kill you if you go ratting to Val or Galina, you big baby."

Vlad hung his head further.

David offered the cigarette to Sergei.

Sergei slapped it back. "What the hell do I want with that stuff?"

David took a short drag and offered it again. "I was younger than you... "

"I'm not you!"

David said nothing, but his eyes held the challenge. As the hand withdrew, Sergei snatched the offensive object and brought it to his lips.

David was startled. He'd only been harassing Sergei; he never expected him to accept. Sergei hung out with Vlad and Sarah, not the older boys, and he never bought into dares. That was half the fun of picking on him. Somehow, though, it didn't seem right. Sergei was too smart to be fooling around with mood-enhancers. "Don't inhale it," he warned. "It's been narc'd. That's why it's bitter."

Sergei coughed hard. He handed the cigarette back quickly, as if just holding it would poison him. "What are you touching it for, then? What'll it do to me?!" He fanned clean air toward his face.

"Don't shit yourself. I'd doubt it's got enough of anything to harm that massive brain of yours. Might make you dizzy, that's all. Don't get all pissy-pants'd out here, Vlad," David sneered. "I wouldn't let you anyway, even if you asked. I don't feel like scraping puke off your shirt."

Vlad wilted. "Why are you being so mean to me again? I thought we were friends now?"

David blew smoke out in as long a stream as he could. He wasn't really inhaling much, either. He just wanted Attitude. Smoking was something illegal he knew he could get away with; knowing the tobacco was laced with a mild narcotic – which he hadn't planned on – made the Bad Attitude better.

"I'm your *brother*, Vlad," he said acidly. "I never said I was your *friend*."

Vlad turned and slunk the ten meters to the far end of the steps.

"What'd you have to go and say that for?" Sergei demanded. "Sometimes you are such a jackass. Come on, Vlad." He climbed the stairs again. "We don't need to *debase* ourselves with *extraneous, pernicious, insignificant peccancy* like that." Nothing pissed David off so much as when he used too many long words in a single sentence.

David crushed out the cigarette and followed them. "You should know, Serg."

The old library strained with hushed noises: the whispers of patrons, the hissing of shoes on carpet, the jingles and clanks and clickings of coatfasteners and jewelry and compads and carry bags multiplied a hundredfold. Four hundred computer carrels spread across the main floor; nearly all were taken. David found one unoccupied in a back corner. He could have accessed everything from home on the 'link, but here there was guaranteed anonymity.

"Show me what I'm doing here," he asked Sergei. "I want to access old city records. What do I look up?"

Sergei reached out a finger. The library relied on touch screens rather than voice commands, to keep the noise level down. "What are you looking for?"

David shrugged. "I don't know. Say, town records from a hundred years ago."

"Archives, then hit City Records." Sergei scrolled down to the Γ's for *Gorodsky,* town affairs. "Scroll for specific category, then the year, 2164, and touch that."

David waved them away. "I can take it from here."

"I'll be down in the stacks," Sergei told him. Vlad followed.

David was stumped. He poked several records, with no success. No vehicle registry. No property ownership. Nothing listed in the 'link directory. No voter registration. Nothing listed in the police blotter for that year, either. He tried the year before and the year after. Nothing. How could a person live in the city and not exist?

As a last resort, he ran a general records search. A full minute passed before the SEARCHING message stopped spinning. One lone match blinked under city employment records, listed for tax purposes. City taxes were pooled to create the state tax fund, which financed the federal fund, a portion of which went to the planetary fund, which supported their portion of the Alliance's galactic operating budget.

David expanded the listing. There it was. He cross-referenced the address; a different name claimed rental of the apartment. That would explain it. A person with no housing, no property, no ties to anything. As close to nonexistence, government-wise, as you could get. Somehow, that fit. He printed the references and a current list of the tram routes, folded the pages and stuffed them in his coat. His work was done. He went to find the boys.

Sergei meandered along the open shelves, scanning titles of aging books and data disks, surviving remnants of a bygone era. Vladimir sat with an electronic copy of *The New 2260 Illustrated Encyclopedia of Mammals, Centauri edition.*

David rested a new boot on the seat of Vlad's chair. It wasn't as much fun as he remembered, ripping up people you were supposed to give a damn about. He'd have beaten blood out of a stranger that talked to Vlad that way. He held out his hand. "I'm sorry I pissed you off. I guess you count as one of my friends."

Vlad ignored the hand. "Yeah? Well, maybe I don't want to be your brother, either." He deactivated the book screen, shoved David's foot off the chair on the third try, and walked away.

They exited the tram in a dark distant section of the city that Mother – or Val or Uncle Tomas or even Father – would never have let them visit alone. Apartment buildings crowded out the skyline, so gray and utilitarian they couldn't be dated. Tired shops lined the walkways and peered up from the bottom levels of some of the buildings. Mud, ice, and garbage banked the foundations.

Vlad fought his urge to hold Sergei's hand. Sergei was twelve and a *half* now, and wouldn't put up with baby stuff, so Vlad kept his hands in his pockets and walked close enough to bump him every step. Sergei looked as nervous as Vlad felt, and even David didn't seem particularly confident.

"You have three minutes to do whatever you're going to do," Sergei whispered. "We're on the next tram out, with or without you.

Will you please tell me what we're doing here?"

"Two more blocks," David promised, picking up his pace.

A school passed on their right, a thick square building with no playground, no sports fields, not even a running track. Across the street, a child stared dully from a third-floor window. No grass or landscaping gave respite to the endless pavement. A scrawny sapling struggled to bud in the spring warmth, its roots, save a small ring of mud, set under concrete. Rumpled citizens wasted away on the walkway benches, as faded as the plastic. They watched the boys pass with sharp, cold eyes.

David sensed his jacket working against him. No one on these streets wore real leather. He stuck out like a space-warp engine at a solar-sail race. A chill wind breezed down the shadowy channels, but he took off the coat and rolled it up under his arm.

Down the flat, ruler-straight side streets to their right, far in the distance, the ten-meter-high orange security fence could be glimpsed. Up close, it would be festooned with two-meter square warning signs in Russian, Polish, and Interstellar English. The border of the Contaminated Zone.

"David?" Sergei whispered. "This is reclaimed land! We're standing on reclaimed land! Is it really safe?"

David checked the building numbers. "Supposed to be,"

Land reclamation. A Herculean task for more than a hundred years as the need for habitable land continued to grow, and current estimates said there were at least thirty years' work left in Minsk. The Russias alone admitted to 150 heavily contaminated sites, not counting the rest of Europe. *Safer than natural dirt!* insisted the politicians, but convincing the public wasn't easy. Land in this section was cheap because for twelve generations it had been unsafe, and no one trusted it enough to live there except immigrants and the destitute.

Radioactive soil. The curse of the past on the future. Fallout from early nuclear-fission disasters, residue from the nightmares of World War III, and unregulated industrial chemicals had helped to destroy a considerable amount of once-arable land. For a hundred years, work crews had scraped the soil and filtered the dust, removing contamination and laying down new topsoil in a massive effort to reclaim vast tracts of deadly land. It was slow, tedious work, testing and retesting the soil to a depth of five meters or more. Every time the government declared a kilometer safe, speculators landed like flies. Apartments sold, but no one yet dared build a private home.

David stopped before a five-story, brown-brick complex. Father had been their source of knowledge on architecture; even Vlad knew that modern prisons were more inspirational.

"What are you doing?" Sergei asked. "You better not have dragged us here for something illegal."

"Nope," David said softly. "This is where Father lived when he met Mother."

"*What?! That's* what you came down here for?"

David nodded. "Think about it. We never knew about Mother's family. We never knew we had an uncle. We didn't know Mother's background – I mean, it makes sense now, but we never knew. But we know even less about Father. Name me two things about Father before he married. Just *two*."

Sergei thought hard, realized David was right. "He was tall, and he worked in a museum, didn't he?"

"That's what the records showed. He must have lived with a friend, because the apartment was rented in someone else's name. Did you ever think about it? I mean, we know Father's patronymic is Grigorevitch, so his father had to be Grigory Kirushenko. There's no one listed by that name in any of the records for Minsk. But what was his wife's name? Our other grandmother? Were they married? Where'd they live? Are they alive? Father has a sister, but is she older or younger? Do we have cousins? We don't know."

Sergei eyed the building and nodded.

Vlad sighed. "It's not very nice, is it. I guess I might get mean, too, if I had to live here every day."

"Should we go inside?" Sergei wondered. Sometimes buildings were nicer inside than outside.

Vlad looked scared at the idea.

David shook his head. "No. We came, we saw, we stared. Let's get out of here while we can. I'm freezing."

They were quiet on the tram home, each lost in new thoughts.

"I take back what I said in the library," Vlad told David. "I guess I can live with being your brother."

David pulled him close, digging his knuckles painfully into the boy's scalp before releasing him. "It's not like you have a choice," he said. "You were born to follow my greatness."

* * * 2 * * *

Dear Sarah,

I'm doing this in the back of the auditorium during a concert. I don't dare write it at home because if David found out he'd kill me dead, but Nikky and me are laughing too hard not to tell you. David's voice is changing, just like Dimi's did! Remember how bad we used to pick on him? David's not laughing now! He's grown 7 cms in the last 6 months. I wish I could grow like that.

Marina's growing too. She can say cookie, and that, and she says Mama Va for Mama Val, because Val really is her mother. Everybody's growing but me!!! I'm going to be a circus midget.

Did I tell you Valeria is pretty much back to her old self? Dr. Carver called last month looking for you, and Kat told him about Val. He had her bring Val to see him and they stayed there two weeks. She smiles now, and doesn't sit in her room all day. Katya said Val just got sad because she blamed herself so much for you guys not coming home. I remember when you didn't want to get out of bed that time, but you weren't guilty of anything, so you couldn't blame yourself. Val's not as bossy as she used to be, but she's mostly herself again and we're all happier now.

Miss you guys.
Your midget brother,
Vladimir

Dear Vlad,
I miss you, too, but I'm always happy when you write. I guess I'm happy for Val, too. It's not fun when you feel like that. I felt really rotten back then. I hated even having to breathe. I used to blame myself for Mother dying – I called for the MedEvac, but I always thought I should have known how to do more. It took a long time for me to believe Dr. Carver that there was nothing I could do, unless I'd been a qualified surgeon. He even showed me the hospital reports. I did everything right. If I hadn't been home that day, Marina would have died, too. So I'm not supposed to blame myself.

I know I'm not to blame for our excitement last week, either. Dmitri says I did the right thing. I was so scared, Vlad! We were coming through a spaceport – I'm not supposed to say where – and got robbed! Somebody put a blast weapon in Dimi's face and told him to hand over his money or he'd vaporize him right then and there. Dimi had about a hundred cash credits on him, too. We were lucky in that they took the money and left us and our stuff alone.

After we reported everything, Dmitri went out and bought one of the biggest, meanest-looking knives I've ever seen. The blade is laser-sharpened and 40 cm long, without the handle. It cost a fortune. Then he bought a smaller one, just as sharp, but the blade's only as long as my hand. I wanted one, too, but he said not in a hundred years. I promised I'd never use it on myself, but he wouldn't believe me.

Tell Sergei I finally found that book by Kingsford and had a print made. I loved it! I stayed up half the night to finish it. Tell him to write me his thoughts and we'll discuss it.

You'll grow eventually. You got the short side of the draw, like Dimi and Kat and Viktor. Which side do you think Nikky got? I haven't seen him in so long. I miss him, too.

I'll tell Dimi about David, and we'll laugh about it with you. Wish we could be there to pick on him.

Sarah

Dear Dmitri,

I'm graduating in two weeks. Grandmother is having a big party for me. I really, really, really wish you and Sarah would come home for it. I want that more than anything. Please? It should have been Sarah's graduation, too, you know.

There's no way you've got her in school, hopping around like that. Tell me you've at least gotten her a program she can study on her own. I'd bet money you didn't think of that. Tell Sarah the Basic Education Exam is a breeze – she could do it blindfolded, standing on one foot while fighting with David. I'll be heading up to St. Petersburg in August.

I miss you. Come home.

Katya

Thirteen

Earthdate: 4 June 2264

"**W**hat's in it?" Sarah begged as they picked up the shipping container at the front desk of their current boarding 'hotel.' "Please tell me! What did you send for?"

"Something," Dmitri said with a fiendish smile. "Something in a box. It's heavy, too."

Sarah danced next to him as they walked to their room. "Let me feel!"

"Nope. Keep guessing."

"I know it's not *that* big a box, but I don't suppose you managed to ship Vlad in it?"

"Not quite, but you're right: it's from Russia, and it's for you."

"ME?! You're kidding! Please, please tell me what it is!"

"Open the room and you can have it." It was worth the exorbitant cost already, to see her so happy.

Sarah unlocked the door, ran to the middle of the room, and held her hands out. "Gimme gimme gimme!"

"Oh, we're greedy now. Maybe I shouldn't let you have it, then…"

"Stop it! Stop it, you vile beast!" Sarah jumped for the box. "*Please?* With an extra thank you on top?"

Dmitri dropped it on the bed, laughing. "Here! Maybe now you'll stay out of my hair." He really couldn't call Sarah greedy – she never asked for anything beyond occasional sweets. If Katerina had only dropped the hint months ago.

Sarah tore at the package with a vengeance. She ripped the lid off and let out a squeal of joy.

Textbooks. He'd ordered textbooks!

Seven fat bound volumes and fourteen computer chips of practice and enrichment for her homework 'pad. She ran her fingers over the spines, drawing them out reverently one at a time. Microchemistry, Astrophysics, Literature – two volumes, Art of the 21st Century, Elementary Linguistics, and Fractal Geometry.

"Oh Dimi!"

He flipped through the linguistics book. "I got the course listings from Moscow State and picked courses from the freshman list I thought you'd like. You said the power cells for your text reader were low, so I ordered printed copies. You can read these anywhere. I thought maybe this way you wouldn't be so bored all the time."

She tackled him over the box. "Thank you! Thank you! That's the nicest thing anybody did for me, ever! *Thank you!*"

Dmitri pushed her back, embarrassed. "Easy. Don't go crying on me, now. Do you like the subjects?"

Sarah wiped her eyes. "They're perfect!"

"Don't expect me to discuss them with you. The art one maybe, but none of that science stuff. Think they'll keep you busy?"

Sarah hugged the linguistics book. "Oh yes! For months! Every one of them! *Thank you!*"

Dmitri pushed the box out of the way and put his arm around her. He held her for a minute, smiling over the top of her head, happy to have done something right at last.

Dear David,

How come you never write me? I hope you're not mad at me. I miss your sense of humor and the way you used to wink at me before you teased Vlad. I wish I could be there in person to wish you Happy Birthday, but, no surprise, I won't make it, so you'll have to settle for an impersonal "Happy Birthday" in print, but trust me, the sentiment is real.

Your hopefully not forgotten sister,
Sarah

Dear Brain,

I wouldn't forget you, you nut! The Fearsome Four are Now and Forever! You're still my Number One Scout. I read every note you send Vlad and Sergei. I don't write you because 1) writing's too much like schoolwork and 2) I'm still pissed you're not here and I'm getting tired of waiting for you to come back. I don't care if that Shit you're with ever returns, but we haven't had a good game of poker since you left. Vlad sucks at poker. How many years we've been letting him play and he still can't remember the order, and every time he gets a good draw he practically claps his hands. I don't think he'll ever grow up.

Thanks for the wishes. I appreciate them.
DAVID

Fourteen

David had just changed for bed when Valeria knocked. Despite her efforts, she remained distant around him. Part of it, he figured, was his own problem. Val may have come to terms with her guilt, but he couldn't get rid of his. He had trouble just looking at her.

"Do you have time to talk?"

"Yeah, sure." David pulled his desk chair out for her, then fled across the room to sit on the bed. Val ignored the chair and to his distress sat next to him.

She fumbled with her fingers. "I've been thinking something over for a while now. When we first got here, and we didn't know where Dmitri was, you seemed to know for a fact they weren't on Navara.

I'd like to know how you knew. I'm not mad – please don't think I came here to make trouble. I just wanted to know."

David hesitated. It was his secret, his alone, but what difference did it make now, all these months later?

"I guessed. I... have the access numbers for Dmitri's bank account. I looked up the account statement, saw there was a deduction made at Shir P'an Spaceport, and it didn't take Sarah's brains to figure out it had to be for flight tickets. It wasn't enough for passage to Earth."

"I never would have thought of that. Can you still access the account? Can you tell where they are?"

David shrugged. "I guess so. It will show the last charges to the account and the location. We won't necessarily know where they *are*, but you can see where they've been."

"Could you? Vlad keeps me up to date, but I'd love to know *where* they are."

"You're not planning to ambush them, are you?" David could seriously kick Dimi's ass right now, but he respected the reason behind the act, and he wasn't about to turn traitor.

"Of course not! I just... It wouldn't feel so much like they're lost to us. If we know where they are, then it's almost like they're supposed to be there."

"That makes sense." David sat at the computer and navigated his privacy encryption. He whistled softly. "Last debit was at Silver City, on Tyrolean IV. He's going through money like water. What the hell's he been doing? How much you want to bet this one was Sarah?" He laughed, reading the spending summary. "Moscow State University Student Supply – 297 Credits. What the hell'd he let her buy – an entire lab?"

Valeria thought of something. "Don't change the screen! I'll be right back." Val returned several minutes later, a comp card in her hand. She gave it to David.

"Can you look up that account as well?" she asked, explaining, "I set up an account for Sarah, in both our names. She has an access card."

David ran the numbers and came up with a blank screen. "How much is there supposed to be?"

"Six thousand."

David couldn't help giving her a nasty look. They'd each received a survivorship benefit after Mother died, in the unfathomable sum of six thousand interstellar credits. They'd thrown themselves at Val's mercy for even a portion of the money to spend, but Val had refused. David knew she'd turned the cheques over to Uncle Tomas to invest, and the money no doubt was doubling as they spoke, but David couldn't help resenting the fact that Sarah probably never asked for the money. Dmitri had stolen his back, one of his many battles with Valeria.

"Six thousand twelve interstellar credits," David read off a different page. "No activity on the account, except interest."

Val lay a hand on his shoulder. "Good. Then they're okay. Could you do me a favor? Give a check every couple of weeks for me? Let me know if they move, or if Sarah touches her account. If she gets low, I can add to it for her."

"Sure, Val," David said. "I can do that."

Fifteen

Earthdate: September, 2264

Dmitri met the group while he and Sarah explored a local park. Parks were free, and Sarah delighted in the grass and trees. The mixed crowd played kembo, a variant of Earth's volleyball. The ball went wild, and Dmitri hit it back into the game. They invited them to play.

Sarah played through a couple of points, then sat on the sidelines, watching. She didn't like it when Dmitri found other people to associate with. It wasn't solely jealousy. Alone, they were more or less equals; when he found friends, she degraded into the pesty tagalong kid sister, nothing more than a mascot to be patted on the head and told she was cute, no matter how much brain she had. Sarah didn't care what she was called, as long as it wasn't *cute.*

They stayed all afternoon, playing and talking, eating and talking, lying in the grass and talking about hanging out that night. Dmitri watched Sarah with an air of disappointment. He knew she wouldn't want to party, and wouldn't stay alone. It didn't matter when *he* had to be bored to tears doing something *she* wanted, but planets forbid she ever let *him* do something without giving him that look: the gnawing look of rejection, of resignation to a boredom so awful it would age her before his eyes. He hated feeling guilty all the time.

He offered their place.

Dmitri answered the door quickly, before the noise could wake Sarah. He'd already explained she needed to make herself scarce, go to bed early and not be a pest. He was having friends over, and they didn't want little sisters hanging around. He was doing it to be nice to *her*, so she wouldn't have to be left alone. She didn't want that, did she? Sarah fell head-first into the trap, disappearing into the bedroom of their dingy two-room apartment.

A giggling girl held up a bottle as Dmitri opened the door, and three girls and two young men entered. "Here comes the party!"

"Shhh! Not too loud." Dimi aimed a thumb at the bedroom door.

"Right! Right," the girl whispered, then giggled again.

It didn't take Dmitri long to catch up to his new friends. "Bottom's up!"

"Truth or consequences," the lighter-blonde girl with the pony-tails and giggles asked one of her male companions. The boy was an albino Caphan, his white hair running down his head in a shaggy mohawk between the short, curved tips of his horns.

"Trut'," he chose.

The girl leaned forward, teasing. "Out of everyone in this room, who do you want to kiss the most?" She wore a shiny pink shirt with straps hardly thicker than string, and her rounded curves invited squeezing.

The boy flushed a dusky blue all the way up his sensitive horns. His male companion elbowed him. "Give it up."

"Raeisse," the Caphan admitted, bluing deeper, and the pretty, dark-blonde girl covered her mouth to hide her smile. The room burst into laughter. The brown-haired girl whispered into Raeisse's ear, gave her a push, and Raeisse crawled across the circle to give the boy a fast kiss before retreating.

"My turn," said the brown-haired girl, and she rolled the die in the middle of the circle. It stopped on Dmitri's number.

"Aw, shit!"

"Truth or consequences?" the girl challenged.

Dmitri felt pleasantly pickled. He wiggled his eyebrows at the pale-blonde girl, and ventured, "Consequences."

The brown-haired girl thought. "I dare you to... go out on your balcony and moon your neighbors." Tipsy laughter erupted around the circle.

Dmitri grinned. "Okay." He hadn't roomed with five brothers and not flashed a couple of moons in his life. He didn't mind this balcony – they were on the second floor, and unless Sarah dove headfirst, she wouldn't be too hurt by the three-meter fall. He dropped the back of his pants, laced his fingers behind his head, and circled his hips to the building across the walkway, humming a tune. Encouraged by the whistles and laughter, he turned around and did a bump and grind to the room. The laughter died.

One of the girls cleared her throat. "We have company."

Dmitri yanked his pants and spun around. Sarah stood in her pajamas, staring at him with her big violet-blue eyes.

He smiled drunkenly. "Sarah! Hi! Sar! What are you doing up?"

Sarah absorbed the scene, the vacant faces, the empty bottles on the floor, the food containers littering the room and the explosion of crumbs on the carpeting that was no longer cleaned daily by a chambermaid. "I didn't know what was so funny."

"Just a game… "

Sarah let him take three steps, then backed up for every one he took. She darted into the bedroom, slammed the door and locked it. She pulled and heaved until her bed slid up against the door.

Dmitri pounded on the door. "Aw, come on, Sar, unlock it! Damn!" He faced his guests. "Guess I'm gonna get an earful tomorrow." He stumbled back to his seat.

Raeisse waved a hand toward the locked door. "She'll get over it. We probably woke her up."

"Here," said the second boy, his sandy blond hair tied behind his head in a curl. He reached into his shirt and brought out a flat tin. He offered it to Dmitri. It contained a number of pearly tablets. "Don't worry yourself about her."

Dmitri eyed the contraband. Even tanked, he knew better, but he didn't want to insult his new friends. "What is it?" he asked cautiously.

"Berenician Moon Glow. It'll double your buzz."

Dmitri hesitated. He hadn't heard of Moon Glow. He knew to stay far, far away from Crystal Faze, which made you feel like you'd been electrocuted, and Reflex, but sometimes chems had more than one name. He liked drinking, drinking was fun, but his one unwitting experience with hard contraband had left him very, very suspicious.

Dmitri shook his head. "No thanks. Some other time when I don't have to baby-sit."

"Sure." The boy shrugged and slipped a tablet under his tongue.

He passed the container; only the pale blonde girl declined, gazing hopefully at Dmitri and holding his eye a little too long.

She *was* kind of cute, in a bouncy, eager sort of way.

Round cheeks. Big round cheeks. At both ends! Dmitri giggled.

An hour later, the other couples paired off and left for more private quarters. Dmitri and the girl slouched together, killing the last bottle, talking until the sky lightened.

He awoke on the small sofa after noon, not feeling half as bad as he feared. Sarah sat, dressed, her back against the door of the apartment, backpack loaded and lumpy at her feet. Her sharp eyes measured his every move.

"What are you doing?"

A deadly glare answered.

Dmitri stretched and stood up. "What time is it?"

"Going on one."

"Damn! We gotta get moving. I promised Hila we'd go to a

concert with her this afternoon. What's the matter?"

Her silence accused him.

"You mad at me for last night? Big deal! So I took a stupid dare. It wasn't something that would have hurt anybody. Like no one's ever seen a bare ass before."

Dmitri sat down next to her. Sarah jumped sideways half a meter, and the look in her eyes changed to fear.

"What's with you? You're supposed to talk to me. I don't read minds."

"You shouldn't need to."

"What? Because I partied a little? Grow up!" Sarah slid a few more centimeters and hung her head.

"Gimme a break, Sar." He offered a hand, but she wouldn't take it. "I'm not Father! Just because I had a drink or two doesn't mean I'm going to take your head off. I made sure I knew what I was drinking and I had nothing but alcohol. I never blacked out, I can remember every minute of it, so I was never derelict in my duties as your guardian. You disappeared so fast I couldn't talk to you. Relax!"

Sarah bit her lip and looked away.

"I'm sorry if it bothered you," he apologized, "but I know what I'm doing. I'm not like that. If I ever raise my voice to you, you have every right to beat me over the head. I wouldn't hold it against you. Truce?"

She reached her hand out slowly, but only the tips of two fingers. It was all the commitment she was willing to give.

An uncountable mob swarmed the concert, deafened by amplifiers spread around the park's grassy amphitheater. The music had been rowdy and often unintelligible, with a pounding beat that made the ground shake. Night fell by the time they returned, Dmitri with the cute and perky Hila hanging on him. Sarah fled to the bedroom.

Hila kissed Dmitri. "How long until she's asleep?"

"I never know," he admitted. "She's a light sleeper. The last thing I need is her walking in. I'm in enough hot water over last night."

Hila kissed him, longer. "You don't *want* to?"

Dmitri kissed her ear twice before returning to her lips. "Of course I want to. I'm just trying to figure out *how*."

Hila released his lip. "Do you have anything left from last night? Pour her a double. She'll sleep."

Dmitri shook his head. Alcohol terrified Sarah; she'd smell it coming a kilometer away. A horrible idea came to him. *Did he dare stoop that low for his own pleasure?* If Sarah ever found out, she'd tear him apart. *It wasn't like it would hurt her or anything....* "I know something that might work."

While she washed in the lavatory, he counted out Sarah's pills. She preferred to take them at night, as they seemed to prevent nightmares. From the bottom of his carry bag he withdrew a small blue bottle and added another tiny tablet to the nightly regimen. He'd swiped the sleeping pills from home, hadn't touched them since. Granted, they were Father's prescription, geared for someone his size, but Dmitri wasn't that much bigger than Sarah, and he hadn't had a problem with them. He hated to do it, but, damn it all! If Sarah wasn't such a pest, if he could count on her to sleep all night without waking three or four times... He'd been with her twenty-four hours a day for seven straight months – couldn't he have a little time for himself? He stuffed the bottle deep in his bag and went to crush the pills until they were powdery. He'd become an expert at powdery.

"Mission accomplished," he said an hour later, straining to carry Sarah's heavy sleeping form to the sofa. "She is out *cold*.

"Now, where were we?" Dmitri put his arms around Hila and gave her a long kiss.

For once, Dmitri awoke before Sarah. He dug through the box they kept snacks in, looking for something that might make a decent breakfast. Sarah heard the noise, stretched, felt the ends of the sofa cramping her, and sat up fast.

She looked around with bleary eyes. Dmitri had settled for devouring a bag of *jwani* flakes and a not-so-clean cup of sweet, cool tea. It wasn't pleasant, but they had no ice to make it iced tea, and no heater to make it hot.

"Good morning!" he said brightly. "You're the sleepyhead today!"

"Why am I out here?" Sarah demanded. "My bed... " She looked around again. There'd been a girl here when she'd gone to bed. She stared at Dmitri, then ran to the bedroom door. The two beds were a rumpled mess as always, but the girl's scent still hung in the air.

"You moved me! I don't know why I didn't wake up, but you moved me! You kicked me out of my bed so your girlfriend could have a cushy place to sleep last night, didn't you?"

Dmitri bit his lip. Better to go with what she already had in her head than make up something worse.

"Yyyyeah, I did. It got really late, but company is company, and I... figured since you were already asleep, you wouldn't care too much, so... I couldn't, um, let her sleep with *me*. I guess I should have asked you first, but I didn't want to wake you." He hung his head in feigned repentance. "I'm sorry."

"It's *my* bed! You had *no right!*" Sarah's hands curled into hard fists, but she turned to the bedroom, slamming the door in his face.

Dmitri could hear the smothered squeals of fury, hear the kicking on the bed. He gave her a few minutes, then tried to enter.

The "tainted" linens lay flung before the door. Dmitri hadn't taken more than a step into the room when a textbook flew at his head.

"Hey! Those are expensive! Ow! Stop!" The second book hit him in the chest; the third gouged his arm as he tried to deflect it. He fought his way into the room.

"*Go away!* Red thief!" Sarah shoved the mattress off the bed, tripping him. She backed up to the wall, slid down and sat, holding her head. "Why do you *do* this to me?"

Dmitri pushed the mattress onto the bed. "I didn't think it was that big a deal. You fit on the couch better than I do."

Sarah rubbed her eyes. "Maybe it is, maybe it isn't. I don't feel right. My head hurts, and I don't understand how I slept through your moving me." She looked small and lost and frightened, sulking on the floor. "I wake up when they palm a light two apartments down, but I slept through being moved? Dimi, it's not good when I sleep like that! It only means trouble! What if my medication isn't working like it should?"

"Hey! Hey! Take it easy!" Dmitri parked himself on the bare mattress. She couldn't fall apart on him now – the night had been too incredible. He knew the headache came from the sleeping pills, they did that to him, but the rest was her own paranoia. That had to be stopped, fast.

Should he tell her the real truth?

He'd have to tell her, sooner or later. If she was going to hate him, shouldn't he just get everything out in the open and let her hate him all at once?

"Come up here."

Sarah tapped her fists on her forehead. "I hate you!"

"Hate me if you want, but I need to talk to you, and I'd rather you were up here." She perched as far away from him as she could.

"I want the truth," he said, in the rare manner he had when he felt responsible and in charge. "How do you feel?"

Sarah crossed her arms with a scowl. "I hate your guts."

"Not that kind of feeling. How you *feel* – any sign of the voices, anything getting the better of you?" She was slowly weaning herself off the Antivox, a highly specific medication they'd had trouble refilling.

"You mean, like wanting to cut your heart out with a spoon?"

"I'm serious."

Sarah frowned with the effort of soul-searching, then shook her head. "No. I just don't know how I slept that hard."

"That's good. Because, I… have a little confession to make." He braced for the impending explosion. "Let me know if you start having anything like that. Because… For the last two months, I've been decreasing the Elavixor. One less pill every two weeks. Three more weeks and you'll be done completely."

Sarah paled as the words sunk in.

"You messed with my *meds*? Without *telling* me? Without knowing the blood levels? How could you do that? You didn't know what that might do to me!" Last time it ran out, she'd had a horrible relapse, unable to get out of bed, unable to eat. The voices in her head returned from the stress, and it began the chain of events that made Dmitri steal her away. Only with ever-increasing doses did she regain control. And he was *decreasing* it?

"You were on the last prescription," he explained. "You hate taking them. The original order said a nine-month course of treatment. You've been on them for a year. I figured I'd try it. If you started getting funny, I'd just bring it back up again."

Sarah stared. "Do you know how hard it is to balance Elavixor levels? Do you know how long it took for me to achieve *stability* on it? Who told you you could mess with it?

"*Who gave you the right to mess with my life!*" Sarah sprang to her feet and fled the bedroom.

He didn't panic until he heard the apartment door open. She took off wearing only her too-short pajamas, Dmitri too many seconds behind.

Dear Sarah,

Happy 10th Birthday! We'd send you a present, but we don't know where you are. We wish you were here to give you one in person. You haven't written in a while, and we wondered how you were doing. We hope you're still getting Vlad's letters. Everyone here's well. Katya is at the School for Higher Education up in St. Petersburg. She promises to write when she gets a break. She's taking extra courses, hoping to graduate early.

I hope you won't be upset that I'm the one sending this. Everyone (except Kat) is standing here while I write it. I won't begin to tell you how much I miss you, even if you don't ever want to talk to me again.

We hope your birthday's a whole lot better than last year's, and the coming year brings you back to us.

Love,

Valeria

& Galina, & David, & Sergei, & Katya, & Nikky, & Marina, & most of all, Vlad

Dear Vlad (& everyone else),

Forgive me for being short, but I'm not in the best of moods. Tell Val I forgave her months ago, don't worry herself about it. I haven't written because our apartment doesn't have any type of comm system. I have to use a public com to get the mail, and so far I've only been able to get there twice. I'm not supposed to tell you where we are, even if it is the only class-M world in the Draconis system.

My caretaker and I have had a bit of a falling out and are not currently speaking. He tried to buy me off with a gift of language books – French literature for Mother's sake, and four semester's worth of beginning ancient Latin for Father's. I'm dying to touch them, but my refusal to do so is really pissing *someone off – and I don't care if you tell Valeria I used that word! I'm sorry I haven't been able to write more often. I printed and read everything you guys sent, and I'm sleeping with all that paper under my pillow. I've read them all 10x already. I miss being able to talk to someone. I wish we had a video account.*

I'll win in the end, because I know I'm right.
(I'm dying to open those books, though!)
    Sarah

Sixteen

Theta Geminorum III
United Planetary Alliance
Earthdate: November, 2264

*H*e forced her to speak at the end of November, five and a half ice-cold weeks. *Stubborn?* Stubborn didn't begin to describe his sister. She needed a good whipping, but he'd never do that. He'd seen her beaten almost to death. When she was little, stubborn had made her cute: the gutsy little two-year-old holding her breath to protest a spanking. The scrappy four-year-old tomboy butting heads with a bossy David. The six-year-old who wouldn't give in to Father, even though it nearly cost her life.

For a week she wouldn't be in the same room with him, wouldn't touch her bed. She camped out in a corner of their dayroom with the blanket from his bed. Dmitri didn't have the nerve to tell her the girl had never touched her bed, and that his blanket was the 'contaminated' one.

He hadn't had a girlfriend for almost a month. Sarah drove Hila and their friends away with fish-eyed stares and bratty tactics. Putting bugs in Hila's hair had been the last straw. Dmitri couldn't get close enough to grab the laughing Sarah while he brushed away insects, couldn't bring himself to haul off and belt her one while teary Hila demanded *some* action be taken. They broke up. Dmitri moved on.

Now there were bigger problems to address. After the last passage, finances were grim. Dmitri would have to look for some type of employment. *But what?* He'd quit school with a year and a half to go, leaving him without any sort of certificate whatsoever. He wasn't even sure what he *liked* to do.

And what about Sarah? No one on a class-one Alliance world would hire a ten-year-old, or let one follow him around while he worked.

No matter how badly she tested him, no matter how hard she pushed him, Sarah never let him out of her sight for more than a second. She still needed him, relied on him for security, and he used that to his advantage in controlling her. But now, like it or not, she would have to face some hard facts: she needed to stay by herself. First, though, he had get her talking.

The next day, ignoring her entirely, Dmitri dressed and walked out the door of their bare-bones room – fourth floor, no balcony, only weekly maid service – without any warning at all. He sprinted around the corner to the slow, grinding lift and waited for the doors. Sarah charged after him, eyes wide.

The lift opened, and Dmitri entered. She tried to follow. "No," he said firmly. "I'm going downstairs for tea, and I'll be right back. Go back to the room." He pushed, but Sarah clung to the doorway, tying up the lift.

He pried the fingers off the doors. "No! I didn't tell you to come with me, and you didn't ask, so – *get – out!*" He wrenched one arm free.

"Out!" Dmitri snapped, hurting her shoulders.

"I want to come!" Sarah blurted at last, and he let her dash into the lift.

One small victory.

Back in the room, Sarah dropped across her bed with her math book and a bag of dried fruit. Dmitri lay his hand, palm up, on the open book.

"Stalemate," he declared. "Draw. No winner out. New hand, new game. Do over."

Sarah shook it. *No blame, new game.* "Start over," she grumbled.

"I apologize for any indiscriminate behavior on my part."

Sarah spoke to her book. "I apologize for being a poop – except for the bugs. That was too funny for words."

"Then I don't forgive you for that!" Hila wasn't as drop-dead beautiful as his old girlfriend Sharinna, or as uninhibited as Lalla, but she was… spunky. He missed her.

Dmitri waited another week to broach the bigger subject. He had a lead, one too good to be true. He'd tapped his fingers over everything for the past two days, remembering his drills.

HIRED, said his application.

"You don't *have* to like it," Dmitri insisted, "but you're going to have to get used to staying on your own for a few hours. We're going to be here a while."

She clutched the hem of his shirt, whimpering. "I don't want to."

"No, but you'll get used to it. You know damned well I'm not about to leave you somewhere. If I was, it would have been a month ago."

Her look of unstated fear bothered him. Dmitri had enough to worry about. It was a hell of a lot riskier for him to trust her than her to trust him.

"How can you not trust me?" he asked. "Tell me I'm not doing a good job."

Sarah flinched at the raised voice. "I'm not saying that. You're good to me, but… I *can't* trust you. It's not *you*," she corrected. "I know you wouldn't leave me behind. I *do*! But Val promised me a hundred times she wouldn't do that, and I believed her. And she still took Vlad and left me. I'll never trust like that again."

Dmitri understood, but it didn't solve his problem. He pulled Sarah to her feet. "Well, like it or not, you're going to start right now," he said with authority. "I'm going down to the café to get us some tea, and you are going to sit here with one of your books and read it while I'm gone, and you will *NOT* panic. Got it? Give me fifteen minutes, in case there're people ahead of me. Go get a book." He gave her a little push.

Sarah's heart shuddered, but she grabbed the Latin text and sat in a corner of the room.

He waited outside the door, watching his chronometer. At fourteen and a half minutes he entered the room with two steaming cups of tea. Sarah let her breath out, as if she'd been holding it the entire time. Her white-knuckled hands closed the unread book.

"See?" Dmitri told her cheerfully. "Nothing to it!"

Dear Vlad,
    Goodness! Thirteen letters in – has it been six weeks already? It was like a birthday, all that mail. I

couldn't wait to read them!

Dmitri and I are speaking again. Dimi got a job! He plays keyboard at a bar across the street from our place. Dimi always could play better than anyone. Can't you still hear Mother telling you to practice, practice, practice, you'd be glad to have had the lessons some day? Dimi sure is. He has to study up on some local favorites, so they let him go over in the mornings to practice before they open. I get to go over with him then. He tried to see if I could sit there at night, too, but they won't let me.

I'm learning to stay here on my own. Katya and Vik – even David sometimes – were staying home in charge of everybody by this age, although they were never all alone. I can see the bar from our window. Dimi gets home very late, but I watch out the window so I know when to let him in. He doesn't know I pile all the furniture in front of the door the minute he leaves

I'm sorry, Vlad, but I can't believe you on that one. There's no way, no way I'll believe David made Honors for the semester. Sergei, yes, Katya, yes, maybe even you, but David??? Even I'm not that gullible!

Try another one!

Sarah

Dear Gullible Idiot,

Screw you, you shit! I told you, I read everything you send Vlad, whether he knows it or not. Without you here to suck up all the brainwaves, the rest of us have finally gotten a chance. Attached is a copy of my grade sheet, so screw you! Plus I made swim team this year – 50m freestyle and 50m crawl. We were 11–4 for the season. Nyah!!

I'm still waiting for you to come back and kick my ass!!

DAVID

They sat in the bar, Sarah picking at the keyboard and Dmitri involved in the morning card game he'd learned about. It had become their routine, three days a week. Dmitri was sharp, Dmitri was skillful, and he managed to break even or be slightly ahead each time.

"Want anything while I'm back here?" the bartender, Jalida, asked. Sarah hadn't decided if his bushy hair was white with steel streaks, or steel with white streaks; both colors were equally present. His hawk-eyes could track a dozen people at once, know what they were drinking, how much they'd had, and their tab – with tip, of course.

"Yellowbark seltzer," Dmitri replied, adding coins to match the raised bid. "Nothing strong before lunch, or I'll never make it in to work later."

"What's your girl want?" Jalida offered, reaching for glassware. "The usual?"

"Yeah, that's fine." Dmitri picked up his draw, frowned, folded his cards and dropped them on the table with a grumpy sigh.

Sarah managed to whisper "Thank you" when Jalida left the glass of pink *bajankip* on the corner of the piano. *Baja* was a sour local fruit, but mixed with sugar and enough bubble water, it made a passable version of lemonade. Jalida had eight children of his own and a heart softer than a pillow, but Sarah wasn't in the mood to socialize.

Chord, two keys, no. Chord, three keys, clash.

Dmitri winced at the disharmony. "Try B minor."

That was it! "Thank you," she said softly,

Toban, owner of the establishment, watched Sarah picking the tune out from memory, and tossed his ante in the center of the table. He dressed conservatively, except for the six flashy jeweled studs he wore like buttons up the side of his smoky-black nose. "Too bad she isn't a little older. I'd hire her, too. Pretty little thing. Give her a couple of years. She'll get better tips."

Dmitri flicked his eyes at Sarah before picking up his deal. "No offense, Toban, but no sister of mine is going to work in a bar. Especially that one."

Toban gave a hearty laugh, and the others followed. "Ah, yes. I have three sisters; I own this place so they don't work here."

Dmitri watched Sarah from the corner of his eye. He'd kept her close the last few weeks. A loud fight in the neighboring apartment gave her a bad fright, and she hadn't bounced back. Dimi worried. He couldn't give up his job; he enjoyed it. The location was perfect, the pay satisfactory, and he got a break from Sarah. He liked socializing with the other employees, even if they were twice his age. He liked to watch the stories unfold in the bar every night, imagining where people came from and where they went: the old blind man who sat in the same seat each time, listening to the latest gossip. The scar-faced man who sat at the same table every night, talking to the same group of men. Jalida made sure they never had to ask for a refill. There was the pretty but overdressed woman who came in at mid-evening, ordered the same drink, and left never more than an hour later with a different man. They were the steadiest regulars.

Separation remained a thorny issue. He updated the power cells to his music player and bought new music chips - if she listened to that, she wouldn't worry about other noises. It worked for a night.

"What if there's a problem?" Sarah fretted. "What if someone's breaking in and I don't hear it? What if there's a fire and I don't hear the alarm?"

"What if I just lock you out and make you wait in the hall so you'll know?" he threatened in frustration.

"Here," he tried again, handing her a small box. "You function on a mathematical plane. Play accountant and keep track of my tips. When we get enough saved, we can move on. It's your pick next time, you know."

The idea of moving on roused her a little. "I can do that." Sarah kept perfect count of the money, reminding him daily of the amount he lost by keeping the cash in a box instead of an interest-bearing account.

Each effort brought a temporary lift to her dismal mood, but Dmitri knew he was losing the battle. Her silences weren't out of spite; this time, she had nothing to say.

"You've been on that same page for an hour," he realized one day. "Want me to read it for you?" He took the book and sat next to her. "Tristan viewt... vee-ut... How do you say that? V-e-u-t?"

Sarah closed the book. She put her head on the table and stared hauntedly at emptiness. Dmitri gave serious thought to refilling her prescriptions.

He didn't have long to think. Two days, and Dmitri awoke to find her staring out the window, weeping. A nod here, a shake of the head there, but he still didn't understand why. She hid something in her hand.

"You can have it back, I promise. I just want to see."

After a minute of push and pull, she released her hold. Sarah sank to her knees, engulfed.

"Aw, man!" It was a picture of Vlad. Today was Vlad's birthday at home. Sarah had been there for every one of his birthdays, from the very first. Except now.

He tried to get her to send Vlad a note, but the tears wouldn't stop. He wrote off the morning's card game. The next day, Sarah wouldn't get out of bed.

Getting her out and about had always helped before – a change of scenery, a preferred activity, a favorite restaurant – but nothing motivated her. She wouldn't eat, never seemed to sleep, wouldn't even sit up. It scared him to leave her alone, and he'd run back during his breaks. He took his knives to work and hid them behind the bar, just in case.

They hit bottom two weeks after Sarah stopped speaking. According to her records, she'd been this low in the hospital, but no one at home had ever seen it.

"Mope all you want," Dmitri told the motionless figure. "You're not lying in bed another day."

He dragged her up and sat her at the small table. Sarah didn't resist, but she didn't help, either, a 41-kilo ragdoll. Dmitri wedged her into the chair with a pillow to keep her from falling over. She'd stopped eating completely the week before. After two days of useless coaxing, he realized if he didn't feed her himself, she would starve. Dmitri consulted the manual the hospital had compiled. As far as he could see, he was doing the right things, but their success still hinged on drug therapy, the one thing he didn't have.

Dimi dribbled breakfast into her, her dead eyes never acknowledging him. He wiped her face with a sigh.

"I don't care how long you tantrum, you're changing clothes today," he pretended to argue. It would take her an hour, but she'd do it if he pestered hard enough. She'd been in the same pajamas for three days.

Dmitri left her at the table while he washed and dressed. He'd run down and grab them both some tea, then nag her into changing. After he finished the quick errand, he left fresh clothes for her in the bathroom, and went to poke her along.

"Come on." He tried to sound upbeat, but he knew he might as well be talking to the chair itself. "Go get changed. You smell." She did smell rancid. He tried to remember the last time she'd taken a bath.

"Let's go." Dmitri slapped her leg, then jerked his hand back. The knee of her pajamas was wet. *Soaking* wet. So was the chair. Vlad had felt like that hundreds of times, usually at night.

Dmitri shook his head. "Oh no, no, no! How can you sit there like that? I can't believe you! *Get up!* Get up and go clean yourself! Enough is enough! That's just plain disgusting!"

Sarah sat like wax.

"That is the end! I put my foot down! You can just clean that up yourself, because *I'm not doing it!*"

Sarah stared, unseeing, unhearing.

"I *won't!*" Dmitri yelled, jamming his thumb into his chest. "I'm sick of it! *You hear me?* I'm sick and tired of being the one who gets stuck cleaning up the piss in life! It's always *me*! D'Misha, your Father puked his guts up! Dimi! Vlad's wet, give him a bath! Here, Dim, be a helper, the baby smells. I've *HAD* it! *IT'S NOT MY JOB!*"

"Get up! Get *up!*" He shoved her. Sarah lost some of her balance and tipped sideways. Her face never changed.

"Damn it all, Sarah!" He knelt where the carpeting was dry. "I can't handle this. I'm not Viktor. I can't do it. I *can't!*"

He shook her shoulders. "*Snap out of it!* You think this is fun for me? Rooming with the living dead? Watching you stare all day, like

I'm not even here? You may hate having to be left alone when you should be asleep, but," Dmitri sighed in self-pity, "I hate you leaving *me* alone when you should be awake. At least I come back to you every day."

He sat on the floor, thoroughly depressed himself. He'd promised no more hospitals, but this was beyond reason. Sarah put so much damned faith in promises, but a hospital seemed like the only option. It would kill him to do it. It would kill her. He had failed in his first and most important promise.

"I'm sorry. I guess it's my fault, huh? Come on. We'll figure something out." He struggled to get her to her feet without contaminating himself.

He sat her in the bathroom, choking on embarrassment. Sarah wasn't two anymore, and he wasn't nine, about the last time he could remember having to bathe her. He didn't even have a tub to soak her in, just a claustrophobic shower. Katya once told him he could do it if he wrapped her in towels.

He took a deep breath, blew it out, and swallowed hard. Beet-red, he closed his eyes and began to peel the wet clothing from under the towel.

    Dear Vlad,

    Bet you never expected to hear from me. I guess you're doing pretty well, huh? I just want to tell you Sarah's really, really sorry she didn't get to tell you 'Happy Birthday' on your birthday. I guess I'm kind of a rat for not doing it on my own, huh? Sarah hasn't been herself the last couple of weeks. Please keep sending your notes, even though she can't bring herself to write back right now, okay? I've been reading them to her. They're the only things that will get her out of bed. Tell her anything – send her your homework, tell her how you tied your shoes, anything. She misses you real bad. Thanks Vlad. I owe you.

    Dmitri

    Dear Sarah,

    Vlad said you were feeling bad again, so I'm hoping my letter cheers you up. I have one more week of break before I go back north. I'm enjoying university tremendously, even though it's so cold up there! I never thought I could miss Navara's heat. I look like a mummy running between classes. I have to take all the boring requirements first. Philosophy is my worst subject. I absolutely hate it!

Can you keep a secret? Promise? I think – I hope! – I might be dating someone soon! But shhh! Nobody knows. He's a lot older than I am, so I don't know if it could ever work. He's not married – a real professional type – but we've become really good friends. He doesn't live here, so I'm afraid most of our association is over the commlink, but we talk almost every day. I don't know. Maybe it's all wishful thinking. But then again, maybe it's not! I wish I knew for sure so I can stop walking into walls and stuff. Am I crazy or what?! Dmitri understands, I'm sure, and some day I know you will, too. Love is so weird, except I don't know if it's really love since I'm not sure what he thinks. Can you keep any of that straight? I guess right now it's just obsession. *Sigh!*

If Dmitri would just TRUST ME with your "top secret" location, I would send you something I guarantee will brighten your day. I promise I won't tell anyone where you are.

Love to you both,

Katya

Dear Kat,

I'm trusting you with our address; please don't be a traitor. I'm at the end of my rope, Kat. She's really down flat. At least she's not chopping herself up. I almost wish she would – at least she'd be doing SOMETHING. Anything you think would help would be great. If you have any ideas on how to bring her around, I'm ready to listen.

I owe you a big one.

Dmitri

* * * 2 * * *

He hadn't been working that long, but Dmitri took a week off. He hoped staying with Sarah might boost her security, raise her interest in the world. He read to her from her books, even though she didn't respond. It seemed to help, just a little. She swallowed easier, she held herself up more, and with his vigilance, no more accidents. He retrieved a long letter from Vlad and Sergei. Sergei sent her a detailed list of writings she would want to read and why, and he sent her a story he had written about a murder in a penal colony that seemed eerily prophetic. Dmitri read it to her twice. He didn't read her the lines scribbled at the end of the letter by David – vicious, hurtful words written as if to her, but directed at him, threatening harm for putting Sarah through such a slump. She didn't need to hear that. Screw David, anyway. When did *he* ever take care of anyone? The words wouldn't leave his head, and it left him in a foul mood the rest of the day.

He had forced in the last of the mashed fruit, waited for the mouth to close and swallow, when a knock rattled their door. The noise jolted him; they'd never had a visitor here. A dark form filled the doorway.

"Toban! I – I – Won't you – come in?" Dmitri stuttered half-heartedly. He hated to have anyone see their dull little room, with the two beds perpetually unmade, clothes and fruit juice bottles everywhere, and Sarah uncombed in yesterday's pajamas and a blanket, staring into nothing with a vacuousness that rivaled space itself. The fear of authority had been emblazoned on Dmitri's psyche for too many years; how could he say 'no' to his boss?

"Dimtri!" Toban's deep voice boomed as he stepped into the room. Twelve weeks, and he still couldn't get the name right; Dimi'd given up. "How's your girl?"

"A little better." Dmitri glanced Sarah's way, but the blank face stared out the window.

"Good! I'm glad to hear. Dimtri, I know you've got ... *obligations*, and I know I told you to take the week, but I'm here to ask if you would consider coming in. People come to drink and be entertained. If they're not being entertained, they don't stay as long. Mr. Narr asked about you last night. He wants to see you back. Mr. Narr's a very... *loyal* customer, Dimtri," Toban emphasized, though Dimi wasn't sure of the insinuation. "I'd really hate to lose his business."

"Mr. Narr?"

"The fancy gentleman at table eight."

Ah! The man with the scarred face.

"I know you're worried about your girl, so I came to see if you'd would leave her in my office while you're working. You can check on her whenever you like. I'm afraid that's the best I can do. They'd pull my license if I let a kid like that out on the floor."

Dmitri frowned. If he'd been able to do that twelve weeks ago... It seemed ideal, but what would Sarah do, sitting alone in a strange office? On the other hand, it wasn't as if she wasn't familiar with the bar, and he would be right there.

"Yeah, I, uh, guess we could give it a try. I'll be in later, then."

Toban clapped him hard on the back. "Thanks, Dimtri!"

Dear Kat,

I owe you a big one, Kat. Thanks millions. It made a big difference. I hope it's all uphill from here. Thanks for the advice, too. I'm trying some of it, but I'm no good at that girl-stuff.

Give yourself a great big hug from me. I hope I can return the favor some day.

Dmitri

Good old Katya, saving his ass once again. It took a week for the little package to get to them, sent on a Davies-speed passenger ship, and he'd rushed it back to Sarah.

Hair ribbons.

Kat had sent *hair ribbons*. Childish, shiny metallic hair ribbons, wrapped around a note, wrapped around several dozen 3-D photos, captions imprinted. Katya must have spent her entire break taking them. Vlad at the computer, Vlad at dinner in an excessively fancy dining room, Vlad asleep, David posed smiling above the sleeping Vlad with a tipping glass of water, Katya's room at school. A picture of a huge building labeled *Grandmother's.* (*Yeah, right!* Dmitri snorted. *Who was Kat trying to kid?*) Pictures of Vlad's birthday. Sergei writing. The four boys sticking their tongues at the camera. A brawny-looking David posing shirtless, showing off the MVP swim ribbon around his neck. Several of Marina, who didn't look much like a baby anymore. An old woman who looked somewhat like Mother, and a smiling man with a laughing Nikky on his back labeled *Uncle Tomas.*

Dmitri forced her to look at the pictures, three times through, reading her the captions. Halfway through the second round, he saw it. The eyes were focused, not vacant. Not a hair had changed, but she had *focused* on the images. She was in there. Dmitri spread some of his favorites on the table before her and put the rest in her backpack with her other treasures. When he looked at her again, she was still focused on the pictures, but tears were forming. He'd never been so relieved to see her cry. Crying was a step up.

Being at the bar at night helped, too. Aware she was among strangers, Sarah pushed herself to be independent. Dmitri spent ten minutes with her every hour. After two days, she moved on her own, observing when she didn't think anyone was watching, shaking her head in response to questions. She couldn't concentrate to read, but she carried Vlad's last batch of notes wrapped around a few of Katya's pictures, gazing at them every so often.

Sarah was slowly functional when Dimi returned to the card game the next week, parking her in a chair next to him. Making her help play the hands kept her focused.

They were down five *otorr* when a loud rapping sounded on the glass door of the bar.

"We open at quarter-dark!" Toban called over his shoulder, but Pesha, the busman, rushed to open it. Mr. Narr entered, followed by one of his shadows.

Toban leaped up. "Mr. Narr! I didn't know it was you, sir! Come in! Come in! What can I do for you so early in the morning?" It was nearly High Sun.

"Just a quick stop." Mr. Narr slid into his regular seat by the wall. "I don't want to disturb your game. I just want a word with your music man there."

Dmitri lifted his head. What could the man possibly want with him?

Narr beckoned. Dimi folded his cards and stood. Sarah moved to follow.

"Just you," Narr called. Dmitri glanced at Sarah; anxiety filled her eyes. He pushed her down in his seat, put his cards in her hands.

"Play for me." He gave her shoulder a pat, ignoring the 'whatever-you-do-don't-leave-me' look of panic. He took a seat across from the enigmatic Mr. Narr.

"Dmitri, isn't it?" Narr shook his hand. Well dressed but not flashy, hair combed back from a Human face in a simple, neat style, his only distinguishing characteristic was the deep slashing scar that ran down the left side of his face, hairline to jawbone. "What do you drink?"

"Uh, iced mint is fine," Dmitri said, unsure if he was expected to order something stronger.

"A wise choice, so early in the day," Narr agreed, and Jalida scurried to bring two glasses. "I won't keep you from your game. I've been watching you. You're on your own? No family?"

Dmitri sipped at the glass Jalida brought. "Yes, sir. Just my sister and me."

"Toban tells me she's been ill. She's better now?"

"Somewhat. She's not up to speed just yet."

"But you take care of her, alone. That's nice. Not everybody would do that. It takes a special kind of man to do that."

Mr. Narr seemed friendly, but he had a piercing gaze, like an icicle skewering Dmitri's skull. As far as he could remember, it was the first time anyone had ever referred to him as a *man,* and meant it. For a few more weeks, no matter what his papers said, he *was* only seventeen.

Dimi shrugged. "I promised I'd take care of her. I'm just keeping my word."

Narr wagged a finger at him. "That's what I'm talking about. You keep promises. You're young, but you're trustworthy. I like people like that. I'd like to make you a business offer, Dmitri. I need people I can trust."

Dmitri hadn't expected that. Everyone in the bar fawned over Narr, though he'd never asked why. Now the question loomed large in his mind. Confidence and power oozed from Narr's pores. But...

"I really can't change jobs. I need to stay close because of my sister."

Narr finished his drink. "I understand that. I wouldn't want you to. I've heard you play. You're good at what you do. It makes people happy. I'm looking for a private courier, someone I can trust. Just an errand for me, now and then. I'll make it well worth your while. Take the girl with you, if you like."

Dmitri opened his mouth, but Narr cut him off with a raised hand. He leaned back like a cobra readying to strike.

"I know that look. You're thinking, 'Why doesn't he use a professional courier service?' Why should I? A company claims they screen their employees, but how do I know that? How do *I* know their employees are trustworthy? I'm supposed to pay for the privilege of trusting someone I know nothing about? I prefer to find people I can trust *first*, and then I hire them directly. I pay my couriers more than they'd make from a company, and it costs me less than a company would charge. I eliminate the overhead. Can I trust you to work for me, Dmitri?"

The man's words made sense in an odd, disquieting manner. The whole thing didn't *feel* right, but what could he say?

"I can still keep my regular job?"

Narr brushed the fears away as if clearing a pesky cobweb. "Of course. Just an occasional thing, that's all. On your own time."

"I guess I could." Dmitri tried to sound more positive than he felt. He didn't feel like *no* was a viable option. "A little extra money never hurt."

"Good! That's what I like to hear." Narr rose and shook his hand again. "You'll be notified when your services are needed. Toban! Thank you for the courtesy of opening your place for me. I will see you tonight."

"We'll be expecting you, sir." Toban let the men out and relocked the door, looking very relieved.

Dmitri rejoined the game to the inquisitive stares of the other players, but he had nothing he wanted to discuss, wasn't sure he was supposed to. His tongue tasted like rusty nails.

Sarah handed him the cards and slid back to her seat. Not only had she won back their five *otorr*, but doubled their starting money.

"You guys shouldn't let her win like that," Dmitri said. The last thing Sarah needed was pity.

"Let her, Hell!" Jalida exclaimed. "She wiped me out fair and square! What are you doing teaching a little girl to play cards like this, anyway, Dmitri? Deal, Pesha!"

For a week, Dmitri started at every noise he heard, expecting a knock on their door or a tap on his shoulder, but all that came of it was nagging indigestion that cut into his sleep. Somehow, Dmitri knew Mr. Narr wasn't the type of person to forget anything.

Sarah was speaking again. He'd said something flippant, and she'd replied, "Not really." *Not really.* Once he realized she had spoken, actually spoken for the first time in almost two months, he had to admit, he went a little crazy himself, grabbing her from the chair and shouting. A half-hour passed before he could coax another word from her, but she was *talking.*

They fought their way through another card game, the second that week and a losing one at that. Dmitri was preparing to leave when Jalida called him over.

"I have something for you, from Mr. Narr," Jalida hushed. He slid a thick envelope across the bar. "The address is on it. That's only four or five blocks from here. It shouldn't take long."

Dmitri stared at the envelope as if the yellow plastic would creep across the bar and climb into his hand of its own accord. Once he touched it, he couldn't go back.

"Thanks," he said, and put the envelope inside his jacket. A cold misty rain had fallen all morning. The envelope would stay dry and hidden in the inside pocket.

Dmitri took Sarah by the hand and stepped outside. Mr. Narr said he could take her with him, and having someone to walk with steadied his nerves. To her it was simply a favor for someone; he hoped that was all. The weather hadn't improved, chilly and damp, but waiting for public transport might take twice as long. He made sure Sarah had her jacket fastened, and set off.

Their destination lay on the thirty-ninth floor of a modern apartment complex, with bright, well-lit hallways and security cameras every so many meters. Dmitri pressed the door chime and waited, well aware someone, somewhere, was watching. He pulled Sarah behind him.

The door opened and a sharp-eyed man stared back expectantly.

"I – I have a delivery – from Mr. Narr," Dmitri stammered. The man motioned him in.

Dmitri pushed Sarah away. She resisted, until he gave her a light swat on the rump. A severe glance warned her not to argue. Dmitri entered, leaving her alone in the hall.

His eyes were taken in by the most perfectly decorated rooms he could ever remember seeing, sleek and ultramodern. Furniture flowed artfully in ergonomic freeform shapes, the lighting indirect and full-spectrum, easy on the eyes. Sweet, subliminal music drifted from somewhere, caressing the bed-sized paintings that gave life to the gallery-white walls. Dmitri forgot his purpose, lost in sight-seeing, until the man cleared his throat.

"You have a delivery?"

Dmitri withdrew the envelope. "Yes, sir. It's for a Mr. Talcot."

The man shoved a hand forward impatiently. "I'm Mr. Talcot."

Dmitri wavered. Narr was counting on him. What if he screwed up? What if this was the wrong man, a test to see if he could do the job? What if it were a trap?

Who did he fear more – this man, or Narr?

Narr won. "I don't mean any disrespect, sir, but, I've never met you before. Could – would you please show me some ID?" He took a step backward, hoping the door wasn't locked.

The man stared. Dmitri was working himself up to run when the man threw back his head and laughed.

"I don't believe this!" he roared. "Where the hell did Narr dig you up? Some schoolroom somewhere? Identification! Son of a bitch!" He shook his head, still chuckling, and reached into his pocket. He held out a computerized Alliance ID. "Good enough for you, kid?"

Dmitri grinned sheepishly. He handed him the envelope. "Thank you, sir. Just making sure."

"You got nerve, kid. You're okay. Here." Talcot pulled several large coins of local currency from a pocket. "Go ahead. Consider it a tip. I've never had anyone do that before. Identification! For Space's sakes."

Dmitri accepted the cash without looking at it. "Thank you, sir."

Sarah leapt at him as he reentered the hall. "What happened? Are you all right?" she asked, but he hooked her under the arm and hurried to the lift.

"I'm fine," he assured her, "but let's get the hell out of here." Outside, it began to pour.

Narr paid him the equivalent of twenty interstellar credits for the half-hour errand. Combined with the ten-credit-equivalent tip he'd received, it was a small fortune. Sarah gave back the ten for the next card game, and stuffed the twenty in the money box.

The 'errands' picked up in frequency – two, three times a week, once even twice in a day. Dmitri had serious regrets, though he couldn't complain about the income. On a busy week, he more than doubled his small salary. On short trips he left Sarah home, taking her with him on the more distant ones. She'd become more at ease with being alone; now it was Dmitri who didn't like the idea. Something – he couldn't say what, didn't know himself, had no proof *anything* was wrong – made him uneasy.

He couldn't fool her anymore, either. By the third trip, she demanded to know, and Dmitri told her. After that, they were partners. He taught her how to watch for trouble, and what to do if it should catch them. He taught her how to tell if someone followed them, what to do, how to memorize faces that passed them in hallways. He made it a game, a memory exercise, and Sarah accepted it blindly, delighting in playing spy with him.

His greatest difficulty proved to be Sarah's undying sense of curiosity, and dreadful boredom. There just weren't enough educational activities in this city to keep her busy. She knew the number of rivets in each of the beds (thirty-eight in hers, thirty-seven on his), the number of steps from the bar to the apartment (three hundred ninety three). She kept track of the angle of sunlight on the adjacent building, trying to calculate the changing tilt of the planet. Dmitri's heart skipped a beat when she informed him the carpet burned with black smoke, but the linens burned with gray, and her socks smoldered white.

"Are you trying to kill us or get us kicked out?" he raged. "Where the hell did you get a flame starter?"

"We don't have one," Sarah replied innocently. "My last science project in school dealt with solar radiation." She showed him the next morning. The bottoms of two of their wide drinking glasses, when put together, made a perfect magnifying lens. She'd used it to concentrate the sun's rays through their window and experiment.

Dmitri disposed of the glasses and bought safer ones.

One day he caught her picking open the corner of an envelope.

"Don't do that!" he shrieked, slamming his hand across the prying fingers. "Do you know how that was sealed? How do you know it's not sending out information it's being tampered with? Or that it's poisoned? Or had some other device in the seal? You'll get us in trouble – bigger than you can imagine!"

Sarah pouted, rubbing her mashed fingers. "Don't you want to know what's in there? Even a *little* bit? *I* think it's money. A big stack of it. I measured it. A stack that big holds around a hundred bills or so, and I'd doubt they'd bother hiring a courier for small amounts, so you know how much you could be carrying?"

He snatched the envelope from the table. "You have no idea what's in there! It could be receipts, pay stubs, tax forms – anything!"

"Or cash."

Dmitri stuck a finger in her face. "Listen good! *Don't touch the envelopes!* Don't look at them, don't feel them, don't measure them, don't think about them, don't talk about them! I don't want to know what's in them. The less we know about them the better. I don't even want to *do* this anymore."

All the envelopes *weren't* the same, that much he knew. Some of them did feel like currency, but some were heavy, some were squishy, some smelled exotic, occasionally some held small containers. Sometimes there were packages. Dmitri had ideas, but he wasn't paid to ask.

Seventeen

Earthdate: August, 2265

*D*ear Sarah,
I know, I've gotten bad about writing lately. It's been a busy summer. Sergei went away to a summer writer's camp. He wasn't technically old enough, since he didn't turn 14 until the week after it ended, but he had enough recommendations that they let him in. Uncle Tomas has David working for him for the summer break. He's spent a lot of time in New York and Moscow, and a couple of off-world trips, too. He's part of Uncle Tomas's research team, learning all about how business is run. He gets paid, too!

I'm finally off the school hook. Grandmother wanted me to go to Northern this fall, but Galina talked with Uncle Tomas. He agreed that since I'm doing so well that it might be best to leave me where I am. I was glad! I have friends here. I've spent a lot of time with them this summer, since David and Serg haven't been around. I'm not used to being lonely! Even Kat hasn't been around. She's left twice this summer for a week at a time to visit her boyfriend. I'm not supposed to talk about him. Val's not happy. She likes him enough, but thinks 12½ years is too big a gap, and that Kat's seeing him for the wrong reasons. Kat's happy, though. I mean, like really *happy.*

Hope you're half as happy as Katya,
Vlad

David tried to stay awake on the two-and-a-half hour transoceanic shuttle flight. This was his last flight back; he'd finish the summer at home. Three weeks, and he'd be heading back to school.

Tomas saw him yawn, stretch, and settle deeper into the First-Class seat. He shook his nephew's knee. "Wake up! Unless you want to be wide awake all night."

"I don't know how you do this all the time," David mumbled, and pushed himself up straighter.

"Years of practice. Your birthday's coming up, David. Sixteen's one of those important years. Would you rather have a big party, or do something else? We could take everyone somewhere for a weekend, maybe a seal watch off the Aleutians. Or do you have other plans?"

David thought for a minute. Nothing burned in his mind. If he was going to party, it wasn't going to be at home.

Or was there? David woke up just thinking about it.

"You know what I'd like? On the other side of the city, over on South Forest street, they have a big bike track – grounders and low anti-grav's. I'd like to rent some bikes. I've always wanted to do that. Sergei and Vlad could come too, but the minimum age is twelve, and Vlad has enough trouble passing for eleven, let alone twelve."

"You're still stuck on those? I thought you'd be over that by now."

David grinned. "No, sir! That's one dream that will not die."

"You're not too tall for those things?" David had shattered the one-point-eight meter mark this year, and he hadn't stopped yet.

"Not at all! You just need a machine with a bigger engine. You ever see the holos on the Aries Elektra 624's? They've got *two* simultaneous cogenerators that can put out a maximum sustained speed of more than 240 kilometers per hour *with* a 204 k-g payload. And *corner*? You can pull more than three G's! The Ganymede 450 IEX is only legal in Siberia – it's got a freakin' *rocket* engine!"

Tomas sounded disappointed. "No, I, uh, hadn't seen that. Okay. Let's plan on that then. I'm sure we can figure out a way to include Vladimir."

Valeria tracked him down that night, long after he'd gotten home. She slipped into his room with the briefest of knocks. "David? Would you mind…?"

David was in the middle of a yawn, or he would have cut her off sooner. "Already did. I knew you'd be hunting me."

"I wasn't – ." Valeria caught his sardonic look. "I just – worry. You know."

"No change since last time," David told her. "Computer, Banktrack program, DMK1, display status." Dmitri's bank account appeared on the screen.

"What about… ."

"Gimme a second, will ya? I know your next question. You never change them."

"I'm sorry. I know, I'm being a pest."

"Computer, split screen, display also Banktrack program SIK1." The two shortcut programs appeared side by side.

Valeria slumped. "Nothing. How could a bank account have no activity for six months? Something's *got* to be wrong…"

"Or something's very right," David said. "Maybe they like where they are. Maybe there's enough cash flow they haven't needed the account. Maybe they started a different account we don't know about. Vlad's still getting letters – dull and boring ones, but still letters. If something that bad happened, Sarah'd have mentioned it. Computer off."

David turned and put a hand on Valeria's arm. "Take my advice, Val. Finish school. Get a life. Do something so you stop worrying about her." He stood up and walked toward his bed. "Goodnight, Val."

Dear Sarah,

Man, I had one of the best days of my life yesterday! David had Uncle Tomas take us to a bike track for his birthday. I was too young to ride by myself, so I had to ride on the back of Uncle Tomas' machine. I don't think he liked it all that much, because he went way too slow, even for me. Sergei did okay, but he's not into it like David is. We were there for hours while David talked tech stuff to the mechanics, but he didn't want to quit yet, so he took me around for a while. What a difference! I was scared to death! David takes hills and corners like gravity doesn't exist. It was stellar! He maxed out one of the ground machines and switched to an anti-grav that went even faster. I backed off on that one. I'm not ready to die just yet. David was happy to get your note. I'm sure he'll write you soon. Uncle Tomas promised him if he graduates with honors, he'll buy David a bike like that of his own. Can you imagine? I bet he'll do it, too, just to get the bike. Won't Val be ticked!

Write me soon,
Vlad

Eighteen

Earthdate: April, 2266

It was supposed to be *her* trip. Sarah sat at the snack bar in the chalet, too warm in her insulated shirt, drinking a lemon-lime bubblewater and filling herself to the point of sickness on a huge dish of chocolate toffee ice cream with cherry-butterscotch sauce, extra marshmallow, and shimmery stars. She stared sullenly at Dmitri's back, two seats away. Two days, and he'd already found a girl to listen to his drivel, picking her literally out of a snowbank. Dmitri hadn't been on skis in years and he'd never been great at it, but he skied better than his present victim and that was all that mattered. He leaned himself against the girl, showed her how to shift her weight, guiding the tips of her skis, helping her stop, impressing her with swooshy turns that had taken him all the day before to remember. Forget that Sarah still couldn't stop very well and almost hit a rock because *she* couldn't turn on purpose, either. No, *that* didn't matter. All *she* got was, "Keep your feet straight!" "Bend your knees more!" "Lean!" "That's just my sister" meant, "Get lost, kid, or else." The tall brunette with the horsey face gave a hee-haw at something he said. Sarah stabbed the scoops of ice cream with a vengeance, stuffed the spoonful in her mouth, and forced it down. This one wasn't even *pretty!* The lump of ice cream was too big, too cold, and it burned painfully all the way down.

Dmitri hadn't wanted to leave their little life at the bar. He'd been happy over the past year. He liked his job. Their dismal little room didn't bother him. His on-again, off-again tryst with one of Toban's waitresses in the storage room of the bar, out of Sarah's sight, kept him satisfied. Both knew it wasn't a commitment of heart, but a convenience of lonely need, and they could live with that.

What bothered Dmitri was Narr's ever-tightening grip. Dimi took people at face value; motives never entered his head. The shame of dishonesty had been planted firmly on the seat of his pants at a young age, and therefore he never suspected it in anyone else. 'Errands' became more involved. They didn't include just deliveries and pick-ups, but the relaying of verbal messages, most of them threatening, and the leaving of packages in odd places. Dmitri couldn't prove his participation, but several hours after he'd been to one delivery, the building exploded.

He joked about retiring at one of the cardgames.

Jalida laughed. "Hah! That'll be the day! You're stuck for life, Dimi my boy! Just like the rest of us. Retirement is not an option."

Dmitri waited. He planned carefully. He lay awake mornings, wondering if he was being watched, or followed, or bugged. They'd saved nearly seven thousand credits – meager poker earnings, tips from the bar, all the payments from Narr. Even hidden inside the casing of Sarah's homework pad, that much cash wasn't safe, but he wouldn't put it in his account, didn't know if the man could trace it. His fear of Narr became paranoia.

He picked his date: the second anniversary of their independence. The date would be a depressing one for Sarah, the second anniversary of being wrenched from Vlad. Dmitri wanted to distract her, keep her from crumbling. He tracked down places and schedules and prices at a public information booth. It would have to coincide with his day off, giving them an extra day before their absence would be noticed.

The night before, Dmitri surprised her with what she'd waited so long to hear: "How'd you like to go skiing?"

"For *real*?" Sarah squealed. "Can we *finally* see snow?"

He smiled at her innocent acceptance, feeling more like her hero than the coward he was. "That all depends. Can you have everything packed by the time I finish work? We'll leave as soon as I get back."

"I can do that! We can really leave? You're not joking? Oh, Dimi! *Finally*!" Sarah gave him a rib-cracking hug. She was growing fast, just seven centimeters shorter than himself.

"Try and squish it all into two cases each, if you can. Nothing we can't carry easy." He wanted to be able to run if necessary.

Dmitri played his best that night, skipping the drinks Jalida usually brought him. His heart pumped adrenaline, trying to ignore Narr at his table. It hurt to ditch his friends without so much as goodbye, but he didn't trust anybody.

Good as her word, Sarah waited eagerly, two cases each packed and ready to go, her tan bag bulging with her collection of textbooks and the overflow from the flightcases. She didn't question the hour of departure, didn't question the short notice, never asked why. They slipped away two hours before sunrise. No one was going to own Dmitri Kirushenko.

Money deposited safely in his account, they traveled again. The week in the snow-bound mountains of Cetus IV. A full week to get to Aldebaran III. Three days at Starbase 34. They backtracked, on Sarah's suggestion, to Gamma Europa IV, the place of Father's great archaeological triumph.

"It's not home," Sarah tried to explain, "but it was home once, even if only for a year. That's *kind* of like going home, isn't it?"

Dmitri couldn't argue that one.

Eight days into the journey to an Aquilan seaport, Dmitri saw the ad on the daily headlines on the ship's hyperspace channel.

Feeling Lucky?
Do you play to win?

Dimi didn't consider himself a bad card player, not in the least. A luxury hotel sure would be nice, after the economy rooms and fourth-class cruiser cabins they'd been living in for the past two years. If only for a day or two, they could watch the experts, maybe catch a theater show. Sarah would like that part.

He sucked his lip, tempted.

He called up the full ad, a slick six-minute presentation. The hotel overflowed with amenities: a swimming pool with a three-story waterfall, exercise rooms filled with the latest ergonomic equipment, massage rooms with attractive uniformed staff, grand cuisine from around the galaxy. The various species of patrons in the ad were physically perfect, richly attired, and of course they were all ecstatic, raking in armloads of winnings in every scene. Dmitri wasn't so stupid as to fall for that, but… He *did* have quite the bankroll at the moment. If he doubled it… Or maybe even tripled it…

He restarted the ad. "Hey, Sar? Take a look at this. What do you think?"

Sarah watched with mild interest. "It's beautiful. It's also expensive. One night is as much as two months in our last place."

He sighed, watching the demo. "Wouldn't it be fun, though? Wouldn't you love to be all dressed up and walk around pretending to be wealthy? Watching people throw away a fortune on a roll of the dice? Can you imagine losing ten, maybe even twenty thousand credits on a single bet? *Man!* Can you imagine *winning* that much?"

"No. It's just the ad trying to lure you in. Probability is stacked against it. Fifty thousand is more than Father made in a whole year. Who could stand to lose that kind of money?"

Dmitri snorted. "People who would live in that picture Katya sent of that alleged house in Minsk. It's just a fancy apartment building."

Sarah shrugged. She hadn't looked at the picture in a while. "You're going to go to that hotel, aren't you? You're going to spend all that money in one place, after it took us so long to get it."

Dmitri wavered. He really wanted to, but she was right. It had taken a year and a half, two jobs, cheap living, and a lot of fighting, pain, and heartache to build their reserves up. If they were careful, they were set for many months to come. On the other hand, if he could win a big hand, they'd be set for a lot longer.

"Let's do it," he decided. "We'll only touch three thousand, that way there'll be plenty to fall back on. Just a day or two," he repeated. "But we're going to do this right, all the way. New clothes, fancy meals, the works! We're going to do it all. This will be a trip of a lifetime."

Nineteen

They arrived at the hotel by public taxi. Jiá Taf, the capital of the United Aquilan Federation, advertised itself as a modern Class-1 metropolis of twenty million people. The Mirabella, no surprise to Sarah, sat nowhere near the park-like center of the planned city. Their hotel stood on the fourth concentric street from the center; close enough to glimpse everything from the upper floors, but a long walk away.

Sarah had watched the ad four times, but it still didn't prepare her for the real thing. She clutched the straps of her backpack as she craned her neck to take in the grandeur. Everything *sparkled,* like a New Year's party. The massive lobby soared twelve stories high, with seven pairs of crystal light columns running down the middle like shimmering icicles and stalagmites, four stories each. A promenade circled the third through eleventh floors, lined with a limitless array of specialty shoppes – a small city by itself. Arching glass skybridges crossed the ether-lobby at the third, fifth, seventh, and tenth levels. Walls and hotel desks gleamed white with narrow strips of mirrored trim, the furniture and accents crystal-clear plastic, and the bright starkness muted by a variety of streaky grays, blues, and purples in the walls, carpets, and upholstery. It gave the effect of being inside an immense ice palace.

Sarah had to give Dmitri credit. Nothing, *nothing* could top this! *Wait til she wrote Vlad!* She hugged her precious backpack in anticipation, unsure she could behave remotely well enough for such a place.

Their room was just as spectacular, but in shades of muted mauves and pinks. The two beds were ridiculous in size, their linens as large as a weather canopy. Sarah chewed hard at a fingernail and tried to control her urge, but the attraction was just too strong. Dmitri emerged from the bathroom to find her jumping on a bed.

He threw her a stern but harmless look. "Aren't you a little big for that?"

"Come on, Dim! Look at this! It's big enough to land a shuttle on!" Sarah begged, bouncing. "Don't tell me you've forgotten how to have fun?" She held a hand out.

Dmitri glanced slyly side to side, then accepted the invitation with a grin. "Wrestling ring!" he declared, taking a corner of the oversized bed. "Last one on the bed's the winner."

Sarah soaked in the monumental whirlpool tub in their bathroom. The tub held four average humanoids; alone, she had almost enough room to float. Dmitri had been the final champion of their wrestling match, three out of five falls, once because she'd overstepped the 'ring' and fallen, laughing, to the floor. They were still a fairly even match, but Sarah knew that, given the need, Dimi was still seven centimeters taller, perhaps five kilos heavier, and in sheer brute strength, he probably had her beat. If she'd been home, those extras would have been an open challenge to better herself; here, she found the facts strangely comforting.

She dried off and began to dress. Dimi had bought her three new outfits at a boutique in the city, the most extravagant things she'd ever owned. Dresses rarely interested her. You couldn't climb or wrestle in a dress, and when your brothers *really* wanted to get you mad, they could gang up and pull your skirt over your head, leaving you helpless against tickling or ink-pen tattoos. Once upon a dress-up time, it had taken her two weeks to get the word *BRAINIAC* off her backside. David hadn't even spelled it right.

This dress, however, made her want to shed some of her tomboy ways – for a few hours, anyway. Hanging against the wall, the long dress with its short, matching jacket looked a dull, boring black. As Sarah moved it reverently from its holder, the somber fabric awoke to a deep velvety blue, and thousands upon thousands of pinpoint sparkles appeared, glittering faintly like stars. Motionless, black. Movement, shimmering electric blue. It was magical.

She emerged in the dress, feeling it slip and slide silky against her legs as she walked, the dark color and tiny jacket hiding any disgusting evidence of a beginning bosom. Dmitri stood up, already dressed.

Sarah stopped. "Nova!" she breathed. "You look grown up." Dmitri suffered enough vanity without being told by *her* he looked handsome in his new clothes, but he truly was. The buttonless black jacket didn't quite reach his waist in front, but the back cut gracefully down to a tailored curve in the exact middle of his backside. He had chosen an intensely blue pleated shirt so incredibly fine and soft it felt more like a breath of air than substance. His hair had been trimmed that morning, and the locks that gave him trouble had been drowned into humble submission with lacquer. A new, expensive cologne made him smell every bit as good as he looked.

Dmitri smoothed his pants. "You really think so?"

"There won't be a girl in the room who won't want to come up and talk to you." Sarah could see it already, Dimi in the middle of a crowd of young girls all giggling and whispering and wanting to touch his hair. He'd wave his money around and pretend to be some bigshot, and she'd be sitting off by herself in the beautiful sparkly dress, waiting for Dimi to tire, which he never would, of course.

Dmitri gave her an encouraging smile, tilting her head with a finger to make sure she saw it. "Not after they see who I'm with. Tonight, *you* are my one and only date; I promise. It's our night for fun, just you and me. Where's that bag?"

Sarah retrieved the cosmetics case that Katya gave her so long ago. She grimaced patiently while he pulled and tugged at her hair, brushing it, pinning it, cursing, then starting all over.

"There!" he said, excited by his handiwork. "Close your eyes!" Sarah sighed with annoyance, but allowed him to lead her to the mirror. "Okay. What do you think?"

Sarah didn't know what to say. She knew it was a mirror, but didn't recognize the person in it. The dark, sparkling dress was like nothing she'd ever owned before; it made her look taller and less boxy in the figure. Dimi had swept her hair to the top of her head and pinned it loosely, holding one side back with the peacock-blue feather clasp they'd bought to go with the dress. On sweaty Navara she'd worn her hair in braids, but never up like this. He'd pinked her pale cheeks with cosmetics – a stranger might not know it, but Sarah did – and brushed her violet-blue eyes with the faintest trace of liner, making them seem a darker purple. Low-heeled sandals of liquid silver wrapped her feet, her toenails flaming with Iridescent Opal nail polish. Sarah stared at the stranger, a girl who looked old enough to be going out with Dimi.

The strange girl stared back at Sarah, terrified.

Dmitri spoke to the stranger. "Like it or not, Sar, you *are* beautiful, and I will be *proud* to be seen with you tonight."

Sarah shook her head, spurring the dress into a million pinpricks of light. "It's not me. I don't look like this. I don't like it." She grabbed for the pins holding her hair.

"No!" Dmitri pushed the hand down. "You can live with it for a few hours. Tonight, you are my date, and you and me are going to *shine*!"

Sarah thought over his words. "If you think you're going to kiss me, I'll deck you right there in front of everybody."

Dmitri glared back. "It's only a little flattery! You're my sister, and, given a choice, I'd rather kiss a goat!"

Their dinner reservations were at a restaurant named *The Golden Egg,* on the ninth floor promenade. Sarah clung tightly to Dmitri's arm as they were shown to their table, trying not to stare at the opulent surroundings and equally lavish patrons. The holographic menu soon took her mind off the room. It was printed in five common Alliance languages, including Standard and Aquilan. Sarah forgot about eating in favor of comparing the two.

She sounded out some of the words. "I wish I'd had more time to study Aquilan."

"You can read Aquilan?!"

"Not really. I understand the phoneme patterns and the morphology, and I know the first fifty symbols, but I have virtually no vocabulary, and even less concept of their grammar. I hope to learn a little of it while we're here. The rhythm and accent, at least."

Their waitress appeared, and Dmitri snatched the menu before Sarah realized she hadn't looked at the selections. "Trust me," he winked.

Nothing made her more nervous than when Dmitri thought she should trust him, but Sarah held her tongue. It was his money.

"What label Porriman brandy do you have?" he inquired, as if he knew something about the subject. He chose the easier to pronounce of the two the waitress named. "And the lady will have an Adorra Nectar, hold the alcohol."

Sarah rolled her eyes.

Dmitri waggled his eyebrows at her, enjoying the game.

"She'll have the Altairan sausage wrapped in pastry, with mushroom sauce and a green salad," he continued, remembering Sarah wouldn't eat any form of meat she could still identify muscle groups in. "And I'll have the Inusian duck with fruit stuffing and the grilled vegetables. Do you have Terran Caviar?"

The waitress thought a moment. "We have something similar, but I don't think it's Terran. It may be Aldebaran."

"We'd like that while we wait."

The waitress returned with their drinks, placing a tall glass of slushy rose-pink liquid before Sarah, its squiggle of topping covered in fine chocolate shavings. To her relief, Dmitri's brandy glass was much smaller.

"I wish you wouldn't drink that," she grumbled when the waitress left. She poked her drink with a spoon and sniffed it.

Dmitri crossed his eyes and coughed. Porriman brandy bit back fiery and strong, just like its makers. "We've been over this. One drink will not kill either of us, so let's not mention it again, shall we? Did you try yours? What do you think?"

Sarah licked the topping off her spoon with the tip of her tongue; it was pleasantly sweet, with an almond-like flavor that mixed well with the chocolate scrapings. Her eyes went wide with delight as she dug in and took a small sip.

"It's good! It tastes like… " She let a larger swallow sit on her tongue while she thought. Something she hadn't had in so many years it more legend than memory.

"Watermelon!"

Dmitri raised his glass to her. "I told you to trust me."

They headed for the gaming rooms, only to be stopped at the sixth floor entry: registered humans under twenty were allowed in the gambling rooms, but could not place bets themselves.

"I'm *eleven*! I'm not a baby!" Sarah smoldered as striped security bands were locked around her wrists. Dmitri filled out identification for her.

She leaned over the edge of the service desk, the dress sparking in protest. "I didn't know humiliation was part of your 'unconditional service guarantee'."

"If you think it's so bad, imagine how it would feel at nineteen," Dmitri said as they left, ever-thankful for his adjusted ID.

Humanoids representing a good portion of the known galaxy filled the gaming rooms, not all of them members of the Alliance. Letts towered over them like small mountains, dainty Wind-sprites darted under foot, Chameloids flashed a rainbow of involuntary colors as their emotions fluctuated. Dmitri and Sarah wandered past dozens of tables, watching, learning. Some games they knew, like Double Draw, Split Shot, and Betelgeuse Fling; others they'd never heard of. Signs flashed in a variety of languages every fifteen meters or so, all saying the same thing: "*Telepaths/Empaths take note: this room is psionically blocked. If this creates difficulty with communications, please see the management.*"

Dmitri stopped at an empty table, a random chance of guessing a number on a spun wheel. "Shall we try a little luck of our own?"

He took his player's card from his jacket. Public law allowed no loose currency in the gaming rooms, all wins and losses were credited through the card. "Pick a number," he said, putting the card in one of twelve play slots.

"Thirteen and twenty-three," Sarah replied without hesitation. She reached out to enter the numbers on the game pad, but an angry buzz from the hateful bracelet made her jerk her hand back with alarm.

"I'm sorry, sir," said the alien woman staffing the table. "Children can't touch the betting pads. She isn't allowed beyond the blue line." The woman pointed to a glowing blue streak around the edge of the table.

"I'm sorry, we didn't know that." Dmitri logged the numbers in, then realized what they were: Sarah's birthday and Vlad's. He shot her a harsh look.

Sarah shrugged in reply. *What else would she pick?*

The table operator waited for all bids to be entered, then spun the numbered wheel. It clicked around until it stopped on one number. "Twenty-three," the operator declared as a hologram of the number lit up over the table.

Dmitri clapped her on the back. "You won!"

Sarah smiled sweetly. "Of course. Vlad's birthday is always lucky."

Dmitri lost his smile. "Once was cute, now you're pushing it." He snatched the card from the slot.

Sarah hurried to catch his sleeve as he walked. "It's the truth!"

He took a seat at a crowded Baxter's Bind table and plugged his card in. He deducted three hundred credits, and received three hundred credits' worth of markers. Sarah stood behind him, watching. She'd never seen the game before. Dimi lost a couple of rounds, then won a big one.

"You won!" Sarah bounced on her toes in excitement. She reached out to rake in the stack of colored pieces before Dimi could grab her. The bracelet sounded again, and she wrenched her hand back, blushing miserably at the people staring at her.

"Sir, children are not allowed to touch the playing surfaces," the Aquilan staffing the table warned. "Please keep her behind the blue line."

"I'm sorry." Dmitri collected the pieces himself. Sarah writhed with embarrassment. He pulled her in front of him, wrapping his arms around her, a silent reminder. She understood, and leaned backwards into him with relief.

Long after midnight, Dimi escorted a sleepy Sarah back to the room. He pulled notes from his pocket totaling three hundred credits and handed them to her.

"Here," he said. "You keep it for now. Hide it in the box with whatever else is in there. If you want, keep half of it for yourself. You told me what to play half the time, anyway. Here, go ahead."

"Really? Nova!" Sarah looked at the cash in her hand. She'd

never had that much money to herself, ever, not even a tenth, and she didn't have a ghost of an idea what to do with it. She dug out the cash box and deposited the addition. Her next move was to peel off the silver sandals. Her toes wiggled freely as she yanked out her hair clips.

Dmitri slouched sideways in the huge armchair. If he sat up, they both could have fit in it. "You goin' to bed?"

"Yeah. Aren't you?"

"Not yet."

Sarah waited for his jacket to come off, but it didn't. She knew, she *knew* what words were going to come out of his mouth next, and she hated him for it ahead of time. The first night – right off the launch! Anticipation squeezed her chest like a tourniquet.

"Sar, if you're going to sleep, and I'm not tired, do you mind if I go downstairs again? Will you be okay? Sleep with the lights on if you want. I promise, no drinking and no girls." He held up a hand to swear by.

There. It was out. She could stop dreading it now. "I guess. Not too long though, please? You know I won't sleep without you here, and I'm really tired."

He kissed the top of her head. "Thanks, Kid." He glanced at the expensive new Cosmochron on his wrist. "I'll be back by 0500 at the latest. I'll stick to the rooms on the fourth floor, in case you have to find me, okay? Catch ya in a little bit." With a wink and a snap of his fingers, he went out the door.

Immediately, Sarah set the security lock. There was no point in going to bed now. She was too tired to study, too disappointed to do anything else. It had been so good to be out with Dimi's full attention, so much fun for a change, but like so many other excursions in so many other places, he'd served his time, cleared his conscience, felt himself free. Maybe she'd write Vlad and tell him about the night. Sarah flicked on the in-room commlink and called up their mailbox. Nothing for her, one message for Dimi. He didn't get mail very often; who would have written him? She changed the screen to compose the letter.

Commlink.

Comm–*link.*

Interstellar Hyperspace Communications Link.

Who was the one person who ever kept her from feeling entirely alone?

Sarah stared at the commlink. The commlink stared at Sarah.

I'm waaaiting, it teased.

Did she dare?

Dimi hadn't said she couldn't. They hadn't been near a commlink system in so long!

Sarah studied the screen as if it would tell her what to do. *Why not? Didn't Dimi just give her money to spend as she wanted?* She wanted nothing so badly as this...

"Outgoing message, hyperspace feed," she directed the flashing screen, reciting the complicated address from memory. It took a minute for the call to connect, dragging out her nerves. She hadn't even checked to see what time it was there. Val would have a fit if she woke them in the middle of the night.

connecting...

A man's face appeared on the screen, startling Sarah. She hadn't thought of someone else answering the call. The man looked like a cross between Dmitri and Viktor, only grown up. A chill shivered her spine.

"*Da, Tomas Ivanov,*" the man answered in Russian.

Tomas Ivanov! Vlad's legendary Uncle Tomas. "Um... uh... *Ya...*" she stuttered stupidly. "Um... *Tam Vladimir Kirushenko?*"

"*May I ask who's calling?*"

"Tell him, it's, uh, tell him it's, Sarah."

The man tipped his head with intense interest. "Not *the* Sarah? That mysterious elusive fragile wandering gypsy that everyone worries about? *That* Sarah?" He smiled warmly.

Sarah had no idea if he was joking or not. "No sir. Just his sister."

The man broke into light laughter. "So you're the missing sister Sarah. I wondered sometimes if you really existed. It's very nice to meet you, Sarah. I'm your Uncle Tomas, and anytime you get out this way, there are rooms here waiting for you and your brother. You're very welcome to stay, as long as you like."

The thought of home and family and staying put brought a strong, unexpected urge to cry, and Sarah fought hard to push it down. "I thank you, sir," she choked, "but I have no control over that aspect of my life. Please, sir, is ... Vlad there?"

Uncle Tomas smiled again, a sunshiny beam that for some reason made Sarah think of her mother. "Don't you go disappearing on him now, little ghost!" He turned and paged Vlad on an intercom.

"Call for you," Tomas motioned to the screen as Vlad appeared in the doorway to his office. He gave the boy his chair. "You can take it here, if you like."

"*SARAH!*" Vlad shrieked, seeing the screen. "See! See!" He grabbed the man's sleeve before he could leave. "I *told* you she's not imaginary!"

"We've met." The man patted the boy's shoulder. He moved to leave, but Vlad pulled him back.

"No! It's okay! Stay! Please!" Vlad didn't know which direction to turn first. Tomas leaned against the desk, at the edge of the videopickup, watching the exchange with fascination.

"Vlad!" Sarah squealed, pressing the fingertips of both hands against the bottom of the pickup. Her delight radiated clear across the parsecs. "You've *grown!*"

"Sarah!" Vlad breathed, touching his fingers against the image of hers. The live hyperspace feed from that distance had a three- second delay, which, after traveling both directions, gave a slight crackling pause before the next transmission. "You think so? David and Sergei have grown so much I'm shorter than ever next to them. I feel like I'm growing backwards."

"I know so! I can tell."

"Where are you? What time is it there?"

"About three in the morning," Sarah said eagerly. "I wasn't ready to sleep yet, and Dimi went out again, so I figured if I called you, I wouldn't be alone. What time is it back there?"

"A little after four in the afternoon," Vlad replied. "I just got in from school. I'm almost done with Sixth Form. Where are you?"

"Oh Vlad! We're at just about the fanciest hotel in the Alliance! It *has* to be! It's like a giant crystal palace at sunrise!" she said in a rush. "I can't tell you where it is, but it's called the Mirabella-Galaxy, and it's just incredible! You could sleep *four* in the beds and not be crowded!"

"Gosh! It must be, if you're dressed like that." Vlad stared, awestruck, watching her dress sparkle. Her hair hung down, but the top had yet to lie flat, making it seem purposely fluffed and styled that way.

Tomas frowned. "Mirabella? The Mirabella on Aquila II?"

Sarah's eyes narrowed suspiciously. "I never said that."

"I understand. Just be careful, that's all."

"Why? What's wrong? What's going to happen?" Sarah demanded. She could just imagine giant arthropods in the basement, feeding on the people who wandered there by accident, like in a horror kino Dimi'd once dragged her to see.

"Nothing, nothing at all," Uncle Tomas said. "I've been there, and it *is* a wonderful place. It's just, with so many people looking for a quick fortune, it becomes a magnet for less honest folk, and the unsuspecting can get shuttled around pretty quick. Just - be careful."

"I understand," Sarah replied gravely. *Just great! Predators lying in wait for the unsuspecting, and Dumb Dimi out there all alone. As long as he stayed out of the basement...*

"*I* haven't been there, tell *me* about it," Vlad begged, and they went on talking, oblivious to anything but each other, as if no time had passed at all.

"I better go," Sarah said at last. "I have no idea how much this is costing."

"Reverse it," Uncle Tomas instructed without hesitation.

"Anytime you want to talk to Vlad, bill it here. We want you to stay in touch, Sarah. You're very important to us."

Sarah shook her head, setting the dress to shimmering like a fireworks display. "I couldn't do that. That would be relying on someone else. Dimi has to do everything himself or he thinks Valeria will rub it in his face."

"She wouldn't do that, not anymore," Vlad said. "She's different now."

"Maybe, but you'll never convince him of that. And he calls *me* stubborn! I'll do my best to call again before we leave. Is this a good time?"

"Anytime! I miss you, Sar." Vlad looked intensely sad, but, thanks to David, he held his tears. "Make Dimi come home soon?"

"I miss you, too," Sarah replied, tears forming without the benefit of David's strict behavior code. Dmitri's rules of behavior amounted to not embarrassing him in front of girls, and not talking about forbidden subjects – like home. The rest was up to her. "Vlad?"

"Yeah?"

"I know I can't come visit you, but... You don't suppose ... maybe Galina'd ... let you come visit me? Even just a *little* while? I'm sure Dimi'd be okay with that. Earth is off limits, but, maybe we could meet you on the Moon ...." Loneliness hung next to her like a shadow.

"I can ask."

Sarah shrugged bravely, knowing the answer. "It's a thought. I'll try and call again. Bye, Vlad."

"Bye, Sarah," and the screen went blank.

Sarah lay in bed when Dmitri knocked at the door. She allowed the computer to release the security lock. Ending the call to Vlad hurt, but she hadn't let herself fall apart. The thought of calling him again the next night gave her something to look forward to, and the idea of not telling Dimi gave her a thrill she hadn't felt since her carefree days with the Fearsome Four.

Dmitri took off his jacket and shoes and undid the soft shirt. He reset the door. "Any problems?"

"No," Sarah replied honestly, allowing herself to relax. "No problems. Just tired."

"Well, I'm back, so go to sleep."

"Any more wins?"

"Yeah! Yeah, I just didn't cash out," he lied, tripping on one of his shoes. "Sleep! Talk to me later."

* * *

Dmitri awoke at lunchtime when Sarah threw her pillow at him. "Get up. I'm hungry."

He opened a single dark eye in the depths of his pillow, and mumbled something crude.

"Did you know you have mail?"

Dmitri sat up ugly. "Don't tell me you woke me up for that? You aren't even dressed yet."

"Only takes a minute." Sarah went to wash.

Dmitri sighed, stretched, scratched, and got up. He poked around the room, adjusted the climate controls, and activated the commlink. Who the hell wrote him? He called up his mail and told the computer to print it. He flopped in the cushioned chair with the paper.

> *Dear Dmitri,*
>
> *I'm writing to you instead, in case you feel the news would upset Sarah. I don't want to make things harder on you. It's good news, Dim. I'm engaged to be married, the week after graduation, next May. Actually, you met him several years ago; he still remembers you. I know Sarah would adore him; he's just her type. He's been so very good to me.*
>
> *Dimi, I want you and Sarah at my wedding, even if only for the ceremony. I PROMISE you, no one will stop you if you leave. I'm begging you, Dimi, PLEASE be there! I want Sarah to be my maid of honor, for reasons you'll see when you get here. I know the whole thing would make her so happy. Please, Dimi, don't break my heart.*
>
> *You both mean so much to me.*
>
> *Love,*
>
> *Katerina*

Dmitri let the letter fall into his lap. He owed Katya a lot of favors. Sure, he missed her, some days more than others. Katya had always been there, for him and with him. She was one of his closest friends in the known world, along with Viktor and David, and his friend John from school. But... to go back... He wouldn't be able to tell Sarah until right before they went – she'd drive him crazy having to wait that long, and how would he get her away again? It would take a lot of thought. He could hear Sarah splashing in the other room. The less she knew, the better.

He went to the commlink, folded the letter, and buried it under a stack of Sarah's textbooks on the desk. Better to tell Kat something now than forget about it and have her tell Sarah later.

Dear Kat,

Congratulations. Honestly, I'm very, very happy for you. You're a good person, Kat, and you certainly deserve every happiness to make up for all the things you've had to deal with. I'll think about what you said. I won't tell Sarah until I make up my mind. It's still way too early to get her worked up over something that big. Man, sometimes I really wish you were here to talk to her. Sometimes she really needs you.

I do miss you, Kat.

Dmitri

* * *

That evening they ate at a less-fancy restaurant, Sarah dressed in a dark pink pantsuit with a floral design on the pockets. She didn't like the color, cared less for the stupid flowers, but at least it wasn't a dress, and this time, Dmitri'd left her hair long, all pulled to the side.

After a theater show, they moved on to several game rooms on different floors, looking for the best chances, until Sarah convinced Dmitri to stick to what he knew best – poker – and they sat for several hours, staying more or less even.

Even though she knew the game, it took all of Sarah's concentration to act normal while time slowed to a creep. At 2:30 she called it quits, and made Dimi take her up. "I suppose you're going back out," she said with a calculated pout.

"If you don't mind. I'll be back same time, by five. Promise."

"How about 4:30?"

"I'll try, but definitely by five," Dmitri swore, tousling her hair. "Wish me luck."

The instant he left, Sarah locked the door and ran to the commlink. This time she knew what to expect.

"Good afternoon, Uncle Tomas," she was able to say when he answered. "May I speak with Vlad again, please?"

"Hello again, Little Ghost. Are things still well?"

"Yes, sir. Thank you, sir."

"Hold on, he's here." Uncle Tomas bid her farewell.

"This is too unreal! Two days in a row!" Vlad gushed. "I was hoping!"

"Isn't it!" Sarah grinned back. She crossed her arms on the desk and rested her chin on them. "Tell me everything you did today. Don't leave out a thing."

Sarah cut Vlad off after twenty minutes or so, though if it were up to her, she would have left the line open all night. Instead of making her sad, the call had been a release. All was still right in the world when Vlad was there, just like always, even if they couldn't touch. It was their little secret, just between them, even if Uncle Tomas knew about it, too. He did seem nice enough, for the few words they'd exchanged. He'd called her a little ghost again.

Ghost.

I guess that's what I am, Sarah thought. *Haunting Vlad's life, but never physically able to touch him.* The analogy fit. She liked it.

She was almost asleep when Dimi came back to the room at a quarter to five.

"Sar?" he asked from his bed.

"Mmm?"

"You like it here?"

"It's cleaner than the last two places. It smells better."

"Would you mind if we stayed another two days?"

"Is that a real question, or just rhetorical?"

"It's real. I'm having fun. If you were, too, we'd stay a little longer."

Sarah rolled over to look at him. The sky outside glowed with the coming dawn. "We have enough money left for that?"

"Well, yeah! Of course I do! I wouldn't suggest it if I didn't!" he said. "That's my worry, anyway, not yours. Go to sleep."

They awoke late as usual. Dmitri left to bring back the food that served as lunch as well as breakfast. Sarah had little to do but wait. There wouldn't be mail on the queue, since she spoke to Vlad just last night, and she wasn't ready to open a book yet. She flicked the commlink onto a music channel and watched the air-traffic out their twenty-seventh floor window.

Thinking of a photo in her bag, Sarah headed for the closet but caught her little toe on the leg of the desk chair as she passed. She stumbled and grabbed for the edge of the desk, knocking her current study books to the floor in the process. Dmitri out of hearing, she let herself say a string of swear words as she sat on the floor, massaging her foot. Convinced nothing broke, she picked up the books – *Principles of Genetics,* and *A Historical Overview of the United Planetary Alliance* – and put them back on the desk. A folded printout had fallen with them, landing open on the floor. The sight of her name caught her attention.

A letter to Dimi. Sarah knew not to read other people's mail, but the signature stood out. She recognized Katya's girlish writing, even without reading the name.

It has my name in it. Why?

Sarah peeked in the printout again, just to see her name, but the word *upset* came before *Sarah. What* was going to upset Sarah? *Who?*

137

Curiosity won out over propriety; her naughty eyes disobeyed and slid across the paper.

Sarah paled, staring at the paper as if it were to blame for her horrible breach of manners, as if the words would disappear like a dream and not be real at all. She folded it and stuffed it under the books, unsure what to do next. She went and sat at the top of her bed, far away from the troublesome secret news, her mind running at light speed.

Katya. Sweet Katya, still thinking of her. She was glad Kat had found happiness, but, that would mean Katya would be leaving home. When Sarah finally got back, Katya wouldn't be there to talk to, wouldn't be there in the dark of night, wouldn't be there to anything; she'd be gone. Katya would disappear on her, never to be the same.

A hole tore somewhere in Sarah's middle.

Two holes. Dimi tore the other one. When did he plan on telling her this? Didn't it matter to him that Katya was leaving for good? First Mother, then Alexei, then Viktor, then 'Byeta, then the two of them, now Kat? Didn't he *care* about Kat? And Sarah knew, knew in her heart, Dmitri would never take her back for the wedding. Not even for just the day. It didn't seem to be about punishing Valeria anymore; sometimes, more and more, it seemed to be about punishing *her*.

Maybe because he's stuck with me. Maybe he hates me because I get afraid sometimes. Maybe he hates me because I never sleep as late as he does. Maybe he resents the fact he has to spend his money on clothes and food for me, too. Maybe...

Sarah knew her thoughts were racing out of control. Her spine crawled with nerves, her heart crushed under *maybe*s, her breath sped up.

Stop! she ordered herself. *Just stop!*

She wasn't supposed to know about the letter. Katya was right to keep that news from her. But how could she forget something chewing on her soul? Sarah shrieked as the door slid open, catching her off guard.

Dmitri carried in their breakfast. "What's the matter? Bedbug bite you or something?"

"No! I was, uh – " She glanced at the books hiding the wretched paper. "I was concentrating on running a four-variable punnet square in my head and the door surprised me. I can't keep track of four variables in my head, anyway. I just can't do it. I can't."

"So stop thinking so hard. You'll make yourself sick." He handed her a cup labeled in Aquilan.

Sarah took the cup, recognizing one of the symbols as *hot*. She gave a wan little smile. "I'm sure you're right."

Sarah stood in front of Dmitri, his arms around her, holding the

138

cards before them. Despite all the traveling they'd done, all the places they'd been, their stays had been on modern Class-1 Alliance worlds, civilized places, more or less. Aquila, too, belonged to the Alliance, but the hotel and its business attracted a far greater range of people than just Alliance citizens. Anyone was welcome, save a handful of races - the Hamalins, the Burin-Jai, the Telwanids, and several other empires openly hostile to the Alliance, but the patrons were bound by Alliance laws no matter where they hailed from.

Dmitri never thought about what happened on such worlds, never really worried himself about the sometimes vastly different cultures. He should have known better, but as usual, he missed the cue, and he and Sarah laughed about it later.

They had been at the table for an hour, ten credits a hand, the wrinkly Pavonian next to them having been there at least half of that, smelling distinctly alien and drinking a strange concoction that assaulted the nose like charred skunk - smoking, not steaming. At a pause in the gaming, he turned to Dmitri and muttered in a thick accent, "You wife there, you sell?"

Dmitri spoke fluent Russian and English, and could sometimes get his point across in badly broken Navaran, but that was it. A translator cube would have helped. "What?"

The alien repeated the offer. "Buy I want, wife that." He pointed to Sarah. He waved a gloved hand toward his considerable stack of playing pieces. "You take money. I many wife have, keep good."

Sarah twisted to stare at Dimi, unsure if she heard right, every nerve poised to run, awaiting his instruction.

As if she didn't have enough on her mind!

Dmitri acted as if it happened to him every day. "This one? No. She is new. She cost me much. I will keep." He pulled her salaciously close.

Sarah didn't need a hint to put her arms around his neck. She wouldn't have let go for anything.

"Why no like you me, Earth boy?" the Pavonian argued, the short twisted antennae on his chin twitching. "Money mine good!"

Dmitri scowled into the dark green face. "Wife mine, no sale!"

The alien met Dmitri's harsh gaze for several seconds, then backed down. He growled in acknowledgment and left the table with his burning brew. When he disappeared into the crowd, Dmitri let go and slapped Sarah on the thigh.

"See!" he laughed in her ear. "You better behave. I could trade you for big cash."

Just great! Now not only could he hate her, but he could dispose of her easily as well! In her heart, Sarah knew it was only a joke, but the thought added more weight to the burden she dragged in circles around her brain.

"You couldn't anyway, *Earth Boy*," she snapped. "It's still illegal here."

"Only if you're caught."

They returned to their room at the usual time, Sarah quiet. She still fumed over the wife-trade remark, even angrier at the fact that Dimi'd ordered himself two drinks in the last hour, both after losing rounds. Added to the anxiety already choking her mind, she didn't know what to worry over first. Dmitri lay back, sprawled on his bed. She changed her clothes in the bathroom; when she returned, he hadn't moved.

"Aren't you wasting time? I thought you'd be gone by now."

"Why? Trying to get rid of me?" he teased. "I told you, you better behave or… "

Sarah's foot slammed the floor. "*Stop it!* I won't have you talk to me that way! Just stop!"

Dmitri sat up. "Don't get all flappy. You know I'm only fooling."

"I don't find you funny! Go play your game, or whatever you've been doing, so you can hurry up and get back. I… I have things to read, and I don't need your cruel jokes distracting me."

"Whatever. I may be back early, though. My luck's lousy today."

She waited ten minutes to make sure he didn't double back on her, then hit the controls for the commlink, cursing the time it took to link a call half a galaxy away.

Vlad answered this time. "I hoped you might call again!" His smile faded. "What's wrong?"

Sarah hadn't realized she didn't look happy. "Nothing!" she said brightly. "I think this is going to be my last call, though. We're moving on tomorrow. I wish I could call you all the time. Want to hear a funny story that just happened?"

Dmitri returned early, but Sarah, already in bed, wished he'd stayed away. He'd been drinking, and he wobbled when he walked.

"Don't start with me," he said, dropping his clothes at the foot of his bed. Sarah turned her back, too heartsick to argue about wearing pajamas as he crawled clumsily across the monstrous bed and collapsed on the giant pillows. Not until Dmitri had been snoring several hours, until the sun crossed the horizon, did Sarah relax enough to sleep.

Three hours had passed when the nightmare hit. She remembered walking somewhere, the scenery a dreamy illuminated black, and somehow, from somewhere, the word *wife* echoed through her head in a voice frighteningly familiar, first as an itch, growing into a whisper, echoing around her head until it sounded like the buzz of an insect she couldn't see to swat.

Sarah woke in an icy sweat of terror. "No!" she cried to the ceiling, straining to hear more.

Not this! On top of everything else, not this!

She'd been off medication for over a year, she hadn't heard voices in two and a half years, she'd been doing so freakin' well! Why *now? Why?*

She didn't wait to find out. Three heartbeats and one foot on the floor, and she crossed the space between the two beds. To Hell with rules! It didn't matter how much or how little clothing her brother wore. It didn't matter that pasty alcohol breath mixed with the fading scent of his wonderful cologne, or that some girl's lips left melted burgundy behind his ear. Sarah tackled him, rolled over him, pressing tight, shaking from head to toe.

Dmitri pushed at her. *"What the hell are you doing? Get off."*

Sarah clung like a leech. "No! They're back, Dimi! The voices! I heard them!"

Dmitri fell back on his pillow. "Whose voice? Where?"

"In my head!" She pulled his arms around her.

"Are they still talking?"

"I don't know. I'm afraid to listen," she whimpered. The voices scared her worse than Father. They spoke without warning, day and night, sometimes soft like an itch, sometimes so loud she swore she'd be deaf. She couldn't put her fingers in her ears to block them; they were already inside.

"Tell 'em to shut up, we're trying to sleep, come back later," Dimi mumbled, and drifted off again.

A wave of deep despair welled up inside Sarah, crashed over her, knocked her flat, slammed the tears from her eyes, left her gasping for air. She clamped her eyes shut, held her breath, fought the tears down unshed, but the fear stayed behind. She rolled over, back pressed against her snoring brother, listening with her entire body for the rest of the morning, awaiting another word.

Twenty

Dmitri dragged himself awake one hour before they had to vacate the room. Sarah had long been up, dressed and packed. She sat silently, curled in the cushioned chair, not doing anything and not seeming upset about it.

"Here," he said, tossing his bags on her bed. "Why don't you pack up for me, and I'll get everything squared."

141

Sarah slid from the chair while Dmitri called up the bill on the room's computer. He frowned.

"Itemize, please," he told the screen.

There was an error in the billing. They hadn't made any calls at all. "Computer, itemize hyperspace charge."

Aquila II Interstellar Communications Service to: Sol III Global Communications Network:

Call 1: 0248 to 0319 31 minutes 4.7 Credits/minute 145.70
Call 2: 0254 to 0318 24 minutes 4.7 Credits/minute 112.80
Call 3: 0300 to 0329 29 minutes 4.7 Credits/minute 136.30
Total 394.80

"Come here," he said, keeping his voice low and even.

Sarah had been trying very hard to master the talent of invisibility. Her nerves were so frayed through lack of sleep and the threat of her voices and the previous day's stresses that she didn't want to know anything else. She approached him slowly, just out of reach.

"Did you make hyperspace calls from this commlink?"

Sarah looked up at him through her bangs. "Me?"

"No! The twin standing next to you!"

"Maybe? You gave me that money. You said I could spend it on something I wanted, and I wanted to talk to Vlad. You didn't say I couldn't."

Dmitri lunged and caught her by the wrist, standing as he reeled her in. Sarah gave a squeal and pulled back. He stood behind her, holding her unwilling head, forcing her to look at the screen.

"I gave you 150 credits, Sar. What does it say under charges? Read it!"

Sarah glanced at the screen. "Uh oh."

"Read it!"

She broke away and whirled to the other side of the chair. "Four hundred." *Damn!* Had *she* underestimated!

He stabbed a finger at the computer. "*Four hundred!* Who the hell told you you could make those calls? It's five credits a *minute*! You spent all your money on the first call! And you had the nerve to make two more? God*damn*it!" He kicked the chair to the side. "That's more than the room costs a night!"

Sarah backed up to the window, then scurried up the alley between Dimi's bed and the wall. "I'm sorry! I didn't realize!" She scrambled up and over his bed with the agility of a deer, a leap over to her bed and across that, circling wide around him, back to the other wall. "The money will cover some of it."

"No it *won't*." He kicked the overturned chair again.

"It'll bring it down to two-forty-five."

"*I said it won't!*"

Sarah cringed against the wall, creeping sideways.

He forced himself calm. "I *wish* you had *told* me." He strained each word through clenched teeth, as Sarah continued her wall-creeping to the outer corner where the bed alcove and closet met. "I – I already spent that money."

"What do you mean? I saw the box in my bag this morning."

He picked her bag from the stack of luggage and handed it to her.

Sarah knelt, one eye on him, and dug until she found the money box. A single credit chip and a handful of coins from various worlds fell out. "That was my money. You gave it to me."

"Yeah, well, I needed it back."

"Then it's your fault," she reasoned, stuffing the box back in the bag. "You should have told me. You didn't call takebacks."

"*My* fault?" Dmitri strode toward her. Sarah dropped the bag and pressed herself to the wall. He stopped, centimeters from her face. "My fault that some sneaky, ungrateful brat ran up four hundred credits in hyperspace charges without asking permission? You touch a commlink again and I'll cancel our mailbox, and you'll never hear from that whining, snot-filled baby again!"

Not Fair! Sarah knocked him away with a double-handed shove to his chest and dashed the last three meters around the closet to the haven of the bathroom, jamming her hand on the doorlock.

She slumped on the floor of the shower stall, wrists pressed to her temples, hearing Dmitri curse and throw things. She allowed the tears five minutes to take the edge off her misery, then made herself stop. She was still okay if she could stop when she wanted. Her mind rumbled faintly, wordless but threatening. Covering her ears, Sarah closed her eyes and thought of Vlad, and home, and the pleasant-seeming Uncle Tomas, and how much she wished she was with them.

Only after the room silenced for an hour did Sarah dare peek out, armed with a hairbrush and a spraycan of hair lacquer. Dmitri lay belly-down on his bed, feet on his pillow.

"You might as well sit down. The room's ours for another night," he mumbled.

She approached timidly. "I'm sorry about the calls. I didn't realize how much it cost. Honest."

He sighed. "It doesn't matter. It's not your fault. It's mine. I had no right to yell at you. I'm sorry if I scared you. I didn't mean it about the mailbox, either. I wouldn't do that. It doesn't help I've got a rotten headache."

"That's no excuse."

"No. No, it's not. There's no excuse for the fact we're almost broke, either."

"*What?!*" Sarah couldn't handle any more surprises. Fear boiled up faster than an atomic holocaust, knifed her heart, weakened her knees, and she leaned on the wall. "We still have three thousand in our account, *da*?"

Dmitri sighed dismally again. "I had no right to yell at you, 'cause I'm really just mad at myself. Sit down. I promise, no more yelling."

Sarah perched on the side of her bed, and he sat up cross-legged in the middle of his.

Dmitri hung his head. "You can't be more mad than I am with myself. Out of the 3,000 we checked in with, 2700 will pay for the hotel – not counting meals for today and tomorrow, add in the 1200 for the clothes, and… the money I took from our bankcard to replace what I lost at the tables, and we have about 1300 left. Total. Everything. I'm sorry."

"Out of seven *thousand*?" *In less than three months?* Sarah ran a hand through her hair, then hugged herself, starting with the twists and twitches she got when upset. Thirteen hundred wouldn't get them more than an ore freighter to the next solar system. "What do we do?"

"I don't know, but I'll think of something."

Dmitri dumped Sarah's pack on his bed and dug through it, searching for anything remotely valuable, Sarah snatching almost everything back. He did the same to his bags, with Sarah rescuing things she knew he shouldn't part with. He would sell off their valuables in the trade shop on the second floor balconade, then turn the cash into a sizable profit in the gaming rooms, sticking to games of skill. With Sarah calculating odds and double guessing his every move, they'd have a real chance.

Sarah hated to lose her text reader, and she used the homework 'pad every day, working out the lessons from her texts, but she had little else that wasn't sentimental value only. "Isn't that how you lost all our money in the first place?"

"Not this time," Dmitri swore. "Not with you with me to make sure. No drinking, no distractions, no girls; we'll do it right this time. Come on, let go before you rip it." He put their fancy clothes on the pile.

Sarah clung to her black/blue dress with both hands, heels dug in so hard she almost sat on the ground. "*Please*, Dimi! Not this! I only got to wear it *once*! It's the nicest thing I've ever owned, and I love it! Even Vlad liked it!"

"Vlad's opinion doesn't count here! This cost as much as your comm charge. Let's hope we can get even a quarter of it back. Now, *let go!*" He smoothed the wrinkles where her fingers had crushed the delicate fabric.

Sarah slammed her hands against the sides of her head and threw herself between her bed and the wall, face to the floor, hands over her ears, hiding. Wretchedness overwhelmed her, and she was trying her damnedest not to cry about it. *To hell with doctors!* She wasn't going to cry anymore. She was sick of crying all the time.

Sarah's text reader. Her homework 'pad. Dmitri's beloved music player and his vast collection of music chips. His stack of palm-com holographic games, and the extravagant Cosmochron timepiece. All their expensive clothes. Two of the five small artifacts Father had collected from his many digs. Sarah watched them go with defeat. At least they didn't want her textbooks – outside of a university, they held no value. The numbness crept in, the dull, dreary feeling that nothing mattered and never would. She sensed the itch that threatened to grow into invisible voices. So far that's all they were – a subliminal itch – but her anxiety only fueled them.

Dmitri found a smaller gambling room on the ninth floor, settling in at a Nine-Square table. Seven hundred credits. Everything they'd had of value – mostly the clothes – amounted to seven hundred credits. Dmitri didn't make a move without asking Sarah first. Sarah knew odds; she couldn't count more than three decks at a time, but every effort helped. After a particularly good hand, Sarah made him leave the table, cash out their profit, and give it to her for safekeeping. They broke for a quick dinner, sharing one larger meal to save the expense of two smaller ones. After ten hours, Sarah held 2,250 credits profit. They'd done it.

"Give me a hundred," Dmitri asked, tapping his hair into precise place as Sarah lay on her bed just before dawn.

"Absolutely not," she replied wearily. "I'm supposed to keep it safe from you. Your own words."

"I'll trade you the bank card. I'm limited to what's in my hand, no risk. Come on, swap over."

Sarah didn't have the will to fight. She untied the sock that held the cash, knotted tightly to the strap of her undershirt. He wouldn't sneak money off her while she slept, that was sure.

Dmitri winked. "Back in three hours."

Without destitution hanging over them, Dmitri changed whims again, determined to regain their fortune. Instead of checking out the next morning, he paid in advance for two days and dragged Sarah back to the tables. After three hours – and a small profit – Sarah refused to play anymore, fretful from the noise and commotion and the sickening combined odors of so many non-humans in the gaming rooms. Her concentration had dwindled, and she wanted no part of anything. She let Dmitri have two hundred credits just to go away.

He appeared two hours later, and handed her five hundred in return. "Nap time," he ordered, kicking off his shoes and flopping on his bed. "I got us in on a private game tonight. It'll probably last most of the night, so we might as well get some sleep while we can. Room: dim window." The room darkened as the glass turned a deep shade of gray.

Sarah knew she'd never sleep. "Is that smart, Dimi? We've never played for big stakes. Even at Toban's, the biggest win ever was only twenty. How do you know they won't cheat you?"

"We'll do fine," he said, already half asleep.

Twenty-one

The card game started at midnight in a private room on the twelfth floor, and still ran strong at three. Dmitri had both won and lost fortunes; how much had passed between his fingers even Sarah hadn't been able to track. Now, not long before dawn, she was too tired to care. They should have left after his last big win, but somehow she didn't think this group would let Dimi leave while he was still able to play. The predetermined cutoff was five a.m..

Sarah's interest rallied as she caught sight of Dmitri's draw. The new cards filled impossible voids. It was the highest possible hand; he would win. Her eyes glanced at the money in the center of the table. The stack of chips stood several centimeters deep, and still the betting continued. Her heart sank as she saw Dimi's reserves; much more and he would be forced to drop the winning hand for lack of cash. That was his kind of luck.

Dmitri could be a cool card player, cagey and quick. They'd all had their moments, but when he put his mind to it, he could beat the pants off anyone he knew – even Father. But Dimi could also bet foolishly, and he had already lost some heavy bluffs.

Sarah didn't like the other five players, didn't trust any of them. The Zenobian with arms as thick as roof pillars seemed to play fairly, but continued to wear several empty weapon holsters. His choice of beverage made Sarah's skin crawl – a beaker of something pink, with a small creature swimming in it. She didn't want to be around to know what would happen to the sad little creature when the alien hit bottom. The hairless, purply Inusian next to them seemed the most trustworthy – which no doubt made him the most dangerous. Every now and then he inhaled an aromatic substance from a metal container; the fumes were strong enough to make Sarah wheeze. The Zenobian was loud and easy to antagonize, but you knew what he thought. The slow-moving Inusian whispered only when necessary, mysterious.

The hotel's arbitrator stayed enmeshed behind his security panels in the corner. He watched his screens and nothing else, making sure no cheating occurred.

The other three humanoids, however, Sarah didn't like in the least. From Carrera VI by admission, elsewhere by accent, they pulled a seemingly endless supply of currency from their embroidered pockets. They were excellent players, but Sarah couldn't get past the fact they just plain *stunk* – of foreign foods and alien breath, of unappealing perfumes, of festering wounds or rotting flesh or something just as bad. They mumbled between themselves in a rapid tongue full of clicks and burps. After a while, the burping made Sarah's stomach hurt in sympathy.

The one in the center seemed to be of higher rank. Older than the others, he wore a brightly colored headscarf in a pattern so intricate it made Sarah dizzy. And he wore eyeshades: a band of mirrored silver glass over his eyes. The Zenobian objected violently, claiming it to be a monitoring device, but they'd all been allowed to examine the shade, and at last he approved. To Sarah it screamed of dishonesty. He couldn't be blind, because he could see the cards, but how could he see with the shades? The lighting in the room was far from overpowering.

The first wealthy gentleman dealt six times around the table. The table bet, a seventh card was dealt, a bet, an eighth card, a third bet. Cards were kept, the rest thrown in, and the deal went out again. Two more bets. The pile of counting chips deepened. The Inusian folded early, then one of the rich gentlemen, then the Zenobian, with a loud wave of alien curses. Another Carreran folded.

Dmitri and Scarfhead remained. Never had Sarah seen so much money in her life, never imagined it.

Please, Dimi! Play smart! she wished hard, forbidden to speak. He would play this on his own. Zenobians didn't allow their females in public, and this one took strong offense to her presence. As it was, she wore a plain black flightsuit, as gender-neutral and unoffending as she could be.

Dmitri gazed calmly into the silvered shade. "I raise, eight hundred more." He pushed the last of his money to the center pile.

The scarfed man paused, but didn't pick up his cards. He leaned to the Carreran on his right and gurgled.

The second man cleared his throat and smiled, baring dirty yellow teeth. He spoke Standard with difficulty.

"Forgive, please. The Potentate wishes to know if your female is paired."

"Huh?" Dmitri frowned, caught off guard. The man repeated the question, enunciating more precisely.

Confusion clouded Dmitri's face. He stared impatiently at the fortune before him, the one with his name on it, dammit. "No, she's never been paired."

More rapid exchange, again the revolting yellow grin, a bilious serpent waiting for a clear strike. "The Potentate appreciates your offer," the translator said, waving a hand at Dmitri's now-empty counter tray. Decaying breath wafted across the table with each word. "The Potentate meets your eight hundred, and raises you five thousand, against one evening with your girl." Several stacks of counters slid forward.

Dmitri's pupils narrowed, but he didn't blink. He licked his lips and consulted his hand casually, as if thinking. The cards were still there, in the order he'd left them. A guaranteed winner. He glanced at Sarah, now hovering near his shoulder in eager anticipation.

Dmitri bit his lip and shook his head regretfully. *Very* regretfully. "Please tell the Potentate I am honored by his extremely generous offer, but I cannot accept. My sister is not mine to bargain with." He hesitated for a tiny second, holding for a last instant the best hand he'd ever had in his life. He dropped it closed on the table. "I fold."

Sarah couldn't help squealing. *"Dimi?!"*

Dmitri raised a finger over his shoulder to quiet her, overshooting and hitting her in the mouth. He rose and bowed to the Potentate, who bent his head in return, and then to the rest of the players.

"As I am out of the game, I bid you all goodnight." He held his hand out to Sarah.

She hounded him as soon as they hit the hallway. *"Dimi!* Why did you *do* that! We *needed* that money! That was everything we worked two days for! Now we have *nothing!* Slow down!"

"Walk, don't talk!" he snapped. They reached a lift in less than a minute. Dimi glanced about sharply as he waved an impatient hand at the call eye. A car arrived, cheerful and bright with its hundreds of decorative lights, and he hauled her in. Sarah's mouth opened again.

"Not now! I'm thinking." Dimi watched the numbers flick by as he tapped his fingers on the glass wall. Sarah crossed her arms with a huff, but she kept her mouth closed.

She wasn't just some dumb kid! She was eleven now! Eleven and *two thirds*! Dmitri dragged her to their room, setting every security lock.

"Okay, we're in the room," Sarah demanded. "Why did you throw all that money away? We needed every last credit of that! And I owe you one for hitting me. That hurt! What are you doing?"

Dmitri hauled his travel case from the closet. He held up several pieces of clothing, stuffing some back and throwing others on the bed. He took one of his knives from the bottom of the case, unsheathed it, ran a finger across the blade, replaced the cover, and threw it on the bed, too.

"What are you doing? Why didn't you take the money?"

"They couldn't be trusted," Dmitri said absently. "For all I know, they were cheating somehow." He searched through Sarah's clothes.

"They smelled real bad, but for that much money I would have dealt with it. What did they want with me? A wife, like that Pavonian? Or someone to entertain them? They don't know how bad I dance, and I don't sightread music that well."

"Take that off," Dmitri ordered, pointing to her flightsuit as he ransacked the room.

"What?"

"This! Take it off!" He jerked her around and pulled open the fasteners.

"I won't undress in front of you!"

"Like I care. I don't have time for bullshit." Dmitri wrenched the fabric down over her shoulders. He hesitated, then cupped a developing breast through the fabric. "Good. Not too big."

"DIMI!" Sarah shrieked. She jumped backwards, trying to protect herself with her arms tangled in the sleeves. "Stop this! You're scaring me, Dimi!"

"Put this on." He pulled one of his shirts over her head and waited for her to free her arms and put them in the shirt. "Come on! Come *on*!" He stuffed pants at her. "These, too!"

Dmitri acted so wild Sarah was afraid to disobey. At least the pants were her own. His shirt hung to her thighs.

"Here." He put a belt around her waist, pulling it so hard and fast it pinched her skin.

What on Earth – on Aquila – was he doing? "I don't like this, Dim. Explain this to me! Why am I in your clothes? This shirt's too big. I look stupid."

"In a minute." He unsheathed the knife once more. The razor-sharp blade gleamed twenty centimeters long and five and a half at its widest. As Sarah adjusted the belt and rolled the sleeves to her elbows, he seized a handful of her hair and cut it free with the knife.

Sarah screamed and tore away, a hand over the gap in her hair. She wasn't sure what was more horrifying – the strange look in her brother's eye, the deadly knife in his hand, or the fistful of hair in the other.

"Why are you doing this to me! *Please*, Dimi! Tell me why you are torturing me like this!" She would fight him if she had to, but not with that knife.

The terror on her face broke Dmitri's frenzy. He scratched at the shadow of beard on his chin with the back of the knife hand.

He took a deep breath. "I'm sorry. I guess I went a little nova,

149

huh? Sit down." He cleared a spot among the clothes on the bed. "Come here. It's okay. Really."

An uneasy minute passed before Sarah shuffled forward. "Give me the knife."

Dmitri handed it to her. Sarah slid onto the bed, cradling it.

"Here." He handed her the half-meter-long swatch of hair with embarrassment. "You better let me finish, or you'll look twice as bad. I won't hurt you, honest."

Dimi took the knife. Sarah opened her mouth, but he silenced her. "You wanted me to talk, let me talk." He retrieved a comb from the bathroom, sat behind her on the bed, and began to hack her hair with the knife.

"I'm sorry I panicked. I suddenly realized I've been neglecting something very important – your safety. I thought by keeping you with me all the time, I'd keep you out of trouble, and maybe I'd stay out of trouble as well. But I know I was very wrong."

Sarah winced as he pulled too tight. He handed her the long pieces; she smoothed them together in her lap. Shavings of hair fell about them, coating the knife blade.

"I should have realized it when that Pavonian wanted to buy you. I forget you're not just my sister, you're a *girl*," he confessed, combing the awful mess he'd made of her beautiful hair. He tried to even it, a little here, a little more there. It didn't help. He'd never cut hair before, and the knife was unwieldy. "You were always a part of Vlad and Serg and David and me, since you could walk. Just one of the guys. But you're really a girl, and you're not that little anymore. Despite what you want to believe, you're *not* the ugliest one on the planet. I've seen the heads turn when you're with me.

"There," he said, putting down the knife and comb. "It will have to do. From now on, you'll be my brother Semyon. At least while we're here."

Sarah looked in the mirror, and felt tears push. Her poor hair was shorter than Dimi's, ragged, uneven, and just plain awful. Tearing it out with her fingers would have been an improvement.

"My hair! It's *horrible,* Dimi! And I hate the name Simon! You could have at least asked me before destroying my hair!" She lay the shorn lengths sadly on the desk.

"Fine! Dress me like a boy if you want! But Dimi! All that *money!* Now what will we do? He added five *thousand* credits to that pile! You knew you were going to…"

"God*dammit*!" Dmitri seized her chin. Her head hit the wall with a thud, forcing her to look at him on tiptoe.

Sarah gripped his arm with both hands, but it didn't budge. From the corner of her eye she saw the knife on the bed, but he would reach it before she could.

"Wake up!" Dmitri raged through clenched teeth. "Stop being so naïve! That man wasn't looking for a dinner companion! That man wanted to *rape* you!" He banged her against the wall again. "Do you understand what that means? He didn't care if you were married! He was asking if you'd been with a man before so he could be your first one! And when he was done, his friends would have been next. *That's* what would have happened if I'd lost that hand! Is that what you had in mind? *Is it?*" He banged her head once more.

Sarah stopped struggling. The wild violet eyes searched him for some shred of black-hearted jest, some possible reason for such a terrible, twisted lie, and she shook violently when she found none.

"Shto?"

"He wanted to rape you," Dmitri repeated softer, slower. He eased his grip, letting her pull his arm down.

"Yes, there were more than *thirteen thousand* credits on that table. Yes, I *did* have the winning hand, and with a little more luck we could have walked out of there with an *incredible* fortune." He sighed, shaking his head sadly. "But what if he cheated? Do you think I would have walked out of there alive if I'd accused him of it? Were you willing to take that risk? Was it worth it to you? I just paid thirteen thousand credits for your safety, Sarah. Do you think I made a mistake?"

She hadn't acted wrong! She wasn't dressed up like a woman! How could the man presume...? Sarah's face contorted in horror as ideas began to connect, the gaps filling until whole images formed. Her eyes searched the floor, but found no refuge from her mind. Backed against the wall, she couldn't even run from it. Around her neck, Dimi's simple chain necklace felt like a noose, and she tugged it away.

"But... He was older than *Father!* I'm not even *twelve...* !"

"Exactly," Dmitri said gently. "Hence the high price he offered as a respect to me. If I had a credit left to bet, I'd say they were slave traders. Who the hell else has that kind of money to throw around?"

Sarah gave another hard shiver. *Too much at once!* That's why Dimi wanted her to look like a boy. *Thirteen thousand credits.* She would have sold herself into a nightmare for thirteen thousand credits. Five minutes ago it seemed the fortune of a lifetime. Now a million times that wouldn't have been enough to make the risk worthwhile. She *was* dangerously naïve!

Her mind spiraled, stirring up forgotten bad memories, thought after thought after thought carrying her downward like falling dominoes. Her hands brushed her body as if wiping off his words. The room faded as her peripheral vision grayed and shrank, as the sound of Dmitri's nervous breathing and her own rapid breath dimmed. The itch of voices swelled into the heavy buzz of a hive of bees, waiting, waiting for the moment she lost the last of her guard.

Stunned silent, she paced the room with ever increasing speed. She raised a hand to tug at her hair, but missed.

Too naïve for long hair! She bounced her fists forcefully off her head instead.

Dmitri caught her arm as she went by. "Oh, no you don't. Don't you think you're going to fade out on me! Look at me!" He twisted around, capturing her head between her upraised arms, until they stood nose to nose. "Look *at* me!

"Stop it, okay?" he soothed. "I know you're scared, but *nothing happened to you*. Well, outside of a really bad haircut. Nothing *will* happen to you. I won't let it." He pulled her close. "When your hair grows some, we'll get it cut better. But until we get out of here, it'll be a lot better if you're my brother instead. I'm sorry about grabbing your... you know... I didn't mean anything by it. I just wanted to be sure this could work."

Sarah nodded, allowing him to hold her, glad that he did but too tense to return the gesture. "I would have made that bet," she whispered. "I would have lost, wouldn't I?"

He squeezed her tighter. "I don't know. Maybe they were honest, maybe they weren't. That's why you've got me to look after you. I might be a little slow, but I catch on. I haven't hurt you yet, have I?"

Sarah's eyes broke away, and she shook her head. "What do we do now?"

"Don't worry. I'll get us money somehow." A big yawn caught him short. "Ugh! It's getting late. What do you say we grab breakfast and get some sleep?"

Any progress Sarah had made over the last two years vanished. She could hear her mind shutting down, the doors of distress slamming a cold, metallic clang one after another around her brain, firewalls against the world. She clung to her brother wordlessly for the twenty minutes it took to retrieve breakfast, one of his caps pulled far down over the Horrible Hair, but she couldn't bring herself to eat a bite. Despite being awake almost twenty-four hours, she couldn't sleep, couldn't begin to. While Dmitri slumbered untroubled, Sarah curled in the corner, clutching her head, aware of nothing but the taunting voices only she could hear.

Twenty-two

*D*mitri tapped the table with his finger. Sarah picked up the half-eaten pastry and left another tiny divot in the nibbled edge. He wanted to be sure she ate something today. Sarah hung on the edge of a major disaster. It was the last thing they needed.

He awoke to find her huddled in the corner, hugging herself and rocking. It took the better part of ten minutes for her to recognize him, to break through the demons in her head and focus her on reality. Lying next to her on the bed, running a hand hypnotically over the remnants of hair, she slept a few hours while he kept guard, a restless sleep tormented by twitches and jerks and muffled cries.

"How bad is it?"

"Bad enough," she forced out, and immediately hugged herself.

Sarah's traditional method of dulling the voices meant tearing herself up – biting her fingers, slashing her arms, or banging her head to the point of unconsciousness – she claimed pain chased them away. There were only so many places to hide his knives in the room, and the hotel wouldn't allow them in public. "You're not going to do anything stupid on me, are you?"

Sarah ignored the tapping finger. "No. Not yet, anyway."

Dmitri grabbed her arm. "Not at *all*! You *warn* me you're about to blow like that! You hear? I'll work you through it, one way or another. Promise me!" He fought to regain her fading attention. "Sarah!"

"Promise," she mumbled.

"Shake on it!"

Growing up, every one of them had put great faith in their promises to each other, always sealed with a handshake. Such pledges were rarely broken, the rest of the group making sure violations were prosecuted without mercy. Sarah still believed in the sanctity of the handshake, and he would have to rely on that faith. She slipped her hand into his and closed weakly on his fingers.

He broke off a piece of the pastry with his other hand and fed it to her. "How long does it usually last?"

"I don't know. Both times I wound up on the medicine."

"We'll figure it out. Just hang in there."

He tried his first idea while Sarah washed.

His fingers drummed on the commlink desk. *Come on, come on! Five credits a minute...*

"Starbase Four Medical Center," a woman answered.

"I need to reach Dr. John Carver," Dmitri explained. "It's a bit of an emergency."

"I'm sorry, Dr. Carver is no longer practicing at the Starbase."

Dmitri's heart skipped a beat. "When? Where'd he go? He's my sister's doctor. She needs her medications refilled."

"I'm afraid I can't give out that information," the receptionist said. "All of his current patients were informed of his change of position. Perhaps you'd like to speak with another doctor? I can connect you to ..."

"No, that's okay. Thank you." Dmitri killed the expensive call.

Now what?

He parked Sarah in front of the video screen with a scientific program and tried again. A hotel this big might have a doctor on staff, if not two. He checked the hotel guide. Sure enough; seventh floor.

The hotel physician eyed Dmitri with uneasiness. "I'm sorry. I can't prescribe that kind of medication without seeing the patient. That's a controlled metabolic compound that requires specific tests first. It's also not commonly prescribed; I'd have to have it synthesized. That takes a day or two. I'm afraid I can't help you without going through the process first."

"I'll see what I can do." Dmitri could guarantee Sarah wouldn't see a strange doctor, or go through some test. *Second idea, shot to hell. Next?*

He was currently out of nexts.

He had forty more minutes of freedom, ten remaining credits in his pocket, and he could hear the bells and gongs and cheering noises of people winning in the gaming rooms. The siren song was strong, calling to him, caressing his name with a lover's hand, tugging him to a place of dirtier deeds. If he could win just a *little* more, he could get her off this rock to a place where she could get the stuff she needed... Just a few minutes... She promised she'd behave.... What harm could ten minutes do?

He followed the flowing crowd.

"Son of a *bitch*." Dmitri slammed his fist on the side of the gaming table. He downed the last of his drink and left, furious with himself both for losing and for succumbing to the call of the game in the first place. A hundred credits up, eighty down. He pushed his way out of the crowd.

"The stars had it in for you, my friend," said a young man as Dmitri brushed by him. "I haven't seen such an aggravating run of bad luck in a long time. You should have consulted a star guide first. It might not be your day to play." He followed Dmitri like an old friend, talking.

The man looked like a half-breed, half human, half Nalkarian, Dmitri guessed. Deep amber eyes surveyed him from under a ball of fluffy white hair. A red jacket hung loose on his painfully thin frame, clashing against his copper skin. He certainly liked to talk, but Dmitri's mood grew fouler with self-loathing by the minute.

"That the last of your money?"

Dmitri stopped and leaned his back against the railing of the skybridge. "What's it to you?"

"Nothing! None of my business," the Nalkarian agreed. "Normally, people don't leave the tables like that if they have reserves left, and you seemed rather desperate."

"Maybe you need to look around more often."

"I'd guess you came for the tournament, since people who run in from the street with a new-found credit usually stick to the game halls on the third and fourth floors; quick in, quick out. They're the cheapest games, and they have the worst odds, those floors. Did you know that? The higher up you go, the more you risk, but the better your chances. It's true. Only the serious players are willing to wait eleven, twelve floors to open their pockets. The stupid ones can't wait to get off."

"This being the seventh, I guess that makes me average." Dmitri turned away. *Shit!* No wonder he got picked clean on the fourth floor.

"You need anything to soften the blow?"

"What?" Dmitri turned back, not sure he'd heard right. Noise roared up the open center of the hotel and spilled out of the gaming halls, making the soft voice hard to hear.

"You name it, I got it, or I can get it for you fast," the alien offered. "Rocks, weeds, pods, pills, powders, injectables, inhalants; up, down, weak, strong, long, short; I got it. Whatever your price."

Dmitri glared with open contempt. "Get the fuck out of here! Leave me alone!" He walked away.

"If you insist." The amber eyes followed him, six-fingered hands sliding into the pockets of the jacket, rattling something unseen. "Sometimes after a bad day, all you want to do is relax and forget. Maybe with Cerilan or something? Pick up a girl from the twelfth-floor lounge, share a little Pheroma, maybe even Passion-8? Mm-mm!"

Dmitri stopped. The word *relax* triggered a forgotten memory. It could be a safe way to test another possibility. How he wished David was here! David knew a lot more about shady things than he did. He'd see how the first deal went, then maybe…

"Okay," he challenged. "Cigarettes. Bloodweed cigarettes from Navara." He'd smoked less than a dozen in his life, but he could still remember the sweet, distinctive aroma, and the utter tranquility they could induce.

The man winced. "Oooh! I think you got me on that one. That's about the only thing I *don't* have. I can get them, but it might take a week."

"Damage?"

"Well, they're mostly legal, so it's just a matter of courier. Twenty each?"

"They're twelve for six on Navara!"

"Export charge, my friend! Export charge! They're not exported at all."

"Forget it." Dimi moved again to leave, only to spin back a second later. "What about prescriptions?"

The Nalkarian coppered up solicitously. "Name it!"

"I need Elavixor, five-milligram tablets, count five hundred, and fruit-flavored Antivox liquid, three 500-milliliter bottles, ten milligrams per measure. And HypnoDex, twenty-mill tablets." HypnoDex was Father's sleeping pills.

"Well, surprise, surprise. Mr. No-No's a pharmacist at heart." The man's sugary tune changed to all business. "Sleeping pills, no problem. Ten credits a hundred. Elavixor... Elavixor... Those are Happy Pills, aren't they?"

"In a way, I guess." Dmitri was happier when Sarah took them.

"No problem. Can do. What's the other one?"

"Antivox. It's an anti-psychotic."

The man whistled, rolling his odd amber eyes as if he'd heard something scary. "Not yours, I hope. Liquid's out of the question, too bulky. That kind of chem's a specialty item. I don't carry it, but I can probably get it synthesized tonight. See me tomorrow."

"How much on the Elavixor?" One drug was better than none.

The man wavered. "Mm, five hundred, you say? They're pretty common. I might let them go for a hundred."

"A hundred *credits*?" Dmitri spluttered. "It's *free* with prescription!"

The alien flicked a bony finger against Dimi's chest. "Ah! That's the catch now, isn't it? You don't have one, do you?"

"Not anymore," Dmitri said dismally. "I can't afford that. Just give me the HypnoDex, then." If she got really bad, he could knock her out.

"You want the pills, or the cash to pay for them?"

"Huh?" It took Dmitri a moment to understand the question. He shook his head. "No. No. I'm no good at that kind of thing."

"Take it in cash or merchandise. Work as often or as little as you want, it's up to you. No pressure. If you know your way around a pharmacy like you sound...."

"Why would you cut into your own business?" Dmitri interrupted. "Won't you lose out?"

"There's seventy floors and 5500 rooms. I have to sleep at *some* point," the man said honestly. "I do like to eat, and I do have friends. I'm just a front man, anyway, and I'm not the only one. More than twenty thousand people pass through here every day. You can make a profit off aspirin, if you try. Hangover remedies are a big sell. Aphrodisiacs sell best floors nine through twelve. Most employees aren't here on the long-term. They get what they want, then leave. Me, I like the lap of luxury, and you can't get much better than this." He stared lovingly up the temple of open balconies.

"I'm not as knowledgeable as you think," Dmitri insisted. "I'm leaving soon as well."

The stranger shrugged. "I offered. Meet me by the sixth-floor lifts in the East tower in ten minutes. I'll get your order."

Dmitri breezed into the room. He pulled Sarah from her vegetating slouch. "Come here. I need to talk to you. Can you listen?"

Sarah nodded blankly.

"I think I've found a way out of our problems, yours and mine. It'll take a little bit, maybe even a few weeks, but I think I can do it. But starting right now, we need new rules."

"Mm."

"Number one: You are not to leave this room alone. *Ever.* You hear a fire alarm, you better see flames coming down the hall before you think of running. Got it? Not for *anything.* Even if you get a message saying to meet me, or there's an emergency, or something else, no matter what. We'll come up with a code phrase so you'll know it's really me.

"Number two: Do not, under any circumstances, ask me what I'm doing, where I've been, who I might be talking to, or what we talk about. Got that? In fact, if someone stops to talk to me, you move away. Understand?"

"It can't be something good if you won't tell me about it."

"Unh-uh. That violates rule number two."

"I don't like it already, whatever it is." She pulled away and fell back in the chair, staring unendingly out the window.

"Too late. A week or two tops, then we're gone, promise. Besides," he admitted, "by tomorrow, I should have some Antivox, so don't say no too fast."

Sarah's head snapped around several seconds before her body followed. "We are on the second mass of rock of this solar system, an unknown trillion kilometers from home, orbiting a star randomly designated Aquila. It is not our planet, our culture, our *biology*. Where in the name of the Universe were you able to get Antivox?"

Dmitri held his hands out. "Rule number two. Not liquid, though. You'll have to take the pills. Before you complain, I remember what they look like. They're *tiny*, Sar! It's not that you *can't* swallow them, it's that you don't *want* to. I'm going far, far out of my way to get them for you. I can't tell you how much trouble I could get into. How bad do you want those voices gone, Sar? *How bad?*" This was a much bigger risk than card games and money. If he got caught peddling contraband, he'd be jailed. He would lose his guardian status, and the fun would screech to a halt faster than a converter-core meltdown.

Sarah pressed her lips together as if staving off tears. "I'll take them," she vowed softly. "I will take them."

Twenty-two

The dividing line of day. Could have been early morning, might have been very late at night. Dmitri had no concept of time. He never left the hotel to know if it was night or day, and he often got up in the middle of a rest.

One youth held a packet to the light and tapped it with his finger. "How do we know it's pure? He doesn't look that confident in his product."

"I only carry the best." In the last two weeks Dmitri'd never had a complaint, only several repeat requests. He learned fast, knew the regulars and carried supplies accordingly, knew which hotel staff to avoid, which ones expected a 'tip,' which people in the halls were actually coworkers. This new group made him nervous. A good delivery needed half a minute at most.

"I got a better idea," a young Aquilan said. He opened the tiny package, no bigger than a thumbnail, and sprinkled a few grains of powder on the back of his thick-skinned hand. "He's gonna try it first."

"I don't use, man, I just deliver."

"Time to start," laughed a third man with a slovenly girl hanging on his neck. She tried to kiss him but her lips wouldn't coordinate, and spit ran in a trail to her chin.

Dmitri moved to leave. "I don't think so."

"I know so," said the first youth. He reached behind and brought forth a palm-sized energy weapon. He pointed it centimeters from Dmitri's forehead. "His hand or mine. You pick."

Sarah awoke a half hour later than usual. Twelve days' of medication had dropped the voices back to a memory, but Dmitri's new 'occupation' drove her crazy with worry. Gone already, goodness knew how long this time. Some days he bounced out of the room almost as soon as he got in, finger on the receiver he now kept in his ear. Every day after he paid for the room, he handed her more cash for their savings, sometimes three hundred, once five times that.

She washed and dressed, hoping he'd return. At last she poked in the box of incidental foodstuffs they kept, settling on a stale pastry. The pickings were sparse; they needed to restock. Flicking the commlink on, she caught up on the latest galactic headlines.

Sarah gnawed the pastry. *Yulk!* She retrieved a glass of water from the bathroom. Dipping the roll in hot tea would have salvaged it nicely, but the room vendor cost more than the lobby café. She'd have to wait until Dmitri returned, and she was hungry now. He hadn't left a note, hadn't left a message on the comm. *How long had he been gone?*

A noise caught her attention as she returned to the vidscreen. Sarah stopped walking, goose pimples cropping up like blisters. It came from the closet. A faint breathy noise, like a stifled sigh.

Ridiculous. She hadn't left the room, and no one had entered.

Had they?

The lock indicator by the door glowed brightly, still activated.

She shook her head and placed the glass next to her breakfast. They were twenty-seven floors up. No one could get in. That was crazy.

Wasn't it?

Sarah broke the pastry in half and read the headlines.

Revolution Imminent on Damaria. Allied Fleet's Admiral Ho Retires. Galactic Sports Report. Storm on Berenicia Enters Eleventh Day. Ivanov Industrial Sells Off Muphridian Mines.

Sarah glanced at the closet. If she spooked herself over nothing, Dimi would tease her for weeks.

The room had only one exit; to reach that she'd have to walk past the closet. A breath, the scrape of her foot on the carpeting, perhaps her arm brushing the doorway…

But what if…

If she had a weapon… Dmitri kept his big knife in his luggage, which was …

In the closet.

"There is nothing in there!" Sarah scolded herself, dipping the roll in the water and taking a soggy bite.

She closed her eyes, concentrating, stuffing her fears down, down, deep inside. *There is no fear*, she reassured herself, and to prove it, forced herself to walk up to the closet. *Fear is a biological reaction. Reactions can be controlled. There is absolutely nothing in the …* She hit the button for the sliding door.

A shriek emanated from within. Sarah echoed it.

"*Goddammit, Sarah! Shut the door!*" Dimi yelled. "Shut it, quick!"

Sarah's heart raced, her whole body trembled from the overload of adrenaline. Dmitri slumped against the back of the closet, clothes hanging down around him, cowering under his arm.

"*Dmitri-Mikhail Alexandrovitch Kirushenko!* What are you *doing* in there! You scared the *life* out of me!" Sarah's foot slammed the floor. "That wasn't funny at all! How long have you been –?"

"Shut *up!* Get in here if you want, but *SHUT THAT DOOR!*"

Sarah climbed into the closet and sat. At least she knew where he was. She stuffed a shoe against the doorjamb, allowing the door to slide shut all but the last few centimeters.

"Shut it!"

"No! Dimi, why are you in here? I thought sitting in closets was my territory? You're not going funny in the head too, are you?" They couldn't *both* be crazy. That was her job. His job was to act like a grown-up.

Dmitri gave a tight little laugh. His voice sounded higher, as if he'd been breathing helium. "I don't even *have* a mind right now! Everything's too loud, too weird. I don't know what's real and what's not. I have no idea how long I've been here."

Sarah eyed him queerly. *He **was** crazy!* He even *looked* funny. It took her a moment to figure out why.

"Dimi? Why are your eyes like that? I know there isn't much light in here, but, they're all dark. I mean like, the whole iris. I'm getting scared, Dim. Tell me what's wrong."

Dmitri stared up the sleeve of his hanging jacket. "Oh God. I am so freaked out! Everything wiggles when I talk. Rainbows happen when I move. They put a blaster to my head. They put a goddamned blaster between my eyes and told me to do it or else!" He gave a high-pitched, eerie laugh. "What the hell else could I *do?* I was so freakin' scared!"

Sarah's heart froze. Dimi was one of the Big Boys. Dimi was brave. He knew what to do even in the worst circumstances, and something still managed to scare the living breath out of him. *Not the basement! Anything but the basement!*

"What are you talking about? *Who* put a blaster to your head? What did you do?"

"I don't know names! They took all my cash. *Shit*, Sar! I am so screwed! Some yellow powder. My ass is so screwed." His voice trailed off, devoid of hope.

"Dimi, you're not making sense. What kind of powder? Did you report it? How much money did they take?"

"*Contraband*, you jackass! You can't report a crime against a crime! They made me breathe in some freakin' yellow powder. Now I'm going to have a price on *my* head because I lost the money to pay up." He giggled again.

Sarah frowned. "*What* money? Pay *who?* Who made you take contraband? Why?"

160

Dmitri let his head fall into his hand. "Man oh man, Sar, you have *got* to get your head out of those books and look around! My *supplier,* dammit! I sell the contraband for them and give them the money. I get a twenty percent cash cut or a forty percent cut on merchandise. That's how I've been getting your pretty little pills!" he hissed in a whisper. Anything louder, and the closet would twist and warp. Dimi wasn't thinking clearly, but deep down in his heart he knew closets weren't supposed to do that.

"It was supposed to be my last drop. Four thousand credits, and they took it all. *Shit!*" he wept. "I am so far beyond screwed!"

Sarah shrank back. *Dmitri was breaking the law!* He could get in big trouble, you weren't supposed to do those things and you could get hurt because only lawless, dangerous people did those things and now one of them had threatened him but he did it for *her*, he took that risk to get her the medication she needed and she felt a tremendous wave of gratitude and love for him but now he was in bigger trouble because he'd been drugged and robbed and couldn't report it because it was illegal money to start with – that meant all that other money was illegal too and now he was just as scared about all of it as she was.

Poor Dimi! He tried so hard to take care of her, and she made nothing but trouble for him. Sarah didn't know a single thing about illicit chemicals, but she knew a textbook's worth on fear.

She rolled to her knees and took his hands in hers, making herself strong for him. "Don't worry about it, Dim. You're safe here. I won't leave you alone. It's got to wear off eventually, and we'll figure something out. We've lived through worse. We'll get through it. We always have. We always will."

Dmitri's eyes clenched, fighting the tears that slipped out. He squeezed her hands hard. "I hope so," he shuddered, not just from the chemicals.

Sarah lay on Dmitri's bed near the window, working through the next chapter of her genetics book. It was more difficult than she expected, and her mind wandered. The practical-use anecdotes were much more interesting than the dry instruction, but without her homework pad, she couldn't access them. She couldn't concentrate as well as she wished. Antivox was neuro-specific; it silenced her voices, but did nothing for the nagging anxiety and restlessness.

For the last two days, she'd tried to be patient about Dmitri's promise of leaving. She knew he hadn't set foot in a gaming room in ages, hadn't followed up on the girls who smiled at him. When not on a 'delivery,' he sat in the room, mouth drawn into a tense line as he stared at whatever program played on the vidscreen. He didn't hand her any cash beyond a small meal allotment. Today he put off leaving as long as he could. She couldn't help but feel bad for him.

Three slow pages of text, and Sarah whipped her head around to face the door, hyperalert. Loud voices argued outside in the quiet hall. Some one or some thing thudded against their door. Again, a hard bang, like a fist.

Or maybe a head.

Instinctively, Sarah rolled off the bed and flattened herself on the floor between Dimi's bed and the wall. Father slammed people around like that – but Father wasn't here. As if to prove her fears, the door slid opened.

Dmitri's voice snarled as footsteps scuffed the carpeting. "I said keep your fucking hands off me!"

"I'll do whatever the hell I want," replied a cold voice, just as furious. "Just get it! No more bullshit! Or you'll be the sorriest thing this side of Andromeda."

Over the booming of her heart, Sarah heard a quick scraping of plastic on plastic. Something slid on the desk and was picked up.

"It's right here, okay? See this? *Right here.* Now get the fuck off me!"

"Shut up and get moving," said a second unpleasant voice. "You better pray you got it covered." The resistant footsteps receded, and the door swished shut.

Sarah lay motionless for ten minutes before peeking over the bed. Nothing looked out of place. She walked slowly around the room before she realized what Dimi came back to get.

His bankcard.

Three hours Sarah waited, ill with nerves. Wherever he was, Dimi was in Big Trouble. She couldn't help him unless she knew where he went, but she had no way to find him. He never left this long without calling her.

Should she go and look? She wanted to, her inner sense said she should, but she'd promised never to leave the room. The hotel was so huge she could search for days and not find him. But then, so could someone else. And if he gave them the slip, they'd surely be watching the hall for his return. Sarah paced the room, helpless, when the door banged again, and she froze in her tracks.

"Open it!" said an impatient voice.

Dmitri's voice came through the door nervous and pleading. "We can work it out! I promise!"

The door gave a thud and a faint grunt.

Sarah looked around in panic, too far from the closet or bathroom to make a run for it. She dove for the gap next to Dmitri's bed again, the farthest corner into the room. It would have to do.

The door slid open as she hit the floor. There was a shuffle of many feet, the heavy breathing of men struggling with something.

Or someone.

"I told you, I'll be gone in half an hour!" Dmitri begged, breathless. "You got what you wanted! Just let me go! Ten! Ten minutes, that's all I need. I *swear …*"

Footsteps echoed briefly in the bathroom, returned to the carpeting. The closet door hissed open, clothing slid, scraped on holders, the door closed. Footsteps circled the room.

"We know you'll go," said an unpleasant voice with a distinctly Aquilan lilt. "We're here to make sure you don't come crawling back."

Sarah was all too familiar with the sharp sound of flesh hitting flesh, the awful, forced expiration caused by a fist planted in an unsuspecting stomach. Fear froze her breath. The massive bed beside her sat on a platform, almost half a meter of bed overhanging the central support. Quickly, silently, she rolled under the edge, wedging into the cramped space behind the hanging bedcover. She hoped to the Maker of the Universe it hid her. Under the edge of the bedcover a pair of hard-soled shoes walk by, hardly thirty centimeters from her head. Someone flicked the long draperies from the window, then turned and walked back, searching for something.

Or someone.

"We'll catch the psycho later," came an angry command above the shoes. "Finish up."

Despite the fingers stuffed in her ears, Sarah heard the sounds of flesh on flesh, too many hits too fast to be the work of one person. The too-familiar involuntary grunts and groans of someone being battered, the muted thud of something soft and heavy hitting the ground, the sound of a hard shoe stomping the floor and the scream of agony that accompanied it. Sarah clenched her eyes until she saw stars, but it did little to make her shrink smaller, invisible. There were at least three other people in the room. The weapons were half a room away. If only she had the big knife! She would fight them, scared or not. Without a weapon, there was nothing, absolutely nothing she could do to save her brother.

Or herself.

"Enough," said the harsh voice at last. "He got the point."

"He won't forget too quick." A hard kick into something soft brought a faint cry.

"Let's go," said a fourth voice. Multiple footsteps receded, and through her plugged-up ears Sarah heard the door shut. Rarely had she known such terror. She wasn't crying, but a single tear forced its way out of each eye. She shook uncontrollably, and prayed the bed didn't rattle as she pressed against it.

For several seconds she heard nothing but the pounding of her heart in her ears and what seemed like an impossible loudness of her strangled breath, half-smothered in the carpeting. Slowly, slowly, she pulled her fingers from her ears.

Nothing.

Silence.

The violence had stopped.

But was she alone? Was someone lying in wait?

Listening, Sarah became aware of breathing: uneven, harsh breaths punctuated by soft gasps of pain. A low moan rose and fell.

Someone *was* in the room.

Dimi! Let it be Dimi!

If only she weren't so afraid! To move would leave her vulnerable, but what if Dimi needed her? Minutes ticked by, locked at an impasse. At last, she wriggled on her belly along the side of the bed, trying her damnedest not to make noise in the dreadfully quiet room. Another moan, and she used the sound to cover up a fifteen centimeter lurch. At the end of the bed, she peeped out under the cover. Her heart stopped as she saw a figure crumpled on the floor. It wore her brother's clothes.

Her thoughts of doom were interrupted by a rough cough and a sharper moan. The figure stirred slightly, then stopped. A cough, a cry, and Sarah slipped out from under the bed. When nothing happened, she rose on her knees to peer over it.

Nothing.

No one.

They were alone.

"Dim? Dimi?" She stood up, dizzy from fear, and moved to where he lay. One good look and the dizziness won out; she sat down hard on the floor.

It *could* have been her brother, the crumpled figure heaped on the carpeting. Sarah wasn't so sure. She shrank back in a different surge of old terrors. The blood – *so much blood!* – threatened to push her over the edge. Several times she looked and saw not her brother and a mauve carpet with drops of dark blood, but her mother and a white floor marred by a pool of bright blood. Mother had bled to death on their kitchen floor, and Sarah had been the one to find her, barely alive. It was hard to separate the images. Blood meant *death*. And Dmitri was bloody.

Nightmare blood splattered his face. Bright blood trailed thickly from his nose, stained the front of his shirt. The print of a man's ring stood out on one swelling eye, the other eye not far behind. Blood covered the back of a swelling hand. He'd dragged it across the carpeting, leaving a streak of brown-red. He coughed again, a choking, gurgly hack, blood spraying through his slack lips.

"Dimi?"

Sarah sat, wanting to help but unable to get past the red. Another gasp, and she crawled closer on her hands and knees. She couldn't help Mother, but maybe she could still save Dimi.

Maybe? She **had** to! She had to do *something,* and she had to do it fast.

No fear. No fear. No fear. No fear.

She forced herself to reach out and touch him. He felt warm and heavy, like he did when asleep. She tried to pull him onto his side, letting go quickly when he gave a faint cry. Their brother Viktor would have known what to do. *Vik would never have let it happen in the first place*, she reminded herself. *Vik would never have hid under a bed.* Oh! She was messing this up! If only she weren't so damned afraid of blood! Using the hem of his shirt, she dabbed cautiously at his mouth, only to stop in horror when she saw the hole where three and a half teeth had been hours before.

Sarah slid against her bed and hugged her knees. *Nothing.* She could do nothing for him, either. He would die there on the floor in front of her, like their mother, like their sister. Wherever she went, people died. She rose, stripped the soft blanket from her bed, and covered him gently. That's what you did when people were hurt. Then when they died, you covered up the rest of them. That's what the coroner had done with 'Byeta. Holding the hand that seemed less injured, she lay on the floor next to him, watching his chest rise and fall, waiting for the moment when it wouldn't rise again.

Twenty-four

The first thing Dmitri became aware of was *cold*. His hand was icy, and something heavy and just as cold sat on his face. He stirred, went to grab the cold, and became aware of a second thing: *pain*. Everywhere, from his head to his shoes, *hurt*. His limbs felt leaden, but he managed to swing an arm up and pull a wet cloth from his eyes. It didn't help his vision as much as he expected; his eyes wouldn't open more than a sliver. Turning his head, he could make out a blurry shadow.

"Shtharuh?" he tried, scratching his sluggish tongue on a broken tooth. He winced as he explored the gaping spaces, and memory returned. With memory came panic.

He tried to roll, to sit up, but grating agony stopped him. He turned his head toward the shape and tried harder to focus.

"Sharuh? *G'dye ti?*"

The dark fuzziness took shape. He made her out, a meter away against the bed, arms around her knees, rocking.

"You okay?" he whispered.

Sarah answered tonelessly, "I'm unharmed. Are you real, or is this a hallucination?"

"If pain'sh any indicator of reality, I'm mosht def'nitly real," he mumbled, bending his stiff knees. "How long?"

Sarah glanced at the clock in the corner of the dormant computer screen, counting in her head. "Approximately twenty-two hours."

"*Fuck.* No wonder my back hurtsh." Dimi breathed through his mouth. His *L*'s sounded funny without teeth for his tongue to press against. "He'p me shit up."

Sarah knelt next to him. "I couldn't lift you, dead out like that. I didn't want to hurt you worse, and the mattress was too big to move to the floor. The pillows were the best I could do. I couldn't bear to take your shirt off with all that blood, so I cut it off. I'm sorry."

"You did great," he said, grunting as he tried to move. Several times he tried to sit, stopping as pain overwhelmed him. His right hand hung worse than useless. Every movement set a wave of agony to his elbow. With Sarah's support and a determined yell, he dragged himself the short distance to lean against the bed, feeling bone grating on bone.

"Mmmmh," he groaned. "Dizzy."

Sarah moved in close, and he put his good arm around her shoulders. He held up the bad hand, squinting at it with the better eye. "Guessh I won't be p'aying piano any time shoon, huh? Good thing they didn't realizhe I'm a lyeffty. You shure you're okay?"

Sarah was biting a knuckle, but she nodded. "I thought you were dead."

Dmitri tried to smile. "Not yet, I'm not. You should know it takesh more than a beating to keep a Kirushenko down." She went to hug him, but he stopped her. "Eashy. I got shome ribsh in there that are moving." He slapped her knee with his good hand. "Hey, he'p me up. I got to pee like an elephant."

With Sarah's traction and one good yell, he stood – barely.

"I can't do thish," he realized, swaying. "You'll have to hold me up."

Sarah shook her head violently. "I'm not going in there with you! Just sit yourself down."

Dmitri closed his eyes and made a face as the floor tipped again. "I got one hand and almosht no eyesh. I can either hold myshelf up or deal with my clothesh. Take your pick. You think thish ish fun? Oww!"

"I'll bring you in there, but you're on your own until you're done."

"'f I could drag you to the lafatory for two damned weeksh when you were down, then you can damn well get in here and help me thish one time," he ordered, feeling for the fasteners to his pants. "Now get over here before it'sh too late."

The trip back went slower without the need to hurry. With Sarah's help, Dmitri stretched on the bed. "Jusht let me resht a bit. Giff me another pillow," he asked, and stuffed it carefully under his hand.

Sarah looked ill. "Can you move it?"

He grunted, barely twitching the curled fingers. "No. They bushted it good." A huge black bruise covered both the back and palm of his ballooned hand, from his wrist to the second knuckles. There were several curved cuts on the back – the same shape and size as the heel of a man's shoe.

Sarah whimpered. "I'm sorry. I wanted to help you, but I couldn't think of a way. I couldn't get to the knives. I was so scared!"

Dmitri grabbed her by her shirt, peering through the slit that was the better eye. "Don't do that to yourshelf! You did everything exshactly right! Cryin' out loud, Shar! There were four of 'em! If shomething like that ever happensh again, you do *exshactly* the shame thing. I tried to keep 'em out of here, but I think they were looking for you. I wash shcared they'd get you. I don't know what they would'a done, but I can tell you, they weren't very fforgiving. I tried to giff you shome warning. Where the hell were you?"

"Under your bed. I didn't even breathe."

"You're shafe, and that's what countsh." Dmitri pulled her head down to his shoulder, kissing the top and roughing up the downy chopped hair. "I don't know what the hell we'll do now, but don't worry. I'll figure shomething out."

Sarah watched him for several minutes, silent and scared. He looked worse than before, face swollen and bruised, propped up on pillows, head back, eyes closed – like a mangled corpse waiting for a casket.

"'Mitri?"

"Mmm?"

"Tell me honest? How much money do we have left?"

"I paid off one debt. It'sh the interesht that nearly killed me... How much you got left?"

"Thirty five and a quarter credits." She'd counted it ten times, searched every drawer, every envelope, every pocket of every piece of clothing they owned.

"Then we have thirty-five and a quarter creditsh left. They took efery other goddamn thing I had, wiped ush clean."

"What do we do?"

Dmitri giggled. "How th' hell do I know? You want the truth, Shar? We're *shcrewed*!" He propped himself up on his good elbow, squinting at her. "I can't walk acrossh the room on my own! Get ushed to being hungry. How well can you beg?"

Sarah cringed. Three cheap meals from total bankruptcy, a zillion kilometers from home.

Dmitri read the fear in her eyes. He fell back on the bed with a loud grunt.

"Don't shweat it. I'll figure shomething out. If worshe comes to worshe, I'll call Katya and shee if she'll loan ush shome money. 'Courshe, knowing her, it will only be in the form of two one-way ticketsh to Earth."

"Is that so bad?" Sarah muttered, but Dmitri didn't answer. He lay still, thinking dismal black thoughts. "Dimi?"

"Mmm?"

"Does this count as a dire emergency?"

"Well, gee, Shar. I don't know. I'm broke to bits, we owe sheveral daysh on thish room, we're down to one shared meal a day for the nexsht three daysh, and then we're pissh-asshed broke! I don't know about your loffty, dictionary-quality interpretationsh, but that shoundsh pretty damn *dire* to me."

"You needn't swear." Sarah retrieved the backpack that held her worldly treasures. She searched until she located a black magnetic envelope, and removed a small yellow card. A string looped through a hole in one corner.

"Here."

Dmitri took the card, holding it close to his eye. "What'sh thish?"

"My bank card. Valeria told me never to touch it, save it for dire emergency only. I know you don't want to go home yet – even if I *do*. This way you won't have to tell Katya you ran out of money."

The broken ends of Dmitri's ribs ground together as he sat up, causing him to cry out.

"*Sharah!* How long have you – You've had thish the whole time? – Two and a half *yearsh*? – And you didn't *tell* me? How much have you *got* in here?"

Sarah slid out of reach. "I thought you'd be happy. Val said not to tell you I had it, not to touch it except for dire emergencies. There's six thousand in there, just like you had, plus interest, of course."

"Shixsh? *T'oushand*! She *gave* you your cheque? The Shurvivor'sh benefitsh from Mother'sh polishy? *Sharah!* How *could* you! All thish time I bushted my assh to keep ush going, and you were shitting there holding out on me? God*damn* you! I put my *life* on the line for you, *more* than oncshe!"

Sarah backed off the bed and stood against the wall, hugging herself. *"Don't yell at me!* Val *told* me not to tell you! I forgot all about it until just now. I'm sorry!"

Dmitri lay down. "Yeah, well, you can jusht march yourshelf downshtairsh and transhfer it to my account."

"Only on my conditions."

168

"What the hell do you mean, *'your conditionsh'*!" he spat, then winced. "There shouldn't *be* any conditionsh! I've ffed you, clothed you, bought you every texshtbook your brain could abshorb…"

"That's your job as my guardian," Sarah reminded him. "Be honest, Dimi! You're lousy at managing money, at least here. All along, you've acted like it would never run out. Now it finally has, and you act like you didn't know it.

"I'll give you half my money, without a second thought. Take it, it's yours, and I wish it could be more. But I'm keeping the other half, in case we ever get stuck again. I think Val knew what she was talking about. My conditions are simple: One: pay up what we owe anybody, so they never come after us again. Two: get yourself to a doctor. You *need* a doctor, Dimi! Get your hand fixed, get some teeth. Make sure you're not bleeding inside. And Three: *I* choose the next place we go."

"I'm *not* going home!"

Sarah sighed painfully. "I know that. I want to go see Viktor. It'll be *like* going home, without really *going* there. It's been so long since we've seen him. Please?"

Dmitri didn't need to think very long. Why the hell hadn't he ever thought of that? Good old Viktor, the best friend he'd ever had. When Vik had been home, they'd been best friends. David had just been the pesky kid brother back then, leader of the tight-knit Fearsome Four that drove the older group crazy. Dmitri belonged to the older crowd, him and Vik and Katya and sometimes the twins, trying to make everything run smoothly as their lives fell further and further apart.

Vik had left home on the hopes that if he worked hard enough, he'd be able to rescue everyone, one by one. He joined a recruitment to man an Alliance border patrol, monitoring the edge of Alliance space against the invasive Burin-Jai Empire. Dmitri could talk to Viktor, tell him anything, tell him everything. Vik would understand. Vik would absolve him of any guilt. And Viktor loved Sarah. He could take over, and Dimi could have a worry-free, Sarah-free vacation. The ache of the emptiness that used to be Viktor hurt almost as much as his hand. He would send a message as soon as they returned from the infirmary.

"Deal!"

Dear Ugly,

That's a stupid question! I'd Kill to see you guys! How long can you stay? Let me know when you plan to arrive, and I'll take some of the time I have coming. How's my favoritest sister? I can't wait to see her! Why aren't you here already! My love to Sarah.

Counting the days,
Viktor

Vik:

Unexpected delay. Explain later. May take a while. Will let you know when able to travel.

Dimi

Twenty-five

"Valeria, can you come here for a minute?" David called on the intercom. Val would want to see this. He leaned back in the chair, rubbing his chin while he tried to make sense out of the data on the screen.

A short knock preceded Valeria. "You wanted me?" She saw the screen. "Something change? Did they move?"

"I have no idea, but something big must be up." David split the screen to show both financial accounts he'd been tracking on and off. He pointed to an entry line. "Dimi wiped his account – every last credit – on this date, and a day later there's a three thousand credit debit *from* Sarah's account that corresponds to a three thousand credit deposit *into* Dmitri's account, same date, same minute."

Valeria checked the remaining balance. "They must be in some kind of trouble. Sarah wouldn't have touched it on her own. I told her to save it for emergencies. If they went this long without it, it must be an emergency. Any idea where they went?"

David cross-referenced another screen. "None at all. The last deductions were 2100 credits to Mirabella Resorts Corporation, Jiá Taf, Aquila II, and two hundred credits cash at a currency transfer station, also in Jiá Taf. Nothing else. They couldn't have gotten off world for that, so I assume they're still on Aquila. Twenty-one hundred for a hotel! Can you imagine? I hope that wasn't just one night."

Val deducted in her head. "So there's less than a thousand in Dimi's account. Get up a minute, Dave. Let me sit. Did you get the banking server yet?"

"Up and running last month." David waited for the retinal ID to scan, then gave his code to access the accounts. They changed places, and Valeria gave the computer a new set of orders.

"That should do it," she said as TRANSACTION COMPLETE filled the screen. "At least they'll have enough to get off the planet. Good catch, Dave." Val patted his hand as she stood up to leave. "I hope they're okay. Has Vlad heard anything?"

"Not a word for two weeks. He's going crazy. Maybe they decided to stay a while and bought themselves transportation," he suggested. "It doesn't have to mean something's wrong."

"No, it doesn't," Valeria said quietly. "It just feels that way."

> *Interfering Valeria,*
> *Attached you will find a transfer order for your 3,000 credits back. It didn't take long to figure out how it got there, since you're the only other person with access to Sarah's account. If you send it again, I will cash it, tear it up, send you the pieces, and you will be out your money. I have closed Sarah's account and placed her money elsewhere, someplace you can't touch it. I did not make off with it – it's in her name and I won't touch it, so you can stop calling me all those names right now. We do not need and do not want any of your charity. In the future, please refrain from sticking your nose in other people's business when it is neither wanted nor appreciated. Rest assured, if we were in need of something, you would be the last person we would ask.*
> *Sincerely yours,*
> **Dmitri M. Kirushenko**

When Val saw mail waiting on the computer and noted the sender, her hopes soared, expecting some sort of thanks, some polite little communication that would show her the rift was mending. But no. Not even the courtesy of an impersonal *Miss Kirushenko,* or a sarcastic *your former brother,* just cold, formal animosity. She hadn't done it to interfere! She wanted to *help,* to make up even a little for what she knew she'd done. Without the account being active, Val had no way to help Sarah if she really needed it. A slap in the face would have hurt less. Valeria put her head on the desk, and let the tears fall.

* * * 2 * * *

"I can't believe you still *talk* to him, let alone want to visit him! Whatever would possess you to play with suicide like that?" David scoffed, lounging in the entertainment room with the rest of the family.

Vlad swallowed around his nerves. "He's right, Val. We're past all that now. Why do you have to go digging up stuff we finally stopped thinking about? Outside of Sarah, we're happy here."

Valeria glared harshly at the boys. "Because I'm older, and I guess a lot more forgiving! He was hurt in an *accident* – they reconstructed his knee, for goodness' sakes! He's laid up in medical for two weeks, and I don't see where I'm evil for wanting to pay a visit. He's still our father."

David stood up. "Maybe because you don't have our reasons for wanting him dead. The only way I might – *might!* – feel vindicated is if they did the surgery with a drunken surgeon, a rusty kitchen knife, and no anæsthesia."

Six-year old Nikky watched the exchanges with interest. "Val? Is that the same father in the pictures in the picture book?"

David answered faster. "*Da.* Did Val ever tell you we had another sister, just a little older than you, but Father beat her to death? Did Val ever tell you *that* little bedtime story of when you were little?"

"David, stop it! You're twisting things …, "Galina hissed.

Nikky frowned. "Is that when all those people broke into our house and shot a bogey man, and we all had to hide in the kitchen and couldn't come out until they were sure we wouldn't tell?"

All eyes turned to Nikky, who had been only three at the time.

David stared. "Boy, have you got *that* backwards! Where'd you come up with *that* garbage?"

Nikky looked unsure. David was so much older, he'd always been a grown-up to Nikky. Without 'Byeta, and with Sarah gone, and if he didn't count his baby sister, the person next closest to him in age was Vlad, now going on thirteen. "That really happened?"

"Not quite like that, Nik," Val said gently.

"'Not quite like that,' my ass!" David exclaimed. "And you accuse *me* of twisting things… !"

"David," warned Val.

"David," Uncle Tomas admonished.

"Come and see me later, Nik, and Vlad and I will set you straight," David offered.

"I'll explain it first," Val insisted.

"At the risk of alienating myself," Sergei interrupted, "I'd like to go with you."

Galina smiled. "I think that would be wonderful. I'm sure he'll be very glad to see you."

"*Kiss ass,*" David couldn't help muttering. "Just don't stand too close. I'm sure his punching arm is itching for exercise."

"Uncle Tomas, will you come with us?" Galina asked. "I'm sure Father would like to meet you. He's really very grateful."

Tomas declined. "The last place a man wants to meet his brother-in-law is in prison, especially if that person is caring for his family in his absence. I very much want to meet your father, but we'll arrange it when he's free and back on his feet. He deserves that dignity."

"He doesn't deserve *shit!*" David sneered.

* * * 3 * * *

Versan Albat Penal Rehabilitation Center
Earthdate: August, 2266

Sasha Kirushenko slid off the bed, putting more weight on one long leg than the other. His face relaxed as the girls entered the room, a hint of smile dawning. It darkened to a more familiar scowl as Sergei appeared behind them. Sasha had not expected to deal with the boys. He'd been against this from the start, wanting and not wanting the visit, mortally ashamed of where he was, and why. It had taken much begging on the twins' part for him to agree.

"What the hell is he doing here! I agreed to see the two of you, no one else! Why the hell would you think to bring a child here?" Sasha may have been a lousy father, but he knew enough not to bring a child to a Level IV Penal Rehabilitation Center. Modern model prison or not, hard criminals filled the halls. He turned his back. "This wasn't the arrangement."

Sergei hung back near the door.

Valeria took a step closer. "He's fifteen, Father. He isn't a child anymore. He wanted to see you. I didn't think Sergei would be a problem."

Somehow it made sense the weird one would want to visit. The boy was six before Sasha was convinced he could speak, he was that quiet.

Sasha glared over his shoulder. "A son should not have to visit his father in prison."

"You're in a hospital, Father," Galina pointed out.

"A prison hospital! "

"I'll wait outside," Sergei said.

"Nyet!" Sasha ordered, the mighty jaws pulsing as he clenched

and unclenched them. "This is not a tourist resort. Young boys do not walk the halls alone." He pulled himself up his full two hundred and seven centimeters and turned around, bearing weight on the healing knee and willing away the torment.

"Well, boy? Am I what you expected to see? Do I fit your memory?"

"I expected to see my Father, and that's who I see," Sergei replied evenly. Sasha was thinner, still as large as a small asteroid but muscular, not bloated and soft with alcohol. The prison-short hair greyed at the edges, as did the dark beard. The eyes, though... the eyes were clear. They were darkest brown, almost black when not bloodshot, so dark no one could read their intent.

"Come here," Sasha ordered gruffly, pointing to the floor an armlength away. He twirled a finger. "Turn. I will see you."

Sergei obeyed.

The boy was tall. He would have the height. Slender, though, not big-boned. He looked healthy. He dressed well enough. He needed to take better care of his skin; the rash of adolescence was more noticeable than it should have been. The thick curls were a harsh reminder of Sasha's own mother, a woman he'd tried his best to forget.

"You play sport?"

"Yes, sir."

"You will look at me when you speak!" Sasha barked. "I may wear prison clothes, but I am still your father. You will respect that or leave!"

Sergei's eyes snapped upward to meet the penetrating gaze. "Yes, sir! I'm sorry, sir. No disrespect was intended, sir. I play intramural soccer, sir, and I will start my second year of fencing. I hope to make the school team this year."

"Fencing? They teach that as sport? Sword play?"

"It's not play, sir. The foils are quite sharp. I've been cut during matches before."

"You are still a form ahead?" Sasha remembered, still sorting Sergei out of the jumble of memories of a jumble of kids. "Your grades – good?"

"Yes sir! I'll start eleventh form. My grade average for last year, all combined, was 93. My low grade was an 85 in Chemistry."

"Then you should work twice as hard at it. You are the brightest of my sons. There is no excuse for one low grade spoiling a strong average. I managed a composite of 96 with a full-time job and three babies under foot. You have no such excuse."

"Yes, sir. I'm sure I'll do better this semester."

"You still write notes to yourself?" Sasha asked. The Attitude slipped a little further. He held out an expectant hand. "Let me see."

Sergei hesitated. He fingered the current volume in his pocket. This had a green plastic cover, molded to look and feel like hard leather. Three-quarters of the pages had softened edges from constant fingering, and loose papers stuck out of it with such frequency that it doubled the original width. He'd tied it with a black ribbon to keep the bits from falling out. It was his entire life for the last two months, but he dropped it in the waiting paw.

Sasha turned the book over in his hands, eyeing the ribbon. He waved it in the air. "You have empty pages here?"

"Yes, sir."

Sasha handed back the unopened book and gestured toward a chair and table at the side of the room. "Write me an essay."

"An essay, sir? On what topic?"

"Any topic. I will see for myself how you write."

Sergei shrugged. "Okay."

The boy sat obediently, lost in thought, a scrap of paper torn from the notebook before him. It didn't take more than a half hour before he turned the paper face down, finished. He went on writing in the book itself while Sasha spoke with the twins.

A computer voice announced the end of visiting hours. Sasha gave the twins a peck on the cheek, and caught Sergei watching. He would never kiss a son like that, but the boy caught him off guard: Sergei looked him in the eye and extended a hand. Sasha sensed the challenge in the simple act. Slowly, almost shyly, he accepted the offer, the huge fingers still almost able to encircle his son's.

"Good bye, sir. I hope your knee heals well."

Sasha dropped his eyes and his voice for a brief second. "Thank you. You will study harder." It wasn't a question; it was a command.

"Yes, sir."

The elder Kirushenko watched them leave. He had eased himself onto the bed when he noticed the paper on the table. He stared at it, distrustful.

What could the boy have written? Or had he left the paper blank, the better to show his disdain? He didn't remember Sergei as being like that. That was more like one of the other boys. Which was the pain in the ass? One of the D's. He rested the throbbing knee for quite a while before retrieving the paper. Only a half-sheet, but clear writing covered one side, some things edited and overwritten. He held the paper in his hand another five minutes before daring to read the words, one line at a time.

> *It is said that a hero*
> *Is naught but a fool*
> *In the right place*

At the right time.

I say the bravest of men
Will fight insurmountable odds
In the face of unbearable pain
When he fears he is beyond redemption.

You will not know such a man
By past or present behavior,
But by the actions he takes
When his aching soul cries for peace.

Sasha read through it once, afraid, then read through it again with amazement. He held it in his hands, chilled, running over their exchanges in his head. He had stood strong, firm. No word or action betrayed him; he'd let nothing slide. The boy could read people instinctively.

Like his mother, he simply understood.

Twenty-six

United Planetary Alliance
Outpost 62
Alliance/Burin-Jai Border
Earthdate: 24 September, 2266

Ten weeks. It took ten weeks to reach Outpost 62: eight weeks holed up in a sordid section of Jiá Taf, and two weeks in a now-or-never attempt to survive the journey to the border zone. Dmitri couldn't wait for the ship to finish docking. If he'd been excited before, he was a hundred times more anxious to see Viktor now. At last! Someone who could give him the break he so desperately needed. If Vik couldn't help him… Dimi'd have no choice but to bring her home. He would not, could not, should not, have to handle her like this. This went well beyond his ability to cope. No.

Dmitri eyed his sister, waiting in line beside him for the pressurization of the airlock to equalize. Sarah peered into a bag of yogurt-covered fruit bits, poking for a specific fruit. She wore a black cap of his over her hair, now grown enough that it covered her ears. The ends had been professionally trimmed, giving the odd cut a more planned look.

"Let me see your face," he ordered. Life had no humor left in it for either of them. Time was their greatest enemy, and both were very aware of the ticking of the bomb that *would* go off. Sarah flashed a bright, eager, adoring smile for his approval.

"Do you mean it?"

The smile disappeared as fast as it had been created. Sarah poked inside the bag, found what she wanted and put it in her mouth.

"Part of it. I will be truly happy to see Viktor. It's the rest of it that's got my stomach tied six ways to Saturn."

"But we're not going to think about that, *are we?*"

Dmitri bored into her with a no-nonsense stare, but Sarah turned away, knowing she was guilty of breaking the new rule, mentally dwelling on *It.* "If you say so."

An indicator light above the airlock changed from red to green, and the portal began to untwist. Sarah closed the bag and shouldered her heavy backpack. She kept a grip on Dimi as the group surged forward.

They crossed onto the Outpost station, following the twenty or so passengers disembarking, when Dmitri felt a tap on his shoulder. He turned, only to be immobilized in a crushing hug.

"Vik!" Dmitri dropped the bags but was unable to return the embrace.

Viktor squeezed before letting go. "You son of a bitch! You haven't changed a bit!"

"You old bastard! Neither have you!" Dmitri pounded his brother on the back. The hair conformed to Allied regs, but he was the same old Viktor, with the soft brown eyes, broad shoulders, and inviting smile, wearing a blue Allied Fleet service uniform.

Vik noticed Sarah watching them with her glowing, practiced smile. He broke away from Dmitri. "Well look over here. Can this big grown-up girl really be my little princess?"

Sarah not only stopped her charge, but reversed direction. The beatific smile vanished, replaced by a look of fear. "NO! I'm *not* grown up! I'm not! I'm not even twelve! And I've never been a princess!"

"Lay off the grown-up stuff!" Dmitri hissed through clenched teeth. *"Tell her she's still a kid!*

"I'll explain later," he whispered at Vik's puzzled look.

Vik tried again. "If it's not a princess, then it has to be Sar'ina!"

At the sound of her baby-name, Sarah gave a shy, unrehearsed smile and ran to him, letting him pick her up. She wrapped her arms around her bigger brother's neck and squeezed back ferociously. Her hat fell off in the hugging.

Vik put her down and ran a hand through the short locks. "Your hair! What happened to your hair?"

"It's a long story," she shrugged, replacing the cap. "It was lots

177

better than the alternative ... ."

"Hey!" Dmitri said, retrieving the travel cases. "Where do you want us to stash these? They're kind of heavy."

"Here, give me half," Viktor said, taking Sarah's bags. "Follow me."

Viktor's quarters seemed kilometers away, down several decks and through a labyrinth of corridors that looked identical to the unaccustomed eye. "This is it," he said. "It's not much, but it serves its purpose."

Sarah stopped to read the label by the door:

KIRUSHENKO, VIKTOR M.
WEAPONS SPECIALIST III

"They give you a door plaque and everything!" she marveled as she entered. "Is a III good or bad?"

Viktor grinned. "Bad! I'm the most unmotivated weapons specialist there is. Three years, and I haven't moved up one class. When I started, I was desperate. I took whatever position they had; I didn't care, and the recruiter talked a good game. I'm not a bad specialist – I know my stuff – it's just that my heart's not in it and I don't push myself for promotion. Now, having been passed up for the second time, I look pretty bad. The commander pulled some strings, and in six weeks I transfer to the medical corps. That's where I really want to be. I know I can move up quick there, maybe eventually try for med school."

Sarah hugged him again. "You'll be good at that. You already know all about taking care of lungs."

"You gave me lots of practice." Vik lifted her off the ground with a playful grunt. No matter what Sarah wanted to believe, she wasn't little anymore, and she certainly didn't take after the dainty side of the family. "Do you guys want to stay here, or you want me to get you an empty cabin for yourselves?"

"Here!" Sarah and Dmitri answered together.

"There's only two beds..."

Dmitri looked around. Vik had a double cabin all to himself. As much as possible had been built into the walls. There were two small desks with computer workstations, and a cushioned bench that served as guest seating. Viktor didn't have much on display – several older family pictures, a popular board game, a small music system, and a few reminders of shoreleave trips off station. A backlit lunar shot of the Earth hung on one wall.

Vik had walked thirteen kilometers into town when he left home, taking only essentials. Dmitri thought of everything his brother had left behind, everything Valeria had sitting in storage somewhere. If only he'd been able to bring some of it with them, return it all to its rightful owner rather than let Val control that, too.

An arching bulkhead separated the sleeping area from the living area on one side of the room; a decorative grille divided the other. Another door led to a washroom.

"That's all right," he replied, stacking the cases at the end of a bed. "We've slept in worse. We can take turns sleeping on your bench there."

"He means *I* get stuck with the bench," Sarah translated, bouncing her bottom on it to test the softness. It was narrow, but better than the floor.

Vik winked. "Don't you worry. I'll make sure he plays fair."

"I didn't come here for the two of you to gang up on me," Dmitri said crossly.

"Lighten up! What would you guys like to do first – sit and talk, or look around the station?"

"Sit and talk," Dmitri said.

"Tour!" Sarah shouted.

Viktor pointed down a side corridor. "…And that's the hydroponics gardens over there. You want to see that?"

"No," Sarah and Dmitri said in unison.

"Can't we see where you work?" Sarah begged.

Vik hesitated. "I don't know. It's a restricted area. Let me check with the lieutenant first."

Dmitri walked backwards, eyes following a passing female officer. Her shapeless, all-purpose jumpsuit left much to his overactive imagination.

"Not a lot of women on the station."

"No, there aren't," Viktor said with a hint of regret. "Eight hundred personnel, and only a hundred and fifty of them women. Ten are married, so you can imagine how the rest get hounded. They're pretty particular, too. Nice girls, though. Dependable. They know what they're doing, out here."

Dmitri whistled. "About five to one. I don't know how you do it."

"Mr. Kirushenko!" A deep voice interrupted behind them. Dark skin was set off handsomely by a blue-and-gold uniform.

Both brothers turned around. Side by side, their relationship was obvious at first glance: the same stance, the same eyes, the same dark hair in the same basic style, the roughly similar faces. Only on closer inspection did differences appear. Viktor stood four centimeters taller, his hair a shade lighter and parted on the opposite side to his brother's. Vik had Mother's gentle smile; Dmitri had Father's rakish, lopsided grin and dark, dark eyes. Vik had Father's muscular build and wide, strong shoulders that had been such an asset on the wrestling team back in school. Dmitri had Mother's slender structure. Vik had

Mother's endlessly patient, calm manner; Dmitri could be rash and impulsive when ideas entered his head.

Viktor acknowledged the man who had spoken, then gave a nod to the man walking with him. "Commander Indala. Lieutenant Commander Morden."

"Is this the family you were expecting, Mr. Kirushenko? Giving the grand tour?"

"Yes, sir. This is my brother Dmitri, and our sister, Sarah."

Dmitri leaned forward to shake the man's hand. "Commander."

"Sir," Sarah managed to whisper, following suit. She tugged Viktor's arm, motioning toward the Commander. Vik understood.

"Commander, I realize the area is restricted, but I wondered if I might show them my station in Section Five?"

"As long as you're not teaching them to run the consoles, I think a quick run through would be acceptable. I'll clear it with the lieutenant."

"Thank you, sir."

"Thank you, sir," Sarah echoed softly.

Indala smiled at her. "You're most welcome. Mr. Kirushenko, since family is rare out here, perhaps you and your guests would care to join me for dinner? I'd be interested to hear their impressions of our outpost."

"We'd be honored, sir. Thank you," Vik agreed.

"Good. Shall we say at 1900, then, in the Officer's mess?"

"Yes sir!"

Commander Indala's warm dignity gave way to an impeccable sense of humor, trading stories with the brothers during dinner. The meal may have come from a replicator, but the salad came fresh from the hydroponics garden.

Sitting between her brothers, Sarah found the meal tense but acceptable. The commander seemed personable enough, but Sarah was so afraid of doing or saying something wrong and subsequently getting Viktor in trouble, she couldn't eat. Vik had tied one of Katya's ribbons around her head, but Sarah knew her hair still looked awful.

Indala addressed her half way through the meal. "Miss Kirushenko, we don't often get young people here at the Outpost. What do you think? What part of your tour did you like best?"

A young person. Not a child or a girl or a young lady, or, Heavens forbid! a big girl, but a young *person,* which was exactly what she was. Sarah basked in the respect, and her tongue loosened.

"I found it quite fascinating, sir. There is virtually unlimited opportunity for learning in several of the science fields. I did find the observation deck unnerving, however. I would prefer to be orbiting a planet."

"Deep space takes some getting used to," Indala agreed. "Not everyone is able to adjust. Did you have any questions?"

Sarah *always* had questions. "The idea of hydroponic gardening made me wonder about closed-systems waste processing and what method you use to …"

"Sarah, I'm *eating*," Dmitri interrupted. "Don't tell me you can't come up with a question that won't turn my stomach."

Viktor smiled. He explained to the commander, "Sarah's a bit advanced academically, and her questions are usually lengthy and involved."

"There's nothing wrong with an inquiring mind," Indala said. "We wouldn't be sitting here right now if no one had ever wondered about the stars and how to reach for them. There's probably no greater asset for a rich life."

So there! she flashed to Dmitri. "I have a better question. When dealing with the operational power supply for the station, how are you able to utilize a controlled transium-particle reaction in a confined space without having a major energy discharge resulting in the station moving several million kilometers at a time? I haven't studied warp-mechanics in detail and I may be misinterpreting my facts, but I thought that's why transium was used in Davies-warp drives, because the resultant energy discharge created by quantum stimulation could warp space itself?"

Dmitri rolled his eyes, but Viktor laughed out loud as Commander Indala stared, stupefied.

"I honestly don't think I've ever been asked that question," Indala recovered. "I could give you my interpretation, but it might not be as detailed as you'd like. Perhaps I can arrange for one of my engineers to take you on a tour of the power plant tomorrow. I'm sure they can answer your questions in better detail."

"Thank you, sir," Sarah said, picking up her fork with a purpose this time. "I would like that very much."

Vik gave her a long squeeze. "You haven't changed a bit!"

The threesome sat in Vik's quarters and talked late into the night. Commander Indala had asked numerous questions about growing up in a large family that the boys were quick to answer. The stories triggered memories, many of which happened before Sarah was born, or at least before she could remember, and she listened with rapt attention.

"Have you ever seen a real Burin-Jai?" Sarah asked Viktor. "Are they really like the pictures in the encyclopedia? Do they really want to take over Alliance territory, or is that just a made-up political thing to keep up the military?"

"It's pretty real. We'll spot a ship now and then watching us from their side of the treaty zone, and once in a while we intercept a transmission, but we've been lucky. There was an attempted raid five years ago, before I came. They harass smaller ships, and they've nailed a few scouts on us. They clobbered Outpost 59 three years ago, but they've been kind of quiet lately."

Dmitri grinned. "Are their women really as ugly as they say?"

Vik gagged. "I'm glad I've never seen one face to face. If you're into yellow skin, alligator teeth and no chin, and don't mind your wife having biceps the size of small dogs, then I suppose you'd be happy. Ugh! I mean, they eat their dead raw, for Space's sake!"

"Talk about bad breath." Dmitri fanned his nose, and they all laughed.

He tried to chase Sarah to bed.

"Please?" she begged. "I've been up way later than this! Let me stay up with Vik?"

"Come on! Maybe I want to talk with him alone, just guys?"

Sarah leaped across the sleeping area, one bed to the other. She landed far short of her goal, but the momentum carried her farther. She ran forward on tiptoe to keep her balance, banging her shins on the other bed.

"It's already 00:30, Sar – *Sarah!*" Viktor barked, catching sight of her. "Is that what Dimi's teaching you? You never did that at home."

"We don't *have* a home now," Sarah said with a touch of sass. "We just travel."

"Take my bed," Vik said. "I'll take the bench the first night, if you promise to get to sleep quick."

"You guys could always share the other one. That's what we always did at *home*."

Viktor frowned and eyed his brother; Dmitri batted his eyes playfully. Vik swept him off his feet in a deep dip.

"What do you say, darling?" Viktor cooed. "Will you share my bed tonight?"

Dimi clasped his hands to his cheek, giggling. "Sorry, but I won't sleep with anyone who's chest is hairier than mine."

"You're right. No tits, and you're not blonde. Sorry!" Vik dropped Dmitri with an ungraceful thud. Sarah burst into laughter.

"I'll take the bench," Viktor said.

Sarah grinned, eyes shining with happiness. "We miss you, Vik!"

"I miss you guys, too. Now, bed!"

A supreme feeling of security – that *two* brothers were with her, that Viktor was there, Vik, who could handle anything from Father's wrath through bacterial invasions; Vik, whose distinctive, comforting scent enveloped her when she mashed her face joyfully into his pillow – made Sarah relax as if she were home again. She fell asleep almost immediately, sleeping through the night for the first time in ages.

Viktor stirred, shifted, heard the soft intermittent *tap tap* of the computer controls. The chronometer read 0800 – three hours later than usual.

Sarah sat absorbed at his computer.

"What are you reading?"

"The general specs on the Outpost. I wanted to brush up before I tour TechSys."

Viktor sat down on the other side of the desk. "Always looking for something else to know. Did you ever finish school?"

Sarah shook her head sadly. "I had about eight months left, and I would have had my diploma eight years early. Not many people can top that. I could have graduated with a university degree next spring, maybe even dual degrees if I'd studied hard enough."

"I'd bet you would have, too. Do you keep up on anything? Read any of the journals you used to follow?"

"When I can. Dimi's spent a lot of money on textbooks for me, so I don't want to pester him for extras. Sometimes we get near a commlink or a library, and I can usually get an hour or two to read something. I'm trying to follow the course requirements for Moscow State," she explained. "I figure, that way, when I get back, I can exempt most of the lower class requirements and concentrate on the really interesting stuff."

"That makes sense. What do you want to study?"

"I like everything, except maybe economics," Sarah pondered, "but I'm thinking about biochemistry, with a minor concentration in linguistics. I could breeze right through that. I wish I could study more music. That's the only thing I can't do right now."

"Why not? 'Mitya's got a better collection of music than I do."

"*Had*," Sarah emphasized. "We… got into a sticky situation, and Dimi sold my text reader, my homework pad, and his music player and all his music cards. I miss all of them. And the most beautiful dress I ever saw in my life."

"Well, that's crazy. I'll take you down to station's stores later and get you a player of your own. You can't study music if you can't hear it. What kind of trouble did you get into?"

"It doesn't matter. He tries very hard, Vik. Don't fault him. He does a good job."

"Selling off your school supplies to raise cash is doing a good job?"

"Yes!" Sarah said with conviction. "He buys me all kinds of texts, he gets me meds when I need them, I never go hungry, he never yells without a reason, he takes care of me when I'm sick, and even when

I'm deliberately horrible, he never hits me, even if I deserve it. How can I say he isn't doing a good job? I'm not an easy person, Vik. He goes out of his way."

"But just the same, you'd rather be home."

Sarah shrugged. "Of course. That's where Vlad is. I blame the twins for that. Valeria because she started all the… *crap*, and Galina because she wouldn't stop her. Nobody would; they were all afraid of her. All Val had to do was say, 'Fine, Vlad, here's your ticket, stay with them, then.' Dimi would never have taken off with both of us. Two of us would have been work. With just me, I'm a partner in crime, someone to give him justification to stay away. He can prove his point to Val as long as he wants. He knows I won't go against him, but I sure wish I could be with Vlad again. We stream text to each other almost every week. It's not the same, but it's something."

Viktor nodded. "I'll talk with him later. How late does he usually sleep?"

Sarah leaned to see the bed. "He's good until lunch, usually."

Vik laughed. "Not in my quarters he isn't! Shift change here is 0600. You ready? I'll hold him if you tickle… "

"Dimi! Dimi? Where are… What are you still doing in bed?" Sarah jumped on him as he pulled the blanket from his head. "I thought we got you up *hours* ago! You should have come on the tour with me! I got to see the intermix chambers, and I learned all about fuels and coolants and evaporators and stuff. And Vik got me a new music player and a dozen chips for it, so we've got something to listen to again, and I got to text it all to Vlad! Get up!" She shook him.

"All right! Stop!" Dmitri said grumpily, rubbing his face. "If you ill-mannered spaceheads let me sleep this morning… "

"Drag yourself, lazy bones," Viktor said. "I told Sarah maybe we'd go down and check out the gym, and if she doesn't mind the open views of space, I'll take you to the Starlight Lounge for dinner, on P-3 deck. The chef's Mirakan, but the food's better than the mess halls. That's where a lot of the civilian traffic winds up."

"I could stand to eat," Dmitri agreed.

The Starlight Lounge reminded Sarah of the Mirabella hotel – sparkly, but this time like a night sky. Pinpoint fiberoptics shifted through the spectrum in a creeping wave over the navy blue walls, the carpeting the same dark blue with specks of white in it. Flickering crystal lamps glowed on each white table. Observation glass made up an entire wall, looking out into the darkness of space. The lights of sub-light transports and freighters drifted across the windows at great distance, and once while they sat, a massive interstellar cruiser passed as it circled to its assigned docking port, its name and call numbers

184

painted in unfamiliar green symbols. A shifting mural covered the interior wall of the restaurant; a ten-phase sequence of waxing and waning moons in various hues.

Vik regaled them with stories of what went on both during and after duty while they waited, stories Commander Indala might not have appreciated. Sarah ordered for herself, but took a mental step back when Viktor ordered vodka from the table's menu screen.

He caught sight of the wide-eyed stare. "What's the matter?"

"I didn't know you drank like that," she said in a small voice.

"Don't pay attention to her," Dmitri said with annoyance. He stuffed himself with another appetizer and spoke around it. "Every time she sees someone with alcohol she thinks they're going to go crazy and come after her."

"I can understand that," Vik said. "I don't do it often. It's kind of like a party with you guys here, that's all. I can have something else. It's no big deal."

Sarah looked at him with amazement. "You'd do that for me?"

"Sure. I can't blame your reasoning. I don't want you to feel uncomfortable." He canceled his drink order and chose something non-alcoholic.

"Well, *I'm* not uncomfortable with it, and I'll drink what I want." Dmitri touched an order for an Irilian Rum Runner. "I can't see babying her on an irrational fear. I can't get it through her head that everybody isn't like Father. She knows I drink, but I've never been more than tipsy and I never so much as yell at her, but she won't quit."

"That true?" Vik asked, concerned.

Sarah nodded to the table. "It's true. He's never threatening. And he doesn't drink that often, or that much. I just wish he wouldn't do it at all."

Dinner arrived in time to change the conversation. As Viktor promised, the food had an alien flair, spicy but delicious. He ordered a large, gooey dessert to share and they nibbled at it slowly, unable to stop picking at the divine concoction. They were relaxed, they were happy, they were having such a memorably enjoyable evening when a waiter brought two glasses filled with a foaming orange liquid, and placed them in front of the brothers.

"We didn't order these," Viktor objected.

"No, sir. They're sent to you from the ladies over there," the waiter explained.

The brothers looked around, curious, until they spotted two young women alone at a table. The girls burst into giggles behind their hands. One of them gave a shy wave of her fingers. Viktor smiled in return and motioned to the empty chair at their table. The girls walked over. Both boys stood up; Viktor snatched another chair.

"Good evening, ladies! Won't you join us? We were just having dessert, but there's more than enough to go around."

Immediately, Sarah broke off a chunk of the delicacy with her fingers – a quarter of the entire thing – and dropped it on her plate. She stuffed a piece in her mouth, choking on it in her furious attempt to chew the oversized bite and swallow it quickly.

How could he! How could he invite them over? They were having such a good time! Only Dimi could ruin an evening that fast. How could Vik turn traitor, too? It wasn't *fair*! This was *her* choice of a place to visit! This was *her* turn to have fun!

Sarah pulled herself in smaller, glowering at the slab of dessert overhanging the edges of her plate. She made a pact to befriend it, a promise to eat the entire rich lump, despite the fact her stomach overflowed with her used-to-be-wonderful dinner. She poked a finger deep into the creamy middle and scooped out a gob, leaving a webby trail from the dish to her chin. She twirled the string of goo around her finger and vacuumed it clean with a smacking noise. Her eyes darted from brother to brother, waiting for reproof, but neither of them noticed. One of the girls wore heavy perfume that made Sarah's nose itch. No one noticed her sneeze.

The tall blonde wore a silver dress, high on the neck and short on the thigh. Honey-blonde hair fluffed back from her face in big feathery waves. Her companion was a blue-eyed brunette, long hair puffed up in soft curls that fell below her shoulders, and eyelashes too long for reality.

"What would bring two such beautiful ladies this far into space?" Viktor leaned forward on his elbows as if actually interested in the answer.

"We're on our way to a colony on Astra VI," the brunette replied. "We have a twelve-hour wait for our connecting flight. It's boring sitting in a flightroom all night, and you all looked like you were having a good time."

"We *were*," Sarah growled acidly.

"Twelve hours is a lot of time to kill," said the blonde. "We were hoping you wouldn't mind talking for a while."

"Not at all!" Dmitri said, studying the girls with more than polite interest.

The brunette flapped her long lashes at Viktor. "Are you from here, or just passing through as well?"

"Well, we're from Earth originally...," Viktor started, only to be cut off by the blonde.

"Oh *wow!* Imagine that! All the way out here!" She elbowed her companion. "I'm from Earth, too! Brell here's from the Martian Colonies. Have you ever been to Galveston?"

"I can't say I have," Dmitri said. "Where is that?"

"You've never been down south to Texas?!"

186

Dmitri thought hard. "I've heard of Texas. That's America, isn't it?"

"'Course it is!" the girl giggled. "I take it you're not from there?"

"Russian, through and through," Viktor said proudly. "We were the first Earth country to reach space, you know."

Sarah suffered through the unbearable pleasantries. After the briefest of introductions and two vacuous sentences directed solely at her, she ceased to exist. She kept her pact with the dessert – she ate all of it, right down to running her finger around the rim of the dish. Her stomach ached with overstuffing. She sat in pain, not a thing to do but listen to the foursome drone on about absolutely *nothing.*

"You two are so *cute!*" gushed the blonde. "Aren't they, Brell? Doesn't he have the most beautiful smile?"

Dmitri flushed red all the way to his ears. "It came with the package."

Sarah couldn't hold back a millisecond longer. "These are the uglier ones. There are five more at home who are much better."

"Five *more?*" Brell exclaimed. Sarah watched her count in her head. "Seven brothers? And only one sister? Why, you must be your momma's pride and joy!"

"Hardly," Sarah sneered. "There were six of us girls, of which I'm only number four, and my mother has been dead for years. *Ow!"* she exclaimed as something smashed her shin. "Vik! Dimi's kicking me!"

Dmitri leaned across the table and spoke softly in Russian. *"Viktor, take her back to your quarters and leave her there! I'll keep things going until you get back."*

Sarah folded her arms and gave the table a vicious scowl.

"That's not really fair to Sarah. Maybe we could all take a walk or something?"

"Five's a crowd, Vik! They didn't come here to baby-sit, you know what I mean? Just let her loose on the computer or something – not the commlink, though."

"Hahchu idti!" Sarah spat in reply. She wanted to leave. Even sitting on the awful observation deck was better than the verbal sugar flying around the table. Certainly Viktor preferred a girl with some intelligence?

"All right," Vik relented. "Come on." He held his hand out and Sarah seized it, nose high in the air. He excused himself to the ladies. "I have to run Sarah back to the room. It'll only take a minute. Don't go anywhere on me, now!"

Brell batted the broom-straw lashes. "Would you mind if I walked with you?"

Sarah's nostrils flared as if Brell had broke wind.

"That'd be great!" Viktor offered her his other hand. He winked at Dmitri as they left.

Sarah led the way, a good eight or ten meters ahead. A corridor from their destination, she stopped. Some things had to stay sacred; somewhere there had to be a safe haven where she still mattered, where she was the only girl allowed.

"I can take it from here," she announced. Dmitri never trusted her, but Vik would.

"You sure?" Viktor asked. "You remember the code?" He checked his chronometer. "It's 2100 now. Give me two hours, and I'll be back, okay?"

Hadn't she heard *that* line before! "Don't rush yourself," Sarah replied, not half as rudely as she'd intended. She fled down the corridor without looking back.

She lay on the floor of Viktor's cabin, an open book before her, but Sarah wasn't reading. Poking around the quarters, she found the book of poetry in the bottom of one of the closets. *Love* poems. She didn't know Vik liked mushy stuff like that. Some were okay, some flowery and grandiose, one or two had overly graphic symbolism. She'd read enough; she was bored now. Bored, angry, and hurt. Why should tonight be any different? Vlad would never do something like that; he'd never ask her to get lost like that. She couldn't even fault the boys this time. The girls forced their way into the group. The boys couldn't be rude in return; they were too old for that. They were almost grown-ups, and had to make nice. Sarah could have cried from rage, but she didn't feel any tears inside. She didn't know if that was a good sign or a bad one. She'd been okay these last two weeks, and when she thought about it, she still felt okay, as long as she didn't think about –

The *shushing* of the pneumatic door saved her from getting herself in trouble.

"Still up?" Viktor asked. "I didn't know if you'd be asleep."

Sarah sat up. "I ate too much." She waited for the inevitable, but he didn't seem to be in a hurry. "What are you doing back so early?"

Vik sat on the bench. "It's 2300. I said I'd be back. You want to go somewhere, or hang out here?"

"Where's your girl?"

"Brell? She was nice, wasn't she? We walked around a bit. I showed her some of the 'post, and then I told her I had to get back to you."

Sarah's forehead furrowed, trying to get the information straight. "You passed on a girl? To come back to *me*?"

"Mmhm. I already had guests. Girls come through here often enough. Some are friendly, some aren't. I haven't seen any of my family in three years. I don't want to miss a single minute. I told Dimi to stay longer if he wanted; I'd come back and keep you company."

Sarah stared at him, dumbfounded. Suddenly she knew where the missing tears were. The word *guilty* seared a path across her forehead. "I'm sorry."

"For what?"

"For everything I thought about you in the last two hours. I was very wrong. I thought you were just like Dimi, but you're not."

"Never was." He retrieved the acrylic game board from the shelf and placed it on the floor before her, sitting down opposite. "Let me show you a new game. I think you'll like it ..."

Dmitri appeared at five after eight the next morning, whistling a popular song and looking surprisingly bright.

"Well look who's back," Viktor mumbled over the rim of a cup of strong coffee.

"Good morning! Good morning!" Dmitri said with more cheer than he'd had in months. He braced himself as Sarah charged and started to hug him around his middle.

Before she could squeeze, Sarah caught scent of his clothes. *Sniff*, his chest. *Sniff*, his shoulder. Perfume. Heavy, sneezy girl's perfume overpowering his own scent. Sarah pulled back, hackles rising. Both hands shot out and shoved him hard in the chest before she fled with a furious growl, locking herself in the tiny bathroom.

Dmitri dropped into the chair across the desk from his brother. "What's her problem?"

Viktor put his cup down. "You don't suppose it's because you didn't come home last night."

Dmitri rubbed his eyes. "So? You were with her."

"Yeah, but she expected you back at some point, too. You couldn't have found a 'com and told her you'd be out late, or at least left a message?"

"The girl and I hit it off. I didn't think I needed to watch the time. Wasn't that the point of you staying with her?"

"Dimi, she was up most of the night, worried about you! I don't mind watching her for you. You want to take a couple of days, I'll get you a separate cabin and you can do your own thing; go right ahead. But you can't leave her hanging like that. You complain she's overreactive, but you disappear like that – it's not fair to her. Just *tell* her if you're going to be gone like that, that's all."

"Yes, *Mother*, next time I'll call."

Viktor grinned. "And my ass you were just talking!"

The comment met with an obscene gesture. "Since when did you become a telepath? Does that happen out here in deep space, or are you picking up on Sarah's paranoia?"

189

Vik pushed his brother's head to the side. "Because I saw the length of those nails, and you didn't have those scratches during dinner. If she'd been any friendlier, they would have made you leave the restaurant. Where'd you go, the observation deck?"

Dmitri blushed hard. There was never any fooling Viktor. "I'm an adult now. I don't have to answer to you anymore." He grabbed Viktor's cup and took a swallow, making a horrible face when he discovered unsweetened coffee instead of tea.

"*Ugh!* How can you *drink* that?"

"Wakes you up, doesn't it?" Vik waited.

"We... never made it that far."

Vik glanced behind to make sure Sarah was still in hiding. He leaned close. "Struck out? I don't believe it! *Man!* You could *feel* the heat coming off her every time she looked at you!"

"I didn't say that." Dmitri raised his eyebrows incorrigibly. "You know that public lavatory on the hall across from the lounge?" He held up three guilty fingers and wiggled them.

Three times?! Viktor mouthed. "No way! The blonde?"

"The blonde!"

"Oooh! She was all legs, too..."

Any further discussion was cut short by the bathroom door opening. Sarah flew out, waspish, heading for the door with a murderous scowl. She moved sideways just close enough to swing a kick at Dmitri, but he snatched a wrist. She pulled back, squealing at the unwanted contact.

"Look, I'm sorry about last night," he said. "Vik's right, I probably should have told you I'd be out late. I figured it didn't matter since you were with him. I'm sorry if I upset you."

Sarah growled and swung her other fist upwards, smashing his elbow backwards.

Dmitri let go with a curse. Sarah fled the cabin.

"Let me get her," Vik said. "I'll smooth it out. Go scrub that grin off your face."

Sarah hadn't run far, sitting in the corridor a dozen or so meters from the room. Her head rested on her knees. "Please let me be," she whispered.

Vik sucked his lower lip. He shook his head slowly. "*Nyet.* Not this time. I don't know what's between you and Dimi, but watching you two I feel like you're hiding something. Dimi told me some of where you've been, things you've done. I want the truth. What's really going on, Sar? Walk with me." He held out a hand. "We need to talk."

"That will depend on the questions," she warned him.

They gave Dmitri six hours to catch some sleep, then Vik cornered him in the tiny bathroom. There was just enough room for two people to stand, if they didn't move. Dimi couldn't escape.

He dried off under the heat lamp and stretched around his brother for his clothes. "Do you mind? I didn't realize you missed my ass that much."

Viktor ignored him, face set with an unmistakable harshness. "We need to have a serious discussion. We need to talk about Sarah."

Dmitri met the baleful gaze with a forceful one of his own as he struggled to pull his clothes on in the cramped space. "I would *love* to talk to you about Sarah. I'm *desperate* to talk to you about Sarah. I've been trying to talk to you for *three days*, but I can't do it in her presence and she's not about to leave either one of us alone long enough for me to say anything. Find a way for us to talk without her, and *soon*. We're almost out of time."

He squeezed past Vik, leaving him even more mystified.

Twenty-seven

Viktor had to think a while on that one. A place where Sarah could see but not hear them, a place where she could keep busy for at least an hour. The poolside lounge off the gymnasium, he decided. The full-spectrum lighting approximated that of a yellow star, tall palms and flowering plants flourished in monstrous tubs, and there were numerous tables where off-duty personnel went to relax and feel more planet-bound. She'd be able to see them, but not really hear. Swimming made Sarah nervous, but the wide shallow end would give her security. He explained the situation, didn't give her a choice, and she accepted his reasoning. Sarah swam.

"Dimi, I had a long talk with Sarah, and I don't like what she told me," Vik started. "Are you crazy? You claim she's mentally unstable, but you bring her to bars? You take her gambling in places so disgusting you shave her head, afraid she might be attacked? What the hell were you thinking!"

"I agree, I've probably done some stupider things, but look at it from my side, too! I deserve a little rest and recreation now and then. I've been with that kid night and day for two and a half years. I've done all the *right* things, too! It's not easy, Vik. It's not easy living with someone who's not always there." Dmitri tapped a finger against his temple. "And I mean as in, 'not of this space and time continuum'!"

"You knew what you were getting into when you took her on," Viktor said sharply. "I have yet to see any evidence of these – *problems* – you keep talking about. She's the exact same kid."

"No! No, I did not know! Not entirely. She was great when we visited her in the hospital, all chirpy like yesterday. Even at her worst, hearing voices and shredding herself, I thought I'd seen it all. But I didn't know half of her. Katya did, but I never thought to ask, like the fear of being left alone, or the fact she doesn't sleep more than four hours a night, or that she can get so depressed she won't eat. I won't even mention the Vlad withdrawal..."

"So why not take her ho...?"

"Look, you want to chew my ass out about where we've been, do that with her around. I've got bigger fish biting me in the ass that are a *hell* of a lot more important, and I *can't* say it in front of her!"

Viktor raised his palms in peace. "Fine. What's eating you, then? You never told me why the big delay in getting here. What's so hush-hush?"

Dmitri turned away. "I *can't* talk about it. It's not really a secret – not from her, anyway. It just upsets her too much. I told her she's not allowed to think about it."

Vik leaned closer, curious. "What is it?"

Dmitri focused on the cream and blue tabletop, scratched by years of use. He needed help, Sarah needed help, but he couldn't bring himself to talk about it, not even to Vik. It was too damned embarrassing.

"What is it?" Vik repeated, poking Dimi's arm with a knuckle. "We're best friends. You know I won't breathe a word."

"I know that. It's just that – *aw, Vik!* It was just so freakin' horrible! You've *got* to help me! *Please!* I can't go through that again! I *can't!*"

"Close your eyes and spit it out," Viktor said quietly. "Whatever it is, I'll do anything I can. You have my word."

"Don't tell her I told you, whatever you do."

"Not a word."

Pain crossed Dmitri's face, and he sighed with a whimper. "Two months ago, the same damned day we were leaving for here, Sarah ...." He rolled his hands around, trying to get them to convey what his tongue didn't want to say. "She got that – *girl* thing."

"Girl thing?"

"Don't do that to me! You have *no idea* what I've been through! You know! *The girl thing!* Every month...?"

"Oh. *That* girl thing." Vik shrugged, unimpressed. "She's what – almost twelve? Did she know about it? I mean, did you ever warn her or anything?"

Dmitri leaped from the chair. *"NO!* Someone should have warned *me!*" He sat down, tormented. "I mean, yeah, after it happened I asked her, and she said yes, so Kat or somebody must have told her, but... "

"She's growing up. Puberty happens. I don't understand."

"Vik! Watch me!" Sarah waved from the pool, ten meters away. She dove and did a clumsy handstand in only one meter of water.

"That's great!" Vik called when she surfaced. "Straighten your legs more. Point your toes."

"Stay out from under the water!" Dimi yelled. "You'll get water in your lungs!" Sarah splashed at them and tried the handstand again.

"Because mentally, she's a basket case," Dmitri insisted. "She can't handle it. Remember how she used to walk around the edge of the kitchen whenever she went in? You know why? Because *she* was the one who found Mother bleeding to death, and she was avoiding the spot on the floor because six months later she still saw the blood! You have *no idea* what she's really like."

"Valeria said once she was having some trouble. She took her to a hospital, but she was coming home the next day. She seems like a normal kid."

Dmitri suppressed the urge to crawl across the table and choke his brother. "*Normal?* That *normal* kid spent three *months* in a psycho hospital because she tried to crack her head open to let the voices out! Read her medical file! Printed out, it's a decimeter thick! Take a good look at her, Vik! A *real* good look! Look at her scalp – right here at the hairline." Dimi pulled his own hair back, pointing. "Look carefully at her arms. Look close at her face. Every one of those scars is by her *own hand*, Vik!"

Dmitri took a deep breath and calmed himself. "She can't handle the thought of growing up. And you know what scares her most, what she can't handle most of all? *Blood.* Seeing Mother hemorrhage, seeing Marina born, cracked her mind. She even avoids the color red. You see what I'm trying to say?"

Sarah kicked the sheet back and jumped out of bed. Today they were leaving on the two-week trip to see Viktor. Today they would leave the beautiful hotel that had brought nothing but nightmares.

Dimi exited the bathroom. "Hey Sar? Do you want…" He stopped, frowning. "What the… ?"

He stared, trying to figure out what he saw. "Ohmigods."

"What? What's the matter?"

Dmitri continued to stare, speechless. He'd heard of it, but never knew any girl admit to it, had certainly never seen it for himself. Guys snickered about it in locker rooms, joked about it at parties. He'd forgotten it happened at all.

Sarah followed his gaze downwards. The insides of her thighs were red, the soft, natural fibers of her pajama shorts soggy.

She touched her leg, eyes flying open in paralyzing surprise at the redness on her fingertips. Realization set in, and with it a building panic. She dug harder with her left hand, only to come up with the same results. Her mind collapsed inward. Dimi could see it, almost hear it, slamming shut with the force of a quadrium emergency door, her mind knowing nothing but the stain on her fingers.

*"No," started as a whisper. "No! **No**! **NO**!" she shrieked, and the scream didn't stop.*

*"I'm going to die!" Sarah clawed at him, shaking so convulsively she couldn't stand. She locked her eyes on his, truly believing what she thought was imminent. "**I'm going to die!**"*

"What did you do?" Viktor asked, unsettled.

Dmitri rested his forehead in his hand. He'd gotten the secret out in the open; it wasn't so hard to talk about it now.

"I dragged her into the shower, screaming, and held her there. I didn't know what the hell else to do. I have no idea how long we stood there, clothes and all. A half hour, an hour, until she started to see other things besides blood. I left her in there and made her give me her clothes. I threw them away."

"She calm down after that?"

"For a little while," Dimi said lifelessly. "I mean, she knows more about it than I do, but that's not saying much, I think."

Sarah sat on the cushy chair with wet hair and clean clothes, silent, unmoving. She stared straight ahead, keeping her mind as empty as possible.

After a while, she wrapped her arms around her middle and bent forward, whimpering. Dmitri knelt next to her, hand on her shoulder.

"It's only for a couple days, right? We'll get through it. You'll get used to it."

"No." Sarah let herself fall to the floor in a ball, holding her middle. She rocked, she stretched, she kicked, then curled back up, moaning.

*"Dimi!" she cried as a new unimaginable terror took over. "It's a baby! I'm going to have a baby and die. I don't want to die, Dimi! **Don't let me die**!"*

*"Sar, unless there's some major secret you're not telling me, you're **not** having a baby." Her belly was as flat as ever. She couldn't be having a baby. Wasn't*

194

*that the whole point of this thing? "You do **not** have a baby!"*

"Baby!" Sarah shrieked, arching her back and letting forth a hair-curling scream. "I'm going to die!"

*"Stop it! That's ridiculous! **There's no baby!** You are **not dying!**" He put a hand over her mouth, trying to stuff the noise back in.*

Sarah would not be convinced. She curled into a ball and with a hopeless wail dug her nails into her cheeks and squeezed. He had no choice but to fight her for the hands.

Viktor shook his head. "Whew!"

"That was just the *first* day. Did you know it gets worse on the second?"

"Vik, did you see me?" Sarah climbed out and wiped her face on a towel on the seat next to him. "I did four whole laps on my back without stopping!" She wore a sleek black swimsuit, cut high and wide in the back to cover as much flesh as possible. The color did its best to hide the changes, but it couldn't erase them. In profile, the top of the suit didn't lie flat by any means; the middle narrowed pleasantly, the bottom curved out over hip bones and ended in a pert heart-shaped backside. The tomboy was shape-shifting, with or without her approval.

Vik smiled as if nothing were wrong. He took her wet hand, swinging her arm childishly as his eyes traveled up it. His heart sank as he noted the forest of faint white lines on the inside of her arm. He pushed her hair backwards as if keeping water from her face, seeing the thicker white scar hiding underneath. For the first time he noticed the faint marks on the fair cheeks, the same width as fingernails.

"Those were short laps, though. Bet you can't do them the long way."

Sarah wavered. "It says seven meters at the other end. I don't like water that deep."

He squeezed the hand. "You can do it. Take the lane near the edge. I can always dive in after you. Go on. Dimi and I are still talking."

Sarah walked back to the pool.

"A credit if you jump in at the two-meter mark," he called. Sarah stood at the edge, gathering courage.

Vik tried to look on the bright side. "Well, at least you had an idea it would happen again. It shouldn't have been such a surprise."

Dimi stared as if boring Vik new eyesockets. *"How!* How am I supposed to know? It's not like you can tell by looking at them! I mean, when you think about it, there was Mother, and the twins, and Katya – we never knew."

"Can you really go through life that unobservant? You could always tell if Kat had it – she'd walk around holding her stomach, and sometimes when it got real bad she'd throw up. I used to cover for her so she could lie down until her pills kicked in."

"Pills?" Dmitri said stupidly.

"Yeah. They take pills for the bellyaches and stuff. It evens out some body chemical."

"I thought Katya threw up so she wouldn't get fat?"

"Well, yeah, she did that, too," Vik agreed, "but that was different. The point is, if Sarah can't remember, *you* need to."

Dmitri sank into depression again. "I don't think it would have mattered. By the time she recovered, she got it again. The second time was worse. I'm a horrible person, Vik," he confessed.

The screams, the endless screams... The other patrons of the low-life building they'd moved to banging on the paper-thin walls and cursing them something awful, stuffing her with sleeping pills that she fought so hard against they made her only groggy, but they eased the screams. Trying to explain it to the law officer at the door.

"I didn't want to do it, I *never* would have otherwise, but I hadn't slept in two days, and I was afraid of what she'd do if I did. I had to sleep, Vik! I tried not to hurt her, honest. Please don't think bad of me. But she tried to dig her eyes out of her head so she couldn't see it."

It was Viktor's turn to look uneasy. Sarah'd been battered enough for one lifetime. "You hit her?"

"No. I couldn't do that." Dmitri braced for a brutal retort. Though Sarah never mentioned it, the guilt ate at him. "I – I tied her up."

Two days he'd held onto her, day and night. Sarah was determined to destroy herself, smashing her head, stabbing herself with whatever she could grab, unable to care for herself, and then he caught her trying to gouge her eyes out.

It took him an hour and a half to cut her nails, wrestling her struggling, screaming form face down on the bed. His hand hadn't recovered; the constant battles left it weak and painful. He struggled to bend the arms backward, one at a time, fighting to squeeze the fingers open, then cutting the nails to spare her face more wounds.

He could tell by the vacancy in the terrified eyes that she wouldn't hear anything he said, but he told her anyway, knowing he deserved to be punished for what he was about to do. It certainly didn't fall under the term care. *She wasn't an animal! She was just scared. He shook the cover from his pillow and wrestled the hands into it, wrapping the drawstring from his pants around the wrists, bagging the prying fingers.*

"I'm sorry," *he kept apologizing. "I can't think of any other way I can sleep and keep you from hurting yourself at the same time. I'm so damned* tired, *Sar! I just can't stay awake any more. If that's too tight, tell me, and I'll loosen it. I swear, it's just while I catch a little sleep. If you need to get up, just wake me and I'll undo you, I promise. I'm sorry!" Using the belt he wore his knives on, he bound her feet.*

"I'm sorry," he repeated, looping the curtain-tie through her locked arms and knotting it to his own wrist. He put a pillow under her head, dropped his arm over her, and fell heavily asleep.

"*Man!*" Viktor whispered in awe. "What do you want to do? Take turns or something?"

"You said you have some ins with the medical department."

"Yeah, I got a couple friends there."

Dmitri gripped his brother's arm. "Then help me! There's got to be a way to stop that thing. There's nothing they can't fix nowadays. It's her only hope!"

"Sure, they can stop it," Vik agreed. "It's also known as birth control, and eleven-year-old girls don't just walk in and request to be put on it without someone asking why. You tell me what will happen if a young stud traveling with a very young girl brings her to a doctor requesting birth control. Think!"

"She's my goddamned *sister*, Vik!"

"Do you think the med department gives a damn who she is?"

"What about for psychiatric reasons? That's the whole point!"

Viktor waved his hands wide. "Prove it. They'll review her records, but they'll want to observe the behavior for themselves. You're looking at one, probably two or three separate psychiatric exams, as well as a physical. Will she go for that? If she's flipping out that bad, they may hold her."

A large splash came up and over the side of the pool, within six meters of where the brothers sat. "I did it!" Sarah yelled from the water. "Did you guys see me? You owe me a credit, Vik!"

Vik waved back. "That was great! I told you you could do it!"

"No." Dimi was adamant. "If she feels trapped like that, I'm telling you, she'll hurt herself good. She'll do something horrible to try and stop it on her own. She'd rather die than go through that, so what's she got to lose?"

Viktor sighed, worry bearing down on him. Now he understood

Dmitri's strain, Sarah's edginess and the fake smile ten times the size of anything he'd ever seen her give.

"Even if I could get around all that, they won't do it for someone under sixteen, fourteen the very youngest. Let me work on it. There's one or two people I might be able to ask, but I'm warning you, it won't be easy."

"She *will* kill herself," Dmitri repeated.

* * *

Dmitri leaned back in the desk chair in his brother's quarters, bare feet on either side of the computer screen, watching a program he'd called up. Sarah raided the computer at the other desk. "You ever see this?" he asked above the noise of laser fire. "*Commando Squad of Lambda Xi*. The battle scenes are pretty good."

"Sounds like a fraternity club," Sarah said absently. As a follow-up to her tour of the Outpost's power plant, she was reading a biography on Campbell Davies and his efforts to develop the early space warp engine. Davies, too, had been a bit of a prodigy, changing the physics of space travel at the age of twenty-six. The current chapter dealt heavily with quantum physics and theoretical math, and she had to think. She liked living civilized again. Outside of blue skies, green grass and sunsets, the Outpost had a lot to offer: security, variety, entertainment, culture, diversity – she could stay a year and not run out of things to learn.

She glanced up when the door opened, and Viktor returned.

Dmitri exchanged a longer, questioning glance.

Vik nodded. *All systems go.*

Dmitri shut the program off and stood up.

"Sar?" Viktor asked. "Can we talk with you?"

Sarah twisted the chair around happily, only to drop her head and turn away a moment later. "Yeah, I guess."

Viktor laughed. "What's the face for? We haven't said anything yet."

Sarah eyed him sideways from under her bangs. "Because I know that look you just had. When Dimi looks like that, it means he's going to ask me something he wants to do that I won't like, but I'm supposed to be nice and say yes anyway."

"It's nothing like that," he assured her, and dragged over a chair.

Viktor cleared his throat. He sucked his lip for several seconds. "Dimi and I were talking, … and … he … told me about your upcoming … *problem*, and… "

Sarah paled whiter than the overhead lighting.

"*What?*" She stared at Dmitri, betrayed to the core. "How *could* you! How could you talk about me like that!" Now Viktor would know she was tainted, that she was ripe for breeding purposes and about to die. *It wasn't fair!* Her hands shot to her shortened hair, twisting and pulling. "You had no right to talk about my privacy like that!"

Dmitri slid onto the edge of the desk. "Vik thinks he can help."

"No!" Sarah fled the chair, pushing through Viktor's outstretched arm. She paced the rooms, tugging her hair.

"It's none of your damned business!" she shouted. "It's *my* problem, and you had *no right* to talk about me like that! *That's* what you didn't want me to hear! I hate you!"

Sarah threw herself on a bed and pulled up her knees. She squeezed her head hard, then banged her wrists on her temples.

"Hey! Hey! Stop that!" Viktor hurried over, pulling the hands down. "Stop it! Come on." Sarah pulled away, curling smaller.

"Who takes care of Sarah when she's hurt? Hmm?" He poked her with a finger. "Hmm?"

Sarah squirmed. "Viktor."

"And who takes care of Sarah when she's sick? Who sits up with her and stays with her until she feels better?"

"Vik."

The exchange stung Dmitri in the heart. "And what am I? Recycled fuel?"

Viktor flashed a dirty look and waved for him to shut up. "That's right," he said to Sarah. "And right now, I see someone I care about who's afraid, and hurting, and I want to help her, if she'd just trust me. If she'll tell me just a *little* more about it, I really think I might be able to help."

Sarah shook her head and tried to melt into the tiny seam between the bed and the wall. "She can't."

"What if... What if I have Dimi take a walk and we can talk, just you and me alone, hmm? Just like old times?"

"Great!" Dmitri sneered. "I do all the dirty work, and then it's 'Get lost, Dimi! We don't need you'..."

"I'll talk with you after," Viktor promised. "Please, 'Mitya. *Pozhal'sta.*"

Dmitri glowered, but he slid his feet into his shoes under the desk. "I'll be back. *Traitor.*" At home, it had been the worst possible insult, meaning you'd sold out and were in league with Father.

Vik tried to turn Sarah to face him, but she stiffened and pulled away with a cry.

"Come on," he coaxed. "I know a little about what you're going through. Who do you think took care of Katya when she had those problems?"

Sarah's eyes brimmed with unshed tears. *"You? She did?"*

"Me." Viktor moved her again, and this time she allowed herself to be slid next to him, his arm around her. She buried her face against his strong side.

"It won't do any good," she sniffed, rubbing her nose on a knuckle. "I can't talk about it."

"Then let me talk. I think I can help, Sar, but it won't be easy. Let me explain first, then you can tell me what you think."

* * *

Sarah shuffled into the sickbay the next day, drowning in cold sweat. Viktor had gone over what she might expect, the people she would meet, the kinds of questions they would ask. The prize for cooperating would be life itself. She felt like vomiting, curling into a ball, and crying for the next month, but the doctors would probably prevent the latter two.

She sat between the boys in the doctor's office, crunching their strong hands with her trembling ones. She focused on her breathing, trying to make each breath exactly the same length and depth as the one before. Someone spoke to her; she tried to pay attention.

"...some questions," Dr. Cronan said. "We'll measure your physiological reactions – pulse, temperature, blood pressure. It's completely painless."

Sarah fixed on his hands, smooth, narrow hands that bore a single silver ring. Father's hands had been huge, rough and callused from working in dirt and rocks. Unless Mother scrubbed them herself – which she did for important occasions – his nails were always dirty.

"You don't believe me," Sarah mumbled in a far-away voice. "You want to make sure I'm not lying. I could have graduated school two years ago, but no one thinks I'm smart enough to make a decision for myself. Why? Why does everyone think Dimi lies?"

Dr. Cronan raised an eyebrow. "I'm not exactly comfortable with this, either. As a patient of mine, I'm responsible for keeping your interests at the forefront. No matter what your intellect or educational experience, Miss Kirushenko, you are far below any possible age for legally informed consent. Hell, I'm not convinced your 'guardian' isn't," he coughed. "If this has been a cyclical problem, I don't see a need to rush into a treatment this very second. Let's wait a week, see what develops, and we can treat it as necessary."

Viktor sat forward. "As I explained ..."

"She won't survive another one!" Dmitri interrupted. "She knows when it happens before I do. There's no guarantee I can intervene before she does something drastic. We can't risk that, even for a minute."

The doctor sighed unhappily. "Let's not pretend here. By statute, I can't prescribe these drugs for someone her age without a team medical review. I would lose my license. I know you, Viktor. I know you wouldn't ask me this without a good reason. I reviewed the transcript and I see where such problems could occur. That's the only reason I'm even considering this. Answer my questions so I can rest easy as to the situation, then Qara here," he nodded at the nurse in the office, "will give you a preliminary exam. If I feel the results are satisfactory, I'll approve the medication. Is that clear?"

Sarah nodded, eyeing the unfamiliar monitoring device on the desk before her.

Vik squeezed her hand and gave her a peck on the forehead. "We'll be right outside."

Sarah clung to his hand with all her might. "NO! Don't leave me!"

"I'm sorry," the doctor insisted. "They have to wait outside. I need your answers, and yours alone."

"Leave the door open," Sarah pleaded. Doctors couldn't be trusted. They held too much power. They could force medications and procedures and restraints on her without her okay, all in the name of 'treatment.' Someone had to be there to speak for her when the doctors stopped listening. *"Please!"*

Cronan gave in. "Okay, but you have to keep your eyes forward. The machine reads pupillary responses, and you can't be looking behind you."

"We'll be right there. You'll do fine," Vik assured her.

Sarah shrank back in the chair, awaiting the first unholy question.

The nurse led them to a private exam room, making eyes at Viktor. "This won't take long. If I can ask you men to wait outside…" She ran a hand across his shoulder and steered him toward the door.

"NO!" Sarah was off the exam table in a flash, pulling at Viktor with both hands. "Don't leave me! I can't do it! Dimi, no!"

"You want your brothers in here with you? A big girl like you? There's nothing to it. It won't hurt a bit, I promise." She put a friendly hand on Sarah's arm.

Hands equaled restraint, restraint equaled panic. Sarah bolted for the door, only to be clotheslined by Dmitri. He held her by the face, forcing her to look at him.

"Stop! You *can* do this. The cure can't be any worse than what we've been through. You don't want that again, do you?"

"No?" she groaned. She wanted no part of either one.

Vik took her hand. "Come on. I'll stay if you want. Qara and I are old friends. I trust her. Come on." He led her back to the table. "Go ahead, Dim. I'll stay with her."

Dimi went to wait in the hall. "Fine! You can get ripped up for once. Don't say I didn't warn you."

Sarah held still for the blood sample. As long as she didn't have to see it, she didn't care. Let them bleed her dry. She fought the next request.

"You have to lie down," Qara insisted, a diagnostic scanner in her hand. "I can't get accurate readings unless you do."

It took several minutes of convincing for Sarah to cooperate. Lying down left her vulnerable.

"Height, 164 centimeters," Qara read off the scanner display. "You've got, oh, maybe another three or four centimeters before you stop. Weight, 62.2 kilos."

"Fifty-six!" Sarah objected hotly.

Qara smiled. "I'm afraid not. Sixty-two it is. That's still just about perfect."

Dmitri leaned against the wall outside the exam room doors. He could hear a louder objection now and then, but he let it slide. The noise rose to a warning wail, and he fought to hold himself back when the screaming began. He ran a nervous hand through his hair.

Vik can handle her. He knows the people here. Only after the doctor ran past into the room did he dash in to meet chaos.

Viktor struggled to hold her, his back to the wall, while Sarah kicked viciously at the nurse. The doctor adjusted an aeroderm and moved in.

Dmitri blocked the way. "NO! *No tranquilizers!* Put that away!" He spun around to pull at Viktor. "Let go of her! You're making her worse!" Freed, Sarah dropped to the floor, hands locked over her head.

"*What the hell are you doing?*" Dmitri demanded of the room.

The doctor shook his head. "I'm sorry, Viktor. I can't do this. This isn't a single obsessive problem. There's more here than that. She needs a complete mental evaluation. If we take care of the mental illness, we might solve the secondary problem in the process. I can't help you without more workup."

Vik blocked the exit. "Doctor Cronan – Perry – *please*! This is exactly what…"

"What do you mean, *no*?" Dmitri said. "What kind of a doctor are you! You upset her like this and leave her hanging? *You're* the one causing her to act like this! You and your unfounded perverted accusations! You promised her help, and now you abandon her? You've aggravated the problem! *She needs those drugs!* She'll be *fine* if you just give her them! I've seen how they do those things. If you won't do it, I'll do it myself!" Dmitri's dark eyes burned with fire. Legal or not, he was her official guardian. No one would terrorize his sister like that, not while he was around. "Vik, you know how to work a skin closer?"

Vik held a hand out to stop him. "Dimi, please! Deal with her. Let me handle this. Perry, I thought we agreed ..."

Sarah lay curled on Viktor's bed, sobbing into his pillow, as she had for the last three hours. Vik went out, then came back, as quiet as before. Now they just sat like a funeral.

The door gave a soft chime, and Vik jumped up to hit the release. The nurse from the morning entered, a rolled package in her hand. To his brother's amazement, Viktor grasped her shoulders and planted a long kiss on her lips. "Thank you."

Qara didn't seem surprised at all. "You owe me, Vik. Like you can't imagine."

"You name it. Anything at all." He led her to the sleeping area, hand in hand.

He rubbed the sobbing back. "Hey, Sar? We got it."

Qara unrolled the medical kit. She gazed sadly at the bed. "You weren't kidding, what you told me.

"It will only take a minute," she said louder, picking out equipment. "Come'ere, Hon." She tried to adjust the girl's position on the bed, but Sarah shot out from under her hands with a cry.

Dmitri knelt next to Viktor at the bedside. "It's your last chance, Sar. Now or never. Vik and I trust her. We're right here to protect you." Sarah gave a warning whine when the strange woman exposed her hip and applied anesthesia, but Dimi held her, whispering.

Qara explained as she sterilized the site with an ultra-violet shield. "This is an older medication, but it should still work fine. We use it so rarely no one will notice a set missing. Bonescan showed she's almost at her full height, so you won't have to worry about growth deficiencies. I'll give you a list of side effects to watch for, but I don't think she'll have any problems. Hold still, Hon. You'll feel a little pressure, but I promise it won't hurt. One. Two. Three. Four. And five," she counted off, loading an instrument five times and pressing it with a pop against the girl's numbed hip. One by one, the instrument made a small puncture and slipped a tiny, flexible tubule of medication into the fat layer. The nurse wiped the five wounds, then ran a skin sealer over them, leaving virtually no trace of the surgery.

"All done," she said, covering the hip and rubbing the spot. "That should be good for five years. No cycles, no bleeding, no fertility. Any problems, though, it *has* to come out," she emphasized to Dmitri. "Don't fool around. Maybe by then you can get a more personalized medication." She rolled the instruments back up in her kit. "And never, *ever* tell how you got it."

"Tell what?" Vik assured her. "It was just a follow-up, but we can't thank you enough."

Qara met his gaze. "I know you can't."

"Hey, Dim? You okay with her? You mind if I walk with Qara a bit?"

Dmitri winked at his brother with a sly half-smile. "Don't let us stop you. We'll be fine."

Dmitri pounced when Vik returned. "You've got a lot of explaining to do, Viktor-Maxim Alexandrovitch! That was no goddamned handshake you gave her. Out with it!"

Viktor blushed, a shy little smile breaking out. "We – had a thing once. We were pretty serious for a while."

Dmitri hung on every word. *"Pretty serious?!* I should hope so, with a greeting like that. I take it you and her were, uh …?"

Viktor blushed anew. "I'm not like you, 'Mitya. I'm not trying to prove myself. I don't have to brag about everything I do."

"Come on! You owe me *something* I can turn into legend about you! You already made me spill my guts." Dimi blocked Viktor every time he tried to step away. *"Talk* to me, man!"

Vik grinned. *"Made* you? If I'd waited one more second, your guts would have exploded all over! If you must know, yes. We had a full-fledged hot and sweaty affair. We were getting serious. *Too* serious. We started talking about commitments, and one morning I woke up with cold feet. I was twenty-two years old, about to be transferred, and we didn't know if she'd be able to move with me. I still wanted to get back home at some point, too. I chickened out. I backed off. We… haven't been together for a month now." He sighed as if still weighing the decision.

Dmitri's longest relationship to date had been his four weeks with Hila, and he'd never considered it to be a long-term arrangement at all. "Self-preservation, man," he reasoned. "Sometimes you have to put yourself first. Why put all that energy into something that's just going to cause you heartache?"

"It wasn't even that. I just… I started thinking about things, you know? About Father and Mother, and watching them go crazy with all of us, remembering Father tearing his hair out over getting grants and contracts and putting all his hopes on things that never materialized, and taking it out on us. It scared me. I just… I don't know if I did the right thing. I'm definitely not over her, but I can't stay in my position any longer. What do you think?"

"About her?" The girl was pretty enough, with wavy dark hair, a pretty smile, and flawless skin the color of coffee with extra cream. "A little broad in the aft for my taste, but I wouldn't mind getting my hands on her upper decks. She seems nice enough. She must still have something big for you, to risk her career like that."

Vik nodded, lost in thought. "We talked a bit tonight. I think we might make another go at it, slower this time, maybe not so intense."

He glanced at his brother. "I can't get her out of my mind."

Twenty-eight

Threat of death gone, Sarah blossomed back into herself. Viktor spent the days with them, but he disappeared each night for several hours with Qara. Sarah started to say something, but the vicious glare she got from Dmitri made her stop. She'd have to ask Vik when Dimi wasn't around. Vik would return to duty in two days, and Dimi toyed with places to go next.

Today Vik had arranged to take them to the station's armory. Every officer and crewman aboard the station had a personally issued EPSAR hand weapon for combat needs, but no one carried them under routine conditions. The big guns – plasma cannons, energy rifles, amplification pods, microwave disruptor grenades, magnetic field particle-bombs – were all stored in the armory, and best of all, Vik promised to take them target shooting in the galleries.

"I guarantee you've never seen one of these up close," Viktor teased. He tapped a code on a locked cabinet in his quarters and took out a palm-sized hand weapon. "It's still off limits to private citizens. On the right setting, it can vaporize an enemy at one hundred meters. Slide it into an amplifier and you triple the range."

Sarah grabbed for it. "Orbital! A real EPSAR!"

Dmitri shoved her away and seized the weapon. "Think again! The last thing we need is you accidentally blasting a hole in the Outpost."

"I wouldn't do that!"

"The hand unit's not strong enough for that," Viktor assured them. "We're shielded against energy weapons, and alarms would go off if you tried. This is your setting adjustment," he showed them. "This here is the trigger. Here, take it. The safety's on."

Dmitri hefted the slim oval and took to it immediately. He held it at arm's length and squinted to sight it, taking pretend shots at various objects around the room.

"Let me try!" Sarah begged, beside herself with anticipation of exploring something wonderful. "I know what it stands for! Electron Particle Stimulation and Amplification Ray … "

Dmitri held it out of reach. "No way."

"*Please?* Please, Vik? Just for a minute? I promise not to mess with it!"

"Hang on." Viktor popped a panel off the back and shook out a wide, thick power cell, a third the size of the weapon. "There. It's empty. No power, perfectly safe."

"Cosmically stellar!" Sarah accepted the weapon with reverence. She turned it over and over, examining every centimeter before pretending to fire. "What's its power source? How long does a charge last? Do you have to carry extra power cells with you, or is there a way to recharge it? What's the refractory time? Does it have a recoil? How does the safety work? What about magnetic interference? Will you let me fire it for real?"

Viktor laughed. "One question at a time! Come on. I'll take you to the gallery and you can fire one. As it happens, I may be a Class III specialist, but I've got a Level I marksman's citation, so I can show you a few tricks."

Dmitri snatched the weapon away. "That's the last thing she needs to learn."

Sarah skipped and pranced along deck nine in her eagerness to get to the armory. Lift J was already in sight when every other overhead light panel turned red and began to flash. Sarah froze at the color, afraid she was the only one who saw it, but Viktor and Dimi were staring up in wonder, too. A whooping squawk made her cover her ears.

"All hands, Red Alert. Repeat, Red Alert. This is not a drill. Enemy vessels approaching. Repeat, this is not a drill. All hands to battle stations. We are at Red Alert. All hands to battle stations. Conflict imminent." The urgent voice blared from unseen speakers as a nerve-shattering siren rose and fell.

"What is it?!" Sarah cried out, searching the ceiling for an answer.

Viktor looked almost as frightened. "Red Alert! *How?* We haven't had a hostile ship within fifty million k's in over a year. I have to get to my post!" He walked backwards down the corridor as crewmen ran past.

"Get back to my quarters!" he ordered Dmitri. "Stay by the comm, and I'll let you know when all is clear. You'll be safe there. Go!" He turned to run. Up and down the corridor before them, microscopic shimmers appeared in the air, as if eyes were short-circuiting. Somehow, someone was using a moley-beam to enter the station outside of the energy-transport room. It shouldn't have been possible; there were shields to prevent such things. The shimmers solidified into a dozen bulky Burin-Jai warriors, their twisted yellow faces reflected in their black battle armor. Gloved fists clenched energy blasters, while blade weapons stuck out at the ready from sheathing built into the thigh plates.

With an inhuman howl, the forwardmost invader charged at the stunned Outpost personnel in the corridor. The blasters aimed but wouldn't fire; some of the station's security measures still functioned. Bladed weapons were drawn, flashed. Someone shrieked in pain.

"RUN!" Vik screamed at Dmitri above the blaring klaxon and shouts of combat. "GO!"

Viktor jumped into the fray, aiding a crewman grappling with a Burin-Jai. He grabbed the warrior from behind, the inside of his arm squeezing the warty throat.

Dmitri stared incredulously at the scene, starting to back up, starting to run, but Sarah stepped forward in the crazy flashing red light, oblivious to the danger.

"Vik?" she called, *flash/red* unwilling to leave when he might need her help. *flash/warning* She always helped him when he was in trouble. If they were running *flash/danger* he needed to come, too. "Vik!" *flash*

"Sarah! Come on! Let's go! Let's get out of here! *flash* Now!" Dmitri ran several steps to grab her, *flash* but she held her ground.

"Viktor!" Sarah screeched. The corridor swarmed with *flash* humans and Burin-Jai, each trying to tear the other apart. Officers from both sides lay *flash* on the floor, some moving, some not. Viktor whirled, grappling and dancing with the *flash* Burin-Jai, when, from behind him, another Burin-Jai drew a wide dagger and drove it downwards into the crease where Viktor's neck met his shoulder. *flash*

Vik let go of the first Burin-Jai, shock on his face. Both hands came up *flash* to grasp the fat black handle sticking out of his neck, blood welling up darkly around it. The Burin-Jai he released spun, *flash* blade drawn, and slashed just once across Vik's exposed middle, from chest to groin. Viktor let go of the knife handle *flash* as his body seemed to split open. He stared in bewilderment, trying to pull the massive wound together, *flash* but instead caught two handfuls of bloody intestine. He glanced up in disbelief, *flash* catching Dmitri's horrified stare. He mouthed the word *Go* before collapsing on the deck. *flash*

Sarah's hands went straight to her hair and she began to *flash* scream. The high-pitched sound *flash* made a Burin-Jai turn to look for the source, noticing *flash* the unprotected pair. His movement roused a petrified Dimi into action. *flash* As Sarah sprang to Vik's side, Dmitri grabbed her by the hair, turned tail, and ran the fastest race of his life.

flash

Twenty-nine

They never remembered getting back to the cabin. The screaming klaxons, the flashing lights, the pounding adrenaline of the speed at which they ran blurred everything into the surreal fog of a bad dream. Years ago, Dmitri had run track in school. At some point he swapped his grip from Sarah's hair to her hand. He focused on only one thing, running, and when he thought about it later, had no idea how she'd kept up. They ran past the cabin in their frenzy, reversing a few meters later and crashing through the door. Dmitri shook so hard it took three tries to engage the doorlock.

Sarah dropped to her knees, gasping and wheezing with her vulnerable lungs. Dmitri leaned against the door. "Oh my god!" he groaned. "Ohhh *shit!*"

Above the door, a light continued to blink red.

"Dimi!" Sarah gulped from the floor. "I think I'm gonna be sick!"

"Not out here you're not!" Sarah staggered to the back of the cabin.

Dmitri's panicked eyes roved the room. A barricade was pointless on a sliding door, and the furniture was built in. His gaze landed on the wall compartment behind the desk, where Vik stored the EPSAR. Vik had left it behind, intending to sign out practice weapons in the armory. Dmitri threw himself across the room, banging on the door-release. It was locked. A touch pad sat next to it; Vik had punched an eight-digit code to open it.

"Sarah!"

She rushed from the lavatory. *"What!"*

"If you had to program an eight-digit code you'd have to remember, what would you pick?"

She gripped the room divider to stay standing. "Vlad's birthday."

"But Vik wouldn't use Vlad's, he'd use… his own," they finished together.

Dmitri's overloaded mind went blank. "*Shit!* What's his birthday?"

"April! The thirteenth!"

"April 1-3, 2-2-4-4," Dmitri punched. The panel didn't move. "What the hell else could it be?" He banged on the panel.

Sarah could smell the fetid stench of doom blowing down the hallway, fanning the tears from her eyes. "Are you sure you got it right?"

He punched the numbers again. "Zero-four-one-three-two-two-four-four."

"You idiot!" she shouted back. "That's *American!* Only Americans do it that way! **One-three-zero-four-**two-two-four-four!" This time a light in the wall blinked green, and the panel slid back.

Dimi grabbed the weapon and herded her backwards. "Get in the bathroom. *Go!"*

They squished into the tiny room. Dmitri locked that door as well. It was the best he could do.

They stood, dazed, each trying to absorb what had happened, was happening. Dmitri wiped his eyes on his sleeve, sniffing.

Sarah hiccupped with sobs. "Di-*hic*-mi? Did *hic* you see… ?"

"I saw it all!" he said sharply. "And we're not going to talk about it right now! Got that? We got worse things to worry about. Get a grip on yourself. We have to calm down. We have to be able to think."

There wasn't much space, but Dmitri felt wobbly. He slid to the floor in front of the door. Sarah knelt on the other side, squeezed between the wall and the sanitary unit.

Sarah eyed the EPSAR. "You know how to work that? *hic* You have the safe*hic*ty off?"

"Yeah, I think so." Dmitri stared at the weapon in his hand. It was no longer an object for play. The seriousness of it started him shaking again.

"That door opens and there's a Burin-Jai face, they're not taking us without a fight," he promised.

Sarah absorbed the thought, holding her breath against the hiccups. She grabbed him with both hands, eyes darkly purple in her terrified face. "No!" she commanded. "They can't take us at *all! hic* That's unacceptable! Dimi! *hic Do you know what Burin-Jai do to prisoners?"*

Dmitri dropped his gaze. "Yeah." Of course he knew. Those were the kind of stories brought up in classroom political-rights debates, the kind of horror stories you tortured impressionable younger siblings with in the black of night, stories too horrific to comprehend. Labor camps, medical experiments, physical and mental torture, and if you were lucky, a slow painful death. And that was a *good* day…

"Dimi, I can't do that! *hic* I won't let myself be captured!" She gripped his arm so tightly his fingers tingled.

"Well it's not exactly first on my list of …"

"NO!" Sarah dug her fingers deeper. *"Listen to what I'm saying!* I won't risk being captured! That door opens, you see a Burin-Jai, you shoot him. *hic* If you see more than one – *Swear* to me, Dimi! Swear you will shoot *me*!"

Dmitri shook his head in horror. "I can't shoot you! You'd die!"

"You *must*, and you *will*!" Sarah insisted. "I won't be taken captive! *Do you know what they'd do to me?* I'm a *girl*, Dimi! *hic* You would let them torture me like that, rather than do something merciful from the heart? It would be quick and painless. That's more than I could ever hope from a Burin-Jai. Tell me you care enough to do that for me."

"You're talking *suicide!* You're asking me to *murder* you!"

"I am."

Dmitri swallowed hard. "I can't do that. If I did, I'd have to kill myself as well. What if I made a mistake?"

"Could you do that?" It wasn't a request, but a question of fortitude. "Or do you want me to do it?"

"No, I do not!" Dmitri snapped with a sick feeling. "I'm older. I'm responsible. I have to do it."

"You wouldn't let me down?"

Bile rose in his throat. Sarah was right. For her, keeping her out of Burin-Jai hands *was* taking care of her, no matter how he did it. The other half... he prayed he'd be able to do if it came to that.

"No."

"Shake?"

With a squeeze of his cold fingers, Dmitri sealed their fate. He leaned against the door, listening with every nerve for any sound, good or bad. The silence made invisible spiders tiptoe across the backs of necks, made imaginations fill with unseen terrors, suffocated listeners as breaths were held far too long, listening for the faintest warning of gator-skinned bogeymen on the prowl.

Sarah took a rough, shaky breath. At least the hiccups had stopped. "Dimi?"

"Yeah?"

Sarah looked away, sucking her lip. "I love you." She'd never said that aloud to anyone, not even Vlad.

"I love you too, Kid." As an afterthought, he held his arm open, but Sarah shook her head. Her hold on herself was too delicate for physical contact.

Dimi understood. He reached out, but instead of holding her hand as she expected, he twisted his arm around hers, crossing wrists and gripping her hand in the affection-disguising handshake the older boys had used among themselves. No one ever did that to her; she was a girl.

"We'll get through this," Dmitri promised. "Strong?"

Nothing in the universe could have boosted Sarah's spirits at that moment as much as that handshake. To her, the handshake was her initiation, the indelible sign that she was officially accepted as one of the boys, not just the tomboy little sister, sometimes a partner, sometimes a pest, most of the time just the source of answers for homework. It was the highest honor she could receive.

A tiny flame of peace ignited somewhere in her middle. "Strong," she agreed,

The new-found strength disappeared as the floor beneath them shook and shuddered, followed by a low, loud rumbling that vibrated almost as hard. The lights cut out for a second or two, came back. Sarah shrieked, her hand clamping over her mouth as it subsided.

"Energy fire," Dmitri guessed, eyeing the walls. "They must be firing on us."

Another shudder rumbled through.

"What if there's a breach?" Sarah whispered. "We'll depressurize!"

"Then, we won't have to worry about Burin-Jai behind the door, will we? Don't worry. The quadrant's crawling with ships. Who knows what's docked. Just because we're sitting blind doesn't mean they're not out there right now, kicking stinking Burin-Jai ass back across the treaty zone." A third rumble shook them.

Sarah held her breath. "Maybe that's them now?"

Three hours they huddled on the cramped floor, barely able to straighten their legs. While Sarah kept her mind busy sending prayers to as many galactic deities as she could remember, Dmitri tried to come up with contingency plans. They'd already covered the very worst. They could be sitting alone in a sealed-off section, perhaps contaminated by some toxic leak, or radiation that was poisoning them this very minute. The station could be overrun and all survivors being removed. Or systematically assassinated. Or the Outpost targeted for imminent destruction.

Or the battle had been won by the Alliance, and they were hiding like frightened mice when all was safe.

What to do?

They conversed a little, nothing important, not about what lurked unmentioned in the corners of their minds. They didn't have time to dwell on that now. Dmitri knew Sarah's strength was temporary, that she was playing little games in her head on purpose, keeping the fragile circuits busy so they wouldn't discover the program collapse until the adrenaline rush ended. Gods help him when the crisis hit.

"We're really just sitting ducks, you know," Sarah thought out loud. "Big ships have pinpoint scanners, there's internal sensors on the station, hand-held bio scanners, infra-red detectors… They could cut off the environmental systems."

"Stop it! Tell me something I don't know. Tell me something you read in all those texts I bought you. Tell me…" Dmitri stopped. He sat up quickly, alert. Sarah froze with resurgent fear.

He rolled to his knees and pressed his ear against the door, the EPSAR clenched in his hand. A whooshy sound, like pneumatic doors opening. He waved to Sarah, and she scrambled to kneel on the cramped floor next to him.

"Ear," said a distant voice. A rattle of equipment grew louder. It stopped just outside the door.

Sweat ran in icy rivulets down Dmitri's back, found its way under the waistband of his pants, trickled itchy down his backside. He glanced at Sarah; she stared through him with a detached serenity.

You ready? he mouthed, his stomach in his throat. This was it, do or die.

Sarah gazed deep into his eyes. She nodded slowly three times.

A finger tapped against the locked door release on the room's side. A knock followed.

"Hello?" called a voice in perfect Standard Interstellar. "Can you hear me? Are you injured? We're from the Allied Fleet Ship *Hoberman*. We're retrieving all survivors aboard the outpost."

Dmitri glanced at Sarah. She hadn't lost the cool emptiness, but she shook her head. Anyone could learn Interstellar. Dimi himself wouldn't know the name of a destroyer from a private pleasure craft.

"Can you hear me?" the voice repeated, and the knock sounded harder.

"Prove it!" Dmitri shouted, unable to bear the strain. "Tell me the first five articles of the UPA Charter!" He looked to Sarah for approval.

Too easy, Sarah said silently as the unseen voice became several voices reciting the answer.

What was something only an Earther would know?

What was the name of the second *Earth ship to explore the moon?* Sarah whispered. Aliens might know the country, but the name of a ship was a picky detail to fish out of three hundred years of space travel. Dmitri called out the question.

"Aw hell!" drawled a voice. "History questions! Ummm …" The voices talked among themselves. "Gemini was two, what was the three? The Trident series? No, Neptune's not right, somebody else. Artemis? Apollo! The Apollo Mission!" a voice called out with certainty.

Even Dmitri knew the answer to that. "What number?" he demanded.

"How the hell do I know? You want to be rescued or not?"

Dmitri glanced at Sarah, who shrugged back. There was no way to tell.

"All right!" he called out, trembling again. "We'll release the door, but I'm warning you! I have a weapon and it's set to kill, and I am pointing it at an innocent child. If you are who you say you are and you are armed, I suggest you put down your weapons. If you don't, I will kill her before I kill you. Understand? Back away from the door!"

"Back off," said a voice, and the noises moved away. "Weapons checked."

Sarah took her position. Her back would be to the door as it opened. Dmitri braced himself against the shower door. He checked the setting on the EPSAR, checked the safety, and took aim. The room was so narrow the EPSAR brushed her clothing. He couldn't miss.

Sarah stood up tall. *Strong*, she coached him silently. *You promised!*

"Okay!" Dmitri choked out with a mouth as dry as dust. Sarah unlocked the door, and it slid open with a soft whir.

Dimi's eyes took in the scene over his sister's shoulder, and the hand holding the EPSAR shook so violently the weapon fell from his fingers and clattered on the floor. He collapsed to his knees with a cry and buried his face in his arms.

Sarah saw him fall as if in a dream. He had failed. He couldn't do it. She spun around to assess the situation, and came nose to nose with four young men in blue-and-gold Alliance uniforms, not one a day older than Dmitri himself. She stepped back and hit the sink. Her back scraped on the edge as she sank in front of her brother, head on her knees, and shut down.

A crewmen tried to squeeze into the room. "Sir? Are you all right, sir? Are you injured?"

"We thought we were dead." Dmitri wiped his face and climbed to his feet, retrieving the EPSAR. He reset it to lowest setting, secured the safety, and dropped it in his pocket.

"We're just happy to find you alive, sir," the crewman said. "If you'll come with us, we're evacuating all non-essential personnel until a damage control team can make an inspection."

Dmitri held a hand out. "Sar? It's over. It's safe. Let's get out of here."

As if made of wax, Sarah reached, and he pulled her to her feet. Arms snaked around his middle and locked there, her face buried against him. He dragged her from their refuge.

Walking through the rooms, Dmitri gazed sadly at what had been their home for two weeks. Reality existed out here.

Could there be a chance?

He stopped walking.

"Our brother is a crewman on the station. He was injured during the attack. I need to find out what happened to him."

"There are medical teams from the *Hoberman* and *Triumph* assisting with triage and emergency medicine," an officer said. "I can take you down to the sickbay. They'll be able to tell you which ship he was brought to."

"I'd appreciate that." Dmitri couldn't remember how to get to the sickbay, couldn't remember their deck, couldn't remember anything before the attack. He felt foggy and blank, awaiting a reboot. He tried to peel Sarah off, to hold just her hand, but she stuck tight, making walking difficult. After much prodding and tugging, he slid her to his side and dragged on.

The station was silent. Too silent. What only that morning had been a bustling center of activity, of crewmen carrying on various duties, off-duty personnel socializing, travelers making inquiries, nothing remained. Two teams of starship officers jogged by, led by the Outpost's First Officer Morden, a raw burn glistening across his shoulder. Chaos blossomed as they approached the sickbay. Crewmen lined the halls half a corridor away. Medical personnel and volunteers moved among them, performing triage, taking notes, and treating the simpler injuries. A raven-haired woman in ship's insignia directed people as they left the sickbay.

Dmitri approached her. "Excuse me. Are you in charge?"

"I am the First Officer of the starship *Triumph*," the woman replied coolly. "I'm coordinating medical teams and assigning evacuation of injured personnel."

"I'm trying to locate my brother, WS3 Viktor Kirushenko. He was injured on deck nine."

The officer scanned her compad. "I'm sorry, I don't have that name here. He may have been in the sickbay before I arrived. You can ask inside, second door on your right."

"Thank you."

Inside, anyone standing was in motion. Every diagnostic bed was filled, every chair held someone waiting for a bed. Five doctors performed surgeries on the spot, while nurses prepped the next cases. Technicians dodged back and forth with lab samples and results. The patients were silent, but the questions and orders and reports of the medical personnel lent a frenetic buzz to the activity. Jumbled smells made breathing uncomfortable: blood of open wounds, the ozone of the laser cauteries, the distinctive medicinal odors of creams and salves, and the plasticky scent of artificial skin. Dmitri stood motionless, watching.

Three beds away, he picked the Outpost's doctor out of the crowd, the one Viktor had asked for help. After several minutes the doctor noticed them, asked his nurse to take over, and approached.

Dmitri didn't bother with pleasantries. "Viktor was injured. We saw him fall. I didn't know if he made it this far."

Perry Cronan grimaced. He put his hand on Dmitri's unoccupied shoulder. "I'm sorry, son. There was nothing we could do."

Dmitri closed his eyes, unwilling to deal with the rush of emotion. He forced out, "I didn't think so, but I had to know for sure. Where is he?"

"Doctor Royce drew morgue detail," Dr. Cronan said. "Through those doors at the end there. I am truly sorry."

"Thanks." He dragged Sarah through the maze of room.

He stopped in the doorway to the makeshift morgue, afraid to enter what should have been a six-patient observation room. Beds were occupied by sheeted shapes, and most available floor space held draped stretchers, more than a dozen. Contrasting the flurry of activity behind him, this room was still.

Deathly still.

Dead.

Dmitri fought the urge to run. The only movement came from a lone man filling out forms on a compad. He looked up at the sound of the doors.

"I think you want a different door out of there."

Dimi shook his head. "I'm looking for our brother. They said I'd find him here. WS3 Viktor Kirushenko."

"I'm sorry to hear that. I'm from the *Triumph*; I'm just getting to identifications. Two weeks from the end of our mission – just two weeks away from home – when Captain Karras got the distress call. Rotten end to a excellent tour of duty. Did your brother have any identifying marks?"

"He would have had a neck wound and a big … wound across the front."

Royce moved to one of the sheet-covered beds. "Over here. Why don't you have your girl there wait outside."

Dmitri glanced down at Sarah, face glued to his side, as motionless as the crewmen around them. "She'll be all right. Nothing short of antimatter is going to get her to let go right now." He dragged her to where the doctor stood, deep among the nightmare shapes.

"Have you ever identified anyone before?" Royce asked cautiously. "It's not pretty, but remember, their pain is over. I want you to be prepared." Dimi nodded. The physician pulled the biosheet back to the figure's shoulders.

Dmitri gave an involuntary shudder. He remembered seeing his sister Elizabyeta when she died. She'd lain on the floor for hours before being carted away like unwanted furniture, to be sliced into photos for evidence. The memory wasn't encouraging, but nothing like what lay before him now. There hadn't been a visible mark on 'Byeta. Drying blood soaked the shoulder of this victim's shirt, a tear in the fabric clinging to the edges of a ragged, wide wound. One side of the angular face was grayish-purple, imprinted with the pattern of the decking, while the other side contrasted unnaturally pale. There was blood on the familiar face, blood matted in the black-brown hair, but it was the open eyes that twisted Dimi's insides, the dullness of the gentle dark eyes staring at the ceiling lights not in pain, not in fear, but in total surprise, as if such a thing just couldn't have happened, just couldn't be real.

A sob caught him off guard. Dmitri nodded convulsively. "That's him." He felt Sarah stir, her head to turn, and he clamped down with all his strength. That was one thing she never, ever needed to see. He didn't ease up much when the doctor replaced the sheet, and she did't protest.

"The bruising's not part of the injuries," Royce assured him. "That's just from lying there. We'll clean him up nice before we release him. Do you know what you want to do for arrangements? Is there anyone we can contact for you?"

Dimi couldn't think. Nothing seemed real, just a slow-moving dream that didn't want to end. He was just a kid, nineteen for cryin' out loud! Teenagers weren't supposed to deal with this kind of stuff.

"Home," he choked. "Can you send him home? Our family's back on Earth. Can you send him there?"

Royce put a supportive arm around him. "We can do that. Come on. Let's get you settled somewhere."

Dmitri lingered. "Why?" he had to ask. "What were they after? Weapons?"

Royce snorted. "The Burin-Jai? Same as always. Chaos and disorder. We want them to stay where they are. They want our space. The outposts exist to keep an eye on them, give us advanced notice. They want the outposts gone. When you hear all those peace-mongers protesting Fleet funding, remember what you've seen here. It's real easy for those Navaran feather-heads to scream peace half a galaxy away. Let'm come out here and see it first-hand, then see how they change their call. Give 'em a day in a Burin-Jai jail, see what they think then." He quieted, embarrassed. "Not that peace wouldn't be nice."

In the main sickbay, Dmitri saw Qara moving between beds. She noticed him; he could tell by her face she knew. His mind screamed collapse!, but Dmitri stopped next to her anyway.

"He loved you, you know. He would have married you."

Qara nodded. "I know. I would have married him, too." She reached a hand out to stroke the girl's hair. Viktor's brother pulled her into a tight embrace that she needfully returned. After several seconds she let go.

"I have to get back to work. We're swamped," she said, running a finger over her eyes. "I'm so sorry."

"Not half as sorry as I am," Dimi said as she walked away.

The officers allowed him back to Viktor's cabin to retrieve their belongings. Dmitri packed some of Vik's things in with theirs. The rest could be sent home. He put some photos of Vik in a folder and wrote Qara's name on it. No reason she shouldn't have something of his as well.

They were assigned to quarters aboard the *Hoberman*. The decision was arbitrary – the *Hoberman* was heading to Starbase 12, the *Triumph* to drydock at the Seattle spaceyards. Dmitri wasn't ready for Earth yet.

216

He sat on the bed in their cabin, numb, Sarah barnacled to his side. The room was silent except for the subliminal thrum of the ship's engines through the structures, maintaining orbit around the outpost.

His mind ticked down the mental list of responsible have-to's. The threat of imminent demise had passed. He'd looked into the face of death and lived to tell about it. He'd protected his sister, kept her safe. He'd braved the gruesome job of identifying a dead body. The body of his brother. His mentor. His best friend. The indelible image of Vik's face as he clutched his middle and fell haunted Dmitri's head, mixing with the ghastly still image from the makeshift morgue. They were aboard a Constellation-class Star Explorer, the finest of the Alliance's vessels, about to flee the Burin-Jai border for safer territory faster than the speed of light itself. Nothing of life-or-death importance distracted him anymore, and he felt himself crumbling.

"Get off me!" he snapped at Sarah, wrenching her from him so forcefully she landed on the floor. Too much had waited too long to be expressed. Dmitri fell back on the bed, buried his face in the pillow, and wept, Sarah clinging wretchedly to his knee.

He didn't know how long he cried, didn't care. After everything that had happened? Dmitri refused to be ashamed. He sat up and hugged his weeping sister, ready at last to share the grief. There was still one more thing.

He retrieved Sarah's pack and emptied it onto a bed. Childish treasures fell out, memories of a lifetime of travel. Stacks of family photos. Feathers from an exotic animal on safari. A striped tracking bracelet from the Mirabella. The big scarf Mother used to drape over the holovision reception console to disguise it, even though the fabric was bright red. A finger-sized tube of sand, probably from Navara. A blue and white shirt that could only have been Vlad's – it still smelled mousy like him. A sealed plastic envelope. Flipping through it, Dmitri found what he wanted, and replaced everything else. Then he opened his own travel case, took out some of Viktor's things, and transferred them to her pack. One more memory never to forget.

He dragged his shadow to the computer screen and sat, Sarah on his lap. He read off the paper he held – a hyperspace address written in Valeria's rushed hand – and waited for the call to go through.

A man's face answered. For a second Dmitri thought he'd lost his mind, as the man made him think of Viktor. Dimi looked away, then back, but the similarity didn't change. He was the man from Katya's pictures.

The man stared at him just as hard. The young man on his screen looked a little like David, a lot more like Vladimir.

The man squinted. "*Dmitri*? Is that Vladimir's Ghost? Ghost?" he called softly. "Sarah?"

"She won't talk right now. I need to speak with Valeria Kirushenko, please. It's urgent."

The man nodded. "Of course." The screen faded to black, to be replaced by Valeria's disbelieving face.

"Dmitri!" she breathed in surprise. "How... How are you, Dimi? Are you all right? Is Sarah okay? Where are you?"

"No, we're not all right." He dropped his gaze from the screen, realizing too late he *wasn't* ready to discuss the matter yet. "We're on the AFS *Hoberman*. Viktor... Viktor's dead," he said as fast as he could, so he could clamp his jaw shut again that much sooner. "We were visiting him. There was a raid on the outpost. The Burin-Jai..."

"No! Oh my...!"

"He was trying to save us when he fell. He died a hero. In the line of duty. He's supposed to get some medal or something. Like that means anything! I should have pulled him out of there, Val! *I should have!* He might have made it if I wasn't so chicken!" Tears welled up against his wishes.

"Don't do that to yourself, Dimi. You don't know that," Valeria said with a heavy voice. "Viktor was always our hero. They can't give enough medals to cover his kind of heroism. How's Sarah? I can get Vlad for her..."

"Don't upset him. I don't think she'll speak to anyone right now. Tell him she misses him every day, and be glad he's not here."

Dmitri managed a deep breath. "I didn't... They asked... I didn't know what to do with... *Vik*, so I told them to send him back to you. At least... he'll be back home." He wiped a cheek on Sarah's head.

"That's good. We'll take good care of him. You're coming with him, aren't you? At least for a funeral?"

Dimi hadn't thought about that. "He's on a different ship than we are. They're supposed to notify you when they get there. I'll... give it some thought. We might. That's all I can say right now."

Valeria gave him a sad little smile. "Okay. We'd be very happy to see you, even for a little while. You *are* welcome here, Dimi. You've been forgiven a hundred times over."

It was Dimi's turn to give a wan smile. "Not by David, I guarantee it. I know how he carries a grudge. I can't blame him. I was a real shit to break my promise. I didn't set out to.

"I'm sorry, Val," he said softly. "Give our regards to everyone, even if David doesn't want to hear it. I think I'm going to take her down to medical and see if they have something that will get her to let go. It's making my back hurt."

"Stay in touch, Dimi."

"We will," he promised, and broke the connection.

Emotionally crippled, mentally exhausted, Dmitri surrendered and brought her to the sickbay on the *Hoberman.* He'd promised no hospitals, not no doctors. The ship's physician was understanding. Dmitri mentioned none of her history, just the events of the last fifteen hours. They filled her full of drugs, weathered her collapse, and gave him script cards for more if she needed them. Dmitri was grateful; he was in no condition to tough her out himself. He wanted to scream with her, to cry and kick and curse the alien bastards responsible, to rip the injustice out of the very fabric of the universe with his teeth, but he couldn't bring himself to do it.

Starbase 12 was a bustling spaceport, a transfer point for a hundred different routes, a shoreleave point for vessels too far from hospitable planets. To support the varied crowds, it boasted a wide variety of entertainments. For the weary traveler, it was a stopover to be remembered, unless you were two young people recovering from a brutal incident. For them, the gaiety was but salt on a wound, the intrusion of people and noise and merriment where it wasn't welcome. They ate their meals at odd times when the crowds were less, and rushed back to their stateroom. Dimi's ever-roving eye never once followed a girl.

Sarah remained despondent, but she could walk and speak when spoken to. *What more could Dmitri ask?* She wouldn't let him out of her sight, not for a second, terrified of another attack, but she was off his back.

The doctor offered Dmitri the same medications, but he refused. What difference would it make? It wouldn't bring Viktor back. It wouldn't erase his guilt. *If, if, if.* If they had grabbed Viktor and dragged him to the sick bay, he might still have died, leaving a trail of innards behind, but then again, maybe he wouldn't, in this modern day of organ bypasses and regenerations and cloning. Maybe it was just bloodloss that killed him. How long did it take him to die? An agonizing minute? Five? Ten? A half hour of lying in unendurable pain, abandoned, knowing what would happen, praying alone for a miracle? Tripped on, fallen on, stepped on by heavy alien feet, each jar a new experience in agony?

His buddy.

His best friend.

His brother.

Vik.

Sarah clutched a pillow on one of the beds, watching his every breath. Dmitri was the drunkest he'd ever been. His words slurred and his light accent thickened until sometimes it seemed he was trying to speak Russian and English at the same time. She knew better than to nag, not now at least. All she could do was watch.

He sat across the room, feet on either side of the desk's video screen, not really watching the travel video running. An open bottle of Centauran *brii* sat on the table near his foot, a sticky glass in his hand. He wore some of the last pour on his knee. Tonight he would sleep, a sleep with no dreams, persistent dreams of being in the morgue, and if Viktor wasn't sitting up and talking to him all gory and dead, then other victims were moving under the drapes and he couldn't find the door, or, the worst one, Sarah lifted a sheet, and he saw himself lying there. Enough was enough.

"I like it," he said, nodding. He grabbed the bottle to examine it. "I like it bedder den da wodka. Sveeter. Sharper bite, I tink. You wan' try't?" He held his glass out.

Sarah shook her head. "I don't think it would be a good idea, on top of the medication."

Dmitri took another gulp. "You're prop'ly right." He stared vacantly at the vidscreen.

"I vish I done dis long time 'go. It'ssenlight – enlightning. I unnerstan' now. I tink I unnerstan' vhy Fadder did dis. I tink it di'n't make sense because I newer drank enough. At leas' not da right stuff. You really shouldt giwe it try. It kills da pain. Doesint botter you attall." He gave a brief chuckle. "No feelingkt, no pain, *da*?"

"I guess I can understand that," Sarah replied. She'd never seen a drunkard yet who didn't turn angry and violent at some point.

Dmitri downed the last of the glass, then turned off the screen in disgust. "Dis *boringk*! I haff no fffreakin' clue vhere I vann' go. I don' vanna go anyvhere! I don' vanna do anytink! I don' vanna *tink!*

"I just vant fforget," he whimpered. "Vhat 'bout you? You vant forget eweryting, or you are juss' gonna … fffile ewerytink avay somevhere in dat endles' – *urp!* – s'brain of yours?" he belched.

"I would like to forget."

Dmitri thumped his feet down and tried to refill his glass. He was mostly successful, sucking the spill from the side of his hand. He splashed more on the table in the process.

"Hokay," he said after a long swallow. "Sinze I refuse to ting about anytink right now, *you* do da tingink for vonce. Vhere vould you sug – shug – *sssuggesht* ve go to forgit ewerytink that ewer happined to us? Vhere do ve go to say 'Do ower!' ? An' don' tell me some goddamm' safari on a trail vit' stinkink aminal shit."

"Nyet." Sarah hugged her pillow, thinking. She gave a hard sigh. He sat between her and the door, but she was sober, and he could only stagger.

"If I wanted to forget," she postulated, "I would find an underdeveloped planet. One in a safe region of space. One without space travel. One that's never heard of the Burin-Jai Empire. Someplace quiet, with no outside interference. A place where you can see green trees, and sunrises, and feel rain on your face. A place to

220

feed the soul, not the mind. That's where I would go. And I wouldn't be in a hurry to leave it."

"Hokay. I drink to dat!" he giggled. "Write down. Write down dose ideas, all ov dem, 'cause I don' tink I'll rebember dem lader. I vill take it to commander of 'base. Or somevone in crew. *One* ov dem damn' unifforms mus' know planet like dat. If it'sh gotta name, ve can get dere." He stood up as if about to run the errand, but fell to his knees on the first step.

"Write down!" he laughed miserably from the floor. "An' I bring dere soon as I feel legs."

II. Slow

Recovery

Dear Vlad,

I'm sorry I haven't written. I have tried. I'm on so much medication I'm dead inside, but right now I'm afraid to be without it. Someday I'll tell you about it, but I can't right now. It was beyond any horror you can imagine, and worse than what you can't. Please forgive me. I am thinking about you.

Yours in grief,

Sarah

Dear Sar,

I feel sick about it as it is. I'm glad you (and Dimi) got out alive. I will tell you what Uncle Tomas did, though. Through Valeria, he got permission from Father to move Mother and Elizabyeta's ashes back to Earth. He got permission from the city to have a monument put on the back of the property, and he had Grandfather, Mother, 'Byeta, and Viktor interred there. It's a beautiful place, surrounded by trees, and he had the gardener put flowers in everywhere around it. We can visit it any time we like. I thought that was about the nicest thing I ever heard of anybody doing. You should have heard the stink, though, when Grandmamá found out we'd cremated Mother and Byeta. I guess it goes against her religion or something. She wouldn't let us do it to Viktor. I don't see how anything done to you *after* you die can keep you out of Paradise. Especially Vik.

Be careful, Sarah! I can't imagine what I'd do if Dmitri called and said you were dead. Probably drop dead right where I stood. You can't die until you've come home again, I won't allow it!! I'm older (I know, just barely), and I said you can't! Promise?

Write me when you can.

We're all grieving with you.

Vlad

Sigma Tau Celi IV
Sun: F—7, yellow—white
System: 4th of 7 planets
Diameter: 12,990 km
Mass: 4.9687 x 10²⁴kg
Density: 5.41
Gravity: 9.4m/sec²; 0.96 of Earth
Type: class M, unrestricted
Moons: 3 — Oes [d= 2,282.4 km], Taber [3,160 km];
Allash [4,353.6 km];
Rotation: 26.3 Earth Standard Hours
Sidereal period: 346.1359 Earth Standard Days
Date of first exploration: 2260 by the AFS *Meritorius*

Data: Four major continents, 21 major islands, all climate types represented. Two polar ice caps. Three continents inhabited by sentient humanoid life forms, technology rating G on Mimba Scale of Cultures [peak Earth technology 1825 — 1900], planetary population approx. 600 million.

Due to technology status, this planet is NOT currently under UPA membership. This planet is currently under covert observation and is considered to be CONTACT RESTRICTED. This planet is protected under Article One [Independent Destiny] which can/will be enforced by UPA/Allied Fleet auspices. Inquiries can be addressed through the Bureau of Planetary Affairs, Department of Developing Planets, United Planetary Alliance, Cormiral, Centauri.

Thirty

Explored Territory
Epsilon Quadrant
Sigma Tau Celi IV
Earthdate: 27 October, 2266

They kept her birthday low key; neither felt like celebrating. A fancier dinner, a slice of cake, a lemonade toast that the coming year might hopefully, possibly, blessedly be better than the past one, a fistful of printed wishes from home, and they let the day slip into history. Dimi made Sarah a special promise: if their luck hadn't changed by her next birthday, they would go home. Another year like the last, and he would need her meds, too.

They studied the statistics of planet after planet, looking for a place to hide. Most were off limits to settlers for political reasons, or health reasons, or technology restrictions. With the help of the

226

commander at Starbase 12, they applied for work status on Sigma Tau Ceti IV, a low-tech, low-profile planet with a team of observers looking for volunteers to join their isolated enclave. They had no specific skills to offer, but a willingness to learn.

The G rating on the culture scale appealed to them, the equivalent of Earth's nineteenth century. Dmitri and Sarah knew the era from history classes. It was a time of romanticism, of rapidly advancing technology, of men and women living in lavish historic homes, the start of modern medicine. A time without pagers or energy weapons or commlinks or disabled defense shields, where an alien was merely a displaced immigrant of the same species. A time of fresh wholesome foods dripping with flavor, and no governmental dietary restrictions. What could be better than that?

Two weeks after her twelfth birthday, three weeks after ... *The Day*, Sarah and Dmitri moley-beamed into the Chessorak Observation Compound. They were becoming old hands at matter-energy molecular conversion beaming. Sarah couldn't remember getting from the outpost to the *Hoberman*, but they'd moley-beamed from the starbase to the transport cruiser, and now from the cruiser to the Research Compound. For Sarah, the process hadn't lost its marvel, but the ooky, shivery feeling of being dissolved and reintegrated somewhere else was losing some of its terror. She couldn't help but wonder just how many of her molecules might have been left behind, wondering where she'd gone. Given a choice, both would have chosen docking.

They reintegrated in the center of a tiny village, checking to make sure all their limbs came with them. Small wooden houses lined the dirt road, one or two of the caliber they remembered in photos. A stone pillar stood in the middle of the street, a wooden handle sticking out one side. As far as the eye could see, the village appeared to be enclosed by a high stockade fence, blocking out everything but the tops of trees. Leafy trees, complete with the chirping squawks of unseen lifeforms flitting branch to branch. Trees under a periwinkle sky lit by a bright, warm yellowy sun still fairly low in the sky. Sarah turned her face upward, closed her eyes, and breathed the fresh air in rapture. More than eight weeks had passed since they'd last set foot on soil.

A scattering of men and women went about in a native costume. The sudden appearance of strangers drew little surprise. A red-haired man jogged up the street.

"Mr. Kirushenko?" he inquired before extending a hand. "Hargan Ennis, communications engineer for the Chessorak compound."

Dimi shook the hand. "Dmitri. My sister, Sarah."

"Nice to meet you. We don't get unscheduled visitors very often. I've been here three years, and I think you're the second surprise.

I'll take you to the camp. It's at the end of the street."

The men began to walk, but Sarah stopped to watch a woman in a long skirt at the stone pillar. Five cloth bands bound her waist-length brown hair into a thick rope. As she pulled the wooden handle downward, liquid poured forth from a spout into a pail.

The woman pulled the handle again. "Hello! Welcome! My name's Nora. What's yours?"

Curiosity won out over shyness. "Sarah. Is that water?"

"Uh-huh. Want to try it?"

Sarah nodded, and Nora stepped aside. She leaned on the handle, amazed by the amount of pressure required. Water gushed from the spout in a wave.

"Not as easy as you thought, is it?"

"Simple hydraulics, or an underground pumping system? Artesian? If it's that difficult, why not use a wind-driven pump?"

"You know something about water! We're too far inland for enough reliable wind to… "

"Sarah!" Dmitri called sharply. The new meds had gotten her off his back – too far off. Without her underlying paranoia, she wandered. Dmitri wasn't used to hunting for her.

"I have to go. Thank you," Sarah said, and ran to catch up.

A yellow-painted building stood last on the street. The road crossed over a rise and headed down a hill, out of sight of the gated end of the high fence. From the rise one could see over the back fence, where a second massive gate opened to huge fields where folk were working. Dotted among the fields were flat carts pulled by a long-necked beast.

"This is the Meeting House," Hargan explained. "If you stay, you'll get to know it well."

Inside, the building looked like an unfinished auditorium, with rows of benches and chairs. Puffs of dust rose as they clomped over the wooden floor; Dmitri sneezed several times. Four doors across the back wall bore labels in a squiggly odd print. Ennis entered one.

"This is labeled as the supply room," he said, gesturing to the three walls lined with shelves of materials. The fourth wall held two more doors; he pulled one open. "In here."

They entered a large closet, complete with hanging clothes and spare boots on a rack. It seemed rather odd until Hargan reached behind the clothing bar, twisted and pulled on what appeared to be a coathook. Sarah gave a squeal and clutched at the wall as the entire closet began to descend.

Dmitri didn't seem overly surprised. "A lift? I thought the village was the complex?"

"All for show. We let the locals into the village, to keep them from dying of curiosity and sneaking in on their own. As far as they know, we're just an immigrant spur. Outside the gates, we tend thirty-five hectares of fields and 150 head of *urpinta*, which are kind of like a cross between a calf and maybe a goat," Ennis mused. "We also have 200 *joubash*, which are more than a chicken but less than a duck." He shrugged for want of a better explanation. "The real stuff is underground, out of sight, built of biostructural materials. If we absolutely had to, we could implode the whole compound, and within six months of exposure to ground moisture most of the complex would biodegrade. Virtually untraceable in this culture." The lift came to a stop, and the door opened on a modern-looking corridor.

Ennis turned left. "Commander Guillaume's office is down here."

Though he was only in his forties, Marcel Guillaume had a full head of silver hair, made brighter by his sun-reddened nose and cheeks. He eyed the young pair before him without much enthusiasm.

"The position is yours if you wish," he said to Dmitri as they sat around his desk, "but I want you to be sure you understand what you're getting into. We pay a minimal salary; the house is yours for as long as you keep the job. Anything more, and you'll have to find local employment yourself. You report back in person every three months, hand in your paperwork, get a medical check, and replace any supplies you may need. If you get into serious trouble, it will take a day and a half to get a message to us, and at least a day and a half for us to get back to you. We can't get you out any faster, even if you're dying. We have no air ships, no ground cars, and no molecular transporters, save the emergency evacuation equipment at the Fithma base. That doesn't mean personal evacuation; it means we've imploded the base and need to disappear fast. The rules and regs make a small book. You break them and we have the right to remove you immediately, with or without your consent. You understand the implications of Article One?"

Sarah nodded. "Yes, sir. The Law of Independent Destiny. Every planetary culture has the right to progress at its own rate, under its own direction. No one may interfere in a culture by introducing knowledge that is more advanced than the culture itself, a philosophy or religion not native to the planetary race, or otherwise exert undo political, economic, or mental control over the population. We must adapt to the local culture, not ask them to adapt to us."

Guillaume seemed pleased. "Precisely. That extends to just about everything. If you stay here, it's as a member of the culture itself. There are no translators and no language training chips; you'll learn the native tongue the hard way."

"I'm currently fluent in four languages, and well-versed in two more," Sarah volunteered. "I'm sure I won't have trouble with a seventh." This was too important a deal to cave in to nerves. She was trying her very best to be courageous and put on a good face. Trying to hide the fact she was doped to the gills on all kinds of neurotransmitters and uptake inhibitors and tranquilizers. Trying to ignore the fact she and Dimi would do just about anything for a chance to hide from the rest of the universe. "If you have a manual, I can start now."

"Six?" Guillaume exclaimed. "Which ones?"

"Standard English, Terran Russian, Modern Navaran, Terran French, and semi-fluent in Ancient Latin and Ancient Greek. I know a spattering of Aquilan, but… I'm not allowed to repeat most of it."

"I'm fluent in two, and can get around in a third," Dmitri added. "It's got to be easier than Navaran. Is the area politically stable?"

"There are no other inhabited planets in the solar system. The present Peloníshalan government has been in power for more than 150 of their years, and there are currently no major factions challenging the system," Guillaume said. "The remote areas are more lawless than others, but the area we would place you in is considered settled territory. You'd be a kilometer or two from the nearest town, roughly half a kilometer from the nearest neighbor."

"So it would be quiet?" Sarah asked.

"There's a cabin and shed on eight hectares," the commander said. "Almost five hectares are fields, which we've traditionally leased out to a neighboring farm. If you want, you can cancel the lease next growing season and farm it on your own. If you want noise, you'll have to make it yourself."

"That's exactly what we're looking for," Dmitri assured him. "Whatever you throw at us, we can handle it, as long as there's peace and quiet."

Sarah had been lost in slow thought. "Three months is a long time. Are we allowed to use the computers and hyperspace and things like that? Do you get mail service here?" She could hide from the world, but not from Vlad.

"Of course!" Guillaume said. "If you'd like, the comm officer can retrieve text mail for you, or transcribe a videocall and send it to you via the local mail service, and vice versa, of course."

Sarah began to nod, then realized, "He'd be able to read them."

"He's not supposed to," Guillaume hedged. "There's only fifty of us here; we're a pretty tight-knit group. You have to be, isolated like this. Any news from the outside world is good news to all of us."

"I'll think about it. Maybe I can create a separate mail channel for important things that can't wait."

"That would work," Dmitri said. "When would we start?"

"If you're still set on it, the next stop would be with our physician for a health check, and if that works out, we'll start with some training, language basics, and get you outfitted. We can have you at your post in as little as five days."

Dmitri stood up. "The sooner the better."

"May I see a language manual while we wait?" Sarah repeated hopefully.

Dmitri's medical exam took half an hour. His health was perfect, but his arms ached from a dozen new inoculations: boosters for previous vaccines, and a host of new ones to combat local germs.

Bolstered by the prescriptions from the *Hoberman*, Sarah tried to cooperate with the idea of an exam. She did enter the room on her own, but no matter how many drugs she swallowed, she didn't like doctors, didn't trust them, and wanted no part of any exam. She insisted on Dmitri's presence before she'd submit to a scanner.

The doctor studied her as Sarah stood pressed against the wall, unable to make herself sit. "You want your brother present?"

"Absolutely," she whispered, knowing that in another moment chaos would erupt, and they would lose Paradise.

The physician shook his head afterwards. "As far as I can tell, she's healthy, but why the hell is she on Norval Estrate? That just shouldn't be. It needs to come out. She shouldn't be on that at all."

They could take away all the Happy drugs, lock her up in an inertia-dampening room with her hands tied behind her, shave her head, pull her teeth, feed her nothing but raw meat, but no one short of the Creator himself was going to take that drug out of Sarah's hip. She wasn't suffering through *that* again!

"They're for nerves," Dmitri explained. "We had a traumatic death in the family, and they put her on medications until she recovers."

Dr. Herzog raised a skeptical eyebrow. "I've been a licensed physician for eighteen years and I've done my share of traveling this galaxy, but I've yet to hear of anyone needing birth control for a grief reaction."

"It's not birth control! It's to stop a... *psychatc prbm*," Dmitri mumbled.

"Yemu daiesh meditsinskuyu kartu!" Sarah said in defeat. *Just give him her damned medical file!* Better to fail now than let hope build.

Reluctantly, Dmitri dug the card out of a pocket and handed it to the doctor. "It's in there. She's fine now. My only concern is her history of pneumonia. I can't drag her back here for treatment if she gets sick."

"I have several vaccines against pneumonias. We haven't had a big problem with that here." Herzog put the file in the computer. "I can run some antibody studies, prescribe some immune boosters."

He gave a long whistle. "This is some résumé you have here, little lady. It's going to take me time to read through this. Let's finish running the tests, and I can take the next hour or two to go through here before I give my final recommendation."

They waited in an empty conference room, reading over the language manuals they'd been given, three slim volumes bound in black: grammar, phrase work, and a basic dictionary. Sarah'd mastered the alphabet and basic sounds in less than an hour. " *'Ch'* as in *cheese*. As in, *<cho gorafesh Ix, fenad domalo?>*, or, 'Where does this road travel to?'. *<gash Imsa dira meralon,>* 'Please pass the salt.'"

Dimi paid vague attention. "Huh? *Gash* what?"

<gash Imsa dira meralon.> Sarah filed the phrase away in her head.

<gash Imsa dira miralon,> he repeated, peering over her shoulder. "Pass the salt."

"Not Gaaash. *Ghahsh eemsa deera merralawn.* Put the G in the back of your throat. Watch your accent."

"What accent? We haven't heard it spoken yet."

Any further argument was interrupted by the beckoning of Commander Guillaume. "Could you come back into the office, please? There are some things we'd like to discuss."

<gash Imsa dira meralon,> Sarah recited, hoping her quick study might convince him she was worth the risk.

"Very good! Primary inflection on *Imsa*, though."

<gash IMSA dira meralon,> Sarah corrected. "Is the accent always on pronouns?"

"Pretty much," Guillaume agreed, leading them into his office. "You do catch on fast!"

Herzog handed the computer card back to Dmitri. "I have some serious reservations about what's in there. We have no psychiatric facilities here, and no frequent traffic to evacuate a crisis. Medical services in the community are less than primitive; they're downright dangerous. A psychiatric disturbance could be seen as a possession by bad spirits, a perverse morality, or some supernatural thing. We just don't know. The people are superstitious enough to fall for witch hunts. It could prove very risky."

Sarah shot Dmitri a worried glance. She wanted to stay, but she had no desire to be burned at a stake, either.

"Please, sir! I don't do any of that anymore. I'll do anything you ask. If you want to keep me on medications, I'll take them. Please, give me a chance?"

"I've handled her through everything," Dmitri said. "I can't see how anything here could be worse than what we've just been through."

The commander looked at the doctor.

Herzog sighed. "I'd like to run a few psychometric tests first."

Sarah squeezed Dmitri's hand. "That's fair."

Sarah passed – not with flying colors, but enough of a margin to win approval. Herzog gave temporary assent, to be continued on a quarterly basis pending mandatory repeat exams. The medications would continue at least three more months, and for once Sarah didn't object. She wouldn't admit it, but this time she was afraid to be without them.

Now started two days of training. As an adult, Dmitri would be responsible for reporting the data, but Sarah could help. Everything and anything had to be tracked: weather, crop yields, crimes, cultural trends like clothing, music, and folklore, technology trends like transportation, communications, and manufacturing. A wood-powered steam engine had been developed, and already applications were spreading fast, mostly in the area of transportation. The planet had few species of draft animals, nothing akin to Earth's horse. To ride a temperamental plow animal was risky at best, and often they moved so slowly and stubbornly one could walk the distance faster. The primary mission needed no prerequisite experience: blend in with the local culture, observing, observing, observing, then reporting everything back with as much detail as possible.

"Ever cook for yourself?" Guillaume asked. "I can have someone run you through the basics in one of the cottages."

"Mother cooked by hand for fourteen," Dmitri replied, full of confidence. "We've learned a thing or two over the years."

The commander didn't look convinced. "If you're sure."

Training was a breeze to Sarah, but outfitting... that was something else. No matter where they'd traveled, they'd always kept the same lifestyle – same clothes, same activities, same baggage. Here, everything they owned, everything they expected to keep, had to pass inspection to ensure technological compatibility. Style didn't matter as much as material content.

Sarah wrinkled her forehead. "Everything?"

"Everything!" Jantzen Dickerson said. As second-in-command of the base, he was well-versed in technicalities. "Any item not deemed suitable must be kept here in your locker. The locks are print-scanners; only you will have access to it."

"What if we came alone and need something in the other locker?" Dmitri asked.

"We can set it to respond to two sets of prints," Dickerson said. "There are a few couples that do that. By the way, be careful how friendly you get with the natives. You can stay here permanently upon approval, but there is no way in hell you can get approval to take a native off-world. Won't happen."

Dmitri shrugged. "Not a problem. We'll take the double locks, though." Sarah nodded.

Dmitri's bags were scrutinized first. Only five shirts made the cut, and two pair of drawstring pants.

Dickerson held up the pants. "They're not a local style, but there's nothing obvious to say they *couldn't* have been made here. The rest of these have illegal fasteners."

Sarah's clothes were worse. "Nope, no, no, no, and no." Dickerson vetoed just about everything. "No pants; dresses only."

"*Dresses?*" Sarah objected. "You can't do anything in a dress! Dresses are horrible!"

Jan's blue eyes flashed with amusement. "Sorry. Women here wear skirts." Even her conservative pastel underwear were dropped in the reject pile.

"What can possibly be wrong with those?" Sarah pleaded.

"Elastic fabric. Can't have it."

"How do you expect them to stay up? Glue?"

"Drawstrings or buttons."

"*Drawstrings?!* What happens if they knot?"

Dickerson laughed out loud. "Then you have a definite problem. Ask the women here. I know they've found acceptable tricks around the restrictions."

The computer chips of homework exercises. Her favorite blue socks. Several mementos from the more civilized places they'd been. The music player poor Viktor had bought her; all to stay locked up at the Compound.

Sarah fought Dickerson over her precious photographs. "No! I won't leave them!"

Dmitri managed to snatch one from her. Dickerson examined it. People pictures were often acceptable.

"I'll tell you what: leave the originals here, and I'll give you gray-scale copies. Keep them to yourself, and there shouldn't be a problem."

Sarah knew a good compromise when she heard one. "All right," she agreed, releasing the avalanche onto the table. "But I want copies of all of them!"

Her foot slammed at the loss of her books. "They're printeds! They're fine!"

Dickerson flipped through pages. "The text itself isn't a problem, it's the photos…. If you can wait a quarter, I'll have them reprint the science texts to eliminate photos; the same with the art texts here. We just have to eliminate the color printing. Keep them under a bed or in a cupboard just to be safe. You really want to carry them that distance?"

"I've been carrying them for two and a half years," Sarah said with determination. "Why would I leave them now?"

The loss of her possessions broke Sarah's heart, but the clothing.... It had to be a joke, a ploy to see how far she could be pushed before she quit. She slapped at the blue jumper she now wore, flapping the full skirt against her legs. Add in the rough white blouse she wore under it, the sleeveless undershirt of her own, a ghastly garment that tied tightly around her ribs to corral a so-called bust line and a redundant skirt liner; throw in the bulky stockings that slid down her legs and made the hairs itch, and Sarah felt like a poorly planned scarecrow.

"I guess I can live with the dress, but I don't need this chest armor, and I want pants under the skirt," she tried to bargain.

Nora laughed at her seriousness. Water-Nora turned out to be Nora *Guillaume*, the commander's wife, and it was her task to teach a reluctant Sarah the ins and outs of local costuming. She showed her how to eliminate the risk of knots by the use of a tiny buckle to hold up the underwear, but it didn't do anything for comfort.

"I'm afraid you don't have a choice on the bust," she said, "but I guess you could wear shorts under the skirt. I'll see what I can get out of the replicator."

As soon as the woman left, Sarah stripped off the underskirt and tried to remove the restraining upper garment. The unfamiliar toggles and hooks and strings took time, and Nora caught her in the process of redressing.

"I hope you're doing that to practice," Nora pretended to scold, carrying several pairs of shorts the same colors as Sarah's dresses. She picked up the shed undergarment from the table and held it out by a string.

"*Required.*" Sarah sighed and began to undress again.

"And you need to grow your hair out," Nora informed her. "Girls wear their hair long, and once they're ready to be married, the hair gets tied back."

"It's *been* growing," Sarah grumbled. "Just tell me how to make it grow faster." It hung below her jaw now, not quite to her shoulder in the back. If it all grew back overnight, it wouldn't be fast enough.

The pair stood before Guillaume and two of his men, Sarah horribly uncomfortable and more than a little upset that Dmitri wore his own pants and a loose shirt that didn't even have a damned tie around the open V of a neck. He sported a pair of boots, the heels of which added five centimeters to his height. A leather belt circled his slim waist, and from it hung the larger of his two knives. The crafting was too fine for a local weapon, but its simplicity let it pass. Their bags lay on the table before them, repacked with acceptable belongings and several new sets of clothing.

Commander Guillaume grinned at the rawest-looking recruits he'd ever seen. He motioned to the blond man next to him. "Dale Reston will lead you out. One day's hard walk to Otaiga, you'll overnight there, and then most of a day's walk to the town of Vandijoc. Dale will help you get supplies out there; no sense in carrying them that far. You're sure you're up to this?"

"Absolutely!" Dmitri insisted.

"Yes, sir," Sarah echoed.

Nora entered the room and whispered something to Dickerson. He gave Sarah a piercing look. Nora gave her a brief pat-down. Sarah took her hands out of the skirt's pockets; they were empty.

Dickerson took her pack and pulled everything out. He uncovered a pair of peacock-blue terylon socks and a paper-bound novel with holographic artwork that had been wrapped in a skirt.

Sarah hung her head. "They're my favorites."

Dickerson pointed the book at her. "*Don't* try it again. Anything like this passes to the surface, you violate Article One and can be held accountable by law. You won't be warned again. Understand?" He handed the forbidden objects to Nora.

"Yes, sir," Sarah whispered. Dmitri reached out and fumbled for her hand, buried in the folds of the wide skirt. She expected him to squeeze it, but instead he dropped something heavy into her pocket. Then he did squeeze her hand, giving her a quick wink of understanding.

What the hell had he given her? She knew better than to look right now.

Dickerson dug through Dmitri's bag, but found nothing illegal.

Дорогой Владимир, Sarah wrote as they readied to leave.
> *Dear Vladimir,*
>
> *This will be the last you'll hear from me for about three months, so please don't worry. I'm fine. We've decided to recuperate on a planet with limited tech resources. When I say it's a two-day walk to the nearest hyperspace transmitter, I mean we're going to <u>walk</u> for two solid days! We'll be making the trip back in three months, so keep writing and I'll respond then. I'll miss them in between. If you absolutely can't wait to contact me, do it care of EXPRESS/ S. Kirushenko /Vandijoc/ Survey Team 4/UPA 63679001–99761/3. It should get to me in a week at the outside, and I should be able to reply*

in another week or less. But write it in Russian or Navaran or something, unless you want it read by other parties. Don't do it too often, at least until I know how well it will work. Do not, I repeat, <u>DO NOT</u>, share the address or our location with <u>ANYBODY</u>, EVER. Top most secret, okay? Not even David or Sergei. Not for anything. I trust you, Vlad.

I promise three month's worth of news!

Sarah

Heavy packs slung over their shoulders, they followed Dale through the wide gates of the Compound, for a countryside they'd seen only on video.

Dmitri studied a crude map. In person, the 'road' was little more than a wide dirt path.

Dale traced an alternate route with a finger. "Eventually you'll learn the shorter path over here. It'll save you a half-day's trudging, but until you're familiar with the area, stick to the main roads. If you get lost, it's a lot easier to get back on track. If you do, ask for the road to Otaiga, and in Otaiga have them point you toward Chanchi, and you'll see our fence long before you get to Chanchi."

<fenad domolo, Chanchi?> Sarah ventured.

"Close! *fenad Ik domolo, Chanchin,*" Dale said. "This road, it goes to Chanchi?"

Sarah memorized the phrase and filed it away. She walked several paces behind, one ear on the conversation. She'd forgotten about the object in her pocket until she slipped on a pebble, making the weighted fabric swing and bump against her leg.

She reached inside the pocket. The object was smooth, metallic, slightly larger than her palm, a squarish oval with an opening in one end that housed a short pointed emitter, with two small pads on one side and an adjustment... wheel... near...

Sarah's hand froze, and she stopped walking. She'd held it before. *Viktor's EPSAR weapon.* Somehow Dmitri had smuggled Viktor's EPSAR past the umpteen checks – and put it in *her* pocket! *Was he crazy?!* How could he do that to her! You couldn't get much bigger a violation than that! No wonder he didn't have a fit about her trying to keep a book. *When she got him alone ...!*

A good distance ahead, Dmitri called, "What's the matter? You still coming?"

She ran to catch up. "Yeah. Just fixing my shoe. What's the word for shoe?" she asked Dale.

Guillaume hadn't exaggerated. Dark had fallen when they came to Otaiga, the village that marked the half-way point. They'd passed fellow travelers and small farms during their journey, but nothing close to the word *civilized*. Otaiga seemed to be little more than a cluster of wooden buildings, some dark, some leaking lamplight from uncovered windows, with a stench like an abandoned zoopark. To the travelers, the local hotel looked like a living museum, but it was clean and functional. The floors were carpeted, printed papers covered the board walls, and the oil-fed lighting lent a quaint charm to the quiet rooms.

Dale handed Sarah a metal key for her room. "One for us, one for you."

Dmitri sighed and seized the key. "That won't work. Trust me. You take the room to yourself. She'll be doing good if she sleeps tonight."

The moment they were alone he demanded, "Where's my EPSAR?"

Sarah couldn't wait to get rid of the evidence. "*Your* EPSAR? What are you thinking! Do you know how *illegal* that thing is? You'll get us in so much trouble *Father* will get free before we will! What if the safety had come off?"

Dmitri wrapped the forbidden weapon in clothing and stuffed it in the very bottom of his pack. "I told you, I never, ever, plan on being caught without a weapon again. Forget that I have it, forget that you saw it, and never let me catch you near it. In fact, let's make that the First and Only Rule of Threat: if I ever catch you snooping for wherever I wind up hiding it, I will – and I mean it! – pull you over my knee and beat you til you can't sit, and trust me, I sure as hell haven't forgotten how it's done."

Sarah eyed him with distrust. He hadn't ever hit her, but she didn't doubt he was capable of it.

"Okay," she agreed, and shook on it. As long as she wasn't the one holding the evidence when the Allied Fleet came to arrest them.

* * *

Guillaume had described Vandijoc as a bustling town on a main trade route, a booming community of six hundred, the perfect place to observe a functioning society. Seeing it in person, Dmitri and Sarah weren't sure they had the right town. Hemmed in by high hills on one side and thick forest all around, the town seemed far more isolated than it was. The main thoroughfare was no more than a rutted, filthy dirt path ten meters wide, littered with enormous, insect-covered mounds of animal droppings. Side streets branched off, the structures less crowded and more dilapidated the farther from town one looked. Most of the buildings were raised up a meter or so, with wide covered porches before them. There was little resemblance to the neat, planned, orderly buildings of the Compound's prosperous false village, or even Otaiga's gaudy painted decor.

Dmitri and Sarah got their first close look at the local idea of work animals, harnessed to a cart in front of a building. The compound had three, but all were in the fields when they toured the animal sheds. Sarah's first thought was of a baby allosaurus in a Siberian coat. The snake-like head whipped high overhead on a long supple neck, with nervous bulging eyes and sharp-looking teeth that snapped disagreeably at nothing. Elephantine legs supported their heavy bodies, three-quarters of which was hidden under a carpeting of shaggy brown and white hair. The creatures ended in thick, balding, two-meter tails. One let out a loud, strangling bray and snapped its teeth at a bat-like bird picking an insect from its hair, while the other lifted its tail and added a vile wave of filth and stench to the street.

"*Porshies*," Dale explained. "They look a lot friendlier than they are. Left alone, they forage on plants and grains, but they'll eat just about anything that wanders in front of them. Unless you're good with animals, I wouldn't plan on getting one immediately. You don't need one, outside of farming. If you can get them to work, two of them can pull a house."

Dmitri blinked his eyes and rubbed his burning nose as they passed. The animals had a strong, heavy, musky odor that made his head hurt. "If," he noted.

"*If*," Dale agreed. "But the best part is, they make a tasty steak."

Dale purchased further supplies in a local shop, and they walked the last kilometers burdened in darkening twilight. The lantern he carried did little to light the forested path; it merely blinded them against the darkness. The pathway opened into a clearing, with the dark shape of a building looming before them.

Dale swung the light in the direction of the shadow. "That's your work shed. Storage, tools if they haven't been stolen, a place for animals if you choose to raise them. I don't know what's left. We haven't had a team out this way for any length of time in months.

"And this is your new home." He held the light up to shine on a wall of stacked logs. The plank door swung open at his push.

Dale hung the lantern from a hook in the ceiling, giving soft illumination to the room. It was a kitchen area, with a metal heating unit, some cabinets, and a massive plank table flanked by benches. A row of cabinets with several open shelves above them divided the room from a sitting area, all but hidden now by the darkness. Dust webs hugged shadows; dirt and dry leaves crunched on the wooden floor. Somewhere in the cabin, an insect protested the invasion. Dale directed Dmitri to start a fire in the heating unit, making sure the pipes still worked.

Lighting brighter oil lamps found on the shelves, Dale took one and showed them around, a three-minute tour. A creaking staircase led to a large bedroom with a single bed. The bed had linens, but when Sarah patted the softness, a cloud of mustiness flew up, sending her into a fit of hard coughing. A doorless hole in the wall formed a closet. Downstairs, a narrow door led to a tiny room under the stairs, fitted with a primitive sanitary unit. It was filled to the top with black water, and supported a thriving colony of waterbugs.

"You don't expect us to use that?" Sarah asked doubtfully.

"Not at the moment," Dale said, pulling the lever that should have rinsed the contents. The lever flopped freely on its post. "Guess I'll show you a thing or two about plumbing while I'm here." He made them flush out the water pump next to the heater before drinking anything from it.

"This is your cooler," Dale explained, pulling up a small hatch in the kitchen floor. The new owners peered into the dark pit while he lowered the lantern in. "Pour enough water in every morning to cover that wire rack there, and then keep anything that might spoil in the bucket on the rack. It's not the greatest system, but it will help. The water will drain out slowly, but it will keep things around five degrees or so most of the day."

After a late meal of watery soup and bread, they tried to sleep. No one was adventuresome enough to take the upstairs bed, so the men camped on the floor of the living area. Sarah slept on the kitchen table.

"It may not be softer or cleaner," she explained, "but until I know what's crawling on the floor, I'll sleep up here."

A relentless shrieking woke the trio as the first faint light sifted through the cracks of the shuttered windows.

"What the hell is that?" Dmitri squinted. "What time is it?"

Dale chuckled, throwing back his blanket. He gave Dmitri an unwelcome shake. *"That,"* he grinned, "is your wake-up call. Time to get moving. The birds start somewhere between 04:30 and 05:00."

Dmitri groaned. "Four-thirty? That's what time we *go* to bed!"

By sunrise Dale had gone, beginning the long walk back by himself.

"You're sure you can find the way back?"

Dmitri nodded. "I'm sure." The two new 'Cultural Observers' gave their guide a tired wave. They were on their own, completely, deliberately, foolishly, a quadrillion kilometers from anywhere.

Dmitri yawned noisily yet again. "Why don't you wash first, and I'll see what I can find for breakfast."

Sarah started across the floor, then stopped. *Come to think of it...*

Thirty-one

Breakfast proved one more disappointing act in an already discouraging day. Dale had purchased a jar of substance he termed butter, but the greasy solid didn't taste like it. Simple toasted bread was all they wanted, but neither had any idea how to make it.

"Heat," Dmitri remembered, starting a fire. "Mother's toasting unit had a heat field in it."

He stuck a piece of bread on a fork and held it over the fire. He cut the first piece too thin, and it fell into the flames. The second caught fire itself, and he burned a finger. The third was blackened on the outside, but he scraped the black off and ate it anyway. Sarah's attempt at pinning bread between two sticks took twice as long, but turned out slightly better.

Dmitri made notes with a charcoal pencil on a piece of real fiber-paper. "Okay. First thing, we look around. Then we'll clean out some of the dirt and stuff. After lunch, we'll head back to town and pick up anything we think we need."

"Maybe I'll have warmed up by then." Sarah shivered, eating her bread by the open stove door. There *was* no formal bath, no bathing facility at all. She'd washed in the upstairs room with a bucket of cold water, dressed – leaving off the chafing rib-strangler and needless skirt liner, and Dmitri helped her wash and rinse her hair with more cold water from the pump, making her teeth chatter and chilling her to the bone.

"We'll work on that problem later," he promised. "We're both stupid for not seeing it last night. Give it a day or two, we'll have it all under control."

The cabin was no more impressive in the daylight, nothing more than a primitive shelter of stacked logs. Odd tools hung in the workshed, but the best find was a sturdy wheeled cart with a handle, as big as a bathtub. They dragged it to town and dragged it back, loaded with things no one had thought about, like a tea substitute, extra cooking pans, and clean blankets.

They spent hours tidying, never having had much practice. Mother's homes always had electrostatic dust annihilators, robotic floor sweepers, germicidal baths, clothing reconditioners, and hired help for anything else. On their own, they'd always had maid service at least once a week, and reconditioned their clothes only when everything they had was thoroughly beyond wearing in public.

By dinner, their idealism scraped thin.

Sarah coughed on the smoke coming from the pan. "I thought you said you could cook?"

"I never said I *knew* how to cook." Dmitri swore as he burned another finger. He sucked on the finger and waved it, then wrapped the pan's handle in the hem of his shirt before touching it again. "I said we should be able to figure it out. This is nothing like Mother's cooking unit."

"You mean in fifteen years you didn't learn anything, watching Mother?" Sarah coughed again, stirring and scraping burning vegetable chunks from the bottom of the pan she tended while Dmitri fought with the burning slice of meat.

He fanned away some of the smoke. "The only thing I remember for sure is to make tea, you wait until the water bubbles, and then it's hot enough. And the last time Mother cooked meat, it was on a flame, but she used a mesh rack, not a pan. Tomorrow we'll go to town and see if we can find one."

They scraped the food onto the plates and sat down with another round loaf of grainy bread. Bread lost its appeal after four meals in a row. At least they now had tea to dip it in. It wasn't like *real* tea; it had a grassy taste. The local version of milk would take longer to get used to – the fat content was much higher, and it had the weedy, herby taste of the butter.

With her fingernail, Sarah peeled the burnt side of what used to be a pale white vegetable, and took a bite. The outer few millimeters were soft, the middle crunchy and tasteless. She made a face. <*gash Imsa dira meralon.*>

<*Axa,*> Dmitri replied, *yes,* passing a glass jar of salt. "There! We just had our first whole conversation in Tau Cetan. See! It won't be so bad." He chewed the edge of his meat, then put the middle on his plate.

Sarah poked the meat, cut into it, then put the knife down. She didn't like meat to start with, and this was charred on the outside and raw on the inside. She pushed the plate away.

"I can't eat this. I can't eat *any* of this. I'm starving and cold and these clothes are cutting into me and all the skin is coming off my hands from that stupid broom. Face it, Dimi, we're in over our heads! How could we be so *stupid*? We don't know how to live like this. No hot water, no skin creams, no baths, no heat, no medicines, no food – our kind of people aren't meant to live like this!" She picked the skin from a blister. "Where are the horse and carriage rides and the beautiful houses and the *good* food?"

Dmitri put down the bite he was gnawing. "Hey! You gonna give

242

up that easily? Since when have we *ever* quit on anything? Did we quit when Valeria left us on Navara? Did we ever quit at the Mirabella? Did we quit when Vik fell? Like Hell we did, and we're not going to quit now. Yeah, I know, this isn't what we expected, and we didn't think of the simplest things like baths and hot water, but we'll get the hang of it. Don't tell me the locals take ice-water baths. This is the worst, the first days. It'll get better, I promise."

"Look," he said, retrieving his pencil. He made a crude sketch of the cabin right on the table. "Here's what we've got. I've been thinking. If we add more building here," he drew on the side of the outline, "we can add a couple rooms in an ell, add me another room upstairs, and down in the ell we'll build ourselves a real bathroom, with another heater and a tub we can sit in, like the one at that hotel. If we keep a drum of water on top of a heater – remember Mother's big samovar back in Kiev? Like that. Wrap the heater in metal coils, we should be able to have hot water for baths whenever we want."

Sarah blew on her stinging blisters. "You haven't built anything since you last played with blocks. You don't know anything about building buildings, and even less about plumbing."

"No," Dmitri said defensively, "but someone around here must. We just have to find and hire them. We can do it." He reached for the bread, thoughts rolling. "We can make this work fine… "

The day had been sunny and warm, but by the time the sun set and the second moon, a sulfurous yellow one, edged over the horizon, the areas away from the heater grew chilly. Exhausted and sore, they dragged themselves up the groaning stairs to the cleaned bedroom.

Dmitri put the lamp on a table by the bed. Every muscle in his body ached from unfamiliar exercise, and the discomfort of sleeping on the hard floor the night before. He glanced longingly at the bed, with its pillows and sheets.

"I guess we can take turns until we get another bed. Go ahead. You can take it tonight."

"You're just as tired as I am," Sarah said. "It's wide. You take one side, I'll take the other. It's not like we haven't slept that way before. Besides, there's no plastiglass in those windows, and no heat up here. We'll get twice as many covers than if we separate."

Dmitri pursed his lips. Sarah wasn't a kid anymore; she was, for all biological purposes, a young *woman*, and he'd been a lot more insistent she sleep on her own.

"All right," he agreed. "But just until we can get another mattress. I don't mind sleeping on a floor, but I'd rather have a cushion under me." Neither undressed except for shoes. Dmitri blew out the lamp, and they collapsed on their respective edges of the bed.

The bed had other ideas.

The mattress sagged, rolling them into a packed mass in the center.

"Maybe this *isn't* going to work," Sarah decided.

Day two, and still only bread and fruit and tea for breakfast. Surely this planet believed in jelly, at least? Dmitri promised they'd go back to town and look for something.

They'd wrestled the mattress to the floor to sleep on. Three sides of the bed stood free; the fourth was the wall. Ropes woven between the sides supported the mattress; over time they had stretched, and needed tightening. Dmitri braced a foot against the frame and pulled; Sarah kept the tension behind him, and just when they had it about right, the rope snapped, crashing them to the floor. The trip to town moved up to the morning's list.

Sarah wanted to help with the bed repair, but there was nothing for her to do.

"It's going to take me a while to restring this," Dmitri said. He tied the ropes together so the new would follow the path as he removed the old one. "Why don't you explore some? I'll call you when it's time to tighten. Stay where you can see the house."

"Whatever." Sarah didn't mind. Nothing, absolutely nothing could bother her except an occasional puffy cloud, and the commotion of chattering birds. Commander Guillaume had been right; this place *was* quiet. After just two days, the word *boring* loomed in her mind. At least in hotels she often had a vidscreen to keep her occupied. What was she supposed to do here? Build mudcastles? Two or three footpaths crossed the yard; she chose the one behind the workshed and set off.

In a minute or two, she lost sight of the cabin. Thick forest grew on her right, to the left was open field, covered evenly with a reedy plant taller than her head. She stopped to investigate. The sturdy stalks had sunned yellow; narrow brown leaves hung down crackling dry. At least a dozen short stems branched off at the top, ending in a flowery arrangement of hundreds of tiny seed pods.

Sarah crumbled one in her hand, blew away the chaff, and examined the hard, ridged seeds, no bigger than a grain of rice. A homogeneous field like this wasn't weeds; it was a grain crop. A scan up the path and a peek through the rows lent strong weight to her suspicions. It must be the land rented by the neighboring farm, and it looked ready for harvest.

Sarah's head snapped up, listening, but all the noises were unfamiliar. The hair on her neck rose. Farming meant people, strange people, and here she was out in an unfamiliar place, all alone. *Damn the medications!* She knew better than anyone never to wander.

Nothing could be seen but the path, the massive trees, and the field of tall grain. A million places someone could be hiding.

How far had she come? Could Dmitri hear her scream from here? Would he know where to look?

She waited, motionless, but nothing changed. The sun beamed bright overhead, baking the grain so it gave off a nutty scent.

"You're stuck here for three months!" Sarah scolded herself out loud. "You can't go getting squirrelly the minute you can't see the house." Against her better judgment, she forced herself farther down the path, mentally holding her own hand.

"Five more minutes and I'll have gone far enough for today." She picked up a stick to mark the place she'd stop. Later she would show Dimi the path, and they could walk it together.

Two minutes passed before she first heard it. A low blowing, followed by a creaking and a metallic jingling, then a faint whistling. Sarah froze in her footprints. Even batty alien birds didn't sing off-key. A garbled shout followed. She slipped between the rows of grain and squatted down, unsure what danger might be near. Daylight glittered through the stalks several meters in the opposite direction. Curious, she hefted the damned skirt above her knees, twisted it tightly, and tucked the twist into her waistband, out of the way. She crept forward on her hands and knees, peering down the row of plants.

Ten or twelve meters ahead in a clearing, a boy was tying up bundles of cut stalks. He whistled lightly while he worked. He scooped a bundle together, tied it with a cord, and stacked it on a cart. The blowing noise sounded again off to her right, a great shooshing followed by an impatient squeal, too close for her liking. Wherever the animal was, she couldn't see it from where she hid. Sarah looked for a gap where she might slip closer. The boy glanced behind him and said something. All she could catch was 'you' and 'be.' Why didn't she think to take the lexicon!

The jingly shaking sounded again, much closer this time. With a crunching rattle of dry plants, a hideous *porshie* lumbered from the side into the uncut grain, directly towards her. It whipped its sinuous neck about, the great scaly head sniffing her scent among the stalks. With an angry bellow, it charged.

Sarah didn't hesitate. Crashing through the grain, she took off for the cabin, the snorting, squealing porshie shaking the ground as its feet slammed behind her in an ungraceful gallop. Her skirt came untucked and fell below her knees.

"Aia!" The boy yelled in surprise as his animal took off. Grabbing a thick pole, he chased after the porshie.

Sarah ran the distance in blind terror. *"Diiiiimiiiiii!"* she found breath to scream as she neared the house, heavy snorting right behind her.

Dmitri was out the door by the time Sarah flew across the yard. She dove behind his legs, grinding the dress into the hard-packed dirt, gasping for breath. The porshie trotted across the yard, stuck its long neck out, and shrieked like shearing metal. It snapped its brown-streaked teeth, the bulging eyes rolling upward to show cranberry rims.

Dmitri couldn't back up with Sarah behind him. His hand went to the knife on his belt. He drew it out and held it with both hands.

"I'll use it if I have to!" he warned the animal uselessly in Russian, and pointed the weapon at the blunt nose.

Ten seconds behind the porshie, the boy ran across the yard. Shouting something, he jumped before the porshie and brought his club down hard on the flat space between its eyes. The porshie reared its head and screamed, came in sideways for a bite, and got clobbered again. This time it gave a grunt and shook its thick head. The boy reached up and grabbed a strap on the bridle. He gave a hard tug, and the head lowered. Taking the strap from the other side, he dragged the porshie to the nearest tree and tied it firmly.

Animal under control, the boy approached them. He bowed low several times and leaned to the side, addressing Sarah as she peeked from behind her brother, chattering in a shushy stream of alien tongue. Then he spoke to Dmitri, pointing to the animal.

Dmitri sheathed his knife. "Any idea what he's saying?"

Sarah stood up. Her face was scratched, her dress covered in soil and leaves. Bits of grain stuck in her wild hair. "Not really, but it sounds like an apology."

<to Aja tuxna,> Dmitri shrugged. *I don't speak.* He figured it was the most important phrase he could learn, next to 'Would you mind if I kissed you?'.

"Sar, grab the dictionary." She disappeared in a flash.

He clapped a hand to his chest. *"Dmitri Kirushenko.* What's the word for sister?" he asked as Sarah reappeared, book in hand.

<Elistri,> she replied without pause.

Dimi pointed. *<Elistri Sarah.>*

The boy stood as tall as Sarah, but strong from labor. Friendly brown eyes looked out from a round face, and brown hair hung to his shoulders – longer than Sarah's. His dusty shirt was damp with sweat, and his pants bore a neat patch on one leg. His bare feet were as tanned as his face and arms. He put a hand to his own chest and gave a slight bow.

<Charshfenakialetneshfaja.>

"Did he sneeze," Dmitri whispered, "or is that a name?"

<Repeat, please?> Sarah dared ask, still mostly hidden behind her brother.

The boy grinned. <Char-shfe-*na*-ki Al-et-nesh-*fa*-ja.>

Sarah repeated it perfectly.

"As long as one of us knows it," Dmitri muttered. Flipping around the dictionary, he tried some simple conversation while the boy endured his mispronunciations.

<Here be us now to live,> Dmitri tried. *<Live before we away, far.>*

The boy gestured toward the path. *<I live. Always live.>*

They stood a long moment in silence. *Please pass the salt* didn't seem appropriate. At last the boy bowed and uttered a few garbled sentences. He pointed to his run-away beast, then back to the path. He had to get back to work. He untied the porshie. The brute reared its head, baring teeth, but the boy seized the bridle fearlessly and yanked with all his weight. The porshie conceded for the moment.

Dmitri flipped pages. *<Me, to help?>*

Charshfenaki bowed again and held out one of the ties. Dmitri approached the porshie warily, keeping a careful watch on the bug-eye ogling him.

"*Dimi!* You know *nothing* about animals!" Sarah hissed.

"Nope. You coming with us?"

Charshfenaki pulled on the strap that crossed the broad nose. The porshie dropped its back end and refused to budge.

"No," she decided. "I'm not going anywhere near that thing. Don't be long, and don't let it eat you."

"Wouldn't be my first choice."

The boy tugged the bridle until he hung from the straps with his feet in the air. He braced them against the beast's chest, fighting the strong neck. The porshie pretended not to notice. Charshfenaki dropped down and gave his club to Dmitri, motioning intent.

"You sure?" Dmitri didn't go around beating on things, especially animals. The boy jabbered encouragingly.

Dmitri poked the beast in its hairy flank, and sneezed eight times in a row. Up close, the musky, mousy porshie-odor made his nose run. He jammed the back of his hand against his nose until the burning stopped.

"Go on! Move it!" He gave the tail a tap. "Come on! Forward ho." *Sneeze, sneeze, sniff.*

Charshfenaki spoke sharper, and swung his arms in demonstration.

Dmitri hated to hurt the beast, stubborn or not. He raised the stick and swung it hard into the base of the tail. "Get your damned ass out of my yard!"

The porshie sat a few seconds longer, then got up and trotted under the guidance of its master's pull as if it had thought of the idea itself.

"I'll be back," Dmitri called behind him, stuffing the dictionary in a pocket and giving his nose a hard rub. "Don't go anywhere alone."

"Not a chance!" Sarah watched him disappear behind the workshed, then darted inside the house and barred the door behind her.

Dmitri banged on the door a few hours later. "It's me, Sar, let me in." Sarah hefted the reinforced board that served as a lock. She gave a soft belch. The house smelled different. It smelled – *good!*

Dmitri had figured he'd start burning something for dinner after he rested. He'd helped Charsh-boy load his cart and hitch up the horrible hairy dinosaur, and his arms and back hurt. The sharp leaves of the plants sliced the skin on his fingers, and they stung. Then there was the pounding headache behind his face every time he sneezed...

"You started the heater? You shouldn't do that unless I'm around. I don't need you catching yourself on fire. You didn't – cook something?" He sniffed at the air with his aching nose.

Sarah couldn't hold back the smile any longer. "Sit! See what I figured out." She steered him onto the bench. "Close your eyes and open up," she ordered, dangling something before his mouth.

Dmitri's eyes opened in delight as he chewed. A vegetable, cooked soft but not mushy, and carefully salted. "Not bad! What'd you do to it? Is there more?" He looked hopefully at the stove.

Sarah pulled him by the hand and showed him a pot half-full of orange-green chunks.

"I got to thinking. When we eat out, we order steamed vegetables, *da*? What's steam but water vapor that's been heated hotter than the surrounding air. So I heated water as if to make tea and I stuck one in there."

Dmitri picked another piece from the pan and salted it. Here was something that herby butter might actually taste good on. "How'd you know how long to cook it?"

"I kept a fork in it and took a bite every three minutes," she explained. "I cooked this batch for eighteen minutes. That's when it seemed to taste right."

He kissed her on the top of her head. "Tastes right to me, too. It's about time you put that brain to use. I told you things would get better. Bring on the bread!"

By the third day a new daily routine had taken shape, centering around exhausted sleep and painfully boring meals. They dragged the heavy cart to the town once more and dragged it back with a new mattress. Dmitri gave the bed to Sarah, and gallantly took the mattress at the foot of the bed. In the afternoon, they explored the grounds in two more directions, picking their way across a stream that ran behind the cabin. Despite the three-hour walk, they found no evidence of any other homesites.

Dmitri sat on a table-sized slab of rock at a bend in the stream. "I guess it doesn't get much more away-from-it-all than this, huh?"

Sarah watched the leaves waving gently overhead, so many trees and leaves all but blocking the purply-blue sky. She listened with rapture to the assorted chirps and squawks of the animal life.

"It's perfect!"

They had just sat down to their dismal little dinner when a voice called at the door.

Dimi waved in Charshfenaki, followed by a shorter, older, much rounder woman, carrying something covered by a cloth.

Charshfenaki gave his little bow. *<Pleasant day,>* he said slowly. He held a hand out to the woman. *<Mother.>*

Dmitri copied the boy's greeting, and Sarah managed a polite nod without looking directly at the guests. The woman held out the cloth-covered object and said a fast string of words. A warm, sweet, meaty smell wafted through the kitchen.

Charshfenaki spoke to her, and she repeated herself much slower. *<For you. We say, 'Welcome in Vandijoc'.>*

Dmitri and Sarah lifted their noses, afraid to hope beyond hope. Something smelled incredibly good.

<mangato, Ahnax.> Dmitri knew enough to thank her, and accepted the warm dish. He lifted a corner of the cloth, and his heart nearly stopped. It sure as hell looked like a piecrust to him. A perfectly formed, golden crust like his mother used to make. He removed the cloth, mouth watering.

Sarah craned her neck for a better view. "Dimi? Tell me that's food."

"I think it's Heaven on a plate." He placed the dish on the table, grabbed the bread knife and plunged it deep into the pie. A wave of delectable steam poured out as he scooped a thick slice from the dish and dropped it on his plate, then did the same for Sarah.

"It's a meat pie," he warned her, as chunks of meat and vegetables tumbled from the crust.

"I don't care! I'm so hungry, I'd eat a mouse." She grabbed a vegetable cube with her fingers, dropped it as she burned them, then picked it up and blew on it before stuffing it in her mouth and burning her tongue.

"It's good!" Sarah gasped. "Oh my goodness! I haven't tasted anything like this in years!" She broke off a piece of crust and stuffed it in next.

Dmitri shoveled in a second forkful, sucking air in around the hot gravy before he remembered their company. He grabbed two more plates from a cabinet, dusted them on his shirt, and placed them on the table. He walked over to the woman, who watched him with a shocked expression.

<*Thank you! mangato, Ahnax! esa mangato, Ahnax!*> Dmitri shook her hand, then kissed it, bowing several times. Her chubby face broke into a smile, and she allowed him to lead her to a bench at the table. She couldn't have been older than her mid-thirties. Her face was still almost pretty, with quick dark eyes and chocolate hair tied back from rosy cheeks. She was no taller than Sarah's shoulder, and as roly-poly as a snowman. Dmitri motioned Charshfenaki to sit, and handed him pie. Sarah pushed her plate forward in turn, even though she hadn't finished the first piece.

The little dictionary passed back and forth as they tried to converse. Charshfenaki's mother merely smiled when offered the book, pushing it back to her son. <*You read,*> she told him, and rubbed at her eyes.

<*You finish field, Charlie?*> Dmitri asked.

Sarah wrinkled her nose. "Charlie?"

Charshfenaki motioned for the book. <*Char Lee?*>

<*Charsh a larsh fenarsh – I no can to say. I say, 'Charlie'.*> Dmitri made a cutting motion with his hand. <*Charlie – you.*> 'Charlie' looked at his mother, and they mumbled a moment.

<*Yes,*> the boy said, understanding. <*Char-lee. Field,*> he held his hands slightly apart, <*done. Need three days.*>

<*You to want to help? We to help!*> Dmitri pointed to himself and Sarah. They had nothing better to do, and they were supposed to make contact with natives. <*Make porshie to stay house – Sarah to pull wagon.*>

Sarah nodded earnestly. She could do that. As long as that dinosaur wasn't there. Charlie and his mother laughed again.

<*How long you travel, to come here?*> Charlie's mother asked.

Sarah held up a handful of fingers. <*Three red months.*> That's what their prepared "background" said. Months were complicated, with three moons circling the night sky. One time frame kept track of the large red moon, whose phases took six Earth weeks to complete. The other tracked the smaller moons, one yellow, one silver, which raced the sky every three Earth weeks. <*Our family live there still.*>

Dmitri eyed the remaining quarter of pie, but Sarah caught the glance.

She waved her fork threateningly. "Touch it and I'll stab you! If we put it under the floor, we'll have a decent lunch tomorrow, too."

Dmitri relented. "You win. I sure as hell won't mind eating it a second day in a row."

Their guests didn't stay much longer. The sky grew dark, and they had a long walk. Dmitri bowed several times more to Mrs. Charlie, then made her a bold offer. <*You come two, three, maybe four days, to cook food? I give money... *>

Mrs. Aletneshfaja bowed, pleased he'd enjoyed the pie. *<You have big girl – she cook.>*

Dmitri shook his head. *<No Mother. I no cook, she no cook. We eat only bread.>*

Mrs. Aletneshfaja bowed again and patted Dmitri on the arm. *<I come back.>*

Thirty-two

Dmitri dragged himself off the mattress when he could no longer deny the brightness coming through the windows. He poked Sarah until she, too, rose sleepily. The sun glimmered low in the trees when they set off down the path behind the workshed, but Charlie had cut several rows of grain by the time they wandered into the field. The porshie remained tethered to the heavy work cart. It turned its ugly head toward the intruders, straining hard at the straps that held it in bondage.

Sarah stopped. "I won't go near that thing, Dim! What if it gets loose?"

"You promised you'd help. These people live with them every day. Come on."

Charlie stopped cutting to bow several times. Dmitri waved back, but Sarah stepped sideways toward the forest edge.

<Elistri no like porshie,> Dmitri explained.

Charlie nodded. He grabbed the animal by the harness loops, and with a mighty tug led it back. The porshie made some progress, then lowered its back half defiantly, showing no intention of ever moving again.

Still Sarah hesitated.

"Move it!" Dmitri called, pausing to sneeze. He, too, was glad to have more distance between him and the porshie. Sarah moved, one eye on the beast.

The ground and grain were dusty, the sun warm on their backs, the work mindless but not difficult. Charlie swung the cutter, a lethal blade as long as his leg, leaving a wide path of fallen stalks behind. Once he was a safe distance ahead, Sarah and Dmitri gathered the stalks and tied them into bundles. After a while, Charlie showed Dmitri how to swing the blade. It didn't take Dimi long to catch on to the rhythm, but he wasn't used to the work, and took frequent breaks. Sarah begged to be given a turn, but even the temper-warning footstomp wouldn't change Dimi's mind. A careless accident could be fatal, and he wasn't taking chances.

By mid-morning ten meters of ground were clear, the entire width of the field. Sarah's soft fingers were sore and shredded, her feet chafed by the dusty shoes. She kicked them off, removed the heavy stockings, and let her toes wriggle free. Her feet were tender against the stalk stubble, but if the natives could do it, she could, too. She sat on the ground, drinking water from a jar, eyes never straying from the porshie now lying on its wide belly, not far enough across the field.

Charlie tipped his head at Dmitri. He waved a hand at all they'd done. *<You work fast. I thank. Me, need work all day.>* He retrieved a stoppered bottle from the cart and drank from it, then offered it to Dmitri.

Dmitri bowed his head and accepted the bottle, assuming it to be water. He choked when the liquid burned at his throat. It tasted like a heavy beer, but with a fruitier overtaste.

Charlie laughed with glee, taking the bottle. He held two fingers backwards across his lips. *<Ee! Mother not know! Think only water. It good? You like?>*

Dmitri broke into a grin. No matter where he went, people were the same. The kid must have been desperate for friendship, or out to impress him, trusting him with a secret like that so soon.

<Axa!> Dmitri said honestly. *<It good.>* Charlie appeared pleased.

"Hey, Sar?" Dimi called to her. "What's the year ratio here? I mean, age-wise? Are we older or younger?" He couldn't keep track of the time juggling. It was bad enough converting things to Unified Stellar Time and back.

"Their year is three weeks shorter than ours," she figured out loud, "but their day is two hours longer, so that's the same as having more than two extra days a month, or thirty days a year, or an extra year every twelve, – oh, just call it even!"

"So locally, I could already be twenty." His age actually matched his ID again. Dmitri pulled the dictionary out of his pocket and searched. *<You how many aged?>*

<Elmench,> Charlie replied, taking another drink. Sixteen. He offered the bottle again to Dimi, who didn't pass. *<You?>*

<Me? Old!> Dmitri tried to joke. *<Shivala.>* Twenty. Charlie nodded. They were silent while Dmitri did more contemplative fingerwork through the book.

<What you like to do, when no to work? You to view much girls?>

<Some,> Charlie admitted. *<I see when I get time for school. I see girls in town, but now everyone working on harvest. After harvest will be big party. Lots of girls. You look for girl to contract?>*

Dmitri gave a little laugh and shrugged. *<I always look...!>*

Two more hours of work, and only Charlie still possessed energy.

<Come!> he said, placing the cutting blade carefully against a stack of sheaves. *<Time for eat! Not sleep yet!>*

Dmitri pulled his aching body from the ground, while Sarah hunted for her shoes. She stopped not far from where she'd started. As they'd progressed the last few meters across the field, so had the porshie. It now stood some six meters away, still harnessed to the heavy cart, chewing contentedly. Something long and pale disappeared like spaghetti into the wide mouth. Something remarkably like a girl's knit stocking.

"Dimi!" Sarah cried, pointing. "It's eating my things!"

Dmitri looked up in time to see the last of the sock disappear. The creature bent its long neck and nosed something on the ground with a breathy snort. When it lifted its head, it was eating a shoe.

Dimi waved at it. "Hey! Hey! Charlie! Porshie!"

Charlie spat an angry string of words that Dmitri didn't quite think he'd find in the dictionary. He grabbed his porshie-stick from the side of the cart and swung it high at the ornery head, shouting. The porshie continued to chew, holding its head just out of reach.

<Stop! No!> Dmitri pushed the boy's arm down as the animal gave a hard swallow and the shoe disappeared for good. *<No,>* he repeated before sneezing caught him. He rubbed fiercely at his eyes and nose. The thought of hitting an animal – even a thoroughly disagreeable one – made him feel sick. It wouldn't recover the items.

Charlie threw the stick on the ground. He bowed repeatedly in front of Dmitri, jabbering without regard. He cursed again at the beast, then bowed before Sarah. He took her hand, shaking it while pleading forgiveness.

Sarah drew back at the contact. Charlie seemed nice and all, but he was still a stranger and he was *touching* her. "Dimi, make him stop. It's only a shoe, for crying out loud! I didn't like them to start with."

<Ganai! Stop!> Dmitri interceded, trying to pull Charlie away without seeming impolite. *<Forget! Forget.>* He waved a hand to brush away the problem, then pointed to the animal nosing the ground for more sweat-salted shoes. *<Look to porshie. Porshie make self – >* Dmitri held his stomach and puffed out his cheeks.

<Aja,> Charlie said with obvious dejection. *<Porshies eat all.>*

There was a pause before Dmitri began to laugh. *<Tomorrow, Charlie – give porshie more to eat!>*

Before they left the cabin the next morning, Charlie and his mother met them at their door. *<I come back!>* Mrs. Aletneshfaja said cheerfully. *<You help Charshfenaki, I help make house* shilak *and teach girl to cook nice.>* She patted Sarah on the arm. *<We make good food for everyone. Come!>*

Today Sarah was barefoot. The only other shoes she'd been given were velvety slippers for best; they wouldn't last long in the stubble of the field. She turned to Dimi. "I'm going with *you*."

Dmitri felt the argument coming like a breeze before a storm. "I think she thinks you're staying here with her."

"Well, I'm not! I don't stay with strangers, end of point."

Dmitri pulled her aside. "Sar, you can't insult her like that. She came over here to do something nice. She's trying to be friendly, get to know you."

"I didn't ask her to be friendly. *You* asked her to come over and cook. You're not leaving me here alone! I can learn just as much about foreign culture out there in the field as I can inside the house. If *you* go, *I* go."

"She's a nice old woman, Sar. You know where I'll be. I'll be back at lunch. You'll be okay. Nothing can happen to us here."

"That's what we thought about an armed Outpost!"

<Come!> Mrs. Aletneshfaja repeated. *<Work will be fast together.>*

Sarah shot Dimi a pleading stare. They didn't have so much as a wristcom to call Guillaume if something happened. *What if an army was on the march right now, bent on destruction? What if Dimi got in the way and Charlie hit him with the blade? What if the porshie trampled him? What if ...*

Dmitri heaved a long sigh. He put his hand out for the dictionary. "Next time, you're staying here," he glared. The woman waited.

<Mrs. Alin... > To Sarah he asked, "What's that name again?"

<Aletneshfaja,> Sarah replied with perfect inflection. It *did* sound like a long sneeze.

The older woman offered her first name. *<Alwhulida.>*

That wasn't any easier. *<Mrs. Al,>* he settled on, bowing. *<I... need... to see girl. I need keep girl today with me. I very sorry. Time next, I make her to stay. Please, understand?>*

Mrs. Al's cheery face furrowed. Her enthusiasm fell a notch, but she bowed her head. *<Next time.>*

At lunch they loaded the bundles and left them; in the afternoon they'd haul them to the Aletneshfaja farm for storage.

Dmitri stared in amazement when he stepped into the dark little cabin. It seemed brighter, even *shiny*. The wooden floor glowed a warm yellow. The dull black stove, formerly crusty with spilled food, sparkled with a reflective patina. The burnt pans, piled on the back of the stove between meals, were scoured clean, the flaky black char gone and the pans hung neatly from hooks that had been in the wall behind the stove the entire time. The sticky table had been washed and rubbed with oil until it glowed.

Wherever Dmitri looked, the grime had been removed from every corner, every crevice, every surface of both rooms. A waterglass sat on the table, holding fluffy yellow flowers and a sprinkling of wider white blossoms. It gave the woodsey kitchen a warm, homey feel. As the crowning touch, Mrs. Al served up a lunch that made Dmitri's mouth water clear across the yard: succulent slices of meat roasted to perfection, a rainbow of vegetables smothered with gravy, and nut-brown biscuits still warm from the oven. Dmitri tore in.

Sarah had seconds on the vegetables, and was on her fourth soft biscuit dripping with buttery-stuff when Mrs. Al prodded her to eat the meat still untouched on her plate.

<Bread make you rise big like me.> She patted her ample middle. *<Meat make you grow, make you healthy.>*

Sarah gave a small, forced smile. "You want the meat, Dim? I can't eat meat like this; you know that. I can still see the striated fibers. Everything else is wonderful."

"Shure!" he mumbled around a mouthful of gravied biscuit. "I don't know what spice she used, but I love it."

Mrs. Al frowned at the girl. *<You must eat meat, make you strong, not sick.>*

<Sarah no like meats – all meats,> Dmitri said, stuffing his mouth. *<She like only that.>* He pointed to the other dishes.

They helped clear the table, following Charlie's lead, putting the dirty dishes on top of the cabinet that held the water pump and readying themselves to go back to work.

Mrs. Al put a friendly arm around Sarah. *<You maybe stay for afternoon?>* she invited, rubbing the girl's back, but something was amiss. Mrs. Al patted Sarah's sides with both hands, feeling jiggly warm skin pressed tight against the fabric.

<Dear girl!> Mrs. Al gasped. *<Where is your* gelhisa?>

Uh oh. If Sarah remembered her Tau Cetan correctly, she was in trouble. Somehow she didn't think she could stupid her way out. Underwear was underwear; it didn't change much country to country. She gave a guilty shrug and pointed to the ceiling. *<In room? It not... Is not... I no like!>*

Standing herself up as tall as she could, Mrs. Al marched over to the man of the house, took him by the elbow, and pulled him outside.

The angry line of her mouth creased her round features. A woman of many words, she tried hard to keep her speech slow and simple. *<Dimi-tri, you must be more ... mmph! with that girl!>* Mrs. Al clenched a pudgy fist and waved it in the air. *<Never, never I see such dirty girl – house so dirty! Dirty pans! Dirty stove! Floor dirty! She big girl. You must demand she clean! And for shame! You not make her wear proper underclothes? She cannot go to town dressed like that! Town people will talk about poor girl with no underthings! School boys will treat bad! Good girls must dress like good girls. If*

you do not,> the woman slapped one hand sharply with the other, *<many big troubles will come!>*

Dmitri sighed, trapped between two females who, it was becoming obvious, were never going to see eye to eye. He spread his hands wide. *<She girl with own head.>*

<And you are man of house!> Mrs. Al shot back. *<She just young girl! You make her obey!>*

Dmitri nodded. Sarah knew the rules; she was supposed to blend in. He marched into the house with authority, caught Sarah by the elbow and dragged her up the stairs. "Come with me," he whispered in Russian.

He glanced over his shoulder, aware that ears would be listening, even if they couldn't understand.

"*Shto?*" Sarah started to say, but Dmitri cut her off.

"What the hell does she mean, you're not wearing underwear?" he shouted. He didn't think anyone could see through the heavy fabric, but then again, he hadn't been looking. Sarah had never been one to do something like that, but since when was she predictable?

"I *am* wearing underwear!" Sarah hefted her skirt and pulled the waistband of her shorts to show him the uncomfortable, unstretchy underwear. "Just not the upper thing. I *hate* that thing, Dimi! I don't even *need* it! Look!" She dropped the skirt and smoothed the dress front to flatten her growing bustline, otherwise hidden under the layers of clothing. "Besides, there's a seam or something that rubs a scar on my back, and it hurts. I'm not wearing it!"

"That's no excuse. You know the rules. You're supposed to act like you've lived here all your life. If that's what you're supposed wear, you have to do it." Dmitri stabbed a thumb toward her clothing drawers. "Put it on, and anything else you're supposed to be wearing. Don't make me have to dress you myself."

The innocent protest faded. "You're not serious?"

"Absolutely. I just got a lecture because you're running around like a Freebie. Get it on, and tonight I'll take a look at it. Maybe we can pad it or something so it doesn't hurt as much. And hurry up," he warned as he headed down the stairs, "or Mrs. Al will probably come up to help."

Mrs. Aletneshfaja wiped the dishes while Charlie leaned against the doorway. Both looked embarrassed. Dmitri patted the woman's shoulder. *<She dress,>* he assured her.

Sarah clumped down the stairs several minutes later. The dirty look she gave her brother was no act. She couldn't breathe in the damned clothing, and leaving it loose just made it chafe more. And she *didn't* need it!

Dmitri made things worse. "Let's see."

Sarah raised her hands, scowling, while he patted her ribs right in front of their company. "Anything else?"

She lifted her hem a few centimeters to prove she wore the under-skirt. If it wouldn't jeopardize their placement on the planet, Sarah had just the mind next time Mrs. Al came over to answer the door wearing nothing but one of Dimi's shirts and her underpants.

Dmitri gave her a peck on the head. "Much better. I'll see you in a bit."

Sarah paled. "What do you mean? I'm coming!"

"You can't work with that thing on. It'll hurt. Stay and keep Mrs. Al company."

A heel slammed the floorboards. "NO! *Dimi!*"

Dimi took her hand and placed it in Mrs. Al's with a devious smile. "Have a good afternoon!" He sped out the door, tagged Charlie, and the two raced each other down the path as fast as they could.

Sarah ran outside. *"Dimi!"* She looked furiously at Mrs. Al standing innocent in the doorway, wiping a cup with a rag.

"This is your fault!" she snapped in Russian. *"You did this to me!"* Anger welled up; Sarah stomped into the house and threw herself onto a bench at the lunch-littered table. She put her face down and crossed her arms over her head, blocking out the world.

Abandoned, the minute Dimi'd found someone to pawn her off on. He would run free all afternoon with Charlie in the fresh air and sunshine, while she was stuck inside with an old doughy woman. What business of it was *hers* what she did or didn't wear? She wasn't her mother, or a sister, or even a friend. She was nothing but a … a … nosy busybody!

Mrs. Al plopped next to her, mumbling something. *What was it Dr. Carver once told her?* Some dumb story about lemonade, but that wasn't what it was supposed to be about. Something about turning a difficulty into an advantage. *How could this woman possibly be an advantage?* She wouldn't even use the dictionary. The woman ruined her afternoon, but how to take revenge in a way Dmitri wouldn't get mad about? The last thing Sarah wanted to do was talk, but the witch couldn't do much else. A light went on in Sarah's head. *Talk!*

Mrs. Al, unable to make contact, had returned to clearing up lunch. She had cleaned the dishes, wiped the table around the inert form, and started on the last of the pans when the girl lifted her head.

Sarah stood up with the silence of a cat, a skill learned young from tiptoeing around Father's volatile temper. She stood behind Mrs. Al, waiting to be noticed.

Mrs. Al glanced up and gave a gasp. She dried her hands, then rubbed the girl's fair cheek with her thumb. Sarah pulled the hand away and held it between her own.

She called up her best look of forlorn. *<You – Help me?>*

Mrs. Al smiled. *<Yes! Yes, I help you!>*

Sarah blinked her violet-blue eyes. *<You – teach me?>*

<Make me very happy to teach you! I teach you good food, make brother very happy. One day, you make husband very happy.>

Not in this lifetime, Sarah thought acidly. She shook her head. *<No. You teach to speak – teach to me all. Dmitri have talk-book – I no speak goodly. One, we learn to speak!>*

Sarah banged the table with the hand that wasn't attached to Mrs. Al. "*Ya govoryu, 'stol'. Shto vass slovar? Shto etta?*" She patted the table again.

<This?> Mrs. Al frowned at the burst of Russian. She ran a confused hand across the tabletop. *<Degsha?>*

Stol/table/degsha, Sarah linked together in her mind. She pounded the bench expectantly.

<Ombiri?>

Degsha. Ombiri. Lampa/lamp/shagee. Pol/floor/akixshra. Lozhka/spoon/attwor. Hot. Cold. Water. Pump. Ceiling. Wall. Wood. Cut. On and on Sarah pressed, dragging Mrs. Al by the hand, every turn of her head bringing a hundred new questions to light. She grabbed paper to make notes on.

There was so much to talk about!

Through the *yard,* from *plant* to *weed* to *grain,* onto the *ground, sifting* through *rocks* and *pebbles* and *dirt* and *insects* Mrs. Al was dragged, at first willingly, then with mild objection over the unfinished work, finally with outright protests, but the girl would not let up, pleading and pulling on her victim. When the *sun* dipped *behind* the trees, Sarah allowed Mrs. Al to return to the house. She followed her like a shadow, intercepting almost every move the woman made with a demand for a word or explanation, blocking attempts to teach any skill but language.

When the boys returned, Mrs. Al walked up to Dmitri and bowed several times. She dragged Sarah to him, pushed her into his arms and pushed them both out the door, shutting and barring it behind them.

Dmitri eyed his sister with suspicion. "What did you do?"

Sarah folded the thick handful of notes, making them look smaller. "Honestly, Dim! All we did was talk!"

Thirty-three

Once alone, Sarah gave Dimi an icy shoulder. She buried her face in her notes, re-writing them in her near-perfect script and putting them into a semblance of order. She'd made great strides in vocabulary, comprehension, and diction, learning words not even in the dictionary. She'd hand in her notes when they went back to the compound, and be proud to have her name listed among those who had compiled the fieldwork. At least she'd get *something* out of all this pain.

She shed the dreaded underthings before Charlie and his mother had even crossed the yard on their way home. As promised, Dmitri examined the chafing undergarment. Little could be done about the troublesome scam but to pad it – they had neither the materials nor the knowledge to restructure it. Until they got back to the Compound, Sarah would have to line the seam with a sock for cushioning.

"You have to stay within the guidelines, Sar," he explained. "If it's just Charlie around, I don't particularly care, but if Mrs. Al is here, you have to be neighborly and act like a local girl. Try and see it from her point of view. They're all alone out there. We're their closest neighbors. She's old enough to be your mother, but she's trying to treat you like a friend."

"The only point of view I see is the one where you go out and have all the fun," Sarah sulked, "and I won't wear anything that uncomfortable. I'm not exactly built like Mrs. Al." She squashed her chest with her palms for emphasis. Dmitri tried to say more, but her fingers traveled up to her ears, and Sarah refused to hear another word.

Morning dawned, and the snit continued. Dmitri made sure Sarah dressed properly.

"I have a good mind to stay up here all day and lie around in my underwear," Sarah threatened.

"Go right ahead," Dimi said as he walked down the stairs. "I'm sure Charlie'd love to come up and watch you tantrum in them."

Round one: Dmitri.

The Aletneshfajas arrived early, and by the time Sarah stalked down to breakfast at the last minute, Dmitri was finishing a valuable lesson on toasting bread and frying a perfect *joubash* egg. Dimi'd forgotten about the beauty of breakfast eggs; anticipation made his stomach cry out in delight.

Charlie bid Sarah a pleasant good morning as she plunked herself at the table. The scowl paused as she bowed and repeated the greeting. Charlie was nice enough, she guessed, a lot like Dimi *used* to be. It was just his tattle-tale mother she couldn't stand.

Dimi handed her a plate he cooked himself, then sat next to Charlie, leaving Mrs. Al to squeeze her roundness next to Sarah. Sarah sniffed the plate; it smelled delicious, and she realized just how hungry she was.

<... *And she dress goodly today*,> Dimi told Mrs. Al with one of his endearing smiles.

259

<She thank you when she older. You see. If we do only what we like, no work ever get done.> Mrs. Al gave Sarah's shoulder a caring rub.

Dmitri laughed. *<That true. Yes, Sarah?>*

Sarah burned, her dignity insulted, her shoulder assaulted. *How much was she supposed to take?* She picked up her untouched plate and dumped the entire thing upside down over her brother's dish before stomping upstairs.

Screw'em, David would have told her. *David* didn't take crap from anyone. *David* would have defended her... No, he wouldn't, either. Nobody ever did, Sarah thought sourly.

Dmitri charged up the stairs. "*What the hell is with you?* Are you trying to kill our mission?"

Sarah lay across the rumpled bed. "I won't sit there and listen to you laugh at me! That woman is not my mother! She has no right to tell me how to live. I don't want anything to do with her, and you can't make me!"

"No, I can't make you like her, no matter how hard she's trying to find a reason to like you. She doesn't have a clue what a terror you can be. But I will insist – no, I *demand!* – that you *will be polite* to her. I mean it! *Grow up!* You looked like a total brat down there. You march down there and apologize. Then you can just stay up here all day, because you're not coming with me."

"I *won't* grow up! I told you I won't, and I'm not going to! You're not Father, so you can't make me do *anything!* I will *not* apologize! Not unless I do it without this ... *strangulator* on!"

"Then I'll – I'll write to Commander Guillaume and he can send *his* people out here to talk to you!"

Dmitri pulled her down the stairs and across the room. He poked her until she stood unhappily before Mrs. Al.

"Apologize!"

Sarah glared at the present cause of all her worldly troubles and snapped, *"Izvenitye."*

Dimi poked her again, harder. "In something she can *understand,* you black hole!"

<Apology!> Sarah forced out. *It just wasn't fair!* She tore away and raced up the stairs.

When Sarah stopped screaming into her pillow, the cabin was silent. She lay on her back, sniffing blackly. Vlad couldn't even send her sympathy; it would be three months before she could tell him.

Why should she have to sit there while Dimi went out? It wasn't like when he worked at the bar; that was for pay, and he needed to do it. This was just a mean-spirited ploy to make her do the dirty work while he had fun. *Who promoted him to Boss?*

So why stay?

The thought was so disobedient Sarah couldn't believe it came from her head. Wandering alone was dangerous. She always stayed put when Dimi said. But this wasn't a hospital, or a hotel, or a low-rent apartment building. Nothing stood between them but blue sky and a field of grain.

Why not join him anyway?

She could work as hard as he could. Hell, she could do *anything* he could! And with three of them working, they'd get done sooner, and then Dimi could keep himself home with her, where he belonged.

A rattle of pans stopped her at the stairs. That fat lump of dough was still down there.

Sarah examined her options. The stairs creaked; the only other exit was the windows.

She leaned out a back window. For a second story, it wasn't very high; perhaps two and a half meters. Her room was narrower than the lower floor, leaving almost a meter of sloping shelf over the kitchen before dropping off. The construction of the cabin formed an architecturally-induced ladder where the logs crossed at the corners – Dale had climbed that way to check the stove pipe. Sarah hiked the horrid dress to her hips and climbed out onto the ledge. She knelt and stretched a leg toward the edge of the roof, the horrid *gelhisa* chafing mercilessly against her ribs.

Easier than she anticipated, Sarah reached the ground and sprinted across the yard to the path. She passed the field they had cleared; that was as far as she'd ever gone from the cabin alone. The forest disappeared on her right, replaced by a field of high grass edged by thick, waist-high poles buried in the ground half a meter apart. Too narrow for a porshie to squeeze through, too high for it to climb over, too strong to be knocked down.

Another hundred paces and Sarah saw Dmitri sitting on the back of the loaded work cart, laughing. Charlie stood before him, singing a song phrase by phrase so Dimi might follow. As he sang, he moved his hands in and out to suggest the curves of a female form, then finished the song with a thrust of his hips. The pair broke into laughter. Charlie started over, Dmitri attempting to sing along.

Sarah slipped between the posts unseen and appeared at the back of the cart. Charlie stopped singing, then blushed deep crimson.

<*Please, sing! I like music. Teach me, too!*>

"What the hell are you doing here?" Dmitri demanded. "How'd you get out? I left orders for Mrs. Al to chase you with her cooking spoon if you showed your face. You better not have hurt her."

"Certainly not!" Sarah said indignantly. "I have my ways."

She turned to Charlie for an ally. <*I want to help work. I work good.>*

Dimi slid off the cart. "I told you to stay home, and I meant it. Go!"

Charlie couldn't understand the conversation, but he knew an argument when he heard one. *<Dimi-tri, maybe she stay? Three people work very fast.>*

Dmitri shook his head. *<No. I very mad her. She not much nice to mother. She go.>*

<I want to help!> Sarah pleaded to Charlie.

"Forget it. Let's go." Dimi dragged her toward the fence.

Sarah fought, step by step. He had towed her eight or ten meters, when her bare feet slipped on the long grass and she sat down hard on the ground.

She smelled it the exact second she felt it.

Sarah scrambled up, pulling the skirt around. Sure enough, she'd fallen onto a fairly recent pile of porshie droppings.

"Ugh! Dimi! *Get it off!* Agh!"

Dmitri burst into laughter. "Serves you right! It perfectly matches your shitty attitude! I haven't seen anything that funny in ages! Hah!"

Charlie rushed up. *<So sorry, Dimi-tri's Sarrah! So sorry!>* He yanked a large handful of grass and used it to scrape away the worst of the offensive matter.

Sarah gasped as Charlie pulled at her clothes. He held the skirt well away from her, but his hand came far too close to her backside for comfort. She froze, waiting to see what he did before she made a bigger scene. Dmitri was a horrible, no-good, mean-spirited ogre, but she knew he wouldn't let the boy harm her, no matter how mad he might be. Sarah searched for the right new vocabulary.

<I happy one of you has good heart,> she said, stung by Dmitri's indifference.

The soil came off, but the fabric still bore a foul mark. Charlie bowed, releasing the skirt. *<I most sorry. I cannot do better.>*

Dmitri grinned. "Guess you'll have to go home now. You stink!"

"Not as bad as you!" In seconds, she undid the fasteners on the back of her jumper. She shrugged the first strap off her shoulder.

"What the hell are you doing? You can't take that off out here!"

"Watch me! I have so many clothes on, gamma rays can't get through!" As Dmitri struggled to hold the dress up, Sarah reversed direction: she dropped to her knees through the middle and crawled out underneath. She snatched the soiled dress away, crumpled it, and threw it at her brother before storming to the path in the blouse and underskirt and shorts and underwear and undershirt and strangulator and sock padding, tears of indignity falling.

Mrs. Al nearly collided with her entering the cabin. Sarah shoved past, crying.

<Stars and moons, child! Where your clothes!>

<i Joso mas PIGS!> Sarah swore as she disappeared up the stairs. *Boys are worse than pigs.*

Fearing something terrible, Mrs. Al turned to follow when Dmitri came around the corner of the workshed. He held up the soiled dress.

Mrs. Al nodded. *<I sorry, Dimi-tri. I never see her leave.>*

<I know. She very ...> He tapped a finger to his head. He wanted to twirl it around his ear, but he doubted the motion translated.

Mrs. Al bowed in sympathy. She took the dress and heaved herself up the stairs.

Sarah sprawled on the unmade bed, the less-soiled underskirt and shorts in a heap on the floor. She sat up quickly at the woman's approach, hiding the backs of her legs. The rough underwear clothed her enough, even by her standards, but she didn't need old scars questioned.

Mrs. Al took in the room with disgust. Sarah's clothes lay where'd they'd fallen; a small mountain of dirty clothing belonging to both sexes festered in the far corner of the room. Travel bags gaped open, their rumpled contents spilling out. The bedside table held a lamp with a chimney so black with soot it couldn't have given much light at all.

Mrs. Al's eyes took careful note of the single bed with two pillows, the covers to which were so disheveled they looked more like a pile of rags than several quilts. Even with the four windows open, the air still held the sweet, musty smell of morning breath and days-old sleep-sweat.

<If you get dirty things,> Mrs. Al said tactfully, *<we can wash all. Bed things, too.>*

Sarah gave a sniff, wiped her face with the backs of her hands, and retrieved a clean dress. As Mrs. Al stripped the linens from the bed, Sarah wrestled into the dress, then knelt down and tugged Dmitri's mattress from under the bed, where they stuffed it every morning to get it out of the way.

Mrs. Al gave a sigh and smiled to herself. She knew Dimi-tri was nice boy.

Mrs. Al sent Dmitri to find buckets and tubs large enough to hold soak water and wash water and rinse water and second rinse water, growing impatient when she realized there wasn't even a rope strung to hang the wash from. Then there was the river of water that needed to be drawn by hand, let alone the fact that laundry had been allowed to accumulate. Everything assembled, Mrs. Al rolled up her sleeves, folded her skirts, and knelt before the first pail. She wet and soaped and scrubbed an item, then handed it to Sarah to rinse.

263

Sarah looked down her nose with a frown. *<I do not wash clothes.>*

A string of loud words exploded from Mrs. Al's lips, none of which Sarah nor Dmitri yet understood. She slammed the laundry into the bucket so hard half the water shot out in a wave, and she rolled to her feet much faster than her shape should have allowed. She marched toward Dmitri, hands gesticulating great arcs of pink soap flecks.

Dmitri backed up several steps. The tirade continued unabated, aside from the pauses Mrs. Al needed to gulp breath.

"Are you getting any of this?"

Sarah's head tipped in concentration. "Not much. *Big, girl, why, you, this.* Enough to know she hates me." She ducked behind Dmitri for safety.

Dmitri put his arms back to shield her. *<Slow, please!>* he begged Mrs. Al. *"Ya vas ni pohnimayu!"*

<You!> Mrs. Al fumed. *<You are cause! Make baby of big strong girl! She not do anything! No clean! No cook! No wash! No sew! Useless! Just want to read and write! Why you teach her that? She not need know that! Spoiled! She cry, you pat on head instead of kick bottom! Look at hands!>* She jerked Sarah's arm and slapped her palm, shaking it. *<Hands soft like baby! Never work! Will never have husband! No man want to contract useless lazy girl. Maybe eyeless man want girl to read, but eyeless man still want to eat! You must make lazy girl work! Spoiled, useless baby!>*

"Lazy?" Sarah located the unfamiliar word in the lexicon in Dmitri's back pocket. "Dimi, I'm not lazy! I'm *more* than willing to work with you and Charlie! She doesn't know what lazy is!" Sarah leaned around Dimi, spouting spiteful Russian.

"I have an intellect *far* too superior to waste time cleaning clothing like that! I could've finished school two years ago! I know seven – *seven!* – languages! Do you have any idea how hard I had to work just to keep *up* with a Navaran school? *You* don't know what work is! You and your whole porshie-packing community belong in a Burin-Jai prison camp!"

Mrs. Al shouted back. She knew insolence when she heard it.

"HEY!" Dmitri whistled for silence. *<Not more!>* he said in Tau Cetan. "Shut up, Sar! I don't care what language you're in, you're saying too much. Watch it!"

<Mrs. Al,> he switched back. *<Please. Girl work hard. She only ... >*

<No!> Mrs. Al snapped. *<I try! Ask for little help, will teach girl rest, expect SOME help, but have none! She will learn wash now!>* She grabbed Sarah and dragged her determinedly to the buckets, handing her the next item from the pile.

Sarah screeched and dropped the cloth on the ground as if bitten.

She wouldn't touch Dmitri's underwear for cold cash, let alone wash it, though for a ticket home, she just might wear it.

"Dimi, I will not *do* this!" she cried, caught on a planet that would not, could not, let her be herself. "My mother didn't raise me that long, but I know she didn't raise me to be a … *charwoman!*"

Mrs. Al tried to force the clothing into her hands. Sarah slapped it away, grabbed her hair and tugged hard twice before spinning around to run.

Dmitri caught her. *"Stop,"* he soothed. "Mrs. Al doesn't know anything of what we've been through, remember that. I'll fix it. Shhh."

Hoping he wasn't killing his golden goose, Dmitri turned to Mrs. Al with the slight authority afforded him as the master of a house in a loosely patriarchal society. *<You cannot understand,>* he said angrily. *<I pay you to cook, I pay you to clean. You want me pay more, you say how much, I pay it. But you will leave girl alone! Understand? Do not make her upset.>*

Mrs. Al's mouth pressed tight, though her eyes held an unchecked fury. She bowed her head and huffed back to the laundry.

"Tomorrow you can come back with me," Dmitri informed Sarah. "But for the rest of today, I suggest you make yourself scarce."

Thirty-four

Dmitri learned basic cooking from Mrs. Al; he taught Sarah. Three days a week Mrs. Al prepared a more complicated meal, left it on the stove, and went home to cook again. Social dinners were a thing of the past.

On one of Mrs. Al's cooking days she came over early and did the wash. The other two days she came over less early and cleaned the cabin. She quadrupled the price she had originally named. This was now strictly business. Dmitri paid it without question.

Dmitri helped Charlie at his house, too. Sarah tagged behind, stubborn as a shadow. The Aletneshfaja home was a neat square of white-painted boards. There were two rooms to their home – a living area whose ceiling was the underside of the peaked roof, and a small bedroom. A ladder led to an open loft above the bedroom; that was Charlie's space. Carved decorations and fancy bits of needlework made the bright, clean rooms fairy-tale charming.

Sarah and Mrs. Al avoided each other. While the four worked together clearing a field of vegetables, neither woman nor girl spoke. Dmitri watched Sarah with a practiced eye, monitoring her level of internal tension by the clench of her jaw and the set of her shoulders. Sarah matched Mrs. Al's pace, pick for pick, bucket for bucket, and refused to stop even when so tired her hands shook and she looked ready to collapse. Dimi worried, but he'd never yet seen Sarah lose a stubbornness contest, even against Father. She would prove herself or die trying.

Second harvest wound down, and the work wasn't so pressing. The days weren't nearly as warm, and soon the rainy season that heralded the new year would begin. The school in Vandijoc would start again.

<You go to school, Miss Sarrah?> Charlie inquired hopefully. <I would walk with you.>

Sarah snorted. What could any school on *this* planet hope to teach her? Even if this empty, mindless planet had such a thing as a university, she would probably still know more than the professors. <No, I not need school. I learn better by self.>

Charlie made an indecisive face. <Maybe I not go, then, either. Am old for school, anyway. Lots of work at home.>

"Why not try it, Sar?" Dmitri suggested. "See what the schools are like. Meet some kids your own age. Find out what they learn. You can report on it for Guillaume from an angle none of us can."

"It's an idea," Sarah shrugged. If nothing else, she would be further immersed in the language.

She did make an effort. With Charlie and Dmitri walking her there and back, she suffered the school for three days. The frivolous girls made eyes across the room at the boys they hadn't seen all harvest season, and the boys did nothing but tease each other and try to impress the girls. Charlie wasn't as quite as crude, and he knew the correct answers when called upon. As she often did in unfamiliar settings, Sarah played dumb, and, as she expected, the others ignored her. She refused to go back, and wrote a scathing critique of the educational system.

Charlie quit the following day.

A month of struggle, and Dmitri caught the flow of the language. His usable vocabulary grew, and he didn't have to carry the dictionary every place he went. He didn't feel like an idiot in front of Charlie anymore.

<We work hard for long time,> he told Charlie several weeks later. <We need one night for fun, just us. Come to town with me; we see what we can find.>

Charlie's eyes went wide. <At night? I never go to town at night without Mother, but, maybe she let me if I go with you.>

<I will ask,> Dmitri promised. <Only one problem, tall as you but

yellow hair. Ask mother how much I must pay so she stay with Sarah while we go. Sarah not run off at night. She behave. I promise.>

Mrs. Al's price was quite steep, but as far as Dimi was concerned, fair enough. Hazard pay, he deemed it.

"I'm leaving now," he told Sarah. "Promise me again you won't start a nuclear war."

Sarah sat on her bed with a book. "You cannot start a nuclear war with flint and steel. As long as that fat-swollen creature keeps her distance from the unjustly accused Unworthy, so shall the Unworthy ignore her. Why are you doing this to me, Dim? Why can't I go, too? I won't be a problem! Every time you go somewhere without me, you get into terrible trouble. I need fun, too, you know!"

Dmitri fought the octopus hands to kiss the top of her head. "Because I need the break from *you*! I won't be back late – before midnight. Mrs. Al sure as hell doesn't want to sleep here. Behave!"

Sarah lay on her bed, head resting morosely on the open book of philosophy. Abandoned again, this time into the hands of a mortal enemy, a woman who hated her very soul. It was almost – no, it *was* worse than being alone. At least being left alone assumed she was responsible enough to care for herself.

Since when did she ever need a baby-sitter? She'd never had one before. Especially one with a burning desire to force the baby into domestic slavery. Every so often a sound rose from below: the tortured groan of a bench, a footstep, a sigh. As long as the hag stayed down there.

Two hours passed before Sarah heard the stairs creak. Mrs. Al appeared at the doorway.

<You so quiet, I make sure you still here.>

Sarah pretended to read. Mrs. Al entered and had the gall to sit on the corner of the bed. Sarah sat up quickly, unsure what she'd done wrong now, or of what she would be accused. They sat in silence, each watching for the enemy to make the first move.

Mrs. Al broke the stalemate. <You – you read to me from book?> she asked shyly. <Is good story?>

Sarah hadn't expected that. <You would not like this.> Closing the philosophy text, she scanned the pile for something that might do. French poetry, she decided. She opened up to Tristan and Isolde, then reconsidered. The story was simple enough, but could Mrs. Al understand it? Sarah didn't think she could translate Old French straight into Tau Cetan yet, and still be comprehensible.

By the time Sarah reached a stopping point, her throat was dry and words spun through her head in four languages, making her dizzy. Mrs. Al seemed to get the idea of the stories despite the gaps in vocabulary.

Sarah saw no reason to skirt the question any longer. <You cannot read?>

Mrs. Al studied her toes, a feat she could do only when sitting. Her low-heeled shoes were more like slippers; it was doubtful she could have bent to lace them. <No. I never go to school.>

<You cannot read your own name?> Sarah was aghast. There was just a minimum amount of basic knowledge one assumed everyone had. You didn't have to read and write, but you *had* to know your own name. Sarah knew all kinds of things long before she went to formal school. To have grown up without any kind of learning was – incomprehensible.

<No,> Mrs. Al said shamefully. <I would ask Charshfe to teach me, but I not want him to know his mother very stupid.>

<It only stupid to remain stupid,> Sarah corrected, paraphrasing a Navaran idiom, something to the effect of *ignorance is a conscious choice*. She located a clean paper and a thick pencil. She thought about Tau Cetan phonetics, and carefully wrote out how she guessed Mrs. Al's name would be spelled, and wrote Charshfenaki's underneath. She knew his to be correct; she'd seen it at the school.

<Take paper home. Your name,> she pointed, <Charshfe's. Write again and again. You not need be so stupid.>

<Thank you,> Mrs. Al said, studying the pattern of curves and dots. <I write many times until I know perfect. Your mother – she read?>

<As Moons Rise! She speak at least three languages. She best cook in world. She have work-woman to clean. She very beautiful woman.> Sarah retrieved her backpack and located the now-colorless copies of her precious pictures. She flipped through the stack until she found one.

<*My* mother,> she said proudly.

Mrs. Al looked at the picture and sighed. Even in gray tones, the woman in the picture seemed angelic. Her long, light hair hung straight down her back, her smile as warm as summer sun on her pretty face. Her eyes shone even in the limited ability of the photo, framed by long, artificially-darkened lashes. It had been taken when she was around twenty-five or so. <She very, very beautiful woman.>

Sarah shuffled the stack, looking for the picture of everyone together. <This,> she pulled a good picture of Vladimir out, <this brother I write letters to. My most best friend.>

She flipped a couple more, and gasped. Sarah raised a hand to her mouth, forcing it to stay shut while she absorbed the shock. *Where the hell did that come from?* She didn't remember it. It must have been Viktor's graduation portrait, with his dashing, shy smile and dark caring eyes meeting hers straight from the paper. She fought the rising flood of emotion.

Mrs. Al squinted in the lamplight that wasn't nearly bright enough for her. <That Dimi-tri?>

<No.> Pain leaked into Sarah's voice. She handed the picture over so she didn't have to see it. <Brother Viktor, older than Dimi. When he die, we come here.>

<Sick?>

Sarah made up a planet-plausible version. <Soldiers come. Start bad fight. Viktor try to save us. They kill him badly, right in our eyes.>

It was Mrs. Al's turn to gasp. <Stars and *Moons*! You *see* it? No wonder, poor girl!>

Sarah nodded, flipping more pictures. <That why we come here. We safe here.> She found what she was after, handing the wide photo to the woman. <This whole family. Mother, Father, most brothers and sisters. This me, that Dmitri there.>

Mrs. Al stared. <How many wives your father *have*?>

<One. Thirteen children. Mother die with last baby.>

<That happen,> Mrs. Al replied knowingly, holding the picture closer to the light. <Nefarjak die when Charshfenaki eleven. We try so hard to have second baby. I want baby girl, too. I would name her Vanavashi, but only I have Charshfe. He good boy. Your mother very lucky woman. You miss others?>

Sarah clenched her teeth and nodded, but a tear leaked past her guard; she rubbed it before it could be seen. She put the pictures back in the bag.

<I tired. I go to sleep now.> She stood by the closet, looking at the floor, hoping she'd last until the woman left. *Damn that picture!*

Mrs. Al smiled and gave the girl's arm a squeeze before she left, carrying her name paper. No wonder girl always argue and unhappy.

<Dimi-tri, my mother get terrible mad! You not know!> Charlie pleaded as they left the tavern, a final bottle of brew tight in Dmitri's hand. He sniffed his shirt sleeve. <Smell! I smell like that girl! Regular girls not smell special like this. Mother very smart! She know I up to something!>

Dmitri walked on, reflecting on some scientific theory he studied once in school, something about the likelihood of similar life forms developing under similar circumstances on various worlds, a theory to account for the vastly different yet recognizable bipedal humanoids that arose on similar-type planets around the galaxy. The fact that Humans and Navarans and Aquilans and Sigma Tau Cetans all had two eyes and two arms and two legs and one head didn't impress him nearly as much as the fact that they all reproduced in a fairly similar manner, and the important parts usually fit, sometimes worse but sometimes much better. Dmitri didn't know if there was a scientific law to take that into account, too, but he sure as hell wasn't going to ask Sarah about it.

All in all, Dimi considered the night a shameful success – he'd learned three new games of chance, lost a dozen games of targets to Charlie, tried five new kinds of intoxicating beverages, and enjoyed the private attentions of a very eager local girl for one very busy hour. His good spirits paved the way two meters ahead of him.

<I have older sisters, think like mothers. I stop Mother. You have fun?>

Charlie's thankful grin blazed a trail from ear to ear, and he blushed. <You are very best friend in world, Dimi-tri! To pay for Charshfenaki to have fun like that. She so beautiful! You think so, too? Beautiful face, beautiful hair, smell so nice, such beautiful – !> He held his hands out to suggest rounded anatomy, sighing with the memory of sweet bare flesh.

Dimi tapped the boy's cheeks. <Hey! Do not be porshie-stupid! Do not leave heart in there! I go back, smile, she say same things to me. Not mean *anything*. Give heart to nice girl, give money to bad ones. Do not bring heart into place like that. When nice girl have heart, she do same things.>

<I understand. What you mean, did girl make 'house call'?>

<I make joke. Now,> he said, breaking the seal on the bottle he'd purchased from the bar, <we take care of Mother. Drink!>

The upstairs window was dark as the surrounding night. Dmitri didn't know if that was good or bad. He couldn't imagine Sarah going to sleep on her own. Sarah didn't do that, ever. More likely she lay in wait, ready to spring. He opened the door, not sure what to expect. Mrs. Al sat at the table with a cup of 'tea.' She folded a paper and put it quickly in the pocket of her dress. The cabin appeared unscathed, so Dmitri went into his plan. He bowed before her, acting far more drunk than he was.

<Mrs. Al? Please, no yell at Chash – Chark – Charlie! I buy him drink for winning game. I lose too many. Please, it my fault.>

<I tell him, Mother!> Charlie swayed without premeditation, looking to his older, wiser friend and bursting into giggles. Dimi-tri had inoculated his clothes with the strong-smelling liquor, overpowering any evidence of perfume. The shirt collar and darkness would hide the kiss-mark low on his neck.

Mrs. Al gave a helpless little smile. <My son not young anymore. If he not going to be schoolboy, I guess he must act more like man. Not often, though,> she warned. <Come, Charshfe, I get you home.> Dmitri lit her lantern as Charlie winked at him with both eyes at once.

<And you!> Mrs. Al addressed Dmitri. <You take nicer care of girl! No more you shout at her! Girl should not be so sad. She need

270

happiness, too.>

<Okay,> Dmitri agreed blindly. He'd figure it out in the morning. <Moonful night!> he called as he shut the door and barred it against the darkness.

* * *

It had taken the better part of twenty minutes, but Sarah found the most out-of-the-way spot in the crowded barn where she could still see everything. The immense structure belonged to the wealthiest family in Vandijoc, and at the moment it overflowed with as many as four hundred people sitting, talking, eating, and dancing. She'd tried very hard to get Dimi to let her stay home, but to no avail. She couldn't disappear, for if she had to be here, she needed to keep an eye on him. Pretty girls teemed like rats, and where there were girls, Dimi couldn't be trusted.

She'd smuggled a notepad and pencil to the harvest party in the pocket of her dress, and made as many observations as she could. Dimi would have a fit if he knew, always nagging her to make friends with people she didn't know and didn't care a cabbage about. Now she knew how Sergei must have felt scribbling notes to himself all those years, impatient at interruptions and sulky when Father took the notebooks away. Her observations weren't nearly as poetic, however. She didn't have his sense of eloquence, his ability to see the same picture on different levels, of seeing with his heart. Even she was bored by her uninspired scientific style.

> *Barn floor @ 35m x 17m, post and beam construction, appears to be hand-hewn. 5 musicians playing in NW corner,. M. 1. – 8-stringed black wooden instrum. reminisc. of a sitar, @ 1m in len., neck @ 60 x 8 cm, ending in a barred metal clamp to hold strings, ovoid soundbox ....*

It was technically accurate description, but it was *dull.*

A shadow darkened her private retreat. Sarah glanced up with fright, then relaxed. Charlie knelt before her, dressed in his best embroidered shirt and bright blue pants, and for once his hard feet sported a pair of soft shoes.

<There you! Why you hide like little *kupu*? Best party all year! You not having fun?> He held out a cup of fruit juice and a plate of assorted sweets. <Mother look for you, afraid you not eat. You like this? I can get other food...>

<No, this fine, thank you.> Sarah put the notepad down and took a pastry. It melted in her mouth, airy, light and crisp, filled with a

271

spicy-sweet cream. It brought back memories of places where she'd eaten such wonderful things on a daily basis. She offered the plate to Charlie, mouth too full to speak. He accepted a small delicacy and squeezed in tight next to her. Their sides and shoulders pressed together, warmer than the barn.

Sarah sniffed as a new scent hit her nose. An earthy cologne, light on musk, heavy on woodsy, with an astringent bite of alcohol, not unpleasant at all. It was *Charlie*. He smelled *clean*, not like he did after working all day in the fields. She hadn't thought anyone but Father could smell like that.

Her heart beat faster from the heat of his body, sweaty and limber from dancing. The warmth of two people in the small space made it hard to breathe, so Sarah eased over to make room, sucking creamy filling from each of three fingers. Dmitri could sit that close, but no one else. Charlie was *kind* of like a friend, though he was much more Dimi's friend than hers, so she didn't object *too* much to his invasion of her space – he did bring her pastry, after all. She picked up the notebook to finish the sentence she'd been writing before she lost the thought.

Charlie waited. <You write more letters to other brother?>

Sarah nodded. It was as good a lie as any. She couldn't tell him the real reason, and he couldn't read Standard anyway.

<Yes. I tell him all about Harvest Party.> She would tell Vlad about it, when she wrote him again. At last, something remotely interesting, beyond *we picked some green berries today and my fingers are full of prickers...*

Charlie watched her expectantly. Tonight she wore a dark-blue skirt with a white blouse, and the soft velvet slippers she'd refused to wear in the fields. Much to her distress, Dmitri pinned up her hair, hiding the shortness and making her look more like the native girls, even though, by their standards, she was too young to wear her hair up. A few of the fine front strands sprung loose, framing her face with their bleached-straw color.

Sarah's blue-violet eyes flicked up. She paused in her descriptions, which didn't mention him at all. <Did you want something?>

Charlie forgot how to speak, and blushed instead. When he found his voice, he asked, <You maybe come dance?>

Sarah looked as if she'd never heard the term before. <No. I do not dance. I can watch from here, though.>

<Oh. You want to take walk? Cooler outside....>

<No, thank you.> Sarah was avoiding the outside, where the gutted carcasses of eight whole *urpintan* and dozens of *joubash* were roasting over pits to feed the crowd. <I quite happy here.>

Charlie's face fell further. <Okay. You need something, you tell

me, I get for you. I go tell Dimi-tri I see you, you okay.> He scooped the last of the creamy filling from his pastry and held the finger before her lips.

Sarah smiled and removed the offering with her tongue. <esa mangato!> It was a very Vlad-like thing to do, sharing not only pastry, but the last bite of frosting, too. She watched him leave. Maybe Charlie was really her friend, too.

She scanned the crowd to make sure she could still see her brother. He stood by the fruit-drink barrel, talking with three *(three?)* adoring young girls and looking very sure of himself.

What would he do with three?

Sarah sighed, shook her head, and went back to her notes.

Thirty-five

"**W**ell, I'll be damned!" Lieutenant-Commander Dickerson swore as he greeted the travelers by the gates of the Compound. "You made it! We were going to send out a party to check on you."

"We agreed on three months, didn't we?" Dmitri replied, cold and tired and dirty from the two-day trip in misty rain. "We told you we could handle it. Is that so out of the ordinary?"

"Ninety percent of the time, it is," Jan admitted. "A lot of people join, only to quit a week later. The isolation gets to some, the primitive conditions to others, some can't handle the language barrier."

<cho Ix rath do nala, sharvesh nath bhanto Ixo falwarak si,> Sarah replied. *Language had never been a barrier to them before.*

Dickerson stared. "I guess not. I don't think any of us were that fluent after only three months."

"*We* were never here before," Dmitri said proudly.

Lights! Bright lights that let one see more than three meters away. People speaking without one having to hang on every word. Glaring white walls, draft-free floors, heated air that surrounded you on every side at once and didn't disappear if you took three steps. And food! They were going to eat food they didn't have to *do* something to first, and it would be good and familiar and properly cooked. And perhaps sleep later than sunrise. Surely, a vacation to remember.

Commander Guillaume shook their hands with gusto. "Mr. Kirushenko! Miss Kirushenko! You look well! I take it you've had some success. Come, we'll get business out of the way, then you can rest."

"If we may, sir," Dmitri interrupted, "we'd appreciate the opportunity to bathe first."

"And access hyperspace mail," Sarah dared add. Some things were too important to be shy about. She had reams of stuff to send Vlad, and hoped at least half as much waited for her. If she sent it fast, he might reply before they left.

The commander laughed. "I think that would be acceptable. Why don't we make it 1900, then? Relax, get something to eat, and we'll have the rest of the evening to go over your reports."

Guillaume combed through Sarah's stack of notes. "These are quite thorough. I wish you'd stayed with the school longer, though."

"I couldn't," Sarah apologized, feeling invigorated and oh-so-thankful for the twenty-minute, steaming hot shower. "I found it unbearable. There seems to be no support of formal learning as a culture. Schools are made up mostly of young boys, and they seem to be sent there more to keep them out of the way than to teach them. I did notice there were almost no siblings. I think there were only six or seven children who had siblings out of forty students. Perhaps the rest are kept home to work."

Guillaume leaned back in his chair with a frown. "We've noticed the lack of siblings, too. Perhaps one in five families has more than one child, about one in twenty families might have three or more, and at least one, if not two of those five families never has children. We've done some surreptitious scans of locals, but so far we can't find a conclusive reason. You can't just walk up to these people and ask them for a genetic sample *en masse*, though our physician does treat locals, and anyone he can get a blood sample from, he takes it. It doesn't seem to be due to a high infant mortality rate, either, for you'll notice there are almost no pregnant women, and those that are pregnant are treated like royalty.

"Right now, we're guessing the problem to be a low rate of fertility. The marriage customs seem to take that into account. Promiscuity isn't a terrible sin. A couple asks the girl's father for a contract of intent to marry. Then, for at least three months, the couple is free to do as they please, including live together. If a pregnancy happens to occur, the union is seen as blessed, and the marriage takes place immediately. If nothing happens, it's the girl's decision to either continue into a potentially childless but happy marriage, or she may back out of the arrangement and choose another. The average age of marriage is twenty, with an average of three trial partners."

Dmitri raised an eyebrow. "That's a custom I could live with."

Dmitri spread his plans out on the conference table before the commander and his officers. "I studied the maps you gave us. Vandijoc is half-way between the Compound and Shilwan in one direction, and Allwesha in another, both towns where other survey personnel are assigned. The addition I'd like to build would add enough rooms that we could act as a way-station, housing those team members on their way back and forth, and that would increase communication among the regionally placed personnel. At times of need, we could also rent the rooms to townsfolk, which would increase our contact with the native population."

"You sound very determined to continue the mission," Dickerson said.

Dmitri rankled. "We didn't make this much effort just to turn around and quit." All he really wanted was a little privacy, and a hot-water bath.

Guillaume passed the crude drawings across the table. "Mr. Lewiston?"

The engineer gave a glance. "It would be easier with boards, but you'll lose a lot of heat that way, probably have to add a heater or two. The extra fuel requirements will take up more of your time. Have to peel some of the original roof back, too, to tie it together this way. Not impossible. Yeah, we can do it in logs, but it's gonna take a lot of them. I suggest you start dropping trees as soon as you get back, no smaller than thirty centimeters thick for this length, fifty or sixty to start. We'll get a crew out there in a month, take us three days, tops. Can do."

Mail? Ennis wasn't kidding! Seventy separate arrivals waited. Sarah strangled on joy. She ordered the computer to print, and started reading as soon as the first page hit the bin. Dear, sweet Vladimir! Faithfully writing and writing when he knew she couldn't answer right away. A wave of homesickness threatened to sink her, but a humorous line on the paper made Sarah laugh before she could be overwhelmed. She had to hurry and send hers out. She put the page down and fed her stack of letters into the scanner.

Too soon they had to pack up for the long return trip. It was harder to leave the modern world behind this time – especially the hot showers.

Sarah sat at the communications console pushing buttons on the hyperspace receiver, wearing a re-engineered but only slightly more comfortable *gelhisa,* and one of three new pairs of shoes. Walking that far in bare feet had been brutal; the velvet slippers weren't much better than socks, and they disintegrated on the second morning. Dimi was about to leave, but she checked communications one last time. She'd responded to all the letters Vlad and Sergei had sent, sent mail to David, upcoming birthday wishes in advance to Nikky and Marina, and a very early birthday greeting to Katya, since her birthday would fall before their next trip in, but so far no one had written back. Maybe they were all on holiday somewhere. What was it, the end of January or so back home? She tried again and sighed. Nothing.

She got up the nerve to ask the communications engineer.

"Am I working the hyperspace wave properly? I sent mail, but I haven't received a reply."

Hargan Ennis laughed. "It's only been three days, Sweetheart. This is the frontier, the edge of explored space! Where are you sending to?"

Sarah bristled over the endearment, but she stayed polite. Her letters depended on this man, she couldn't tick him off. "Earth."

"Then of course you haven't gotten a response. It takes at least a week to get a message that far, if you hit the relay beacons right, and another week to get a response back. This is the middle of nowhere."

Sarah stared at the blank screen, feeling the world fall out from under her. Never would she have direct contact with Vlad, ever, even if Dimi said yes on a special occasion. He might as well be a figment of her imagination. A friend she knew through letters only, not a brother she'd spent almost every living moment in direct contact with for more than nine years. Her disappointment must have shown, for Ennis spoke again.

"If you want, I can scan for messages once a week, print them, and send them out in the local mail. I won't read them," he promised. "A week to get to me, a week to Earth and then back, and you could get a return response in a month, maybe less. That's the best I can do, outside of hand delivery. I can't change physics. With all the modern warp and hyperspace technology, we tend to forget the immensity of the distances involved. Hell, without hyperspace, you could forget any communication for generations."

"I understand," Sarah said, homesickness chewing at her insides like a swarm of Muphridian carrion beetles. "Could you do that for me, now and then? If I mark something special, or send it to you directly to send out? I would let you know if I expected an immediate reply."

"Sure. It's not easy being this far out, is it? I don't know why the commander let you guys stay; we aren't supposed to allow children. I'm not sure we should allow anyone under twenty-five. This kind of isolation has driven more than one person crazy."

"There's a lot to be said for that," Sarah agreed.

Thirty-six

Sergei laid the printout on the desk in front of his brother.

"What the hell's this?" David asked.

"You always say you don't know anything about him. I found it while researching a biography for a paper I had to write. It doesn't tell much we don't already know, but it's a little more. And no, I didn't set out to find it. I was in the K's anyway."

David studied the page.

2261 WHO'S WHO IN THE ALLIED FLEET
KIRT–KIRW

KIRUSHENKO, ALEXANDER GRIGOREVITCH – *Associate Professor of Archaeology, Allied Fleet Academy, Gantankar Province, Navara 2260–* B. 2216, Sochi, Georgia, Russian Federation of States, Earth. *Married,* Maryana Ivanova, 2239; 12 children.

EDUCATION: Bachelor of Science (Archaeology & Ancient History) *Summa Cum Laude,* University of Tbilisi, RFS, 2242. Masters of Science (Archaeology) Moscow State University, RFS, 2244. Doctorate of Science (Archaeology) – Moscow State University, RFS, 2247. Doctorate of Science (Ancient Cultures) – Moscow State University, RFS, 2259.

COMMENDATIONS: Recipient, 2258 Presidential Medal of Honor, Gamma Europa IV. Recipient, 2259 Pentara Award for Outstanding Contribution in Archaeology. Recipient, 2259 Argon Award for Excellence. Recipient, 2260, G. L. Franklin Award for Outstanding Contribution to History. (See 5 more)

Professor Kirushenko is most noted for his excavations of the Hantovalle Temple sight on Gamma Europa IV and his discovery of an extinct species of flying lizard (*Eodraconis Kirushenkus, Gamma Europensis*), the presumed basis for an early form of religion on that planet. Recently published papers include:

2259 – Tracing the Rise of Early Religious Culture Among the Hantovalle of Gamma Europa IV. *Galactic Archaeological Review.* Vol. 121, 7.

2258 – Discovery of Dragons on Gamma Europa IV. *Modern Paleontology.* Vol. 84, 9.

2258 – Excavating the Hantovalle Temple. *Archaeology and Anthropology.* Vol. 200, 2.

2257 –

David handed the reference back coldly. "Am I supposed to be impressed? Maybe we should see about leveling the town so nothing like that can ever come out of there again. Remind me to add that to my list of places to avoid at all costs, right underneath Navara. Maybe we could put up a plaque: 'On this spot was born a homicidal maniac'."

"You're in a foul mood."

"Yeah, well, you looked at the date?" David gazed darkly out the window. That Bastard still had her out there. He could only hold Val accountable for so much now. The rest of the blame now lay somewhere out there in space.

Sergei nodded. "Yeah. Three years today and counting."

The seventh of February. How could any of them forget? There were still those days that tore open festering wounds, year after endless year. Birthdays, holidays, and the day they left Navara; the day they left Them.

David toyed with the idea of the three of them getting out to take their minds off it. *Where to go, though? What to do?* What would involve them to where they wouldn't think about why they were doing it? "What's Vlad doing?"

"You don't want to know. Lay off him, will you? The kid's allowed to be a basket case one day out of the year. He's still got ten weeks 'til her next batch of mail."

David stood up with such energy he knocked over his chair, tripping on it in his haste. If he stayed any longer, he'd be a basket case, too. "I gotta get out of here. Uncle Tomas around?"

"Moscow. Gal's hoping he'll be back today, since he can usually get Vlad to cheer up."

"Val around?"

"I think so,"

"Well, since this is the one day a year I refuse to speak to her, you can tell her I'm taking the Grounder out for a while."

Sergei snorted. "Are you crazy? You can't take the Grounder out in winter. There's fifteen centimeters of snow out there. Go buzz the snowcrawler."

"Busted a rod going over a jump last weekend. The Grounder's got the heavy tires on it," David reasoned, pulling on a coat and finding his bike gloves. "I know what I'm doing. Running the Grounder forces me to concentrate. It clears my head."

Sergei leaned against the desk and crossed his arms. "You've had a suicidal streak as far back as I can remember, from getting in Alexei's way to deliberately pissing off Father, to contraband and speedbikes. Did you ever of think of having your head examined?"

David took his safety helmet from the shelf in the closet. "No. But I've thought about having it done to yours. And nobody was ever crazy enough to deliberately try and piss off Father. If I'm that suicidal, I'm sure as fuck awful at it." He slapped his brother on the shoulder. "Relax. If I'm drunk as Father and dancing on the roof, pissing in the gutters, you have my permission to call any doctor you want. Until then, get off my back."

Sergei answered the commlink call from the trauma center. When the twisted bike was hauled away and David's wrist pieced back

278

together, Sergei went with Val to retrieve his brother, but try as he might, he couldn't get the *I told you so* off his face.

Thirty-seven

*H*ow to turn a dismal existence into something salvageable: make a plan, get it approved, spend two weeks in back-breaking manual labor, add six people who knew what they were doing plus a friend willing to lend a hand, tear your hair out trying to keep sharp tools away from your little sister, and a week later you have a palace.

Dmitri soaked in the hot water up to his neck, eyes closed, feeling the tension flow out of his body. The metal tub could have been longer, but it was wide and deep and it was in his own home. He and Charlie spent three days tinkering with pipes and a makeshift water heater, and the system worked perfectly. A newly installed hand pump pulled water into a metal tank balanced atop a small wood-burning heater. Through a simple valve, the heated water poured into the stoppered metal tub, and could be drained out through a hole under the floorboards.

Charlie scratched his head when they finished. <You sit in that with no clothes?> The Aletneshfaja's cold-water pump was outside by their workshed, and they had no working sanitary, just an outhouse. Clothing got soaked, not people.

<Try!> Dimi urged, and at last Charlie gave in.

He shrugged when finished. <If that what you like, I guess it okay. It still silly, to have swimming hole in house.> Mrs. Al just laughed, but she thought it a wonderful effort-saver for laundry.

Dimi had his own room now, too, with his own bed and closet and clothes drawers. Sarah writhed with the change. For the past week, she'd reverted to crawling into his bed. He'd wake up to find her next to him, or across his feet, or, after he complained, curled up on the floor next to the bed.

She trembled, stomach twisted by tension. "Dimi, outside of hospitals, I've *never* slept in my own room, ever! It's not like I can leave the lights on quarter-power."

"You're going on thirteen, Sar! Time to grow up." She was trying – sort of – but he knew she wasn't sleeping nearly enough.

He waited, very impatiently at times, and little by little she began

279

to sleep. He knew better than to rush her, but he couldn't wait forever. He was only human.

* * *

Sarah awoke for the first time that night, unsure how long she'd slept. She'd been going to bed while Dimi was still awake, since hearing him scrape a chair or cough or feed the stove reminded her she wasn't alone. Now the house hushed, crypt-like. Somewhere outside in the ghostly light of the silver moon Taber, an insect sang softly, cree-EEP, cree-EEP. Another answered, shriller, CREE-craw.

She rolled over and pulled her quilts tighter around her neck. Her breath caught before she relaxed. A faint light came from the stairs; Dimi must still be awake. Either she hadn't slept as long as she thought, or he was working late on something for the Compound. Now that he had a desk to work at, he often worked upstairs, closer to her, and she was grateful for that.

She slid out of bed. She would keep him company while he worked, and they could talk. They did their best talking late at night, when the concerns of the day weren't there to obstruct the flow of thoughts. At night Dimi didn't act so much in charge, and they could be real friends. She wished he would talk about important things – like home and family and visiting – but she knew better than to mention that. Someday wasn't yet.

Sarah padded across the room. The light came from under his closed door. Dmitri promised when he installed the door that it was merely for decorum, not to shut her out. Maybe he didn't want the light to wake her. The door to her room dragged against the uneven floor; it took two people to close it, and made an awful scraping noise if you tried.

She stopped, hand on Dimi's doorlatch. She swore she heard a giggle. Dimi's voice said something she couldn't make out, and it sure sounded like someone answered him. Charlie didn't stay this late, and he didn't generally giggle.

Sarah lifted the latch and pushed the door open on its silent new hinges.

"Dimi?"

The room imprinted itself on Sarah's mind like a nightmare, never to be forgotten. Dimi lay propped on an elbow in bed, blanket to his shirtless waist, an opened green bottle and two – *two* – dirtied glasses on the lamp table. He was looking down at the bed, a – a *hair pin* in his hand. His head turned at the sound of her voice. As he turned, Sarah caught a glimpse of a *girl* wrapped in the bedsheet next to him, a *strange* girl with bare shoulders and wavy auburn hair, only half of which was held up in pins. She pulled the covers over her

280

head at the sight of Sarah.

Dmitri's eyes locked on Sarah's as time stood still. His smile faded.

"That door was shut. You didn't even knock. Get out."

He didn't offer to walk her back to bed. As he shifted position, the blanket didn't move with him. Sarah glimpsed a low section of bare belly, and suddenly understood why.

Dmitri was naked! Nagoi. Au Naturel. The Way Nature Intended. *Zorenchaf,* Charlie would say.

Come to think of it, there were girl's underthings on the floor so the girl must be naked too they were lying in his bed naked together why why would he be doing that when girls and boys only got naked together when they were going to make ba... . Oh no no no no no!

Sarah filled with a greater horror, eyes wide as two purple moons.

"Get out!"

No! Not Dimi! He wouldn't! No! He wouldn't do **that** to a girl – Who was she? He was naked and she was under his blankets! Why? When did she – ? Why did she – ? What?

Sarah's brain locked up, unable to think.

"NOW!" Dimi bellowed, lashing an arm toward the door. The blanket moved, and Sarah's eyes locked on the haze of black hair peeking above the hem. The implied potential of violence broke through the shock, and she disappeared in a billow of white nightdress.

Sarah dove onto the bottom of her bed, burrowed to the top, cocooned the covers tightly around her. She heard the scrape and click of a metal lock sliding into place.

Alone. She was truly Alone in the world. Dmitri was doing something else he wasn't supposed to do. That was an *adult* thing, between *adults,* and Dimi was only a kid like her. Why would he *do* that? They were supposed to be a *team* – friends, crewmates, partners – and a partner didn't leave the other behind! It wasn't fair to grow up without her, when she wasn't ready!

Sarah burst into hard tears. It took a while to figure out why. She was scared. Herzog cut back her anti-anxiety medications on the trip to the Compound, and now she was scared. *Terrified.* Alone in the universe, a galaxy away from Vlad. She didn't matter anymore to Dimi, not at all. He'd never, *ever* locked himself away from her before. Someone could come in through a downstairs window, accost her like he was accosting that poor strange girl, and he would never-ever come to see why she was screaming, never protect her, never rescue her, because he cared more about adult things. She couldn't even close her door!

Locked. Out.

Was this one of her nightmares? The ones that never wanted to stop? *Let it be a nightmare,* she cried hysterically under her blankets. *Please let it be a nightmare!*

Home! she gasped. *I want to go home!*

She tiptoed down the stairs late, never making it to breakfast. She couldn't have eaten anyway.

"Good morning!" Dmitri said as if nothing were amiss. "I wondered if you were getting up today."

No sign of the strange girl. Sarah sat on the bottom of the stairs. She dropped her head in her hands, pushed them across her face, and hugged herself.

Dmitri came to sit by her. "Hey. I guess we should talk about last night, huh?"

She lay awake all night, and he never once came to check on her. She pulled a defensive shoulder up, possessed by the twitches that signaled a bad upset. "No."

"Let me say something anyway." He rubbed her shoulder.

She twisted from his hand, the evil hand that had defiled that poor girl. "Don't touch me!"

She fled to the bench under the west-wall window. Any touch right now was physically painful, let alone the abhorrence she felt toward him. He'd touched *that girl*, that *naked* girl, with malicious intent; he wasn't touching her. She wedged her hands between her knees and hunched herself in tight.

Dmitri sighed and moved to the far end of the bench. "Look," he said to the floor, "there are some facts you have to face. Whether you want to believe it or not, Sar, I'm not a kid anymore. I'm twenty. *Twenty*! That's an adult, free and clear, on almost any Alliance planet, *without* padding my ID.

"What I did last night, that's – that's what adults *do*," he blushed. "I'm *allowed* to do it. It wasn't the first time, and it won't be the last. I'm sorry you had to find out about it like you did, but the rule has always been if the door is shut, you *stay out*. I'm not mad at you. I'm *not*," he insisted, "but you never even knocked. She would have been gone before you got up. I never intended for you to find out; it was my private business."

He'd done it before! All this time, and Sarah'd never realized what kind of person he really was. Her faithful image of her brother – of Dmitri the Hero, Rescuer from Hospitals-for-Those-Who-Were-a-Few-Impulses-Short-of-a-Space-Drive; of Dmitri, Friend and Comrade and Entertainer of bored sisters; of Dmitri the Protector, whose crazy schemes to get her medication nearly cost him his life – shattered. If she looked at him now, all she'd see would be Dmitri the Kidnapper, who made sure he kept her as far from Vlad as he could; Dmitri the Traitor, who promised he'd only keep her away from the family a week or two at most – a week that was now three years and growing; Dmitri the Predator, who allowed himself to act out carnal yearnings with girls who couldn't possibly have known what they were agreeing to, or they wouldn't have agreed. Flirting was one thing, even kissing, but ...?

"Are you going to marry her?"

"No." Dmitri seemed quite certain. "I might see her again, I might not. I don't know."

"Will she have a baby?"

Dmitri snorted. "Hah! Not by me, she's not. The point is, Sar, I *am* an adult, and especially now that I have my own space, you need to pay more attention to respecting my privacy, and I will do the same for you."

"And I'm just a lousy dumb kid who doesn't count anymore," Sarah mumbled. "I – I think I need to lie down for a while," she choked, and fled swiftly back upstairs.

A knock at the door kept Dmitri from becoming as morose as Sarah.

Charlie poked his head in the cabin. <You ready, Dimi-tri?>

Dimi sighed and stood up. <No, Charlie. I not go. Sarah not feel well. I need to stay near house today.>

<She sick? I can get Mother... >

<No, no. She okay.> The last thing either of them needed was Mrs. Al poking around. <She be all right. I just need stay here today.>

But it took several weeks before Sarah recovered, Dmitri's Declaration of Age leaving an unbridgeable gap between them.

Thirty-eight

Moscow
Russian Federation of States
Earthdate: 29 April, 2267

Valeria sat in the Headmaster's office, arms crossed so she wouldn't get all touchy-feely and embarrass her brother. David sat next to her, tall and impossibly broad, all of it muscle. She could tell by his silence that he, too, was anxious to get the meeting over with, but he sat patiently, his angular jaw high. He did not run from his mistakes. Uncle Tomas sat, just as formal, on David's other side.

The headmaster sighed. He poked David's computer file with a finger, steering it in a little arc before he stopped. "This is a very

283

serious matter. Your record at Northern, until three days ago, has been exemplary. Compared to your record before Northern, it's what some people might term a major miracle, the kind we like to take credit for whether we deserve it or not. But I'm afraid our policy is very, very clear on the subject."

"We understand that, sir," Valeria said. "Coach Durgin agreed to drop the assault charges. We were hoping that might have some bearing."

"Based on the statements of the student in question and those of the other members of the team who came forward as witnesses, Mr. Durgin and the Board of Directors – minus Mr. Ivanov, of course – decided it would be in Mr. Durgin's best interest if his contract with us terminated immediately. Regardless of Mr. Durgin's current employment status, the fact remains that Mr. Kirushenko, by his own admission, did hold a faculty member to the wall and threaten him with bodily harm. Whether it is four years, four weeks, or four hours before graduation, that kind of action cannot be tolerated or condoned."

"We understand," Val repeated with a heavy heart. Three years of unwavering determination, three years of watching her brother do an unbelievable turnaround into a respectable, intelligent, hard-working young man, would be shot to hell with only four weeks to go.

"Do you have any words to say in your defense, Mr. Kirushenko?"

"As in an apology? No sir," David replied. "I did what I did, right or wrong, and given the same circumstances, I'd probably do it again. If I learned one thing at Northern, sir, it's honor, and there is no honor in standing by and allowing a fellow student to be hit and screamed at. Nevshenko's a good player, a good *team* player. He'd gotten word that morning his mother was seriously ill. He was flying home right after the game. He didn't need to stay for us, that was his choice, his team loyalty. He didn't need Durgin slamming him like that over a trivial play that had no bearing on the outcome of the game. If Coach Verislavsky were here, he would have just benched him.

"I'm sorry, sir, but I won't stand by and watch a student be abused by a soccer coach. I did what I did, and I'm willing to accept your decision."

"Very well," the headmaster said. Few students were as physically imposing as the brash and energetic Mr. Kirushenko, not even his taller younger brother. Fewer still would ever have had the nerve to intervene as quickly – or as rashly – in a difficult situation, to throw away a promising future on the basis of a personal principle. The other members of the team were certainly in awe.

"Despite the close proximity to commencement ceremonies, such an act would normally result in immediate expulsion. However, based on our investigations, and some very strong lobbying by the Nevshenko family, the Board has decided to reduce that to a three-week suspension. Mr. Kirushenko will remove himself from the dormitory immediately and will not be allowed to return until exam week. This will become part of his permanent academic file. He will be stripped of his athletic team membership for the spring semester, nor will he be allowed to speak at commencement ceremonies. He will lose credit for the missed classwork, and in addition he will spend no less than sixty hours of his suspension in service to the school. I expect you here in this office at eight a.m. Monday morning, Mr. Kirushenko."

A look of relief spread over David's stoic features. "Thank you, sir. That's more than fair. Thank you!" He stood up to shake the man's hand, all hundred and eighty-seven centimeters of him.

"Thank you, Vasya," Tomas said, shaking the headmaster's hand. "You can be sure those three weeks won't be wasted."

Thirty-nine

Sarah hunted her brother down in the workshed and took refuge behind his knees. "Dimi! She's doing it again!"

"What now? Mrs. Al trying to domesticate your independent spirit again?" The two females had more or less worked out their differences. Mrs. Al no longer bothered Sarah with such vexing non-academic tasks as cooking and cleaning, and in return Sarah agreed to perform a few menial daily tasks, such as wiping her own plate.

"Worse! Flowers! She's planting flowers everywhere, and she wants me to help. She must have a million of them. Can't she just throw seeds in the dirt?"

"What's wrong with beautifying our yard? You've seen how nice their house is. She grows those indoors all rainy season, so they'll be further ahead when planting starts. Mother had flowers back on Earth."

Sarah folded her arms crossly. "She also hired someone to plant them. I hate plants!"

Dmitri put down the cutting tool he was sharpening. "You're the genius. Meet her half-way, make a peace offering. Use that head of yours. You know she likes those particular flowers, so why not see if you can cross-breed them to make a new color or something and present it to her as a gift? That's something she might go monkey over."

"I'm not great at botany. Plants are boring, and they take too long.

Bacteria are much quicker."

Dmitri laughed. "Somehow I'd doubt she wants a cold. I'm sorry. I thought it was something you knew how to do."

"I know how to do it. I just said plants are *boring*."

Dmitri went back to sharpening the tool, scraping and smoothing the metal with a special bar. "Well, why don't you plan it out and show me. I'll help you if you get stuck. I'm sure Mrs. Al would be more than happy to help you with the plants." He dangled the bait, knowing full well the starving fish would snap it up in an instant.

"Hah! That'll be the day when I need your help on a science problem." Sarah crossed her eyes and managed a small smile, thinking it out in her head. "Yeah, I could do that."

Mrs. Al cornered Dmitri as he came back to the cabin at dinner, fists resting on her ample hips. <What you do to Sarrah? I hope you not yell at her.>

Dmitri rinsed his face and dried it. <Why? What she do?>

<She no wash for dinner, say she not want to eat. First she run and hide when I say dig flowers in, now she want all flowers, all seeds, and ask for more. Ask me all kinds of questions about plants. She outside digging new ground right now.> Mrs. Al waved a hand at the door. <She make self crazy!>

"It's not the first time," Dmitri said under his breath. <I go get her.>

* * *

He was glad Sarah was on the other side of the store picking out candy when the man behind the counter handed him an actual piece of mail. It came from the Compound, addressed only to him. He made sure Sarah was occupied, and tore open the envelope.

Transfer URGENT to: Kirushenko, Dmitri, Vandijoc, Sigma Tau Ceti
Message as follows:

Mrs. Andrea Ivanova
requests the honour of your presence
at the marriage of her granddaughter
Ekaterina-Anastasia Alexandrovna Kirushenko
Ceremony at Noon
Saturday, the Twenty-Fifth of May,
Two Thousand Two Hundred and Sixty-Seven
Ivanov Residence
6213 Velikaya Ploshchad Extension
Minsk, Byelorus, Earth

Received/transferred by Hargan Ennis, Communications Engineer, Unified Date: 361675

Dmitri read it through twice, folded the paper and put it back in the envelope. He tore it in half lengthwise, put the halves on top of each other, and tore it in half again. He handed the pieces back to the storekeeper and asked him to throw them away.

Forty

Minsk, Byelorus
Russian Federation of States
Earthdate: 25 May, 2267

Valeria opened the bedroom door, one hand adjusting the ring of fresh flowers on her hair. "Are you ready? There's three hundred people out there. David's getting impatient, and Marina's tearing up the rose petals. We need to go."

Katya gave a quick dab to her eyes. "Yeah," she sniffed, though her voice said otherwise. "Let me get my flowers. You wouldn't have any last-minute good news, would you?"

She stood up and smoothed her white dress. Her blonde hair swirled softly on her head, wreathed in a ring of white flowers and green leaves, every third flower a pink rosebud. She retrieved an enormous trailing bouquet from the bed. Though he was only seventeen, Katya had asked David to give her away in marriage. She felt so indebted to Uncle Tomas – beyond the fairy-tale wedding – that it was difficult not to ask him to do the honor, but Father didn't have the option of accepting, and she didn't wish to offend him. Viktor was departed, Dmitri wasn't there, Alexei's whereabouts remained unknown, so that left David to speak symbolically for the family. Uncle Tomas thought it quite prudent. And David was prouder than a peacock.

Val pulled her sister into a comforting embrace. "Don't do this to yourself. This is supposed to be the happiest day of your life. You did everything you could. You *tried*. Short of kidnapping, there is nothing else you could have done. Cooperation takes two. They may not have gotten the invitation in time. Vlad says they're at the edge of explored space."

"I know. And I *am* happy. I just can't help wishing ...." Katerina

287

broke off before more tears could fall. "I've been keeping my secret from her for so long. I know she'd be thrilled to see him, Val! I know it!"

"Shh! Enough now." Val wiped Katya's eyes herself. "Come, let me fix your face. You can't go down there like that; everyone will think you've gotten cold feet."

Katerina managed a wan smile. "No. That's one thing I'm sure on."

Val eyed her critically as she touched up her sister's light makeup. "As long as it's for the right reasons. Sometimes I wonder if you're not doing it for her instead of yourself. A man doesn't leave an established career and start over in a foreign country, doesn't try to master a new language if he doesn't really love a woman, age differences aside. Would you have been willing to do the same for him if he hadn't? Do you love him as much as that?"

Katya blushed. "Yes. You know me better than that, Val. I couldn't ever marry someone if I didn't love them first. I've been waiting almost two years for this day. I think that's plenty long enough to know my own mind. I knew the other was a long shot, but the secret won't spoil. It hasn't yet. It was just a surprise I wanted to share."

Valeria squeezed her sister's hand, knowing every bit of her pain and disappointment. "You wait, Kat. Four more years. Four years and five months. I guarantee she'll be here the day after her birthday. He won't be able to keep her away after that. You wait and see."

"No more! Put it out of your head now." The substitute Maid of Honor adjusted the bride's dress one more time. "You have plenty else to think about today. Now, move it! You mustn't keep your new husband waiting, Mrs. John Carver!"

Forty-one

Sigma Tau Ceti IV
Earthdate: January 2268

Dmitri dug around last year's tree stumps with a flat shovel, while Charlie hacked the roots with a long tool. Once loosened, they chained the porshie to the stumps and tried to get her to pull them up. Dmitri had grown comfortable around the beast – allergies abated by Dr. Herzog, enough that Charlie let him pull it place to place around the fields. Today, using the porshie's new baby as bait, they had cooperation an incredible seventy-five percent of the time. The current stump gave a wiggle, a creak, then eased out of the ground in a shower of damp soil.

Charlie leaned on the handle of the *navichet*. <Dimi-tri, I ask you something?>

Dmitri wiped his face on the hem of his shirt. <Sure.>

<You know me good for while now, no?>

<Yeah, I call year and half while.>

<You think, maybe, I, maybe sometime, I, maybe, walk Sarrah to town or something?>

<Sarah? Why? You need trip to town? Or just someplace to walk with her?>

Charlie nodded, and Dmitri nearly fell over with the force of his laughter. <You must be Moonless!> Sarah wouldn't talk with other girls, let alone boys, and she stuck by him tighter than a Bellatrixian barnacle when someone came around.

Charlie wasn't laughing. He looked hurt. <Why? She not like me?>

Shit!

Dmitri's smile faded fast. <You serious, yes? No, she not hate you in particular, Charlie, but in case you not notice, she hate *everybody*. I try to make her find friend, make her not so lonely, but she not talk to anyone. You trying to hold fire.>

<But it okay with *you?*> Charlie pressed. <To ask her?>

Dmitri wavered, wishing to spare Charlie the pain of the inevitable belligerent response. <I... not know, Char. She still some young. She just hurt feelings.>

Charlie placed a hand on Dmitri's arm. <I *swear*, Dimi-tri, on Moons above! I not do anything bad. You know I not! I know she not that kind of girl. If she say yes, I can?>

Dmitri gave a low whistle. Not so long ago he was seventeen and lovesick, too. <Man, you have it bad, no? Head over heels for the *pit viper* herself. I feel bad. You have more luck teaching porshie to sing.>

Charlie nodded sorrowfully, even if he didn't understand the term *pit viper*. <She have prettiest eyes I ever see, not like eyes on any other girl. When I first see her – when she run from porshie and hide behind you on first day – she stare at me with big pretty eyes. Even with hair like boy, I think she pretty. Now her hair long and soft, and she wear it down so it swings and shines in sun – I never see hair so like *sunshine* before!>

There was truth in the statement. Dmitri'd seen one or two locals with a burnished sheen to their hair, but most had shades of browns, brownish reds, or black. None could come close to Sarah's shade of pale, the color of the shimmery light from Tau Ceti's smallest moon.

<You not know what you mess with,> Dmitri insisted. <She even *think* she smell that kind of idea, she break every bone in body.>

Charlie gave a short laugh. <I know her, Dimi-tri. She not that bad. I understand. I not rush her. As long as I can try.>

Charlie leaned in the door of the cabin early one morning. <Ai, Dimi-tri! I go to town, buy things for Mother. Come, too?>

Dmitri closed his mouth just in time. The question wasn't meant for him. <I really not plan to go this morning. I – have other work to do. Hey, Sar?> he called, and she poked her face between the spindles of the stair rail.

<Charlie goes to town, but I must finish work here. Go with him for me?>

Sarah ran the idea through her mind. <Not without you, Dim. You know I not like town. It far to go alone.>

<You how many old? You cannot run simple errand? You not be alone; Charlie will go. I trust him.>

<Change schedule,> she insisted, clomping down the stairs. <We all go.>

Dmitri gave Charlie an *I tried* look, and got ready to make a needless trip to town. He tried to back off, to give Sarah a chance to answer Charlie's simple, conversation-starting questions, but, true to herself, Sarah waited for Dimi to answer, not saying a dozen words. When they got to town, Dmitri couldn't help whispering to Charlie, <*I warn you!*>.

* * *

Charlie stepped carefully over the rows of plants. <Here you!>

Sarah sat barefoot in the warm sun. Her shins and skirt were black from crawling down the rows of her experimental 'garden' on her hands and knees. A handful of tiny pollination brushes and her dirt-streaked notebook dragged along with her. She'd rolled her sleeves past her elbows, skirts hiked almost to her shorts as she floundered in the dirt, revealing long, shapely legs.

<Dimi-tri say almost dinner time. He come back to house now.>

Sarah didn't look up, marking in the notebook. <Mangato. Tell him I almost done; I be in soon.>

Charlie squatted across a flower from her. The low sunlight sifted gold through the trees, caught the back of Sarah's head and filtered through her tousled platinum hair, electrifying it.

<Mother think you crazy, but you never tell me why you put hats on flowers.>

Sarah sighed, but put down her pencil. The plants *did* look funny, the whole plot of flowers wearing little paper cones around each and evey blossom, but so far so good. She untied a paper off a purple bloom and showed Charlie the fat flowerhead. <You know how plants make seeds?>

<Flower dust spreads to other plants, makes seeds.> Charlie was much more intent on the scientist than the science. He tipped the flower toward him, wrapping his work-worn hand over her slightly smaller one. He leaned his head close to hers, so close their hair touched. The warmth of her sun-drenched cheek radiated onto his, her breath fluttering soft on his chin. Out alone in the heat, the tormenting *gelhisa* buried somewhere in her room, Sarah had undone the first few fasteners to her blouse, and Charlie glimpsed an exquisite cleft of young flesh through the low neckline. It amazed him that she could work so hard – as hard as a boy – and never smell strong like other girls who worked outside. She always smelled like – fresh washed.

He leaned forward, nosing the sun-gold strands behind her ear. <With right touch, beautiful things can grow.>

<Pretty much,> Sarah conceded. She let go of the flower under his hand and pointed to the fancy center. Charlie sat back, blushing. <But I very fussy. I not want just *any* flower dust, only *certain* flower dust for certain flowers. Paper hats keep out extra dust. I spread dust where *I* want it to go.>

Charlie was about to say more, but Dmitri's call interrupted him. He extended his hand to help her up, but Sarah bounded to her feet on her own, hiking her skirt to brush the dirt from her legs.

Sarah looked over the last half-row that wasn't recorded yet, and started toward the cabin. <I guess I finish after we eat. Come on.>

* * *

The hot haying season. Dmitri now owned his own cutting blade, so he and Charlie made good time in cutting back the tall grass, while far out from underfoot Sarah raked the previous day's work into piles they would gather onto the cart after lunch. It was warm, even for the dry season. Sarah braided her hair up, and secretly left off her *gelhisa* and underskirts. After an hour, Dmitri shed his shirt, and Charlie followed suit.

"I hope you're not doing that to impress anyone!" Sarah called across the field. "Wait until the circus comes to town, and see if the sideshow needs a new attraction."

"Jealous!" Dmitri taunted back, knowing she was melting under the layers of clothing. He'd grown more muscular, but his physique was still no match for the sturdier, stockier Charlie, whose sculpted form had been forged by much harder, much more constant labor. Charlie didn't work for fun; Charlie worked to live

<You have dirt on face,> Charlie told Sarah at the morning break.

He licked a finger and rubbed a spot on her cheek.

Sarah pulled away. It was bad enough when Valeria used to spit-polish their faces, let alone some sweaty, half-naked neighbor boy. <Thank you, I can do.> She picked up the hem of her skirt and wiped her face.

<You get it!> Charlie smiled his very best, trying to catch her eye. He dipped a cup of water from the covered drinking bucket and offered it to her.

<*esa Mangato.*> Sarah accepted the cup, drank almost all of it, and poured the last onto the hem of her skirt, wiping her face and neck with the cool wetness. She gave a short nod of appreciation and handed the cup back, stretched, then returned to raking.

<*What I do wrong?*> Charlie asked miserably.

Dmitri shrugged back, watching his sister work. <I warn you. She break heart.>

Dmitri took matters into his own hands over their lone dinner. "You were rather rude to Charlie today."

Sarah speared a vegetable with her fork. "Me? How was I rude? I hardly said two words to him, and both of them were polite."

"That's what I mean. The poor kid's been trying to make you notice him for ages, and you not only ignored him, you turned your back and walked away. He likes you, and you won't even give him the time of day."

Sarah put her fork down. "Likes me? You mean, like Vlad likes me? Or like *you* like girls?"

Dmitri reached for his glass. *"Da."*

"What! *Why!*" she cried, horrified. "Why would he like *me*? I don't dress fancy! I don't show myself off! I'm much too young for him to think of like that!" She crossed her arms over her chest, hiding her body from the eyes inside her head.

Dmitri swallowed the mouthful he was chewing. "No, you're not that young. I mean, yeah, you're too young for some things, but you're going on fourteen, Sar. That's not too young just to go and hang with someone. He's only three or four years older than you. He's a good kid. He thinks you're pretty, and a hard worker. That means a lot in this society. It wouldn't kill you to humor him and just *talk* to him a little – at least acknowledge his efforts to impress you. You hurt his feelings today. He's trying to be nice."

Sarah stared at her half-eaten plate in angst. A hole seemed to have opened under her seat. The wind rushed by cold and sharp, stealing her breath as she fell through the center of the planet, stomach first.

"No one asked him to be nice to me. I won't tolerate it! I'm not going to marry him, so he can just stop looking at me! I won't degrade myself like that for *any* man!"

Charlie was okay – as a friend of Dmitri's. As a friend, he'd always seemed harmless, and that's how Sarah'd thought of him. Being with the two of them was like hanging with the boys back home. Charlie could be as aggressive and impatient as David when wrestling a stubborn porshie, as contemplative and attentive as Sergei when she explained science to him, as nervous and mousy as Vlad when Mrs. Al yelled at him, but most of all he reminded her of Dmitri when they'd been home, an easy-going kid who was full of fun. Now, like Dimi, he, too, had a darker side, and he wanted to turn those dark desires to her. That couldn't be allowed. Not at all.

"Tomorrow you can just tell him I'm not interested and he can stop wasting his time, because *I won't do it*!" Sarah insisted, tarnished and soiled at the thought.

No. Oh no. Unable to breathe, unable to scream, unable to free herself from the fingers ruthlessly burrowing into her naïve flesh... Not again. Not *ever* again.

"Nope. I won't do that," Dmitri said around another mouthful of *joubash* stew. "This is the perfect opportunity for you to develop some social skills. If you want him to stop, you need to tell him. And make sure you do it nicely. He's done nothing wrong, and us guys are kind of sensitive about rejection."

Sarah was gone by the time Dmitri awoke the next morning, avoiding the problem by running from it. She appeared silently in the field at mid-morning, face blanched, eyes wide, shoulders scrunched up to her ears, carrying fresh cool water mixed with sweetened fruit juice – her effort at being nice. Cool was good; it had been hard to adjust to a climate that never got cold enough to make ice a commercial business, and didn't have machinery to make it without the weather's help.

Dmitri waved a finger to call Charlie's attention to her, and headed towards the forest edge on the pretense of a nature call.

Sarah saw him leave and nearly lost her nerve, the pressure in her chest so tight no air could enter. She put the water bucket on the ground before Charlie, shaking, sweating, her terror so strong she prayed she wouldn't vomit. She stared at the bucket, focusing on nothing else, forcing herself to breathe against her crushing ribs.

<*esa mangato, Ahnax*.> Charlie smiled, taking the cup from its hook on the bucket's handle and filling it. <You want first drink?> he offered, but she shook her head. <It very warm again today. That good for hay.>

Now or never. Now or pass out from nerves and leave herself completely vulnerable here in the wilderness, where no one could hear her scream.

293

Sarah whispered to the ground the words she'd spent the morning composing. <Dmitri say you want to talk with me. I think you very nice, but if you talk long to me, you find you will not like me very much, and I too young for you to think about like that. I sorry. I cannot be girl for you. I cannot make you happy, not like you want, I cannot. I just cannot. *I sorry!*> she cried, losing her nerve. She turned to run, but he reached out and caught her hand.

<Wait!> Charlie pleaded. <I just want – >

Sarah spun with a terrified shriek, digging her heels into the ground and pulling on her arm with considerable strength, her frightened eyes large and darkly blue in the daylight. <Please! Let go!> *Where the hell was Dimi?!*

He no longer protects you, a distant part of her subconscious reminded her. *Adult games, remember?*

<Please stay! We cannot be friends?>

<Yes! Yes! Whatever you want! Please *let go!*>

Hands, entrapment, helplessness, fear, the horrible touching, the shameful pain …

Charlie released her. Sarah ran down the path faster than she ever thought she could.

For two days, Sarah wouldn't leave the house. She hid in her closet, refusing to eat or wash, unable to sleep, with fresh, ominous nail gouges on her face. Dimi knew a bad thing when he saw it, but Sarah wouldn't say a single word when she wasn't weeping, wouldn't let him within arm's length without kicking at him until he left her alone. He slept across the doorway to her room.

On the third day he brought his knife and a bucket of soapy water upstairs, and told her if she didn't at least wash, he would cut her clothes off, dump the bucket on her, and scrub her right there in the closet. After some consideration, Sarah decided she didn't have the energy to fight, and went reluctantly downstairs to bathe.

He dragged her to the fields on the fourth day, knowing the amount of work to be done and not daring to leave her alone. She made it into the field, his arm around her, but on seeing Charlie the perceived pressure swelled so intense Sarah ran to the edge of the field and collapsed, hugging herself and rocking while tears of hysteria fell. Charlie watched, near tears himself knowing he was the cause of such distress, watching Dmitri comfort her and knowing he couldn't. Sarah curled at the edge of the field the rest of the day, in Dimi's sight but unable to work.

For more than a week, Dimi worried. He watched and waited, poked and prodded, and if he worked right next to her, away from Charlie, she would slowly help. That was good. Down, but not out. Gone, however, was the humorous banter that had made the tedious work seem like play. Now the only sound in the fields was the creak of the cart and the whooshes of the porshie. It wasn't until after haying season that something would happen, something so big and bold and bothersome enough to upset Sarah in a completely new direction, enough to make her count Charlie as an ally.

Forty-two

Sergei opened the door of the study and entered. "You wanted to see me, Uncle Tomas?"

"Yes, please! Come in, sit." Tomas shut off the screen and motioned to the chairs before the desk. "You're an elusive person, Sergei. I've been meaning to talk to you for more than a month now. I'm afraid our schedules haven't coincided."

"No, sir."

"You're graduating soon. Have you given thought on how you'd like to celebrate? David went out with his friends; I didn't know if you planned on doing the same, or if you wanted something here."

Sergei twisted his mouth sideways, thinking. "I don't know. Maybe something here with the family. Nothing fancy."

Tomas nodded. He'd expected that out of the boy. Trying to pin Sergei down was like trying to capture a radiowave with your fingers. Tomas knew David well. Valeria had been legally in control until he turned seventeen, and David accepted that, but there had been little question as to whom the boy considered to be in charge. Tomas felt close to Vladimir, too, and perhaps even closer to eight-year-old Nikky, whom he'd known for more than half the boy's life. But Sergei... Tomas knew what he liked and what he didn't, had long, scholarly conversations with him, knew he had a fierce loyalty to his brothers and a sly, caustic wit that surfaced when you least expected it, but as far as what drove him, Tomas could only guess.

"Okay. Consider this, though: I graduated sixteenth in a class of thirty-four. Nothing spectacular, I admit. Incidents aside, David graduated third in a class of thirty-three. Much more impressive. Unless you manage to fail every one of your exams, you will graduate at the top of a class of thirty-six. That's pretty special. Only one person in every school has that distinction each year. Are you sure you don't want something bigger? Invite a few friends; your whole class, if you'd like?"

"I guess that'd be okay," Sergei said reluctantly. "There's a few people I could invite."

"Good. Go over things with Marya, and she'll take care of the arrangements. Galina said you opted for Moscow State. I'm a little surprised. She said you were accepted at St. Petersburg. That's a much better school for your interests."

"Yes sir, technically it is, but Moscow has a more diversified program, more opportunities for me to branch out if I want. There's a hundred areas I can sub-specialize in. I plan on doing at least one semester in 'Petersburg. It's better, if I do minor in fine arts. And besides," he winked, "someone needs to keep an eye on David."

What Marya pulled together was a far cry from the private family dinner Sergei desired. The back lawns swarmed with fifty students, parents, family, and extra help hired for the occasion. Noise shook the trees to their roots from a quintet of musicians familiar with the current concept of teen music. The loaded buffet tables stretched eight meters long.

Galina interrupted Tomas where he sat at a table with several other adults. She held an embarrassed-looking Vladimir by the elbow. David stood behind them, arms crossed in supreme annoyance. "Excuse me, sir. I'm sorry to disturb you, but I need to speak with you privately. Now, please."

Tomas excused himself. "Of course. What's going on?"

"She's blowing things out of proportion, that's what!" David objected while he still could.

"I am no less pleased than you are over Sergei's graduation," Galina started, "and I wouldn't dream of denying him his party, but I'm afraid I have to draw a line. If Sergei wants to drink, it's his party, his business; I won't stop him. But if I catch David near Vladimir again, I will have to make a scene. David is pushing Vlad to drink, and I *will not* allow that to happen. It won't be David sitting with him when he gets sick."

"I thought you didn't drink, Vladimir?" Tomas said. Vlad never even finished the New Year's toast. The man hired to tend bar had explicit instructions not to serve alcohol to anyone under sixteen, and fourteen-year old Vladimir hardly looked eleven.

Vlad tried to stand taller. "I had beer, that's *it!* I'm not a baby!"

"It's not *what* he drank I'm objecting to as much as *how*," Galina said curtly. "David's got him over by the trees with a group of friends, pushing to see how fast he can drain a glass."

David rolled his eyes with the injustice of it all. "I was not timing him! I just so happened to be *looking* at the time when you came over!"

"And congratulating him on besting his previous time. I'm not stupid, David. Val and I did the same thing at your age. I just hope when he gets sick, it's all over you, in front of your friends. He's already got Sergei under the table."

"Sergei's *fine*!" David pointed across the yard to where his brother stood with two arms around the girl in front of him, a glass in his hand, talking to a group of friends and laughing. "It's his party, man! All I did was loosen him up. Now he's enjoying himself. Everyone in this family is so damned uptight!"

Tomas sighed. Both parties were probably telling the truth, as each saw it. Tomas knew, as did Galina, that the danger lay in the fact that Vlad worshipped David like a hero and would do anything he asked, follow his brother down a path of destruction and see nothing but his own faith, never questioning. David rarely took advantage of his position, but this seemed to be one of those times.

"I'll take care of it," Tomas assured Galina. "Take care of Vladimir. David, come with me." He turned and walked across the lawn. David followed, his protests falling on deaf ears.

Tomas stopped at the set-up near the rose arbor. "I would like you to stop serving alcohol for the next hour," he told the bartender. "No wine, no beer, no vodka, nothing, for one hour. Let's bring the cosmonauts back to Earth. When you reopen, take careful note of this gentleman here." Tomas put a hand on David's shoulder. "He is not to be served again, no matter how much he cries or kicks his feet. If he tries to bribe you, pocket his best offer and I will double it again that you don't serve him. He has abused his privilege and is cut off as of this minute. Is that understood?"

The man behind the table gave a nod, memorizing David's face. "Quite clearly, sir."

"Uncle Tomas...!"

Forty-three

Sigma Tau Ceti IV
Earthdate: May, 2268

Sarah couldn't bring herself to dine at the table the nights the Aletneshfajas ate with them. After accepting Dmitri's simple explanations the first two absences, Mrs. Al pushed him aside and puffed up the stairs to see for herself. Sarah huddled in her closet under a blanket. Mrs. Al unwrapped her and gave her as thorough an inspection as she could, refusing to take *aja* as an answer. Satisfied when she found no physical marks, no painful spots, no fever, no 'women's complaints,' she allowed Sarah to return to her cocoon. Despite Dmitri's pleadings, Mrs. Al returned to the room after dinner and tried to force-feed the girl. Dmitri practically sat on Sarah, blocking the closet after the well-intentioned plate hit the floor and the head banged on the wall in frustration.

Mrs. Al's eyes sparked angry fire. <She need to eat! She need medicine!>

<I *give* her good medicine!> Dmitri insisted.

<*I* will see.>

Dmitri thought fast. He went to his room and returned a moment later with the small blue bottle of sleeping pills. They were out of code by several months, but they shouldn't be harmful.

Mrs. Al examined the small print with care, unaware not even Charlie could have understood the squiggles. She opened the bottle, poured several tablets into her hand, and held them out to the barricaded girl. Dmitri danced behind Mrs. Al to get Sarah's attention, nodding madly for her to take them.

Sarah missed most of the cues, but no matter. She had long been a champion at hiding pills in her cheeks and pretending to swallow them. Mrs. Al smiled and patted her on the head.

Dmitri forced Sarah to call a truce with Charlie. More on his lap than off it, his arms around her, she stared at the table and whispered the answers he prodded out.

<I could not *ever* hurt you, Sarrah!> Charlie said, choked by heartache. <I think you funny – in good way. I hear you talk to Dimitri and I feel happy. I just want maybe talk to you myself, maybe feel even happier.>

<I sorry,> Sarah mumbled, bent over so far her nose almost touched the table. Dmitri lifted the chin, but the eyes went sideways, anywhere but toward Charlie. <I much too young for that! Please, *do not* think like that!>

<Okay,> Charlie conceded. <But you must stop hiding, yes? I still Dimi-tri's friend, and I still friend to you. Just plain friend, yes?>

Dmitri pushed her hand out to shake on it, but Sarah pulled back before they could touch. <You make mother stop feeding me?> she asked first. Mrs. Al had been making all sorts of fancy dishes to tempt her to eat. Sarah nibbled here and there, but Dmitri suffered terrible indigestion, trying to consume everything before the next wave.

Charlie and Dmitri broke into laughter. Charlie held her trembling hand. <Yes. I stop Mother sending food.>

Dmitri and Sarah made a grocery run into Vandijoc, in need of fruit, bread (Sarah turned out to be a satisfactory bread-baker, but only on a whim), bottles of a local hard beverage that Dmitri had become fond of, and, as always, a small bag of sweets to keep Sarah happy. They stopped to see if Charlie wanted to join them, but Mrs. Al explained that the Moonless porshie had gotten loose, and Charlie was off tracking it. Mrs. Al wasn't terribly upset by the fact; last time the porshie got loose at night, she'd come back pregnant. To the Kirushenkos' horror, the Aletneshfajas butchered the young porshie. Sarah stared murderously at Charlie during meals and went completely vegetarian, and even Dmitri laid off porshie meat for a while.

The bag of candy never left Sarah's hand, but Dimi carried the loose items in a bag over his shoulder. He paused in the street to pull a piece of fruit from the bag. Sarah stopped behind him. She wasn't allowed to hold his hand anymore, lest a town girl not realize she was only his sister. Before he could take more than a bite, a girl exited the store facing them, arms overloaded with fat parcels. She felt her way down the steps one by one, kicking her skirts out of the way, but she miscounted and missed the last step entirely. She fell in an ungraceful heap, packages bouncing across the dirt.

Dmitri dropped the fruit and fell on his knees next to her hardly a breath later. <Moons above!> he exclaimed. <You unbroken? That quite a fall!>

<Yes, I fine, thank you.> The girl blushed, dusting off her dress. She stood ten or eleven centimeters shorter than Sarah, as slim and fine as a porcelain doll. Light-brown hair hung to a slender waist, tied back by a single gold ribbon. She tucked the loose hairs back behind her ears. <I not always so careless. I walk on these stairs all my life.> She glanced up at Dmitri with a coy, embarrassed little smile. Her dark green eyes caught his, and Sarah *swore* she could see the lightning strike.

Dmitri gave a slight shake, and his face went blank. His eyes opened wider, and they held her gaze much longer than polite.

<It seem to me like you just have more than your little hands can carry,> he said softly, and the girl-killer smile wove across his face. The girl blushed again and dropped her eyes, glancing at him through long, dark lashes. Dmitri bent and gathered up the packages.

"Sar!" he hissed, motioning for her to help.

Sarah picked up their bag and wrapped her arms around it. "Sorry, Dim, my little hands are already full."

Dmitri scowled, but better things demanded his attention. He stood up, arms brimming. <Perhaps I carry them? I not want you to hurt yourself.>

The girl blushed deeper still. She pointed to the side street that ran up the western rise out of Vandijoc. <I live far up hill. I cannot ask you to go so far out of way.>

<It not so far. And you not need ask, I offer. Show me way!>

"Dimi!" Sarah squealed several meters behind. "What do you mean, not far? That's the exact opposite direction from home! It'll take forever!"

"You can run home and help Charlie hunt for his porshie. I'm sure he'd love the company."

Sarah's eyes burned, but she shut her mouth. Growling, she stuffed her bag of candy deep into the groceries, shouldered the bag, and ran to catch up.

Jaycelani. Jaycelani Sivalaxa. Jay-cel-*ah*-ni. Jay-cee. Jayceelani. Jays. Jay-cee. Dmitri couldn't get the name out of his head. He rolled it around one way, rolled it back another, listening to the sound of it. *Jaycelani.* He thought about the pretty face that went with it. The slender hands, the slim waist, the lively green eyes that sparkled when she looked at him, the shy little cherry-lipped smile. Dmitri didn't talk much the rest of the day but he sighed a lot, and wasted an entire hour combing his hair a hundred different ways before putting it back the way it started. He picked at dinner, mind elsewhere.

It took Charlie only a minute to notice the following day, the recovered porshie chained to a tree.

<Dimi-tri, you up to something! What you know that I not? I know when you look like that. You see pretty skirt!>

Dmitri blushed. <Pretty girl fall at feet. I have no choice but look.>

Sarah rolled her eyes in disgust. *At least this one fell forward.*

A knock sounded at the door while Sarah grudgingly helped clear dinner. Dmitri opened it, and Mrs. Al craned her neck to see two giggling girls. One was the girl from the store. Dmitri stepped outside. Charlie followed, checking out the girl's friend. Sarah wasn't nearly as polite, shoving and squirming her way between the boys.

Jaycelani blinked her eyes at Dmitri and held out a metal box draped with an exquisitely embroidered cloth. <I wish to say thank you for kindness of yesterday.>

Dmitri glanced at Charlie; Charlie's eyes dared him to push on. He accepted the box with a short nod and removed the cloth, revealing a dessert with fluffy topping, perfectly swirled.

Dmitri let slip that damned smile. <It look delicious, but I bet it not half as sweet as maker.>

The girl blushed harder, her toe tracing lines in the dirt, while her friend suppressed an envious grin.

Ugh! Get real! Sarah wanted to fall down laughing. This was toooo disgusting! She spun toward Charlie and puffed her cheeks out, making gagging motions.

Charlie was conversing with Jaycelani's friend. *<Stop!>* he glared.

So Charlie was a ninny, too. Sarah crossed her eyes in contempt a second before she found herself dragged suddenly backwards by her hair. Mrs. Al shut the cabin door and pushed a cloth into her hands.

<Dishes must be dry,> Mrs. Al said in a voice that dared to be defied. *<Your business in here.>*

<My business to make sure Dmitri stays from trouble,> Sarah scowled. She stepped sideways, but Mrs. Al matched her every move like a shadow.

Mrs. Al propelled her to the dishes. *<Boys not have trouble, so you can help in here.>*

It was heavy dusk when Dmitri thanked Mrs. Al for staying, and she and Charlie left just after the girls. Leaving the lamp burning, he went wordlessly upstairs and shut his door. Sarah sprinted after him. She banged on it, lest she be accused of not knocking.

"Go away."

"What do you mean, *'go away'*? I want to talk to you. You haven't talked to me all night."

Dmitri opened the door. "Maybe I don't want to! Maybe my name is Sarah, and I'm a spoiled brat! Maybe I stick my fingers in other people's desserts and lick them in front of a roomful of company, and then insult the cook."

He stamped his foot, waved his fisted hands, bottom lip sticking out. "Maybe everybody's just unfair to me and I'm going to sit and sulk in my room until I get my way, so leave me alone!" He slammed the door.

Sarah stared at the planks. "Is that supposed to mean you're mad at me for something? Be mad, then! You want to act like the world's biggest idiot because a girl has a nervous tic that looks like a smile to you, go ahead! *And I'm not spoiled!"* She kicked the door before flouncing off to mope in her closet.

How the tables had turned! Charlie delighted in torturing the love-struck Dmitri, at last finding a way to make Sarah smile at him. He'd backed off as promised, but his heart hadn't given up. He sneaked behind Dmitri and made sniffing noises until Dimi chased and wrestled him to the ground. Sarah jumped around them in delight, cheering Charlie on.

Charlie grinned, lying across Dmitri's back. *<Say so!>*

Dimi laughed despite his arms being pulled from their sockets. *<All right! Am kissing fool! But I not kiss her yet!>*

<Porshie-kissing fool!> Charlie insisted, winking at Sarah, who pinned her brother's legs, giggling.

"Ugh! Moons no!"

<Say so!>

<*Ow! Okay!* Am porshie-kissing fool!> Dmitri gave in, too happy to care about simple harassment between friends.

Dmitri found a dozen excuses to see Jaycee. After all, he needed to return the plate she brought the cake on. As he and the kid sister left, Jaycee reminded him he'd forgotten the cloth. She'd stop by tomorrow. He *had* to run an errand to town, and, just the damnedest thing, she was running one, too. She wrote him a note and left it at the post exchange. Dmitri could speak Tau Cetan fluently now, but he'd never had a call to write it. He struggled for hours with the dictionary, copying the correct spellings, refusing to let Sarah translate for him – and of course, he had to go back to town to leave it for her. She paid him several calls, sometimes alone, sometimes with her friend, always seeming to time the visits on the days Mrs. Al stayed late and could run intercept around Sarah. Jaycee tried to include the girl in the conversations, but Sarah stared like a fish from the first sentence and fled upstairs, peering through the cracks of the floorboards and sprinkling dust onto the people below.

This evening was no different. Mrs. Al grabbed Sarah by the hair as she tried to slip out the door scarcely five minutes after Jaycee arrived. <No you not! I say you stay, you stay!> She barred the door.

<Mother! She by window!> Charlie called. Mrs. Al pulled Sarah off the west wall bench, closed and locked the shutters. Sarah scowled and kicked air, then sidled toward the bathroom.

<Moons above, you awful girl!> Mrs. Al swore in vexation, turning Sarah away before she could sneak off to the front windows in the addition. Mrs. Al dragged a chair over and sat in the alcove at the bottom of the stairs, able to view the whole downstairs at once. Aggravated, Sarah ran to her room.

Deepening twilight played across the southern horizon. The big red moon Allash glowed large overhead, and a waning yellow half of Oes peeped over the trees. <What beautiful sky!> Jaycee sighed. <I love to watch night-lights come out.>

Dmitri held her dainty hand as they sat on the bench outside the door. <Do you know stars' names?>

<No, do you?>

<Once I did,> Dmitri said wistfully, <but I live so far away, even stars there look different.>

<How could stars be different? Stars are stars.>

<Many things different, far away. I live one place, the land so hot, no trees grow. No grass, no farms, everywhere just dry dirt. I live another place, it get so cold in rainy season that water outside turn

hard like rocks, and stoves must burn day and night to keep houses warm.>

Jaycee leaned on his arm, gazing at a purple-dark cloud against the gleaming blue of the evening sky. <I cannot imagine such a place. You would take me there, some day?>

<I will never go back to place of hot sand,> Dmitri assured her. He put his arm around her, cushioning her tender back from the rugged cabin. She slid closer, warm against his side. His face rested centimeters from hers, her breath cloud-soft on his cheek. Her head tipped ever so slightly, presenting her ear to him, her trusting eyes begging him to make a move. He felt her shiver with anticipation; the moment was *there*, it was *perfect*, it was *right*, and he leaned in for the kill.

<Do you know what time white moon rises tonight?> said a voice that came strangely from above.

Dmitri jumped to his feet, beet-red in the darkness, looking for the body that went with the voice. He saw no one, until his eye wandered upward. It was so dark he couldn't see much more than a black shape – leaning over the first-story roof edge.

"What the hell are you doing up there!" Dmitri bellowed. "Get back inside before you fall!"

"Don't be such a worry-wort. It's perfectly safe."

"Inside!"

Jaycee laughed. <Let her be, Dimmy! She funny! She just young girl who wants love in her heart, too.>

<*Hah!* That *last* thing she want,> Dmitri scoffed. <She get offer; she run crying other way.>

Dimmy? Dimmy?! Sarah squealed with glee. Oh, that was really too much! Wait 'til she let that slip to Charlie! <I resent that – Aaah!>

Sarah's retort ended as she slipped turning around on the slanted ledge. Her bottom half fell over the side, feet pedaling the air with no hope of reaching a hold on the door below. Only her elbows kept her from falling. Jaycee gasped.

"Oh for crying out loud!" Dmitri swore. "Hang on!"

"I can't! I'm slipping!"

He grabbed her knees. "Quit kicking! I've got you. Let go." Feeling his arms, Sarah eased her weight downward, letting go when his hands reached her waist. He dropped her safely to the ground, held her by the back of the neck, and knocked on the door until Mrs. Al opened it.

<Dimi-tri! *How?*> Mrs. Al stared, mystified.

<Fall off house,> was all he could say. He marched Sarah to her chair in the sitting room, a big rocking chair he bought her some months ago. She'd discovered a similar one when she finally entered the Al's house, and she'd fallen in love with it.

Dmitri took his smaller knife from its sheath on his belt. He handed the knife to Charlie, sat him in the padded chair near the rocker, and told him, <If she move even one *enab* from chair, cut heart out.> Charlie nodded.

Sarah watched Charlie with distrust. She couldn't win an honest wrestling match against him, especially with the knife. Mrs. Al would never allow him to hurt her … but Mrs. Al ordered baby porshies to be slaughtered, and she cut the heads off live poultry herself. Sarah pulled her knees up under the skirts and rocked slowly. *Round one, Sarah. Round two, Dimi.*

Whoops! *Dimmy*, she giggled to herself.

Dmitri rejoined Jaycee. <We need time alone. I think I know how.>

Charlie was game. He'd never babysat anything before, but he didn't think he'd have trouble keeping Sarah home for just two hours, so Dmitri could meet Jaycee for lunch. In Charlie's experience, girls were no worse than porshies, and he could handle porshies.

On pain of death, Sarah was relegated to her room. Charlie sat in the open door of the cabin, Dmitri's knife in his hands. He couldn't help but admire such a fine blade. He had a good knife; it was dull gray and scratched with constant use, the handle a polished wood now stained by years of faithful service. The blade on Dmitri's shone with a mirror finish, the edge so fine and sharp Charlie could have shaved a porshie with it and the porshie wouldn't have noticed. Decorative scrollwork covered the blade, engraved in a language Charlie assumed was the one Dmitri spoke to Sarah. He would ask Sarah about it, if she came down.

He felt honored, entrusted with such a highly expensive tool; Dimi-tri was a good friend. Charlie had played with it for an hour, carving and flaking bits of wood from a small stick to see just how fine the knife would cut, when he heard a rustle in the open yard. He glanced behind to see Sarah waggle her fingers at him before taking off like an *urpinta* down the path that led to town.

Sarah's legs were two centimeters longer than Charlie's and she had desperation in her speed, but Charlie'd traveled on foot all his life; he had stamina and muscle and endurance; he knew tracking and hunting animals in the forest. Twice he almost caught her, her clothing slipping through his fingers. Sarah ran down the main street of the town in a breathless streak, collapsing on the steps to the tavern in exactly twelve minutes, her personal best.

Charlie rushed up seconds after, just as winded. Unable to speak, he scowled at his ex-prisoner.

<Touch me … and I scream … so loud … your mother hear me … at home,> she choked between coughs.

<I promise I watch you – I do that,> he panted.

They hadn't caught their breath when the tavern door swung open and Dmitri held it for Jaycee. He stared, speechless.

<So sorry, Dimi-tri,> Charlie said. <I try. She climb down house, run like escaping porshie. I chase, but she have head start.>

Dmitri glared at his sister. <It not your fault, Charlie.>

Sarah looked hurt. <Why you stare at *me*? I not disturb your meal.>

Jaycee smiled sweetly and took Sarah's hand. <I have best idea! Everyone walk home with me and I make dessert. It can be like small party. You see!>

Dmitri said nothing on the long walk home. Sarah waited, but he said *nothing* to her, talking instead with Charlie, comparing the Aletneshfaja farm to the Sivalaxa's. No doubt it was another snit like the other week. *She hadn't bothered him*, so what was the big deal? At home he gave minimal answers to her questions, opening a bottle of local liver poison and having a glass with dinner. Worse, he poured a second glass, and carried it to his room.

Sarah gave him some time, then went upstairs. Dmitri wrote out papers at his desk, door open. She rapped on the doorframe and entered. She sat in the middle of his bed, and still he didn't look up. The glass on the desk was empty.

"Want to talk?" she volunteered brightly.

"Nope."

That's right, he had Jaycee to talk to now. No doubt Jaycee knew his plans for the next day, the next week, the next month. Dmitri *always* had something to talk about, even if only about something Sarah'd done wrong.

"What'cha working on?"

"Stuff for Guillaume."

Oh. "Want to play cards? I'll spot you five points…"

"Nope."

Left. Out. Sarah sighed, watching the back of his head. *What now?* She *didn't* interfere today!

"Have a lot of work left? Want some help?"

Dmitri gave an angry huff and put his pencil down. "Your *help* is the one thing I *don't* want." He stood up and leaned his bottom against the edge of the desk. "You want to talk? We'll talk.

"I want you to stay out of my business! You hear? Jaycee is a very nice girl – a *really* nice girl, the kind you like to be seen with, the kind you're proud to bring home to meet your family. I'm trying very hard to do this right, Sar! I don't need you screwing it up on me."

This wasn't the right lecture! It was supposed to be about her disobedience, not more of Jaycee this, Jaycee that. Something evil rose up inside Sarah, an overpowering, black-hearted serpent-self, frightening her with its strength, whispering things she'd never even think on her own.

Should she say it?

Of course not. It was far too rude and terrible. *Could* she say it? No. She'd never used that word. Goodness gracious! She *could*, because the words slid out on their own too fast to stop them, icy and black and coldly antagonistic.

"I thought screwing was *your* specialty."

The words cut Dmitri through the heart. In seconds his face ran through no fewer than eight separate emotions, starting with shock and ending with murderous rage. His jaw clenched, his body shook, his fists tightened. Too far away to hit her, Dmitri raised a fist, turned and swung it hard into the door of his closet with a loud howl.

"God*damn!*" He rubbed his knuckles, no less angry. "You better run."

Sarah flew down the stairs, two at a time.

He cornered her in the kitchen, boxed between the broom cupboard and the table. Both were shoeless, leaving Sarah just two centimeters shorter. They stood motionless, watching, waiting, the smell of Dmitri's panting bringing back tortured memories of Father's breath, sometimes so thick with alcohol you could get drunk on the fumes.

At once, Sarah realized the danger she could be in, all alone in the middle of the wilderness. She stared into his eyes, which were furious but not shiny or bloodshot or yellowed. Still, she felt a deep fear. Humor, attitude, anger all disappeared, every nerve tuned to his next move.

"You listen to me and listen good," Dmitri hissed. "*You stay away from her.* You hear me? I won't have you ruin this on me, Sar! This is *real*, and I won't put up with your tantrums over it. You blow this on me and I'll hurt you! That's a promise! Whether I put you over my knee and plant fear across your ass, or we go man-to-man five rounds in a ring, *mess with Jaycee and I* will *hurt you*. No more bullshit! Is that clear?"

Sarah stared him in the eye. "Perfectly."

Let him punch her teeth in. She'd be damned if she'd call him 'sir.'

Dear Mr. Ennis,
Please send following URGENT to standard address.
Thank you.
S. Kirushenko

Дорогой Владимир,

I wish, I wish, I wish I could call you just one more time, but I wouldn't dare even if I could. Vlad, if I tell you something, can you keep a secret? A not-tell-a-soul-secret? Uncle Tomas, Val, Sergei or anyone secret, even if it bothers you? If you don't think you can, tear this up tiny now, don't read it, just recycle it without looking and make SURE you delete any traces from the mail cache. Please? I don't want anything to be misinterpreted that might make something stupid happen and make things worse. I just wanted to talk.

Vlad, have you ever worried that bad things might happen again? I mean, like Father? I started thinking about it, and I'm scared, Vlad. Really scared. If I show up suddenly at your door, you'll know why. Dimi drinks, Vlad. Not as bad as Father, just now and then, and he's almost always amusing. I've never once seen him drunk like Father, he never gets that look in his eyes. Don't be upset – he's never hit me, never even threatened to, not where I believed he actually would, but I'm still worried. He got a little upset the other night – he didn't even get loud! – but it made me think how isolated we are out here, and it scared me, being all alone like this if he ever does have "problems." Does anyone else do that, Vlad? Do you ever still get scared like that?

PLEASE don't say anything to anyone. I'm not as worried as I make it sound, I'm really not. I guess I just feel awfully alone, and I miss you guys something terrible. I can handle Dimi from here. If I think I can't, you can be sure I'll be home, on my own, one way or another. Don't sweat about it.

Sarah

She *tried*. There wasn't a God in the Universe that couldn't have seen how hard Sarah tried. Too soon it was *Jaycee* helping Mrs. Al make dinner three nights a week, chatting and laughing over mixing bowls. *Jaycee* helped Mrs. Al hang out the laundry, singing little songs to herself, her brown hair shining in the sunlight. Sarah grabbed some of Dimi's clothes and knelt by the bucket to soap them, but Mrs. Al chased her away.

<Go! Not enough wash to bother three people. Go find book and read to us while we work.>

Sarah wormed her way into the kitchen. <I make good bread.>

Mrs. Al pushed her back out the door. <Yes, but not today. You

in plants all morning; hands too dirty. Go, find our boys and pester them.>

After much begging on her part, Dmitri agreed to leave Sarah alone if he went for a walk with Jaycee, and she kept her word to behave, locking the door the moment he stepped through. The first two times he had Mrs. Al come by to check on her; Sarah spoke to her through the window and insisted she was okay. Dmitri kept his part of the bargain and never came back late, not even by a minute. He praised her for showing responsibility, praised her for staying alone, praised her for behaving, brought her treats from town, but he didn't have much else to say. All his dreams and ideas and stories and smiles were now used up on Jaycee. Sarah was perfect during the day, but at night she buried herself at the bottom of her bed and wept.

She could hold on. This too would pass.

She tried to stay upbeat and cheerful. "Aren't we cutting wood today?"

Dmitri pulled on his boots. "Nah. You might as well stay here and check your plants. I've got to help Charlie repair the cart before we can haul wood. Nothing you can help with."

"I checked the plants yesterday. Can't I come watch?" she asked hopefully, lonesomely, eager to do anything with him, anything at all.

"What's there to see? I'll be back by noon. I'm meeting Jaycee at three."

Sarah stayed behind. And wept.

In the depths of her misery, she did what she thought was the most daring thing she'd ever done, bolder than standing up to Father, and potentially far more dangerous.

Sick with desperation, she walked to the Aletneshfaja's late one afternoon by herself. When she really thought about it, Charlie *was* kind of nice. He liked to joke and wrestle, and though he certainly couldn't be called educated, he wasn't stupid. He never failed to give her presents, be it a fruit drop or a new pencil or even a pretty pebble he found while walking. And all he said he wanted to do was *talk*. She could handle talking.

She stood silently in the doorway to the big shed, waiting to be noticed, while Charlie fixed the stock for the night. He spread extra grain in the porshie's feedbox. Sure enough, the porshie'd gotten pregnant again the night she'd run loose. Apparently porshies had no fertility problems. Mrs. Al promised they wouldn't butcher this one.

Charlie gave a big smile. <Sarrah! Why you come here? Dimi-tri come too?>

Sarah shook her head. <You need help?>

<Too late. I just finish.>

<You want to talk with me?> Maybe, just *maybe* if he promised

308

not to touch any other part of her, she might let him hold her hand.

Charlie smiled sheepishly. <I want to, Sarrah, but, music is playing at town school tonight, and, I ... supposed to meet someone there. Maybe tomorrow? We can play game of *duwhalikae*.>

Sarah blinked hard. She forced a smile and a little nod. <Perhaps another time. Please, enjoy music.> She fled home but stopped half way, darting behind a tree and letting the tears pour out.

Дорогая Сар'ина,
Dear Sar'ina,

I'll keep your secret if you keep mine. Don't ever tell Dmitri, because if it somehow gets back, I'll be dead before you get home.

Sure I still get scared like that. It took us a long, long time to believe Uncle Tomas when he said he'd never hit us. I still get bad dreams, and I panic at people shouting. I hate that. It's worst during the week when Sergei's at school and there's no one else in the room with me. A lot of nights I just sleep with the light on. Yeah, I hate being alone, too. Guess we still belong together, huh?

David drinks. I've seen him. He drinks with his friends at University, too; Sergei told me. I've seen him with contraband, too – twice. That stuff scares me. Not Sergei, though. I've never seen him with more than a glass of wine, I think. If he does, he doesn't brag about it. I worry about David, though. He's big, like Father was big. Ever since that time with Valeria, everyone's been a little afraid of him, but since then he's been just the nicest person in the world. I believe he could do it again, though. You never know. Sergei's just as tall but he's not as big, and he never bothers anybody. Uncle Tomas has wine with dinner, he says it's good for you like that, but he's okay with it. I've had it, too. It gives me a bad stomach ache, so I only have a sip to toast the holidays. David dared me to drink a beer once, and it was so disgusting I threw up in a flowerbed when he wasn't looking. I think Kat's the only one that refuses to drink anything at all.

Your secret's safe, Sar, but just give the word and I'll send in a troop force. Dmitri lays a hand on you, David will break him in half. That's a quote, word for word. Uncle Tomas knows an awful lot of people, Sar, all over the place. IMPORTANT people. He can have you rescued back any time you want. He offered, but Val said no. Not because she doesn't want you here, but because she's afraid if it failed, Dimi'd take you deeper into hiding, or that you might get hurt. As long as you keep in touch.

Awaiting your word,
Vlad

* * *

Dark came but they didn't want to move, sitting on a downed tree at the far edge of the fields, nearby but out of sight of the cabin. They sat seamlessly close, Jaycee leaning against Dmitri, his arm encircling her, watching the silver quarter-moon grow brighter in the darkening sky. The night air weighed cool and damp but Jaycee was warm against him, soft and full of life. If Dmitri could have had one minute of his life to live over and over, it would be this very one. He bent to trail his lips across her neck, then to her lips, a thirsting, aching kiss that thrilled him to his soul and left him starving for the precious next.

He nuzzled his nose behind her ear, the Tau Cetan equivalent of kissing. Tau Cetans had scent glands behind their ears that released pheromones when stimulated. It didn't have quite the same effect on Dimi, who lacked the same chemistry, but it sure didn't hurt. <Do not leave! Stay with me. Do not let this night end. Let this night be forever.>

Jaycee stroked his cheek and kissed him his way in return. <I feel magic in tonight, too. I wish time would stop, right now, nothing ever change. Just you,> she kissed him lightly, <me,> she kissed him again, <and the Moons.> She gave a final kiss. <I want to stay with you forever, Dimmy! My heart *cries* to stay, but I cannot stay tonight. You must make contract with Father. I know he agree. He like you, Dimmy. I was contracted before, but was very bad contract with horrible man. I leave as soon as I could. This time, I never want to leave.>

Dmitri stole an endless kiss, pulling her closer, tighter, not wanting to stop, not ever wanting to stop. His hands ran over her back, her shoulders, her hair. He wanted to possess her completely, to devour her alive until she dwelt inside him, to merge with her until they were one being, mentally, physically, spiritually. This wasn't the lust he felt when he saw a pretty shape walk by. It wasn't virginal adventure with the uninhibited. It wasn't a game with a willing teen counterpart. This was a true love, a love to *die* for, a love to rearrange who he was and what he wanted to be for.

<I will be at house before sun is over trees,> he swore.

Dmitri approached her while she lay reading in her room. "Sar? Can I talk to you? I mean, really talk?"

Hope rushed up from its refuge in Sarah's feet. A genuine smile spread over her face, driving back the unbearable sadness that hung over her like a shadow. "Of course! We haven't talked in ages."

He sat across from her on the bed. "I want to get your opinion on some things."

"Sure! What's up?"

"What do you ... think of Jaycee?"

Sarah puckered as if she'd swallowed an unexpected spoon of salt. The beacon of hope crashed down so fast her toenails stung with the force. "You must narrow down your parameters and be more specific before I can give you an accurate statement."

"Come on, Sar! Stop talking like a damned Navaran! I asked you a simple question as a friend. You know! What do you think of her as a person? Do you think she's nice?"

Sarah's nostrils flared. "As compared to what or who? She can't hold Transium against someone like Katya, but I'd room with her over Father any day."

"Can't you just answer the question? I'm serious. Bullshit aside, what do you think of her?"

"In my limited dealings with her, I did not find her to be unbearably unpleasant."

"You don't mind her, then. That's good. I – I *want* you to like her, Sar. Please, I know it's hard, but I want you to try and be friends with her. At least don't be hostile, okay? It would mean an awful lot to me if you could try." He gave her his best cheerful smile.

"I think I love her, Sar. I mean, *really* love her. I think I might marry her. She's going to move in here tomorrow."

Sarah could not have been more shocked if she'd suddenly floated off the bed. The words echoed inside her head, not making sense. *"What?"*

Light poured from Dmitri's face like a saintly Icon. He held Sarah's hands in his, squeezing them. "I want to marry her! I know it's a lot for you to think about, but it will work out great! You'll see! You won't have to worry about all those households things you hate. You can put more time into your studies. Maybe we'll take back some of the land from Charlie and farm it ourselves, get a porshie of our own. You can play with increasing crop yields and insect resistance, and things like that. That's right up your alley!"

Sarah stared, numb. He was so excited, so very excited. It showed in his face and his eyes and his voice, and he was so very happy to be telling her this.

"Aren't you a little young to be getting married, Dim? I don't think Charlie wants to lose the acreage, and you know we don't have a clue how to take care of porshies. And I *hate* plants. I couldn't care less about crop yields and soils – if I did, I would have used the information to help Charlie already."

"Mother was seventeen when she married, and Father was twenty-three," Dmitri rationalized. "I'll be twenty-two next birthday. Jaycee's eighteen, and she's already been married once, so she knows what she's doing."

"I won't raise your children."

"I don't expect you to," Dimi promised. "I don't know if we can have any. Even Guillaume doesn't know if the genetics are compatible enough to cross on their own."

Something tickled the back of Sarah's mind, something they'd been told once. *What the hell was it?* It had to do with romancing locals. It was in their rule book. *What was it?* You could marry a local, but… Sarah's heart stopped as she remembered the quote. She couldn't think about it. Not without having a total breakdown.

"Dimi! If you marry her, you can't ever leave! We'd have to stay here *forever!"*

Dmitri shrugged. "That's … Something we'll work out."

Forty-four

And so it began. Jaycee moved into Dmitri's house, his room, his life, to begin her three-to-eleven month trial before the marriage would be formalized. Dmitri couldn't sit, jumping up to help Jaycee with the stove, to fetch her wood, to pump her water, to retrieve her sewing case. He knelt adoringly at her knee, listening to her explain how she took such tiny stitches.

Sarah stood frozen in the sitting room, eyes begging Dmitri for help. Dmitri came back from the clouds and realized the problem.

He patted his upholstered chair. <Uh, Jaycee? Why not come sit here? That Sarah's chair.>

Jaycee moved over. <I sorry, Sarrah! Why you not tell me? I would move for you.>

Sarah perched stiffly in the rocker for three full minutes, then ran upstairs. Later, after the lights were out, she could hear the lock on Dmitri's door slide shut, hear muffled voices behind the wall. Jaycee was in there with him.

In his bed.

Under his blankets.

Sarah pulled a pillow over her head and prayed for the elusive unconsciousness of sleep.

<Good morning, Sarrah!> Jaycee greeted her when she came

down to breakfast each morning. She always had a ready compliment – either Sarah looked nice, or her dress was pretty, or she had shiny hair, or she looked eager for the day. Jaycee'd stroke Sarah's hair or squeeze her hand, and one dreadful morning gave her a hug. Sarah stiffened harder than stone and tried to stifle the cry that caught in her throat.

Dimi heard it.

He pulled the arms down. <Jays… It much better if you not touch her.>

Jaycee looked upset at the mistake. <So sorry! So sorry, my new sister!>

<You never show me flowers you like,> Jaycee asked one day. <Tell me about flowers. If you like, I will weave some in your hair, nice and pretty.>

Sarah rocked in her chair, stone-faced. She had nothing to say. Mrs. Al and Charlie came around only once a week for dinner, since Jaycee could make the meals now. The dreaded emptiness returned like an overdue comet, and nothing mattered anymore. Day and night differed only in the type of agony they bore, and time was friendlessly slow.

<They just dumb flowers,> she replied hollowly. <I not even like them. I just grow to see how tall they get. You can walk in them if you wish.> It was the most she'd said to Jaycee yet.

The scream brought Dmitri running from the bathroom. He tore up the stairs, shirtless, to find Sarah rocking on her knees, hands wrapped in her hair and pulling hard.

"She touched it!" Sarah wailed in Russian. *"It's all moved! She had no right! My samples! My samples! MY room!"* she screamed, and banged her head on the floor. *"Red!"*

Dimi and Charlie had built Sarah a workbench between her windows two seasons ago, with shelves above. For her thirteenth birthday, Dmitri'd had the engineer at the Compound put together a simple, reflected-light microscope. Sarah found new things to observe by the hour, filling pages with notes and sketches. As a result, her workbench hid under a blanket of biological samples, papers, crumbs, jars, and slides.

Except today.

Dmitri's eyes roved the room, shocked at the difference. The bed was made. No clothes littered the floor. The papers were stacked, pencils stood ready in an empty cup, the crumbs cleared away, the shelves straightened, the floor washed. There were *curtains* – cheery *red* curtains over the bare windows, giving the wood-brown room a cozy, homey feeling. Jaycee stood near the bed, confused and frightened.

Dmitri knelt and held Sarah tight. "I'm sorry, Kid. I'll take care of it. Shh! She didn't know. All you have to do is *tell* her these things, okay? She just tried to be helpful. Relax. It won't happen again, I promise. Just put everything back where you had it. I'll see if I can get your samples back." He rocked her until he was sure she wasn't destructive, then let her lie despondent on the floor.

He took his fiancée aside. <Jays, you should not do that.>

<*Dimmy! She dirty girl!*> Jaycee whispered apologetically. "Floor dirty, table dirty, bed not neat. And *bugs*! Dimmy, there *dead bugs* all over table! And she stab bugs with pins! Make my back shiver! I clean and clean, get rid of dirt and bugs, make room nice and pretty as if she had mother. I give her surprise to make her happy, and she *cry!* She very *strange!*>

Tell me something I don't know, Dmitri thought. How to explain this? He didn't want to hurt Jaycee's feelings. Since she began an experiment with plants, Sarah expanded on it by collecting samples of the insects she found pollinating them. Finding it more interesting than the flowers, especially after she got the 'scope, she collected every insect she could find, classifying and pinning her samples to small labeled boards. Jaycee had destroyed a year's work.

<Jaycee, I know you mean right, but, please, if Sarah want to live in messy room, ask *her* to clean. Please, do not touch things. She like to look at different bugs, see how many bugs she find. Curtains very nice idea, look very pretty, but color make her think of blood of dead things. It best you not come in here at all, okay? If room not clean, tell me, *I* make her clean. Please, dear?> He kissed her pretty nose.

Jaycee looked at him queerly, then nodded. <If you wish.>

Dmitri found Jaycee leaning against the workshed, watching the red and silver moons rising together. <Find you!> he said, putting his arms around her and holding her close. He buried his face in her hair. <I wonder where you go. Moons again, huh?>

Jaycee sighed. <It peaceful out here.>

<It peaceful inside, too.> He nuzzled her ear from behind, then kissed it, swaying as they stood in the dark.

Jaycee heaved a deep sigh. <She hate me, Dimmy. She never say word, never look at me. I do nothing right. I sit in wrong place. I cook meat, she cry. I make room pretty, she frightened of curtains. I throw away bugs she like. I try! I talk and talk, be nice to her, I *want* to be friend to her, but she never even *smile!*> Jaycee looked ready to cry herself.

<I told you, will take long time. Has only been three weeks. You will see. Besides,> he laughed, <you will know if she hate you. Ask Mrs. Al! Sarah hate her like end of Moons, yell and scream and

spit for months. Now she love Mrs. Al. You see.>

Loneliness. Life-crushing loneliness. Sarah'd been horribly lonely during her three months in the hospital, and she'd had bouts of loneliness on and off during their travels, but always, always she'd had *hope.* Hope they'd move on, hope they'd go home. Now even hope lay moribund, and there was no such thing as life-support here in the Stone Age. Dmitri had settled. He didn't ever want to leave. And she was stuck with the consequences.

If she had the nerve, she could pack her things and return to the Compound on her own. The short path to the Compound saved time, but it meant camping out in the wilderness overnight. She would have to take the longer path and stay in Otaiga. But she couldn't bring herself to do that to Dimi. He'd kept his promise; even when things had seemed darkest, he'd never given up. Sarah could do no less for him. She would have to bear the hard times, too, and wait for him. When he got over this – *infatuation,* she would demand they go home.

If it wasn't for that damned Jaycee! Live together, fine. For a little while. Let Dimi have his fling, work out his demon urges, and then they could move on, but it couldn't go so far as marriage. Vlad would never forgive her, giving in like that. She wasn't a traitor! How long should she wait, though?

Sarah rubbed her eyes in futility. It would take some time. Her insides were so dead she couldn't think. For now she'd have to survive on sheer determination, and the possibility she might make it home before she turned fifty.

<It not personal, Jaycee! I tell you, she do this! Ask Mrs. Al!>

Jaycee wanted Sarah to like her so *badly,* but she couldn't understand the moods, couldn't understand how someone could stare into space hour after hour without speaking, and not be spiteful.

<I tell you, it nothing to do with you. If anything, she mad at *me.* Come on, Sar! One bite!> Dmitri poked her in the mouth with a loaded fork. <There no meat in it, I *swear!*>

Sarah sat hunched at the table, rocking herself. She honestly wasn't hungry. She had only wanted to slip away unnoticed, not disturb anyone, but Jaycee got upset that Sarah never ate *anything* she made, and that made Dmitri all buttery nicey-nice to Sarah so Jaycee would be happy instead of staring out the window while she dried the dinner dishes. Such a divine opportunity couldn't be wasted. There was no way she'd eat now.

Dmitri smiled. "Please, Sar? For me? I know my girl is in there!"

"I *can't,*" Sarah whispered.

"Fine, then!" Dimi threw the fork onto her untouched plate. "Starve! See if I care! Go! Get out of here!" Sarah fled to the safety of

her closet.

Dmitri opened a cabinet, took out a bottle of whatever was in front, and poured himself a glass.

Mrs. Al stopped by in the middle of the week. Sarah's refusal had stretched to three days. <Jaycee worry Sarrah no eat. I come by to see. I tell Jaycee, Sarrah big strong girl, eat like growing boy. She can go several mealtimes with no food.>

Sarah glared at Mrs. Al like a stuck porshie. Yes, she was bigger than she wished, sturdy and square and big-boned and graceless, not willowy and delicate and slender like *Jaycee*. But she certainly wasn't soft and flabby like Mrs. Al, either. When the hunger pangs got bad, she nibbled at food stashed in her room, but when Mrs. Al made her a plate of fried bread and spicy vegetable paste, Sarah couldn't resist, and devoured every crumb.

Mrs. Al smiled, smothering an unusually affectionate Sarah in her rubbery bosom. <That my girl! You just miss Mrs. Al, yes? I miss you, too.>

Jaycee said nothing, but she looked hurt.

The main room wasn't a restricted area, like the bedrooms or bathroom. Sarah had no reason to expect otherwise. She saw the light and honestly thought Dmitri was up late and might care for company. Obviously he did, just not hers.

Dmitri sat in *her* rocker, *That Jaycee* straddling him, skirts spread out, long, long hair tumbling down her back like a soft curtain. Jaycee's hands combed through his dark hair while they slobbered on each other. The bib to Jaycee's jumper hung loose, her blouse untucked, unfastened. Dmitri squeezed handfuls of female backside through the skirt.

There hadn't been a sound, not a shadow, but as he leaned his head forward, something made Dmitri look up. He froze, and for an awful eternity they all stared at each other.

Jaycee turned away and covered herself, mortified. Dmitri's face twisted to a furious rage, holding his wife tight against him.

"Get out of here!" he shouted. "Get the *Hell* back where you belong!"

Sarah vanished, heart breaking.

* * *

Please send the following immediately and forward any reply immediately upon receipt, faster if you can. Thank you.
    S. I. Kirushenko

316

TO: Vladimir V. Kirushenko\Ivanov\RFS\Sol III
66015-98-93514-8ZX.

My dearest, dearest Vladimir,

*Please, please tell me you haven't forgotten me, Vlad! I'm feeling a little skittish right now, and I just need to hear from a friend. I'm okay, I'm not in danger, don't worry about me like that. I just need to hear from you right **now**, okay? This very second. Don't wait a breath. Send your reply via the express address you have, okay? Even one sentence is enough. They'll be looking for it.*

Miss you guys.

Sarah

Sarah folded the letter, sealed it, and addressed it in Tau Cetan to Hargan Ennis at the Compound. The afternoon marched toward evening, but she wanted it sent today. Misery exhausted her, left her numb and listless. She needed to hear a kind word from someone who cared, who really, really gave a damn about *her*. Surely Vlad still did?

"Dimi, would you run quick with me to town?" Sarah asked when she located him. "I have to drop this off. It will just take me a minute."

Dmitri hung the pail on its peg in the shed. "That's twenty minutes there and twenty minutes back for a one-minute errand. The sun's about to set. Jaycee's probably got dinner almost ready. How about first thing in the morning? I promise."

"Sure."

Sarah slunk out of the shed. She should have known. Dimi never cared about Vlad, anyway. She gave a long sigh. She had wanted this posted *today.*

How badly? her inner self dared.

On her own? Without someone to protect her? She'd run the whole way to town once, but that was with Charlie in pursuit, it wasn't really *alone.*

You can do it! Sarah's brain coached her. *You know the path!* An imaginary hand slipped into hers, giving her strength. She eyed the town path between the shed and the house with trepidation.

You've done brave missions for David before; some of them were dangerous and alone. Afraid, but strong.

Yes, I have, she answered. She'd done things lightyears beyond brave in the name of the Fearsome Four! Clutching the letter, Sarah darted down the path at reckless speed, before her cowardice could catch her.

317

<Will Sarrah come to dinner?> Jaycee said without a smile.

Dmitri peered into the steaming pot on the stove and sniffed with delight. <I thought she already in?>

<Not that I know.>

<I find her.> Dmitri gave a yell out the door.

No one answered.

He stood in the yard, hands on his hips. Shadows crept into the clearing, but it was quite dark inside the trees. Sarah didn't stay out at night. *Ever.* Not alone.

<You checked by stream?> he asked Jaycee.

<No, not recent. Maybe she not answer because she hate me.>

<She not hate you! She just need time. *Sarah!*> he yelled into the darkness. A sleepy bird answered, *chee-wee.* <Run, get Charlie,> he told Jaycee.

<I tell you, she porshie-sized pain in bottom end, but she scared blind of dark! She *not* be out unless something wrong,> Dmitri emphasized to his small search crew. The three lanterns made a feeble glow against the blanket of night. The red moon Allash was of little help, and tonight the bright moons wouldn't rise until late.

<You stay with her, you know! She not leave house at night,> he reminded Mrs. Al. <When she scared, she hide. Look in little places, covered places. Maybe she hurt. Maybe she lost. But I know by Moons, if she outside, she very scared. Jaycee, take Mrs. Al, look behind house. I check fields and this side of house.>

<I take paths,> Charlie volunteered. <I run toward town, then come back and try different one.>

<Go,> Dmitri ordered. *If this was a joke...* He hoped it was. He didn't want to think of the alternatives.

The path opened up wider, merging into the main street of Vandijoc. No trace. Charlie didn't want to run lest he miss her, but he didn't want to waste time dawdling, either. He'd come this far, he might as well look around. A few townsfolk milled about, heading for the taverns.

<You see girl, tall girl, hair like moonshine, eyes like sky? Look lost?> Charlie stopped to ask several times, but no one could say they had.

<*Sarrah?*> he called, holding the lantern high. No one else should answer; he'd never heard that name before. <It Charshfe, Sarrah!> He walked the more populated section of Main Street, down one side, then slowly up the other. He was almost back where he

started when something made him stop and listen.

Charlie? came a whisper so faint it could have been the scrape of a leaf blowing across the dusty street.

Charlie whipped around, ears prickling, squinting into the blackness. He headed nearer the row of closed buildings, holding the lantern out. Maybe she'd been locked inside?

Wait.

There! Fingertips stuck out between the open stairs of the post building. He took several steps closer and saw the glint of eyes.

<*Sarrah?!*>

Charlie rushed under the side of the crude steps. It *was* Sarah in the lamplight, dusty, dirty, eyes red from tears that were still falling.

<*Moons above*, Sarrah! You hurt? Why you hide in town? Dimitri scared to *dying* about you!>

Sarah cried harder, pressing the heels of her hands to her eyes. <I fine! I just – *stupid!*>

<*Ah-ah-ah*. Do not cry.> Charlie wiped her face with the end of his sleeve. <All good now. Tell Charshfenaki what happen.>

She pressed her hand over her mouth, trying to slow her sobs. <*I stupid!* Dimi not want to go, but I want to post letter. I run very fast, hope to get letter in before runner leave. I get here so late, but I get letter in. I start back to house – I get to path, but sun already set, and path in trees very dark. I have no light, no knife to make me brave. I start to walk, but I *stupid!* Stupid! Moonless-dark-dumber-than-*porshie*, stupid!> Sarah paused to cough; Charlie dabbed her eyes again.

<I get too scared, run back to town. Now everywhere dark. I scared of town, I scared to go home. I find place to hide, think: wait for morning, run home at first-light. I so *scared*! And *stupid*.>

Charlie smiled lovingly. <I would walk to town, if only you ask.> Touching her teary face with his hands, he pressed his lips quick as lightning to her forehead as he'd seen Dmitri do, heart breaking when she jerked away.

He gave a soft laugh. <You right. Porshie-stupid.> Aware of the humor in her predicament, Sarah smiled back between the tears.

<Come, I take you home,> he said, climbing out from under the stairs. <We hurry. Everyone worried to sickness, what happen.> She followed him out of her hiding spot, scrubbing shamefully at her eyes.

<Here, take hand. I not a porshie, Sarrah! I not bite you. I not hurt you, *ever*! We move faster if you hold me.>

Still Sarah hesitated, then reached out and put her hand in his.

Charlie broke into a grin, pleased to pieces that *he* had found the damsel in distress, his very favorite one. <Come!> he said, and began to run.

<I get her!> Charlie shouted when they drew close. <She here!> Shouts relayed across the property.

<Sarrah!> Jaycee ran to meet them at the end of the path. Without thinking, she grabbed Sarah in a hard hug of relief, but Sarah didn't fight. A breathless Mrs. Al smothered her next, until Dmitri came charging across the yard.

Sarah pushed Mrs. Al away and ran to him, the last vestiges of bravery dissolving. She clung to him as the terror of the previous hours gushed forth in a flood of tears. As scared as she'd been, as relieved as she was, Dmitri's arms were around *her* again, he held *her* tight, he spoke to *her*, he kissed *her* head, just like he used to. She hadn't done it on purpose, she would *never* have done that on purpose, but if only for a moment, Dmitri remembered *her*.

"Where *were* you!" he demanded with anguish. <What *happen?*>

<I think she okay,> Charlie said. He repeated Sarah's story.

Dmitri squeezed his shoulder gratefully. <Thank you, Charlie. Come on, Kid.> He dragged Sarah to the cabin. "You dumb, crazy kid."

Sarah clung to him in a grip that defied release. Dmitri sat in her rocker and pulled her onto his lap, murmuring in Russian.

Mrs. Al headed for the kitchen. <She probably cold. I make everyone hot drink.>

Dmitri eyed the figure sobbing uncontrollably on his shoulder. She was beyond calming herself, and he didn't have any medications to help her … *or did he?* It was worth a shot.

<Just water,> he gambled. <Jaycee, go upstairs to desk. In left drawer, in back, find little blue bottle. Bring for me, please?>

He knew Sarah hated people staring at her, hated this kind of attention worst of all. Dmitri'd refilled the sleeping tablets some months ago on a trip to the Compound; he'd be able to knock her out, let her calm down while she slept. He could talk to her in the morning. The sooner she calmed, the sooner the room would.

Jaycee brought him the bottle.

"Here, Sar. Swallow," Dmitri said, pushing two tiny pills between the gasping lips and following them with water. "There you go. Thatta girl. You're okay. You'll feel better soon." Sarah, aware of nothing but suffocating sobs and her brother's caring voice, swallowed them faithfully. Dmitri and Charlie struggled to get her upstairs a half-hour later.

Jaycee leaned against the doorway to Sarah's room. <You coming to bed, Dimmy? It late. We need sleep, too.> She wore the sleek nightdress Dimmy had bought for her, a blanket wrapped around her shoulders for warmth. They'd eaten late, and even then Dimmy rushed back upstairs.

He lay on the bed next to Sarah, watching her sleep. She gave a twitch now and then, and he'd rub her arm. Even in sleep, she didn't look peaceful.

Dmitri adjusted the covers. <Look at her, Jays. She make it all the way to town by herself. You know what big thing that is? *Huge* thing! She try so hard to do something right, even though she mess up at end. If only she leave earlier. She ask me to walk with her, but I tell her no. I wrong not to go. Letters mean everything to her. I not fair.>

He frowned, weighing the chances of trouble. Stress often did it, and Sarah'd definitely been stressed. <I think – I think I stay with her tonight. I afraid she wake up in dark, be twice as scared, not know where she is.>

Jaycee ran her hands over his shoulders and neck. <You say medicine make her sleep good. She be okay. You just in next room. Come, I take thoughts off worries.> She breathed something in his ear.

Dmitri's face pinked, and he kissed her hand. <Not tonight. I need be here. Sometimes when she have bad scare, she have terrible dreams, scare her worse because she cannot wake up. Tomorrow, I promise.>

Jaycee studied him with increasing disappointment. <Okay,> she conceded. <Sleep well, my love.>

Dmitri awoke late. Jaycee had breakfast cooking when he came down the stairs. <Good morning, my early bird!> He kissed her under her ear and squeezed her from behind as she tried to keep the toast from burning. He ran his hands hungrily over her curved sides, from her ribs to her hips and back again. He glanced back at the stairs. *If he didn't expect Sarah up…*

<Miss me last night?> he whispered, grinding his hips against hers.

Jaycee pulled away to put breakfast on the table. <Yes. She still asleep?>

<Yeah.> He eyed Jaycee questioningly when she sat at the table with her back to him. <Something wrong, my Jaycee?>

Jaycee put her fork down. <Dimmy, I think a lot last night. I worried, Dimmy. I know she not get lost on purpose, but it just one more thing in long *line* of things! Every time I look, she there: 'Dimmy, I need help,' 'Dimmy, come here, I scared,' 'Dimmy, come see,' 'Dimmy, I upset,'… Every time *I* need you, *she* need you worse! Every time I alone, I feel like she watches me, but I turn around and she not there. Sometimes I think she make me crazy! I *love* you, Dimmy,> she smiled at him adoringly, <but – I not know if I can ever love *her*.>

Dmitri knew that feeling all too well. Sometimes he himself wished Sarah would just go away, but a promise was a promise. He stuck her around his neck in the first place.

<I understand. I will talk to her. She tries to behave. Going to town by self – if you only *knew* how hard for her, Jaycee! Like climbing ladder to Moons! And she made it! That such a good, big step for her! But I understand what you mean. Lately she very – demanding. I talk to her. You see.> He gave her hand a confident squeeze. <We work it out.>

"You're kicking me out?" Sarah whispered, white as a new sheet. She'd been good! Outside of one, at most *two* little things, she hadn't done a thing wrong!

"Of course not!" Dmitri reached for her arm, but she wrenched away. "That's *not* what I'm saying at all! All I said was *back off* a little, give Jaycee a little space. You're suffocating her. Just try to stay out of trouble, okay? Stop hanging on me so much. You're a *big girl* now! You're almost fourteen! Just be a little more *independent*, that's all. Okay?"

Sarah couldn't begin to think of what to say. Not only wouldn't he acknowledge her efforts, he didn't want to know about her at all! She'd been... replaced.

"I think I understand," she said, refusing to give him the satisfaction of seeing her cry. "If that's what you want, I won't bother you again." She grabbed the top book from her stack and ran out of the cabin.

"Sarah!"

Damn it all! He was blowing things again.

Forty-five

Good as her word, Sarah disappeared. When Dmitri awoke next morning, she was long dressed and outside with her plants.

<Breakfast ready, Sarrah!> Jaycee called pleasantly.

<I eat already, *mangato*,> she replied, just as pleasant, and focused on her work.

Sarah often skipped lunch when absorbed in something, but for days she was nowhere to be found at lunchtime. She left before anyone awoke and stayed away until dark, rushing up to her room the moment she returned. Several times Dmitri brought a plate to her, but she refused.

"Sar, we need to talk. You're taking this all wrong. All I meant was ... "

Sarah closed her notebook and laid the pencil down. "I can't talk

322

now, Dim," she said with a haunted look. "I'm dreadfully tired and I'm falling asleep on my feet." She stirred her blankets until she located her nightwear, and began to unfasten her dress.

"Just two minutes," Dmitri pleaded. "No one is mad at you, I swear… "

Sarah shrugged off the dress and started on the fasteners to the blouse. "Another time, okay? I really need some sleep. Would you mind? I can't close my door."

Dimi left, Trouble chewing at him.

He awoke one morning to a strong, steady rain pounding on the roof. *Surely she'd stay in the house today?*

Only by chance did he find her mid-morning, face-down asleep in a book, hidden in the back of the workshop loft. He slipped back to the house and returned to cover her with a blanket, always afraid a chill might work its way into pneumonia. When he went to wake her for lunch, she'd moved on, the blanket mysteriously folded on his bed. No one saw her come in.

Dmitri and Jaycee were consumed with love, full of knowing smiles and touches and fawning endearments, tripping each other in their effort to please their partner, but both were very aware of the invisible physical presence – or absence – that hung over the table when they ate their romantic little meals for two, or sat together in the long quiet evenings, watching the skies. Neither would ever deny their world wasn't perfect, but the pressure of *nothing* weighed them down.

"Hey, why don't you take a break and come downstairs, and we'll play some three-handed Nine-Square?" Dmitri offered, riffling the deck of cards invitingly. The pips were different, there were two extra face cards and a mysterious tree card, but the concepts were similar.

Two lamps burned on the workbench to give Sarah enough light to peer into the microscope. Several slides were arrayed to the side. She was attempting to make drawings of her findings, but studio art was one of the few subjects that eluded her.

"No, thank you, Dimi," she said. "I want to finish this and get to bed. I get up early, you know. Maybe some other time." It was the first she'd spoken to him in two days.

<I follow her today,> Jaycee said over their private little dinner. <She never see me. She walk way down by stream – you know where big flat rock is, near bend? She sit on rock, open book, but pick up skirt instead and cry heart out. I feel so *bad,* Dimmy! I afraid to go to her, sit with her, tell her I *do* like her. I afraid she run farther away. I not know what else to do.>

<I have no idea anymore.> Dmitri pushed his half-eaten dinner away and got out his 'medicine' bottle. A glass or two after dinner,

and it eased the permanent knot that had formed in his belly. It helped him to sleep.

It helped ease the gnawing of his guilt.

Sarah slipped through the door at sunset, quiet as a mouse, and made her beeline for the stairs. Jaycee pounced, ready.

<Sarrah, please wait! I have letter for you.>

Sarah froze at the bottom of the stairs, hand on the railing, watching distrustfully from the corner of her eye.

Jaycee approached, something flat in her hand. <Charshfenaki bring this today from town. He say it for you.>

Dream-like, Sarah turned in slow motion. <For me?> she whispered, not daring to hope. <That for *me*?>

Jaycee smiled as Sarah took the envelope and read the address. <Yes! For you!>

The very bottom bore the script, Re: V. Kirushenko. *Vladimir.* Sarah's heart skipped a beat.

<*esa mangato, Ahnax!*> she breathed, the faint potential of a smile casting a different shadow on her long-dreary face. <Thank you! Thank you for giving to me!>, and she meant it. Jaycee couldn't hate her *too* much, or she wouldn't have given her the letter; she would have thrown it in the fire. Sarah sprang up the stairs.

<Sarrah?> Jaycee called again. Sarah stopped part way. <Maybe you sit in chair to read?>

Sarah missed her chair. <I not know what letter say, so I will read up here, thank you.> She didn't doubt Vlad, but everything had been so wretched lately she didn't dare raise her hopes. Maybe Vlad found life at Uncle Tomas's house such fun he started to forget her. She sat at the workbench, opening the letter with hands that shook so hard she dropped the envelope, twice. Even after she unfolded the paper, she was afraid to read it.

Received UPA 63679001-99761/3 Unified Date: 379940
Transfer URGENT to: Kirushenko, Sarah I, Vandijoc

Dear Sarah,

Forget you? I'd have to have my brain erased to forget you! Wanna know how bad we miss you? Promise you won't talk about it, because it caused a real big stink here. Last Feb., on the anniversary we left Navara, David went and got himself a tattoo – the real kind that never goes away. It's not very big – maybe 5x5cm – but it's four ships flying in missing-man formation, with two intertwined F's under it for Fearsome Four. It took a lot, but me & David talked Sergei into getting one, too. I went with them, but I was under age, so when we got home Sergei drew it on my arm with ink. He has to touch it up once a week because it wears off, but it looks just as good.

You should have seen the commotion – a supernova of epic size! David's an adult now, Val couldn't stop him, but boy, did she blow a seal! Galina calmed down when she found out mine wasn't real, but she wasn't happy when I refused to remove it. Uncle Tomas was mad as hell because he knew David had done it not just for you, but to make a permanent dig at Val, and he chewed us out for a good long while. David didn't care. He was really proud that he came up with the idea. I think it's the best idea he's EVER had, and I can't wait until I can have mine made real. Nikky's in awe of the whole thing. He still remembers you some, and we don't let him forget.

So you see? We haven't forgotten, and we never will. We think of you every time we take off our shirts. Keep your faith up. It can't last forever.

We love you, plain and simple.

Vlad (& Sergei, & David, & Nikky)

The tears started half way through the first paragraph. They hadn't forgotten her! *They* still loved her. She wasn't alone in the universe, just on this rotten planet. Loyal little Vlad! Sarah could *feel* his hand holding hers across the incredible distance. Tattoos! Leave it to David! If *that* wasn't the best idea! She could hear Valeria's scream of fury in her head. Well, she wouldn't be left out! When she managed to get home, no matter how old she was, she would get the same tattoo. She *was* the fourth member of the Fearsome Four, after all. Maybe she'd get the writing ink from the cabinet and draw an ^F_F on her arm, too. The thought of Vlad, spindly little Vlad, so afraid of everything, being willing to sit through a tattooing brought a laugh. How funny he must look, with his skinny little arms! Sarah put her head on the workbench and let tears of relief escape.

<Bad news?>

Sarah looked up with a start. Jaycee stood in the doorway, concerned.

Sarah hugged the letter to her chest. She gave a wet sniff and allowed a polite little smile to emerge. <No. Is very, very good news. I cry for happiness.>

Jaycee smiled broadly. <I glad you receive happy news. I worry it not be good. You always so sad, you not need bad news, too. Sarrah,>

she sighed, <dinner almost ready – please, I ask nice – come eat with us? If you don't like, I make something different, whatever pleases you.>

When you came down to it, it really wasn't Jaycee's fault that Dmitri was a magnet for estrogen. The girl was too naïve to understand that kind of thing. Jaycee gave her the letter, she didn't destroy it, therefore Sarah would repay the kindness, in case another letter ever arrived. <Okay. I come down.>

Dmitri raised an eyebrow when he came to the table. "What's the occasion?"

Sarah blew on her forkful of food, then put it in her mouth. While she thought of a retort that would both convey her anger yet politely tell him to mind his own business, an unexpected surge of fury rose inside her, so intense and bitter it left a foul sting in the back of her throat. She didn't feel that angry toward *Father*, but *dam*mit all! There were people at home who *loved* her, who *wanted* her with them, and Dimi persisted on keeping her away from that forever! In that one instant, Sarah knew that whatever she did, she could not, *would* not, allow that to happen.

"Not that you'd care to know," she growled. "I do believe I live here as well."

Dmitri raised his eyebrows and pretended to whistle. "Excuse me for asking. Anyway, it's nice to have you join us."

"It had nothing to do with you. I owed Jaycee a favor, and I returned it, that's all."

She scraped the last of her meal off the plate, wiped her mouth, and stood up. She bowed across the table to Jaycee. <I thank you for gracious hospitality.> Clearing her dish to the wash bucket, she stalked upstairs.

* * *

"Get up," the voice ordered.

Dmitri blinked. Jaycee slept on his arm, naked and peaceful. The room glowed with the imminence of dawn. He must have dreamt it.

"I said, *get up.*"

Dmitri's eyes opened to see Sarah standing by his feet, already dressed.

"What's wrong?" he asked. Jaycee stirred and clutched the covers. "What is it this time? You're supposed to knock before coming in here."

"Like I care what you might be doing! And you already did it last night, anyway." She picked his pants up from the floor and threw them at him. "Get up, *now!*"

"Sarah… ."

"Hurry, or I'll drag you out of bed myself!"

Dimi kissed Jaycee and sat up. "Could you leave the room, please?"

"I've seen you in your skin-tights before, Dim, and ones a lot tighter than those. Come on!"

"I asked you to leave the room, and shut the door behind you."

"Oh my goodness!" Sarah's nostrils flared in disgust, and she turned her back. "Don't tell me she doesn't even make you wear *underwear* to bed! That's *repulsive!*"

Dmitri pulled on his pants. "What I wear is none of your goddamned business. All right. What's this dire crisis?" Sarah grabbed his hand and towed him outside.

"What are we doing out here? I'm freezing." The sun's first rays twinkled through the leaves. Their breath steamed, and he didn't have shirt or shoes. She dragged him across the yard to her rows of flowers.

"Look!" Sarah knelt in the cold dirt and pulled him down to see an opening bloom. "I did it!" she breathed, holding a ruffly, speckled white-and-purple flowerhead. "It took five full generations, but *I did it!*

"There were only four colors – white, yellow, ruby, and a deep red-purple, and they all had straight petals. I crossbred the yellow and red and got an orange, which isn't unusual, I guess. *But!*" Sarah explained joyfully, "based on the information I gathered running a DNA map at the Compound, I became even more selective. Two generations ago, by interbreeding the white ones, I came up with four plants that had ruffled petals. I crossed *them,* and I now have *twelve* plants with ruffled petals. Okay, nothing major, a simple recessive trait. But look! I wanted to see what crossing white and purple would do, and instead of a solid lavender, I got a co-dominant trait of *marbled* petals! Nowhere, *nowhere,* not even among the plants in town, have I seen a marbled color! And I managed to do it with the ruffled petals, too!"

"Son of a bitch!" Dmitri squatted to marvel at her work. He hadn't seen that kind of radiant excitement from her in a long time. "I'll be damned! That's really incredible." He'd never be able to do such a thing even with a step-by-step guide, and she'd done it all from her head. "I told you you could do it!"

"I should have two more like it," she grinned. "They haven't opened yet, but they should this week. You think Mrs. Al will like them? I want to go one more generation and see what happens, but I'll concentrate just on the white, the marbles, and the purples. I'd like to know if it happens to the other colors, but I'm so sick of plants. I can try proposing a couple of theories once I run another DNA sequencing next time we're at the Compound."

Dmitri gave her a crushing embrace. "I think you better get ready to eat yourself silly. You know how Mrs. Al thanks people!"

* * *

Sarah made an effort for an entire week, the look of utter dread gone from her face. She swept out her room, helped Jaycee with the dishes, and smiled when she saw people, even Charlie. She allowed herself to be dragged into a game of cards. Dmitri couldn't have been happier, convinced all she'd needed was that little boost of confidence to get on track again, and Jaycee bubbled once more now that Dimmy was cheerful.

Too soon, the tarnish crept back. Jaycee clutched her chest when she opened the broom cupboard and a dozen insects flew at her. Something entirely natural in a wood cabin – or did bug-loving Sarah put them there? Smoke billowed into the cabin when Jaycee lit the stove. It was nearly dark by the time Dmitri came home, climbed on the roof, and pulled a nest out of the flue. Did an animal build it in an afternoon, or did the twigs have human help in choosing their new location, a human who scampered in and out windows and over roofs like a monkey? It was impossible to tell, but the suspicion remained.

Blossoms disappeared off vegetable plants, leaving them barren. Jaycee gave a screech when she hauled up the cooler basket and found a dead rodent among the stored items. Dmitri carried it out between two sticks. Jaycee's cloth strip of sewing needles disappeared. Sarah denied knowing anything about it, and sure enough, on wash day the strip turned up in the pocket of one of Jaycee's less-worn aprons. It was entirely possible Jaycee had forgotten it there.

But had she?

All could have been legitimate coincidence. Dmitri knew Sarah would never drown an animal, but how the hell else could it have gotten under the heavy cover of the cooler?

<I cannot have much more… surprises,> Jaycee admitted as they lay in bed. <I think I go Moonless. I scared to touch anything. Is terrible on heart, always afraid.>

Dmitri cuddled her close. He'd been putting it off, dreading the scene. Out of ideas, he'd spoken to Dr. Herzog the last time they'd visited the Compound. Of course, Sarah'd seemed fine to everyone there. Herzog assured Dmitri teenage girls were notoriously moody, and that was normal. She'd outgrow it. Dmitri shook his head. *Normal* was the one thing he knew Sarah wasn't.

Dimi kissed Jaycee on the head. <I take care of it. *I* know she behind it, and *you* know she behind it, and *she* knows what she does. I think I have idea. You ever hear saying, 'Fight fire with fire'?>

<No. That not make sense, Dimmy. Fire cannot put out fire.>

<No, not put out. But if forest burns, you make small fire that

328

burns toward big fire. By time big fire comes near, little fire has already burned up ground, and big fire has nothing left to burn, so it dies. I mean I will fight bad tricks with bad tricks of own.>

<That not very nice.>

<No, but can be a lot of fun. You know what?> He gazed down at her troubled face and slid his hand across her thigh, making her squirm and smile. <I know something else both nice *and* fun.> His lips sought hers in a lingering kiss. <And I bet you agree... >

Sarah drew peace from her evening bath. She preferred to bathe in the early morning, before anyone else had risen, giving her an extra sense of privacy. Dmitri had not planned on installing any lock on the bathroom door, since the traditional rule held neither of them could use it anyway, Just In Case. But as they began to entertain fellow "Cultural Observers" on their way to and from the Compound, Dmitri yielded to Sarah's desire for a more secure door. The new rule said it was okay to lock the door if there was company, but on a normal basis it would remain unlocked, for all parties involved. Hence, Sarah found bathing in the evening an infinitely more stressful experience. Tonight, however, she felt rank from sweating in the fields; an evening bath was unavoidable.

She rinsed her hair and soaked in the water, watching her flexing toes create waves, watching the waves collide and absorb each other in a new, larger wave. She contemplated the possibility of using gene splicing to further manipulate her Stupid Flowers, but she wasn't sure Commander Guillaume would approve. Using natural selection to force-cross strains was one thing, but deliberate laboratory exploitation could interfere with the cultural and biological development of the planet. A new mutant strain could overrun native species, and a unique, highly desirable plant owned by just one person could create an economic monopoly. Sarah could hear the vetoes across the board. Her attempt at forming a possible rebuttal was cut short when the door opened without warning, and her brother strode boldly in.

"What are you doing!" Sarah shrieked, pressing her nakedness to the side of the metal tub. She couldn't reach the towel or even her dirty clothes. "You're not supposed to be in here when I'm in here! You didn't even knock first!"

"Yeah, well, you've walked in plenty on me when you shouldn't, and not even in the dignity of the bath. I need to go and I'm tired of waiting." He grabbed the strings of his trousers.

"You can't do that while I'm in here! At least hand me a towel! Dimi! *Stop that!*" She stared at his back, dumbfounded, as he stood at the sanitary and relieved himself.

"I've used the sanitary with you in the room before."

"Only *twice,* when it was absolutely, positively, impossibly unavoidable! You didn't even ask me to get out! If you were that desperate, you could have gone outside!"

Dmitri retied his pants before turning around. "But I didn't." Immune to her discomfort, he stopped before her clothing on the floor.

"I've been to Earth, I've been to France…," he recited wickedly. He scooped the dirty clothes from the floor and held one piece high. "Now I've got Sarah's underpants!" He swung the garment just out of her reach. "I wonder how much Charlie'd pay me for them. And still warm, too!"

Sarah made a short, desperate grab. "Dmitri Alexandrovitch, that is *not funny! Stop* it! Give those back!" she cried, knowing full well Charlie was due that evening. That was all she needed! Dmitri *couldn't* be that cruel! He just couldn't!

Dmitri relented with a tremendous pout. "Okay. I'll be nice. In fact, I'm *so* nice, I'll put all of these away for you." He grabbed her clean clothes and towel along with the dirty things and ran out of the room with a little wave.

"'MITRI!"

"That's not funny!" Sarah screamed, banging on the door. *"Give me my clothes!"* To get more, she would have to walk wet and naked through the short hallway, out to the main room, and dash up the stairs. The only portable thing left in the bath was the colorful mat Jaycee had placed before the tub, so small it wouldn't cover Sarah's whole front unless she bent over. *Damn him!*

"DMITRI!"

A light knock took her by surprise. <Sarrah? What wrong? I can help? Or do you need Dimmy by himself?>

Sarah opened the door a crack. <He take my clothes! I have nothing to hide me!>

<*Moons and stars!* I am so sorry! I step outside, empty dishpan,> Jaycee apologized. <I get you clothes. Which place you keep clean dresses?>

<Bottom drawer,> Sarah said gratefully. Thank the Moons for Jaycee's rigid sense of decency.

Jaycee returned and passed Sarah a folded towel, a fresh dress, and underthings.

<Thank you most gracious!>

Jaycee smiled back. <You most welcome, my sister! I will go yell at brother.>

<*esa mangato, Ahnax!*>

Sarah ran upstairs the first moment she could, hearing Jaycee's normally gentle tones chastising her beloved. When she felt she had recovered some dignity, she returned downstairs where Dmitri and Charlie sat at the table, playing *duwhalikae* on a narrow board.

<Hey! I know you!> Dmitri teased. <You look different, though. I know!> He snapped his fingers. <You have clothes on!> He burst into laughter. Charlie blushed, but he snickered, too.

Sarah held her head high. She knew how to handle brothers. She filled a pitcher with cold water. Getting herself a glass, she filled it from the pitcher, but instead of drinking, she turned and dumped the pitcher in her brother's lap.

"Next time, take the water, too," she said icily as he jumped up, sputtering. She returned upstairs, honor intact.

Forty-six

Earthdate: 16 October, 2268

*H*onor intact, but not avenged. Such a heinous act deserved careful retaliation. Fury prevented her from acting fast. Dmitri'd be on the lookout. She would have to wait until he no longer expected something. Sarah thought about it for two weeks, conceiving dozens of ideas and discarding them as too simple, not severe enough, too difficult, too bizarre, or just plain stupid. She needed something devious, something that would convey her level of irritation.

She'd acquired the habit of walking the lonely path through the woods behind the house, hiding in places no one would bother her, places she didn't have to listen to Dmitri coo-cooing at Jaycee, watch them grope each other. She'd learned the way slowly, a little farther over the stream and down the path each day until the terror of *alone* faded, never seeing another soul or any evidence someone had passed by. She found trees to climb, and would sit high up for hours, hidden safely from view, keeping compulsive tally of any wildlife. Sometimes she'd spread bait on the path, waiting to see what appeared.

It was on such a day that Sarah perched in a wide crook of a *shaparika* tree six or seven meters off the ground, watching a mother *tuturima*. The creature stood shorter than a housecat, with honey-gold fur over a round little belly, eyes like two drops of black glass, and a brown hairless tail that waved back and forth while it walked. It waddled along the path, followed by four smaller versions of itself nosing and rolling over each other. She smiled, watching the babies play, and from nowhere Sarah got a devilish idea for revenge.

What was the one thing Jaycee wanted out of her marriage? Babies. Tau Cetans worshipped them but didn't always have them, for

331

whatever reason, and Dimi wasn't sure he *could* give them to her.

Certainly not for lack of effort, Sarah thought dryly. She hadn't realized people did *That* that often. Maybe it was time to let Jaycee know the truth about her partner's potential sterility.

* * *

Jaycee crawled outside in the vegetable garden, armed with a stick and a jar containing a centimeter of lamp oil, picking bugs. Sarah and Dmitri had little interest in gardening, it merely provided the convenience of not needing to run to town if they wanted something fresh to eat. Left to themselves, they settled for trampling the weeds if they happened to be out there; Jaycee kept it neatly hoed. Either way, every farmer in the area had problems with a spiny yellow beetle that devoured leaves. Minimizing the damage meant picking off every bug by hand. One or two plants weren't a problem, but thirty plants took up the better part of the three weeks the beetles were feeding. Sarah used to have that job; Jaycee took it over.

Jaycee gasped in surprise as Sarah seemed to appear out of thin air among the knee-high plants. *I should be used to that by now,* Jaycee thought, since Sarah startled her almost daily. If Jaycee knew it to be deliberate, she'd have been upset, but she couldn't honestly tell. The girl was *always* that quiet. Dmitri insisted it was shyness, but Jaycee wasn't sure; the girl just didn't seem *right* to her.

Sarah stood before Jaycee with her typical indifference, a little sad, a little nervous, a little afraid, as if she expected someone to bite her. Jaycee was always extra nice, to see if Sarah would ever stop looking so mournful, but nothing ever helped.

Jaycee tried yet again, cheerful and inviting. <Hello, Sarrah. Will you make company with me?>

The impassive purple eyes blinked. <I may talk with you?>

<Most yes!> Jaycee's smile shone brighter than the afternoon sun. *Wouldn't Dimmy be happy!* The official marriage date loomed just two months away. This would make things even better.

Jaycee sat on her heels in the dirt. <Come, sit by me, my sister! Tell to me what on mind.>

Sarah stepped over the rows, as mournful-looking as ever. <I must tell to you something you will want to know.> She took two photographs from behind her back.

* * *

Dmitri stared at the bags inside the door. Jaycee wore town clothes, a dark plum dress that nearly brushed the ground. <What those for? Where you going? Something happen to family?>

332

<I sorry, Dimmy. I cannot do this anymore. *I love you!*> Jaycee pleaded. <I love you with *every beat* of heart! I love you so hard I cannot *breathe* without you, but I cannot live here one more night. I not know *what* to believe anymore! She – she tell me terrible things, Dimmy! She say you won't tell me you have wives before – show me picture of beautiful woman, woman having baby who already have *two* babies. She tell me you leave that woman, leave babies behind, marry another. She tell me you have other baby with strange woman, not even under contract, that you come here to hide. She say you will not give me babies. She say you will leave me, like you leave other wives.

<I *love* you, Dimmy, but I cannot any more live with *her*! Maybe she tell terrible lie to me, or maybe she really friend who warn me of disaster. Maybe she so sad because she know you say sweet lies. *I cannot understand her!* I cannot *fight* any more! You cannot leave her, and I cannot live with her. I will die inside, but I release you from contract.>

<*What?!*> Dmitri's stomach lurched as if the planet had suddenly stopped rotating and he was flying off into space. Was this a dream? A nightmare born of worry? *Wake up! Wake up! Goddammit, WAKE UP!*

<What you mean? I *never* married before! Jaycee, I swear to you by Moons in sky! *I never have other wife!* You must believe! I never have children! *Ever!* Not with *any* woman! I not know how to prove to you, but you *must believe* me! She tell you horrible story – but is *just bad story*! I get her – make her tell you truth. You cannot go! *I love you!*>

Jaycee stroked his beautiful face, eyes mirroring the pain that now touched his heart, too. <Do you not see, Dimmy? She will *never* tell truth! I will *never* know who lies to me. Always I will wonder. I think all afternoon, and still I not know truth. I yell, I scream that she lies, but what if it not? I know what my heart says, but I cannot stop hearing my head ask for truth. I cannot spend rest of my life like that. I so sorry!>

Dmitri grabbed for her hands. <Jaycee, *no!* We can fix this! I *promise*! I will send her away! I can do that! Take me one, two months to leave her with other brother, but I come back and marry you without her. *Please*, Jaycelani! *Do not – please* do not give up! Today! I can take her away today! Or I can marry you today! Or both! Whichever you want!>

Jaycee took his face and gave him a last sweet, sorrowful kiss on the lips, a last heart-wrenching snuffle behind his ear. She hefted her bags. <It would not work, Dimmy. She too far in your heart. She need you, you run, and I lie alone in cold bed. You send her away, you will worry every day. She write you letter and cry to come back, and you

will let her. I very selfish girl. I want to be alone in your heart, and your heart already very crowded place.>

<Jaycee! *NO!* Do not do this! Do not leave me! *PLEASE!*> Dmitri dropped to his knees and grabbed her skirts. It wasn't a gesture of servitude as much as the fact he shook too hard to stand. The third? fourth? time he could remember his life shattering to pieces around him without warning – when Mother died, when he realized that Valeria actually meant to strand him on Navara, Viktor, and now this. And this hurt worst of all, an unbearable agony that ruled out recovery.

<I can fix it! Stay!>

Jaycee gave a heaving sob and shook her head. <Good bye, Dimmitri. I love you forever in my heart!> With a tug to free herself, she seized her bags and ran for the path, disappearing in the trees.

Dmitri watched her leave. He bent over, head on the floor, and began to gasp.

"Goddamn you you motherfucking *bastard!*" he screamed to the planks. "*Goddamn you to hell,* you backstabbing, ungrateful, rotten son of a *bitch!* I'll *kill* you! I'll *kill* you! I'll fucking rip your heart out and shove it down your goddamned lungs until you *choke*! Why? Why, Sarah! The one perfect thing in my life, and you killed it! *Why?*

"*SARAH!*" he screamed out the door.

Nothing. The same way his life now was. Empty nothingness, save for unbearable pain and betrayal.

Dmitri crawled to his feet and clung to the doorframe with both hands, hands that still held the scent of her. He had to do something. He had to set this right. He would find a way. He tore up the stairs two at a time.

The sight of Sarah's room being so... *her* brought rage to the surface. Two could play at being Sarah. With a growl of fury, Dmitri cleared her precious workbench. The beloved microscope bounced on the floor amid the shattering of glass. Seconds more, and the mattress flipped to the ground; three manic slashes with a laser-sharpened Denebolan-steel knife and the ropes that suspended it dangled. The drawers from her dresser bounced off the far wall. Textbooks flew from the shelves, hitting the floor critically injured with twisted spines and torn covers. The contents of the closet sailed one by one until he hit the backpack. The damned backpack, the first thing he had ever bought her.

Dmitri ripped open the straps and dumped the contents in a heap, kicking the mess until he found it. The dog-eared stack of photos, all black and white or sepia'd to look authentic, the oil from fingerprints and probably tears beginning to distort the simple pigments. He looked through the stack one by one, tearing each at least in half, more if he thought it might be a favorite.

Son of a bitch. Sure enough. God*damn!*

A picture of beautiful woman having baby, who already have two babies.

An old, idyllic picture of Mother, maybe not even twenty yet, hands on a very pregnant belly, two blonde toddlers next to her with their chubby hands also pressed to her belly. The toddlers had to be the twins, and the belly must have been Alexei.

But would Jaycee believe him?

Dmitri searched until he found another picture with the twins in it – much older, much too old to possibly have been his children. He would have to try. He took three pictures for evidence and confettied the rest. He'd give Jaycee time to get home, to calm down. Time to calm himself, start to think. And he had a rat to trap. There was a time for everything, and this time, such intense pain could only be answered by equal pain.

* * *

Sarah pushed open the door and entered the cabin. Dmitri sat at the table, hunched over as if resting; he didn't turn around. She'd been having second thoughts about her revenge. Jaycee'd been angrier than she'd expected. Should she apologize for her dumb idea before Jaycee had a chance to tell him? He'd rip her apart for sure, but better to catch him before Jaycee did. She would drop her things upstairs, then kiss the porshie and explain to Dmitri while he was alone.

She stepped into her room, just one step, and surveyed her precious haven. Not a single thing wasn't out of place, not thrown or shattered or ripped or broken. *Who would do such a thing?* Surely not Jaycee. The wispy girl didn't have that kind of violence in her. *Who –?*

The hair on Sarah's neck rose. *Gavno!* Uh oh.

Her spine crinkled, cold and itchy. Jaycee hadn't been downstairs. She wasn't sulking in Dmitri's room. Sarah tiptoed down the stairs.

She stopped three meters or so from Dmitri's back, waiting to be noticed, a habit ingrained since toddlerhood. You never interrupted Father, even if he was only staring into space. You waited until he spoke first. It was safer that way.

"Dimi?" she said when he failed to acknowledge her. "What's going on?" She realized with a fright he held a glass of liquor in his hand, two open bottles before him. He didn't do that in the middle of the day. He just *didn't.*

Sarah's scalp shriveled like dry leather against her skull. Where was Jaycee?

Dmitri gave her a fast glare from the corner of his eye. "Don't use a name like that with me. The name is *Dmitri*. Only my *friends* may use diminutives. Maybe in your case, we should keep it to *Mr. Kirushenko.*"

"What – ?"

Dmitri swung his legs over the bench until his back leaned against the table. "Maybe you should ask my children and ex-wives."

Sarah's heart gave a nauseating flop. She couldn't run. She couldn't hide. She couldn't even lie to get *out* of the lie; she couldn't find the words. She deserved to be whipped; there was no doubt in her mind. Dmitri still hadn't forgiven Valeria – how long would it be before Sarah might be forgiven? She'd really have to kiss up to Jaycee now.

"I'm sorry. I can explain. I was just really … "

"I don't get you," Dmitri interrupted. He took a swallow from his glass, watching her with an air of bemused detachment. "What is it you have against me? Against everybody? Every time I form a relationship with someone, you flip out and act like a brat until I'm alone again. What's your problem? I'm entitled to friends. I *enjoy* people's company. I've never met anyone who *doesn't* want friends. Except you."

"That's not true," Sarah mumbled. "It's just very hard for me…" It was a terrible, weak excuse. Only part of it was a fear of strangers; the other half was just plain Navaran-styled snobbery.

Dmitri scrunched his face in disagreement. "You're not shy, Sarah. You're just plain *weird*. Shy people aren't go-getters. They want what everyone else wants; they're just afraid to do it. Shy girls still dream you'll notice and ask them out. But *you!* You don't even dream of people talking to you, do you? Charlie tried so hard to make you notice him – even if you only told him he was acting like an idiot – and you couldn't even do that.

"I don't get you. Are you trying to punish me for something? Or are you so stuck up in that … lofty little cloud your head sits on, do you so *disdain* those of us who don't have your *extraordinary* abilities to memorize and process information and spit out insights to academic questions, that you can't bear to lower yourself to associate with a regular person? Is that it? Is Charlie not good enough for you because he's an ignorant farmer from a civilization that hasn't caught up to ours yet?"

"No! Of course I don't. Charlie's as nice as anybody! My value of a person doesn't depend on their intellectual potential."

Dmitri gave a brief nod. "I suppose that's true, 'cause goodness knows Vlad was always as dumb as an erased file. So what is it, then? What makes you go around destroying my life? I don't get it."

Sarah wanted desperately to defend herself, but her tongue wouldn't work. She couldn't say what she felt. Not to Dimi. He didn't understand things like that. He didn't understand loneliness and boredom and stranger-fear and family loyalty. He didn't understand heartbreaking homesickness, and a crushing fear of losing the only people she *could* relate to, the only people in the world she trusted. Dmitri enjoyed being on his own. Like Mother, he made friends just by walking down the street. He was all she had left of her old life, the last dying link. She had to hold on to him or die.

"That's not true!"

"Of course it is."

He approached her. Sarah's nose curled at the stink of the vile liquid on his breath, but the door was shut and Dmitri stood too close for her to open it. She backed against the door, muscles tensed.

He planted a hand on either side of her shoulders, blocking escape.

"Have you *ever* had a decent feeling toward another human being? Just *once*? Have you ever looked at a boy and felt your heart pound with interest? Even a screen star? Are you even *capable* of that kind of feeling? Have you ever *wanted* to be kissed by someone – *anyone*?" he goaded. "I'd bet my entire savings you've never been kissed – I mean, outside of piss-assed Vlad."

"I've *never* kissed Vlad!" she hissed. "*Ever!* Nor has he ever kissed me."

Dmitri gave a soft snort. "So you've never been kissed by anyone."

"I didn't say that." Charlie kissed her on the forehead that once.

"*Huy!* I know you better than that. I had my first real kiss behind Klemitsky's garden trellis the summer I was twelve, and I think I dreamed about it for two years before it actually happened. Are you *afraid?* Is that it? Are you *that* screwed in the head? Are you afraid of something so goddamned *normal*?"

Sarah flinched, giving away the fact he'd struck a sore nerve. He knew her difficulties, he knew her fears – What did he want to hear her admit? That she was terrified of her emerging *adultness*, a fact he was painfully well aware of? How deeply did he want to shame her?

"Dmitri, I-I've told you before, how I-I tend to associate certain – *things* – with a long string of… "

Any further explanation ceased as Dmitri leaned forward on his hands and pressed his mouth firmly over hers.

It took two or three dreadful seconds for Sarah to comprehend, and panic engulfed her.

She couldn't move, couldn't scream, pinned to the wall, unable to touch the ground, his gangrenous foul mouth over hers and the hands, the well-practiced hands already under her clothes, brutal hands scraping across her skin, digging and pushing and forcing their way as he'd done to so many others, and even though she fought, she fought in every way she'd been trained, the hands were going where they had no right to be, to the places she'd been warned and warned no one should ever touch, and she was absolutely powerless to stop them ...

But that wasn't *now*, the back of her brain realized. Her feet *were* on the floor, and she *could* breathe, and she *wasn't* pinned, and she *could* move, and move she did. Up and out came her arms between his, knocking them off the wall. Her head twisted out from under his. Her knee came up and found the vulgar place she'd been unable to reach so many years ago. Two hard backfists to the nose as he crumpled forward, fists, fists, fists to the sides of his head and a brutal kick to his knee finished the job. Dmitri curled on the floor, trying to protect all of himself at once.

Sarah burst into tears and slid down the door. She banged her head backwards several times, trying to chase away terrors she thought she'd buried.

Until now.

"I'm sorry!" she wailed. "I'm sorry! *Why did you do that!"*

Dmitri rolled on the floor until he could speak, nose bleeding.

"What the fuck did you do that for?" he gasped. "God*damn* it, Sarah! I ought to kill you for that! I can't! I just can't handle you anymore! You're too goddamned crazy!"

Sarah sobbed in disbelief. *"Me? You're* the one who kissed *me!"*

Dmitri sat up, waiting for his assaulted nerves to settle. "I just fucking thought if you knew you didn't need to be afraid, you'd get over it! It was just a damned *kiss*, for cryin' out loud! It was no big deal! You didn't need to beat the shit out of me."

"You should've told me you were going to do that! There – there are things you *don't know*, Dimi! You should never have tried to do that!"

"Like what? I've been with you day and night for four and a half years. What can I possibly not know?"

Sarah huddled against the door, but the door had no comfort to offer. She couldn't tell Dimi her worst secret, her nightmare that wasn't a dream because it really happened. She couldn't! She didn't want his sympathy or his pity or his sarcastic derision, or worse yet, his speculation and curious questions. But she'd have to. She owed him *some* explanation for beating on him like that. Sarah couldn't bear to look at him; she spoke to the stove instead. Inanimate objects held a bizarre safety, a bizarre comfort in their inherent non-judgmentalness.

"It happened before that. Valeria doesn't know. Not even Vlad. It's my very worst secret, and you must swear never ever to mention it! Not to *anyone! Ever!* I don't even want to tell *you*, but I will. *Swear it!* Swear it on Mother's grave!"

The alcohol sinking into Dmitri's blood didn't help his confusion, but he nodded. "Swear."

"Even Dr. Carver doesn't know all the details." Sarah shrunk ever smaller against the heartless door, forcing the words out by sheer will. "When I was in the hospital that time? I walked away from my staff person once and I – I ... I was *attacked* ... by a man. He crushed me to the wall and he ... kissed me. He kissed me so hard it hurt. I *tried* to fight, and I *tried* to scream, but all he did was stick his tongue in my mouth until I threw up. He *scared* me, Dimi! *I was barely nine!* I wasn't even sure what he was doing, but I knew it was wrong."

She could share that much with him. She couldn't tell him about the hands. She never told those details to anyone, except in a yes-no manner to Katya, the one and only person in the universe she'd ever told. Katya kept secrets. Katya understood, because Katya had been caught like that once, too, and Katya could be trusted. Dimi knew enough to get the idea.

"You doing that brought it all back like it was still happening."

Dmitri bored into her with a penetrating gaze, searching for truth.

"All this time, you kept a secret like that from me? I guess I know where I rank in your long list of friends," he said bitterly. "It might explain some things, but it doesn't excuse them. Maybe it was a dumb idea, but you didn't need to kick the shit out of me." He dabbed his nose, but the bleeding had stopped.

"I strongly suggest you get out of here," he warned. "Because if you don't, I'm going to kill you, Sarah, plain and simple. You have managed to destroy any chance I ever had for a happy life – a happiness I freakin' *deserved!* What did I ever do to you?! What did *she* ever do? I'm going to close my eyes and count to ten, and so help me, you better not be here."

He rubbed his thumb over the curled fingers of his clenched fist. "*Adin*! *Dva*!..."

Sarah was out the door before he got to three.

* * *

Dmitri was stuffing clothes into the bag on his bed when Sarah climbed in her window and tiptoed to his door. He glanced at her with foul, shining eyes, and continued stuffing. He'd had two hours to be alone with his thoughts, two hours to think, two more hours to drink. The liquor bottle sat on his lamp table, down to the dregs.

He'd thought about Jaycee, warm, sweet, gentle Jaycee, with her soft brown below-her-ass hair, smooth skin, teacup breasts capped by dark nipples, and a ready laugh that made his heart beat faster just to hear it. Jaycee, who knew just how to read his mind, who wouldn't dream of letting him do work she could do herself, who always woke with a cheerful face and a kiss so sweet the taste alone would sustain a starving man.

He'd thought of Sarah, too. Of silent, brooding Sarah, who sulked when your plans didn't coincide with hers. Sarah, who was now fourteen and couldn't run an errand without a nervous breakdown. Sarah, who didn't quite get the concept of privacy when it pertained to persons other than herself. Sarah, so obsessively jealous she never did – and he realized now, never would – allow him to have friends or lovers, nor seek them for herself. Hatred boiled in his blood. He gave her the best years of his life, and she couldn't give a shitty damn less.

She watched from the foot of his bed. "What are you doing?"

Dmitri gave a final shove, closed the bag, and buckled a strap over the top. "If you must know, I'm leaving." He grabbed a jacket, and he was done. The rest he could come back for if he wanted.

"Where are we going?"

"I said *I* am leaving. What you do is up to you, but you are *not* coming with me. If you follow me, I *will* kill you."

"Dim – Dmitri," Sarah corrected herself. "Where are you going? You can't just leave me here. You're supposed to be taking care of me."

"Care? *Care*? You don't know the meaning of the word!"

Blind fury rose inside him, an explosive, murderous frenzy at the unending vain demands, and he knowingly, willingly let it take over. In a second, Dmitri had a hand around her throat, then two as she gave a choking shriek, shoving her until she backed into his desk. He pushed her over backwards, flailing across the desk, his hands tight but not yet tight enough around her throat, her hands clawing uselessly at her neck. He took diabolical gratification at the terror in her eyes. He hurt, and he wanted to hurt, to torture, until she realized the depth of his pain.

Dmitri pressed downward with his thumbs. "Move one hand against me and I'll cut your air off completely. Understand?"

Sarah sprawled on the desk, toes not quite able to touch the ground, head jammed against the wall. She couldn't pull her feet up because he stood between her knees, pinning her skirt to the desk. His hands covered her entire throat; she had hardly enough room to give a frantic little nod.

"Take *care* of you? *You don't know the first thing about caring!"* Dmitri spat. "I *took* care of you! I held you when you were afraid. I fed you when you couldn't feed yourself. I freakin' *bathed* you when you didn't have enough sense left to do it yourself. Every step, every time you needed something, *I was there*. I felt your joy, I felt your sorrow, I felt your pain, I gave you my *everything!"* he hissed, pressing his body over hers to stare into the terrified eyes, feeling her heart thumping fast and hard in the veins of her neck. "*That's* what caring is about! *But I don't care anymore, Sarah!* It's never been enough for you! You've taken everything from me and I have nothing left!

"What did you give *me*? What have you done for *me,* Sarah? Lies? Jealousy? Vindictiveness? Arguments. Dependency. Immaturity. Insubordination. Betrayal. How did you care for *me?*

"No, I *don't* care about you anymore. I *hate* you! *I hate you!* From the bottom of my heart, I don't care if you live or die! You have managed to destroy the – the one *perfect thing* in my life!" His voice caught, and he breathed fast to keep control. "In my entire life, nothing has ever been this *right*, meant *so much* to me, as what I had with Jaycee.

"*Why?* Why couldn't you let me be happy*?* You're a lousy waste of an intelligent brain tied to a personality who's only goal in life is to make others as miserable as herself. *Grow up!* Get over the bad things that happened to you! I grew up in the same house, too! You weren't the only one getting your ass kicked! And you know the key to surviving that? Do you know the little fact you failed to uncover? That if all you dwell on is the *un*happiness, you'll never, ever see the happiness in life! Bad things happen. You clean up the mess and keep going."

Dmitri twisted his hands again, arms rock-hard and sinewy from work, feeling her writhe and squirm in mortal terror as he pressed just a little bit more, making it difficult for her to swallow, impossible for her to speak, but allowing enough room to breathe if she held still.

"I won't have you rule my life any more. *I can't live with you!* No one can! Maybe you don't want to grow up, but I *do. I want my life back*! You're on your own, just the way you like it. I have to go find a way to get Jaycee to give me one more chance, promise her a life not complicated by a traitorous, ungrateful, spoiled brat."

With a glare of utter loathing, he released her, unharmed, and picked up his things. He headed down the stairs.

Sarah leapt aside the second he moved, coughing and shaking. She raced down after him.

"Wait!" she called out hoarsely. Dmitri paused at the doorway.

"When will you be back? You can't just leave me here. I'm not old enough to be on my own. Whatever I've done, I'm sorry! Give me a chance to fix it, at least!"

"I don't believe your apologies any more. You have ripped my heart out and stomped all over it, and there is no room left in it for *you*!" He walked out the door.

Sarah ran after him.

"DIMI!" she screamed as he walked down the path. *"What am I supposed to do?!"*

Dmitri turned around, but kept walking backward. He gave a short laugh, a chilling sneer of satisfaction on his face.

"I.
Don't.
Care."
And he walked away.

Forty-seven

Sarah knelt in the yard for the longest time. She couldn't move. She couldn't think. She knelt, forehead in the dirt, crossed arms protecting her head. After a while she got up, walked in the house, shut and barred the door, and sat in her rocker. Just sat. Dimi'd left her alone before. She'd be okay. He'd be back. He always came back.

Night fell. Sarah started a fire in the heater. She closed and barred all the shutters and lit the lamps. Dimi'd never left her alone at night here before. Ever. But he'd be back. And she'd apologize. And things would be okay again.

Deep breath again it'll be okay just have to wait for him he was upset but he'll be back when he's ready and when Jaycee comes back with him I'll have to do some heavy-duty butt-kissing to make up for it but it will all work out in the end it always does he will *calm down I'll prove how really really sorry I am I never meant to upset him that bad I just wasn't thinking and it was a stupid thing to do I never thought Jaycee would take it like that it was just a joke really if he wants to punish me he can take a good swing I'll understand he'll be back soon enough.*

Sarah sat in her chair like a good girl, forgetting completely about dinner. After a longer while she remembered the chaos upstairs. Taking a lamp, she climbed to her room.

She observed the destruction with detachment, an encompassing numbness protecting her like a shell. She found two mismatched shoes in the rubble and put them on, then retrieved the broom from the kitchen and swept up the broken glass. The microscope twisted at its joints, but seemed undamaged. She picked up the hundreds of pages of notes, dirty and trampled, and placed them in the correct order in the notebooks. She smoothed the bent and wrinkled pages of her beloved textbooks, realigned the damaged covers, and placed them on the shelves in their proper order. She refused to look at the shreds of photographs as she swept them; it was much better to imagine them as bits of paper.

Little by little she reassembled the room to its former state in the tiniest detail, except for the bed. That Sarah could do nothing about. She straightened the mattress next to the empty bedframe and fixed the linens neatly, as Mrs. Al had taught her.

She returned the broom to its place and looked at the clock. 25:20. She would normally be awake in four hours. Blowing out the lamps, she carried the last one upstairs. She was safe. She was brave. She could do this. She'd been alone until dawn before. Not completely alone, not where there weren't other people around who might help in a real emergency, but still, alone wherever she was. This wasn't that much different, was it? If she thought someone was breaking in, she could flee out the window.

Not bothering to undress, she took her pillow from the mattress, tossed it in the comforting box of a closet, nestled herself among her things, and settled down to wait for morning.

When it seemed light enough outside, Sarah got up and changed her clothes, not because she wanted to, but because that was the routine, and nothing could be wrong if the routine still worked. She opened the windows, rekindled the fire, and made herself breakfast. She was wiping her dishes when a knock at the door made her jump.

She peered out a window.

Her heart sank when she saw Charlie. She had to let him in. She had to talk to him. Anything less and he might think something to be wrong, when it really wasn't. She opened the door.

Charlie still smiled whenever he saw her, waiting for the day when she might change her mind. <Bright morning, Sarrah! I not see you around house for while.>

Sarah managed a twitch that passed for a smile.

<I – had things to do today before I go out.> She could do this. She knew Charlie. He wasn't a stranger, and he had yet to prove himself untrustworthy.

Charlie nodded in understanding. <Dimi-tri nearby?>

<Um, *no*. No, he not. He get early start. I – I not sure where,> she managed to say. It was mostly the truth. Dimi wasn't there, and she didn't know where he was. <I tell him you look for him when I see him.>

<Okay. Nothing important. When he has time. Mother want to know how other plants doing.> Mrs. Al now thought Sarah the smartest plant person in the world, and asked her opinion on every seed.

<They growing. She can take what she like.>

<I tell her. You come by and visit, sometime? Mother complain she never see you anymore. She miss you.> Charlie leaned against the doorframe, unhurried.

<I try,> Sarah promised, growing faint with the mounting strain of prolonged conversation. She sank against the door with relief when Charlie left. This was harder than she thought.

After three days the strain showed, with the most minimal of sleep and the constant drain of denial. But she was up! She was functioning! She hadn't cracked!

Yet.

You are still brave! Sarah ordered herself. *He* will *come back!* Nobody abandons a child on a strange planet!

Except Valeria, echoed over and over in her head.

No. Not Dimi. NOT DIMI! He knew what that felt like, and HE WOULDN'T DO THAT.

<Sarrah, something wrong?> Charlie asked when Dmitri wasn't to be found for the third day in a row, or Jaycee, for that matter. <Tell it to me! If it secret, I can keep. If it bad news, I want to help. Dimi-tri not disappear like this and not tell me. *What wrong?*>

An overpowering urge swelled inside Sarah, a compelling desire to tell him everything, confess what a blasted, horrible thing she'd done to an innocent person, admit how fatally poisonous she was to everyone she met. She wanted to put her arms around Charlie, cry on his strong shoulder, have him hold her tight and tell her she wasn't as bad as she feared, that everything *would* be okay, that he'd take care of her if Dimi no longer would, and she knew he'd do it, too. She *would* let him hold her hand, because he *was* nice enough to be allowed to do that, and she would maybe even let him rub her back, because she knew he *could* be trusted to let her go if she asked, and nothing would make him happier. When she thought about it, she *did* like the attention he paid her, and the way he laughed when she tried to be funny, and how much she looked forward to his token treasures. And he had the most gentlemanly manners around her, and he wasn't afraid of *anything,* and she'd gotten so used to how he smelled after work she almost looked forward to it, and surely he could appreciate the fact that she knew how to pronounce his name correctly …

NO!

interrupted her head. *Don't you fall for that! You start to believe that and you're better off dead! You WILL NOT allow that to happen! Allow yourself to fall for that and you're no better than the girls you make fun of. Stop it! You will not EVER trust him like that! No man can ever be trusted not to touch.*

Yes. Her meeker side hung its head, and Sarah obediently pushed down, deep down to her feet the first decent feelings she'd ever had toward a boy that weren't just brotherly.

Her head lifted with renewed confidence and she gave Charlie a smile. <They wanted to get away for while,> she said smoothly.

<They spend few days with Jaycee's family. They not want to be

bothered. I expect them back soon. I learning to be brave on my own.>

<Oh. If you need anything – anything from town, more wood cut – tell me and I get for you,> he offered. <I check on you again, make sure you okay.>

<No need, thank you! I be fine,> she lied, reaching out boldly to squeeze his hand. <No need to worry.>

But the minute he left, she lost control, spending the rest of that day and night crying into her pillow.

Tired but satisfied, Sarah headed back to the cabin. Her feet and knees were black with dirt, her back and shoulders ached from swinging a hoe, her dress filthy and sweat-soaked. She carried a few of the riper vegetables back to the cabin. The mindless, repetitive work had helped set her back on track after three days huddled in her closet. It helped clear her head so she could think.

Nine long days she'd survived. If Dimi didn't appear by tomorrow morning, she would take a change of clothes in her backpack, her most treasured items, all her notes on the plants, something to eat, and she would force herself to return to the Compound. Dimi had left her no currency; she would hide somewhere in Otaiga at nightfall and continue onward as soon as it was light enough to see. She would have safety and shelter at the Compound with people she knew, while she waited the weeks before her call to Valeria might be answered. If Val didn't want to come get her, maybe David would. Maybe Vlad could beg his Uncle Tomas to fetch her. Uncle Tomas had seemed rather nice. If they didn't want to deal with her particularly nasty brand of poison, she didn't know what she'd do. Maybe Valeria would tell Uncle Tomas about how bad she could be, and he would decide he had enough to worry about. She refused to think about that.

Sarah wiped the sweat from her face, leaving more dirt behind. *Bath* was on her mind far more than dinner. She went wearily into the cabin and stopped cold. The produce in her hands dropped and rolled across the room.

Dmitri sat askew in her rocking chair, one leg over the arm, foot swinging in the air. A powerful wave of relief flushed through her. She started to smile, then stopped herself.

Dimi was as filthy as she was, maybe worse. Sarah had no idea how fast he could grow a beard. He'd always kept his face clean – a requirement on Sigma Tau – but now his cheeks and chin and lip were covered in a dense layer of black hair. The sight was unnerving enough for its strangeness, let alone the memories of Father's beard. He stared resentfully at her through cold, wounded eyes, and took an antagonistic drink from a bottle he held in his lap. Sarah couldn't see the label, but she knew it wasn't likely to be fruit juice. Not unfermented, at least.

She stayed rooted by the door. Father's eyes were blacker than Dimi's, his hair and beard thicker, but the attitude that faced her was all Father's, and it chilled the marrow in her bones.

"If that is to be your permanent companion, please tell me now. I can be gone in five minutes. Less, if you insist."

Dmitri rocked the chair slowly. He took a short swallow, never taking his eyes from her. He shook his head. "No. This is it. I just needed something to give me the courage to come back." He waved the bottle. "This stuff doesn't make me the beast Father was. It only gives me the power to do things I can't bring myself to do on my own."

If Sarah believed that statement, she was crazier than *she* gave herself credit for. "Like talk to me."

The bottle raised again. "Like talk to you." He sighed.

"You and me, Sarah, we need a Do-Over. We blew the last round. Completely. Poof!" He waved a hand up and away. "Both of us. We need new rules if there's to be any chance of starting over. Things have to be different."

Sarah watched him sharply. She didn't know how full the bottle had been or how hard the liquor, but a quarter was gone. He seemed calm for the moment, so she sat on the west-wall bench, alert for the slightest change of demeanor. "Like what?"

"Like grow up and stop destroying my life! I tried to do something once, out of the goodness of my heart," he said, devoid of feeling, as if the words had been rehearsed for days. "I thought I was helping a friend. A kid who needed a break from a bully. Even when I knew I was in way, way over my head, I tried to live up to my promise. Even if they weren't legal, the promises were real. No one forced me to do it. I believed I was a man of my word, and I wasn't afraid to try. And I succeeded – to a degree. I put up with an amazing amount of bullshit, above and beyond the call of duty, long after I should have called quits. But I didn't count on the vindictiveness, and the jealousy, and the outright selfishness." He stared forlornly at the floor, the chair *creak, creak, creaking* as he pushed it.

"You hurt me, Sarah. You hurt me bad. I've tried. I've tried to forgive you for the last week, but it's not in me. I *loved* her! I wanted to *marry* her! To spend the rest of my *life* with her! And I would have!" Dmitri's voice cracked, and up went the bottle.

He rubbed his nose with the knuckles of the bottle hand. "She won't see me. She won't talk to me. She won't let me try again. She doesn't think she's strong enough to fight you for me. I told her I'd send you home, stay on this ass-backward planet without you, and she still said no." He gave a wry little laugh and upended the bottle. "I guess you blew that for yourself, too, huh? 'Cause there went your little ticket home."

"I'm *sorry*," Sarah whimpered. Her heart ached at the idea of going home, but she deserved punishment, she knew it. "I know it isn't enough, but I am truly sorry."

"Yeah, well you're right about that," he snorted. "It isn't anywhere near enough." They sat in pregnant silence for several minutes.

"I'm *twenty-one years old!*" Dmitri exploded. "Whether you approve of that fact or not! I am legally, physically, mentally, emotionally, economically, and morally an *adult!* If I choose to have a physical relationship with a consenting woman, that is *my business!* I'm through babying you! I'm not asking you to participate, just accept that it happens and respect my right to do it! If you can't do that, we can end this conversation right here and now."

Sarah shrank on the bench, chin to her chest. Every word was true, every bit of it. She couldn't handle relationships, from the idea to the first word right on up through that abominable consummation part. But it was *her* problem, not his. He *had* done her a tremendous good deed – at the very start – and she did owe him gratitude for that. Dimi was seven and a half years older and she had to accept that, good or bad. *She* had screwed up this time, a very, very monstrous screw-up.

"I'm sorry," she repeated. She walked to the chair, head bent, hand outstretched. *The damned beard!* It gave her the creeps.

"Truce?"

Dmitri eyed the dirty hand and shook his head. "No. No truce right now."

Sarah took a step backwards. No one had *ever* refused a truce offer. The strength of his anger left her without a frame of reference. She sat on the floor, suffocating under the tension.

"Okay. I acknowledge and respect the fact that you are an adult, and that you are entitled to the rights of an adult, with or without my permission. As long as you are not breaking any laws, I respect and acknowledge your right to adult relationships, provided you carry them on behind closed doors and not in front of me, as the whole thing makes me vastly uncomfortable."

"Okay. Term accepted. *You* will acknowledge the fact that you are no longer a baby and need to develop some personal skills to function in the adult world," he countered. "You will attempt – make a visible effort – to form social relationships with persons other than myself, preferably your own age."

"I have nothing in common ...."

"That is my term!" Dmitri bellowed. The dangling leg slammed down.

Sarah shrank and stared at her dirty toes. "Yes, Dimi. If the operative word is try*,* I accept the term. *You* need to acknowledge the fact that you are not my boss, and as you insist I am no longer a child, I want you to grant me the respect I deserve as an equal partner in this venture."

Dmitri had raised the bottle again, but had barely a taste before he lowered it.

"You think I'm taking orders from *you*? You forget, *I'm* legally in charge here! This is legally *my* house, you're legally *my* responsibility. You take orders from *me*!"

If she wanted to carve new rules, it was now or never. Sarah dared to meet the frozen stare. "We both know the original documents were signed under false information. I have no *legally* appointed guardian. You've been in charge because I let you. I trust your judgment. I know I can't always take care of myself."

Dmitri's anger rose like acid in his throat. He rose and walked to the door. Sarah flew behind the empty rocker. He gazed out at the trees, raising his bottle several times before throwing it out the door as hard as he could. It bounced off a treebranch, hit the trunk, and shattered with a popping noise. He spun to face her.

"You ungrateful bitch! All the *bullshit* I put up with because of you, because you can't handle the littlest twists of life, and you're telling me you only *allowed* me to be in charge? Forget it! I don't need that shit! Especially from you." He shook his head and walked out.

Sarah dashed around the chair. "No! Wait! That's not what I meant!" He stopped, and she ran in front of him.

"Please!"

"Then you acknowledge the fact I am in charge here. Of business, of routine, of *you*. I will no longer tolerate insubordination. What I say will be followed to the letter."

"I just … "

He raised a warning finger. "No! All or nothing. I'm either in charge, or I'm not."

Sarah felt trapped, and her face showed it. "I just want you to include me in the decision making, whenever possible. If I remember, that's all you were after when you took my guardianship in the first place."

Dmitri gave a grim sigh. "Fair enough. Acknowledge the fact I am unconditionally in charge, and I will try to include you in the decision making whenever you will be affected by the decision."

"As long as you include me as a partner in decisions, I will acknowledge the fact you are older and in charge of me, papers or not."

"I want that in writing."

"Okay." Anything to keep the tentative peace.

"All right. It's a start, I guess. We'll work out the details later.

Write it up and we'll sign it."

Sarah relaxed, immediate crisis averted. The rift in her universe had closed just slightly, but it was inertia in the right direction. She reached out to hug him, but he shoved her off.

"No. I am far too angry for you to touch me. As you like to say, it's going to take time. I don't trust you anymore. Don't think of me as a friend, because right now I'm *not* your friend. There aren't enough apologies in the universe for that right now. That may come back in time, but I'm not about to guess when. Let's just shake on the future."

Sarah seized his hand. The hand was her lifeline, no matter how weak. She could wait.

"Okay. To the future, then."

End, Part 2

Appendix:
Overview on Pelonishala Region Sigma Tau Ceti IV
(accent on bold print)

Moons of Sigma Tau Ceti: The three Moons are important to the native population : *Oes* (**Oh**-ays) (the little yellow one), *Allash* (the biggest, with a red hue to it), and *Taber* (the big silver one). Oes and Taber chase each other at the same speed, appearing in the sky at roughly the same time. Allash moves in a different plane, and takes twice as long to wax and wane. When in the right phase, Allash can be faintly seen during the day due to its coloring. Folklore puts great emphasis on the moons, giving them omniscient, God-like powers. The blood-red rays of Allash are said to heal the sick and give strength to the weak. Taber gives comfort and lights the way for travelers, and Oes answers prayers and gives insight to those who seek its help. Because of all the moons, many Tau Cetans are avid night-sky watchers, though when all three moons are full, it's hard to see any stars.

Pelonishalak towns, cities, villages:
Pelo**ni**shala : a regional political division, less than a full country but more than a state. Because the population is relatively small, no one is really concerned with the size of the continent or country, just the local area and the law governing it. Capital is **Kor**shin, @ 500 miles north of Vandijoc, population 17,000.

Arviji**ca**nti - between Vandijoc and Ezoshala, pop. 400.

Chanchi - village nearest Chessorak Research Compound, @ 3 miles north, pop. 600

Char**tai**ga - Northwest of Otaiga, pop. 800

Chessorak - continent of Sigma Tau Ceti where Pelonishalak language is spoken, location of an Allied Fleet Research Compound, complement of @ 40 people.

Demorak - village southwest of Vandijoc, east of Sharfaxil, pop. @ 450

Ezo**sha**la - east of Vandijoc, pop. 300

Fithma – the largest Allied Fleet research compound on Sigma Tau Ceti IV, the one with evacuation transport equipment. Fithma is on the **Mi**mbo continent, approximately 4000 miles from the Chessorak base. Complement @65 people

Kinonah – Another Allied Research compound, located on an island approximately the size of Greenland, but with a climate resembling that the Gulf coast. Approximately 1800 linear miles from the Chessorak camp. Complement @ 40 people

Lozintal - south of Vandijoc, pop, 576

Otaiga - town in Pelonishalak district, half way between Vandijoc and the Chessorak Compound, population @1500

Rizoshanti - around 50 miles due east of Chessorak Compound, pop 2,800

Sharfaxil - southwest of Vandijoc, in high hills, pop. 330.

Vandijoc - forest town in Pelonishalak district, approximately 40 miles from Chanchi, population @ 5-600

Common animals:

porshie - large draft animal with a body like a small elephant, hair like a yak, but a neck, head, and tail more like a brontosaurus. Strong as a freight engine, they are vicious and obstinate in character. With great patience, a strong arm, and a hard club, they can be trained to pull carts, logs, plows, etc. A gelding can be taught to carry a rider, but most Pelonishalak women don't have the strength to control them. Porshies prefer fresh grasses and grains, but will eat just about anything they come across - small animals, crops, laundry on a line, farmer's backsides, etc. They are also raised for meat and hides. Hair is buff to rust in color, but grays and dark browns are not unusual (black is rare, pure white never seen). Hair can be spun and woven into coarse, water-resistant yarns. Porshies are mammalian in nature and give birth to single live young weighing @ 50 kilos, after a gestation of @ 10 months. They nurse for approximately five months, but are not sexually mature for 18 months.

galishnixa (plural, galishnixan) - a ground-dwelling rodent half-way between a squirrel and a prairie dog, with no tail and big black eyes.

urpinta (pl, *urpintan*) - a small goat-like herbivore, but more delicate, like an antelope. *Urpinta* means 'hardy little bugger." Raised for meat, milk, and soft leather.

joubash - a domesticated land bird used for food, as fat as a duck but more like a chicken in character. Joubash eggs are pink speckled with brown, and highly flavorful.

tuturina - cross a kinkajou with a possum; a common tree-dwelling animal with golden fur, eats plants and insects. Pesty if they get in barns because they'll eat grain.

kupu – small mouse-like rodent, often hiding in buildings.

Pelonishalak Language

There are 22 written consonants and 5 vowels in Pelonishalak, the dominant language of the Pelonishala region of which Vandijoc is a town. Most letters have one equivalent sound, though local dialect may put different edges on them.

Roman-letter equivalents to Pelonishalak phonemes:

$\mathcal{M}$ - **mem**, as in more, many

$\mathcal{A}$ - always says **ah**

Ch - **chen,** the hard ch of <u>ch</u>air, <u>ch</u>icken, <u>ch</u>ur<u>ch</u>

$\mathcal{B}$ - **bay**, as in *ball*

$\mathcal{V}$ - **ev**, as in vacuum, valiant, verve

$C/\mathcal{K}$ - **kee**, always hard, as in <u>c</u>ake or <u>c</u>at.

$\mathcal{E}$ - **eh**, always short, as in *egg* or *elephant* or *extra*

Sh - **sheh**, Sh! Lots of soft sh'sh's

G - **ghah**, always hard, as in girl or glass. Never soft like a J, but gargle it a bit, so it sounds like you're clearing your throat. Closer to a Russian *X*. A hard *Hah!*

ι - **ea** - always like a long E, as in *pilaf* or *ski*.

$\mathcal{F}$ - **feh**, as in *feather* or *phish*

$\mathcal{P}$ - **apeh,** as in paint, pepper

$\mathcal{J}$ - **jiuh,** as in jump

$\mathcal{L}$ - **loe**, as in load

$\mathcal{T}$ - **toe**, as in turtle

$\mathcal{Wh}$ - **wo**, as in what, where, why

$\mathcal{D}$ - **du**, as in Dmitri

S - **sah**, as in snake

$\mathcal{Z}$ - **zin**, as in zipper

Zh - **zhen**, the soft j sound found in plea<u>s</u>ure, mea<u>s</u>ure, lei<u>s</u>ure

$\mathcal{O}$ - **aw,** usually a long *O*, as in <u>o</u>we and t<u>o</u>tal, but occasionally a softer *aw*, as in Vandijoc.

$\mathcal{U}$ - **oor**, as in moon or broom, never short as in book.

$\mathcal{R}$ - **rhea,** as in rabbit. Rolling it is not uncommon.

$\mathcal{N}$ - **nah**, as in Newton

Th - **thin,** a voiceless th as in <u>Th</u>orazine, weal<u>th</u>, <u>th</u>ought, never voiced as in then, wither.

$\mathcal{K}$ - **ka** - as in kite

X - **ksah.** Yes, you can say this. The same *ks* as in a<u>x</u> (aks) or loo<u>ks</u>y or Tur<u>k's</u>.

7 pronouns:

Ima (I, me)

Imarak (We, us, specific to you and me and him, a "local" we)

Imarakashi (a global We, as in We the People, All of us here at home, everyone at school, those of us in town, etc.)

Ahn (you, meaning just you)

Ahnax (You, plural, meaning both or all of you and your whole family, too, or a very respectful you, as in you, your body, mind and spirit included.)

Ix (He, she, or it; there are no genders, no differentiation)

Ixo (they, them)

Pronouns or subject nouns receive the primary stress in a sentence, no matter where in the sentence the word winds up.

Articles don't exist in Pelonishalak. There is no *an, the, a*, etc. Example: "*have You good porshie, it go far before it stop at* (the) *river to have* (a) *drink*." Intonation will tell you if the words are a statement or a question.

In written language, sentences do not start with capitals. Pronouns can be capitalized, but most often, the main noun of the sentence is capitalized. Pronouns can start sentences, but most often they fall somewhere in the middle.

Known Pelonishalak words and phrases:

Aggenta -sanitary facility, toilet, outhouse *(polite form)/ aggit (slang, very rude; lit. shithole)*

Aj, aja, No

Akixshra - floor

Attwor - spoon

Axa, yes

Banati, Bata - father, daddy

Banatishi - Uncle

cho gorafesh Ik, fenad domalo? Where does this road travel to?

cho Ix rath do nala, sharvesh nath bhanto Ixo falwarak si. Language had never been a barrier to them before.

degsha - table

Elistri – sister

Enab – a unit of measurement, equal to 1.84 cm, or a hair less than three-quarters of an inch.

Farrash Ixa? - Who's there? (Arrives who?)

Filash - local currency

Ganai- stop

*gash ix **dira meralon*** - Please pass the salt.

*i **Joso** mas* "PIGS" - All men are pigs

*Imad Ahn **risak*** - I love you

Ispa - Please

ki – and

*koffo-ti **shan**weh **Shojeni** lorach stirinas **Ahnaxin:*** May the Light of the Moons Brighten Your Way *(short form: shanweh Shojeni/*Light of the Moons: Have a Good One/See ya round/Good Luck!/Peace be with you/Good Night!

*Mangato / esa mangato, **Ahnax*** - Blessings (thanks) / many blessings (thanks) to you/ Thank You

*na**vichet* – hacking tool, similar to an adze.

ombiri - bench

*shag**shwe** - lamp

*shi**lak* - spotlessly clean

*Sho**jai/sho**jen* – Moon/Moons

*Sho**jen noti!* Moons Above! (mild invective/ Holy Cow!)

*Sho**jen ki Cha**ven!* Moons and Stars! (mild invective/ Oh my God!)

*ta**vana, **Ta**ta* - Mother, mama

*tava**nishi* - Aunt

*tin**tima, **Ispa* – repeat, please

*"to **Aja **tux**na,"* I don't speak [the language]

*to **tux**nu Ahnax Pelonishalak?* Do you speak Pelonishalak?

"tozhto Ahnax ti kappera!"   It is pleasure to see you.

Vonash - Go (away yourself)

*Zap**pirash* - an intoxicating beverage

1 **Ob**	11 **Ob**en	21 Oben **shival**
2 **Shi**	12 **Shi**vash	22 **Shiva**shal
3 **Ched**	13 **Ched**nash	23 **Ched**na'**shival**
4 **Tog**	14 **Tog**antesh	24 **Tog**ant **shival**
5 **Chi**chi	15 **Chi**chivash	25 **Chi**'shival
6 **El**men	16 **El**mench	26 **El**men'**shival**
7 **Jom**	17 **Jom**bash	27 **Jom**ba'**shival**
8 **Shen**a	18 **Shen**avash	28 **Shen**ava'**shival**
9 **Dos**s	19 **Dos**san	29 **Dos**san**shival**
10 **Kiv**	20 **Shi**vala	30 **Ched**nala

40 **Tog**ana	50 **Chi**china	60 **El**menala
70 **Jom**ba**sha**la	80 **Shen**avala	90 **Dos**sala
100 **Tef**orag	0…**Sho**jak	

igma Tau Ceti IV. An idyllic, underdeveloped planet currently under secret study by the United Planetary Alliance. A planet 400 years behind Earth's technology – except for three separate reports of a modern energy weapon in use. Who would dare introduce such a weapon and violate one of the Alliance's strictest Constitutional rights? How could it happen? It is up to Captain Jazak Sullivan to find out how, and why.

His investigation leads his crew to set up a temporary base near one of the reported sightings, with a young Alliance Cultural Observer and his brilliant but eccentric younger sister. Eccentric – or just plain crazy? Jack Sullivan can't decide, and the skittery girl won't let a doctor near her long enough to find out. The longer they stay, the more lies appear – and the more secrets are coming to light. Sullivan is convinced the girl may hold the answer – if only he can get her to trust him. What happens next will take all of Tomas Ivanov's formidable pull to try and save the Kirushenkos from themselves.

Broken

Trusts

Someone's changing the rules

Book 3 of *Best Intentions*
Susan Staneslow Olesen

Susan Staneslow Olesen is a graduate of Chase Collegiate School and studied psychology and writing at Wells College. She is a special-needs foster parent with more than 20 years experience in autism. She has worked all aspects of special education from birth to adult, taught creative writing and beginning Russian language for adult education, spent several years fostering kittens for a local shelter, won several awards for art and costuming, and is a perpetual pest at science-fiction conventions in the Baltimore area. When not writing or intervening, she works as a Tech Assistant for her local public library. She lives in Connecticut with her husband, five children, three dogs, five cats, and a Dumbo rat named Fatticus.

On occasion, she has been known to sleep.

For info and trivia, or to contact the author, follow along at Best Intentions book series on Facebook.com